MANSLAUGHTER PARK

A JANE AUSTEN MURDER MYSTERY

Also by Tirzah Price

Pride and Premeditation

Sense and Second-Degree Murder

MANSLAUGHTER PARK

A JANE AUSTEN MURDER MYSTERY

TIRZAH PRICE

An Imprint of HarperCollins Publishers

HarperTeen is an imprint of HarperCollins Publishers.

Manslaughter Park
Copyright © 2023 by Tirzah Price

Library of Congress Control Number: 2023930918
ISBN 978-0-06-288986-7

Typography by Corina Lupp

23 24 25 26 27 LBC 5 4 3 2 1

First Edition

To all the readers who think that
Fanny Price deserved better.

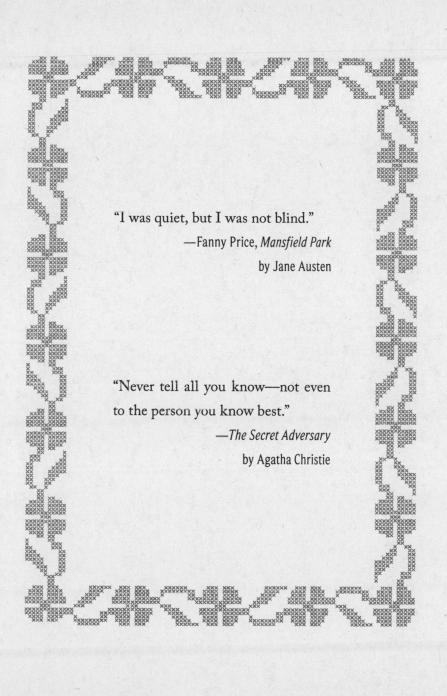

"I was quiet, but I was not blind."

—Fanny Price, *Mansfield Park*

by Jane Austen

"Never tell all you know—not even to the person you know best."

—*The Secret Adversary*

by Agatha Christie

ONE

*In Which Fanny Price Engages in a
Little Light Eavesdropping*

"FANNY!"

Fanny Price's paintbrush slipped at the sound of her own name, leaving a streak of brown paint across the canvas.

"Dash it all!" she muttered, careful not to raise her voice. She cast a furtive look over her shoulder anyway, as some habits were hard to break. Mansfield Park, her home for the past nine years, was an estate of five square miles with a spacious manor house, multiple stables and outbuildings, and a large storehouse that housed the family business, Mansfield Emporium. One would think that with so much space, it shouldn't be difficult for Fanny to carve out one small corner of said storehouse for a bit of peace and quiet.

One would be wrong.

1

"Fanny Price! If you're in here, come out this very instant!"

Fanny hurriedly wiped her paintbrush and set to work feathering out the brown streak she'd left on the canvas. If it dried, it would be impossible to cover up or blend into her painting without having to start from scratch, and Fanny was too proud of the work she'd done thus far to set herself back. Of course, that meant ignoring Aunt Norris, who was sounding more and more cross—and closer and closer—by the second.

"If you're ignoring me, girl, then there is extra sewing as punishment!"

Fanny tried not to shudder—she had almost finished blending the line of paint. For as patient as she could be making tiny brushstrokes in front of a painting, sewing was not one of her strong suits, and Aunt Norris knew it. She swished the paintbrush back and forth, carefully inspecting the pigment of the paint and then stepping back to get a fuller look. There. Hardly visible anymore.

A creak sounded behind her as someone approached, and she whirled around, an excuse wrapped in an apology already flying to her lips. But the person standing behind her wasn't Aunt Norris at all.

"Edmund!" she exclaimed in a whisper.

"Fanny Price!" Aunt Norris shouted once more, exasperated.

Edmund lifted one finger to his lips, which were twisting in a delighted grin. Fanny bit her lip to keep from asking him what he was on about as he turned around and shouted, "She's not here! Go bellow for her somewhere else!"

"Why, I never!" Aunt Norris exclaimed, and then in a louder shout she added, "Is that any way to speak to your aunt, Edmund Bertram?"

"Hardly *my* aunt," Edmund said in a whisper to Fanny. But he shouted back, "We're trying to work here and you keep disturbing our progress!"

There was some muttering and stomping and then the sound of retreating footsteps. Fanny's shoulders sagged in relief. "You didn't have to do that," she said, but she could hardly hide her smile.

"Oh, I know. But I wanted to. Vexing her is so much fun."

For you, perhaps, Fanny wanted to say. Edmund could sass Aunt Norris all he wanted and never face more than a withering gaze or mild admonishment from their uncle, Sir Thomas Bertram. However, there would be hell to pay for Fanny when she finally faced her aunt, and it would be even worse for her if Aunt Norris found out that Fanny had been holed up in the loft of the Mansfield Emporium storehouse all along.

But that was future Fanny's problem. For now, she had a measure more of freedom, and Edmund was smiling at her in a way that made her pulse quicken. "Well, thank you for the distraction."

"My pleasure," he said, and Fanny shivered at his choice of words. Ever since Edmund had returned home from his time at school, Fanny felt as though something had shifted between them. His looks felt more significant, and she dwelled on every sentence he spoke, searching for deeper meaning. "I have been meaning to venture up here and see if you'll show me this mysterious painting you've been working so diligently on."

"Oh!" Fanny suddenly remembered her canvas, which now sat in plain view. "It's not finished!"

"It looks finished enough," he protested, stepping closer. "Come on, I just want a peek!"

Fanny realized she'd shifted herself in front of the painting so that she was blocking it, and her arms stretched out as if she could stop Edmund. He hesitated and Fanny wavered. "Fine," she relented, lowering her arms. "But you mustn't laugh."

"I would never!" he said in mock outrage, bringing a smile to Fanny's lips despite her nerves. Edmund had in fact laughed at some of her more childlike attempts at art over the years, but he was never cruel, unlike their shared cousins. Now he assumed a contemplative pose that might have made her giggle if he'd been examining anyone else's work.

"I can't watch this!" she said, and made to turn and flee. But Edmund's hand closed around her elbow before she could run from whatever humiliation was about to unfold.

"Stay," he implored, so gently that Fanny's pulse resumed its galloping beat.

So she did. The painting she'd been working on wasn't her original work, but rather a copy of her favorite acquisition of her uncle's from the past year. It was unlike his usual fare of pretty landscapes and still life paintings that were popular for society drawing rooms, nor was it a depiction of the more famous personae of Greek or Roman mythology. Instead, the painting was of a domestic scene, a family receiving a caller in their modest yet comfortably middle-class drawing room.

The family consisted of a mother and father, three sisters, and a brother. The caller in question was male, and he was clearly a suitor of the oldest daughter. His hat was in his hands, and the mother stood, welcoming him. The father and brother looked bored and curious, respectively, and the oldest daughter's eyes were downcast and demure. The youngest daughter, no more than a child, was watching the suitor approach with eagerness.

But it was the middle daughter's face that Fanny had been unable to finish. In the original painting, her brown eyes were unreadable. Searching, but not emotionless.

Fanny couldn't quite put a finger on what they were trying to say, much less how to paint them.

"This is . . . ," Edmund began, and Fanny nearly fell over in anticipation.

"A modest attempt, and nowhere nearly as good as the original, I know," she rushed to say. "It's not meant for other eyes, really. I do love the original, though, and it was a good opportunity to practice my shading skills."

"I was going to say it's rather good," Edmund said, casting her a surprised glance. "And that it wasn't what I was expecting."

"Oh." Fanny knew without having the benefit of a mirror nearby that her cheeks were turning pink. Her features were unremarkable, her hair a plain light brown, but her skin was pale and very clear, and it betrayed her every time she felt even the slightest bit flustered. "That's kind of you to say."

"It's the truth," he added, emphasizing the word as if doing so could convince her. "Although it is on the unconventional side."

"Isn't it?" Fanny was happy to divert the conversation away from her own talents and to discussing the painting that had inspired her. "Sir Thomas found it in a small gallery in London. Not much is known about the painter, a Mr. Millbrook, but he paints the most intriguing scenes of domestic and everyday life . . . or, that is, to my knowledge he does. I've only seen this painting and one other Uncle brought back with him, but he sold the other one."

"How could he?" Edmund asked in horror.

Fanny rolled her eyes and elbowed him good-naturedly. "I know, sometimes I wish . . ." She stopped herself before she could go too far. There wasn't a point in wishing that all of this art were hers. Not when she was so lucky as to get to be around it day in and day out. Wishing that Mansfield Emporium were a museum rather than a business, that all of the wonderful art she encountered could stay for her to take in rather than be sold to pay for their living, was not just greedy. It was *impractical*. And when you were the penniless ward of a gentleman who had a son, two daughters, and another nephew for a ward, the very last thing that Fanny could afford to be was impractical.

Edmund didn't press Fanny to finish her sentence. Instead, he eyed her painting and said, "I daresay that our uncle will be selling your paintings to his clients soon enough."

"Oh, I don't know about that!"

"Why not? You're clearly very good."

His praise made Fanny's cheeks grow even warmer. She was suddenly very cognizant of the fact that they were quite alone in this corner of the storehouse. And while they'd grown up alongside each other on this great estate, Edmund the son of Sir Thomas's deceased younger brother and Fanny the daughter of Lady Bertram's disgraced younger sister, they were very much grown now. And *technically* unrelated.

Fanny was saved from having to puzzle out a response to Edmund's compliment by the sound of shuffling footsteps behind them. She turned to find her uncle himself, Sir Thomas Bertram, meandering through the aisles of shelved art and miscellaneous paintings, looking about as if he had lost his way.

"Oh, hello," Sir Thomas said, seemingly unperturbed to have interrupted what was shaping up to be a *moment* between Fanny and Edmund. "I didn't know you were stashed away up here. Fanny, your aunt Norris has been looking for you."

"Has she?" Fanny's tone was all innocence, except for a slight nervous pitch.

But he was thoroughly distracted by the canvas behind

7

Fanny. "Have you made much progress?"

"She's being shy," Edmund said, raising his eyebrows at her as if daring her to disagree.

Fanny did not. She *was* shy. It was difficult enough for her to admit that she enjoyed sketching and painting when she lived with her Bertram relatives, who were well-known in upper society for being art dealers and connoisseurs. To have her work judged by her uncle . . . it was almost enough to make her faint.

"Let's have a look," he said, adjusting his spectacles so they sat more firmly on the bridge of his nose.

Fanny did not allow herself to faint. It might have been daunting to hold her chin up as her uncle raked his eyes over her canvas, comparing the two paintings, but Fanny was no wilting flower. Besides, Fanny had requested that she be allowed to take the Millbrook painting up to her corner of the storeroom and practice replicating it. She'd been so enchanted by it, and she wanted to somehow capture just a whiff of the same artistry and intrigue that had gone into the painting. She'd been surprised when Sir Thomas had acquiesced to her unusual request—no painting hung in his storeroom a minute longer than necessary, and the next buyer was always lined up.

Fanny tried very hard to brush away the hope that Sir Thomas's willingness to let her try her hand at replication meant something.

"Hm," he said finally, and Fanny darted a glance at Edmund. Was that a good hm, or an *I am fishing around for a proper comment because this is actually terrible* hm?

Edmund shrugged.

"Very good," he finally pronounced, and Fanny felt the breath whoosh out of her lungs. She hadn't realized just how tense she'd grown in the few moments that had passed.

"Really?" she asked. "You aren't just saying so?"

Sir Thomas's spectacles slid down his nose, and he pushed them back up and cast a reproving look at Fanny. "Now what would be the point of that?"

She gulped. "Oh, well, I—"

"I see no benefit in flattering you, Fanny. You have some measure of talent. That is a matter of fact. The replication is quite good, although unfinished. I look forward to seeing the finished result. If you apply yourself, who knows. . . ."

He let his sentence dangle, and it had the effect of holding out a crust of bread to a hungry beggar. Fanny nearly fell forward in her excitement. "You mean to say that perhaps my paintings . . ." She could hardly get the words out because it felt like an impossibility, as if he were offering her the chance to one day *fly*.

"Let's not be too hasty," he said, but a small smile tempered the words. "You'll need to practice quite a bit, and perhaps lessons. . . ."

Fanny looked to Edmund, who was grinning at her. The full force of his happiness mingling with her own elation made Fanny feel curiously light-headed. As though she might faint, but out of happiness, not because she wanted to disappear. It was a curious sensation.

A curious sensation, shattered by the sound of a newcomer's voice. "Who needs lessons?"

They all turned to find Sir Thomas's eldest daughter, Miss Maria Bertram, standing framed between an overcrowded shelf of ceramics and a flimsy wall bearing the weight of stacked paintings. She had crept upon them on cat feet, so quietly that Fanny hadn't heard her until she spoke. Now, much like a cat, she looked upon them with vague suspicion and disdain.

"Fanny," Sir Thomas answered. "If she wants to improve her skills."

"What skills?" Maria demanded. "Just because she dabbles about in pots of paint and spare canvases doesn't mean she's an artist."

"I'd say she does a fair bit more than dabble," Edmund interjected.

"Oh, Fanny, you know what I mean!"

Unfortunately, Fanny did. Maria did not like it when someone was better than her at something, and so she'd diminished Fanny's artistic skills since she was ten and could draw horses that looked like actual horses and not goats on stilts, like Maria's drawings. She swiftly placed a quieting hand on Edmund's arm, to keep him from defending her artistic talents any further.

"Of course," she said. "I am no professional artist. And I'm very grateful to you, Uncle, for allowing me this space and the chance to improve myself."

Sir Thomas waved a hand, as if it were no bother. To him, maybe. But Fanny knew better than ever that while Sir Thomas might not have cared if she spent all day covering every canvas she could get her hands on in paint, other members of the Bertram household did care. And they had an awful lot more sway on Fanny's day-to-day happiness than her uncle did.

"Father, I need to speak with you," Maria said, clearly already moving on. "And Fanny, Aunt Norris is looking for you."

"Oh really?" Fanny's attempt at nonchalance was somewhat tempered by the waver in her voice.

"Better run along now," Sir Thomas said, as if she were eight and not eighteen. "Don't want to keep Aunt Norris waiting."

There was a moment of silence, as if all four of them were thinking upon the horrors that would await them if Aunt Norris had to go a single step out of her way.

"Of course," Fanny said, making a move to gather up her brushes and palette.

"Leave them," Maria said coldly.

Fanny looked to her uncle for guidance. If she left them, and the paint dried, they'd be ruined. But that must have been a trifling concern compared to whatever Maria needed to say, for she was waved off. Edmund took her arm and pulled her along, leaving behind her paints and the unfinished canvas.

"Is it my imagination," Edmund whispered as they wended through the aisles of shelving and partial walls hung with paintings, "or has she gotten more insufferable in my absence?"

"Not your imagination," Fanny confirmed with a whisper. "She can't be married soon enough."

"Uncle still hasn't consented to the marriage?" Edmund asked, surprised.

Fanny shrugged. No one shared details with her. "I suppose not, although he did give his blessing for them to become engaged."

"Why do you think he's dragging his feet?"

Because Maria's fiancé, Mr. Rushworth of the neighboring estate of Sotherton Hall, was insufferable and boring, and he had poor taste in art. It was obvious to anyone that Maria was marrying him only for his money, but no one would actually say that part aloud.

"I'm sure he has his reasons," Fanny said instead. "And I'm sure Maria will do her level best to badger him out of them."

Edmund's laugh was a quiet almost-snort, and Fanny smiled to hear it again. "I'm glad you're home," she said.

He squeezed her arm once. "Me too," he said after a beat.

The moment felt weighted with promise, and Fanny felt her pulse speed up once more, but before she could decide on what to say next, Edmund asked, "Any other family secrets I ought to know about?"

"Oh, well . . ." Fanny didn't normally like to gossip, but

there was hardly ever anyone she could gossip with. And it was Edmund, who was, technically, family. "Aunt Bertram is prone to taking sherry for her nerves."

Edmund snorted once more. "Right, for her nerves."

Fanny continued, "And Aunt Norris makes a decent effort at acting as if she doesn't wish to just move into the house and abandon her cottage."

"Is she still pocketing candles and whatnot?" Edmund asked.

"Yes," Fanny confirmed. "And the occasional provisions from the kitchen. She says it's so nothing goes to waste."

Edmund guffawed. "More like she doesn't want to waste her own income on such trivial things as food and candles."

Fanny was getting into the gossiping spirit now. "Don't you know that when she shuffles off this mortal coil, all of her worldly goods must be divided up among her dear nieces and nephew? And she must be economical so as to benefit their future happiness?"

"You mean Tom and Maria and Julia? What use will they have for her money?"

"Everyone always has use for money," Fanny admonished. "Especially money that's given to them rather than earned."

"You know what I mean. They won't *need* it. They've got the Bertram fortune, the Bertram estate, and Tom will have his father's title. You're her niece, too. And your siblings . . ." Edmund trailed off, and she studied him. So, he hadn't completely forgotten how things were, then. "I'm not her blood relation, so I don't have any reason to expect anything. But the way she and Maria treat you . . ."

Fanny felt a swell of feeling—gratification that he recognized the unfairness, mixed with anger. She pushed it aside. It was no use getting angry at things she could not change, and if she dwelled too long in her feelings, she might not be able to push on.

"Yes, well, never mind that. Aunt Norris is not the only one known to take something that doesn't belong to her."

It did the trick of distracting him as they came to the open railing looking out over the first floor of the storehouse. "What! Who?"

"Julia," Fanny whispered, naming their youngest cousin. "There's a reason the shopgirls down in the village keep a close eye on her, you know. And it's not because they offer impeccable service."

Edmund let her take the stairs first, so she wasn't next to him as he muttered something behind her, but she did pick out the word *thieves*. Before she could say anything more, he said, "And what about Tom?"

"What about me?"

Fanny and Edmund startled to find Tom just a stone's throw away from the bottom of the stairs, sitting on a workbench, jacket off and boots up on a cherry end table that Sir Thomas had recently acquired from Thomas Hope himself.

Next to him stood his friend Mr. Yates, a skinny fellow with a tendency toward dramatically cut black jackets and bright cravats. Today's was a plum color.

"Nothing," Fanny said. "Edmund was just wondering what you were up to, is all."

"Working," Tom said with a sardonic smile. "Can't you see, cousin? I am hard at work."

"Clearly," Edmund agreed, not even trying to hide his sarcasm.

"You don't believe me?"

"I didn't say that, did I?" Edmund's tone managed to sound both congenial and biting at the same time, which Fanny had to admit was a special trait of the Bertram family.

"Yates and I are brainstorming new clients," Tom said with a touch of defensiveness. "We might know a fellow who would be interested in this end table." He indicated the one where the heels of his boots sat.

"Not if you scratch it," Edmund muttered.

Luckily, Tom didn't hear him. "What are you doing to aid in the family business today, Edmund?"

"Sir Thomas asked me to tune the pianoforte," he said.

"Hmph," was all Tom had to say, for who could argue with such usefulness? "By the way, Fanny, Aunt Norris—"

"Is looking for me, I know." Fanny heaved a sigh and turned to go. "Time for me to meet my judgment. I'll see you at dinner, Edmund?"

"I'll walk you back to the house," he said, and Fanny felt something in her melt a little.

"Egads, the two of you look like suitors, smiling at each other like that!" Tom proclaimed.

Fanny spun back around to face Tom. "Don't be absurd, Tom!"

But her cousin and Mr. Yates were laughing and exchanging knowing looks. It was enough that Fanny almost wanted to reveal that she did indeed know a secret of Tom's—that she had observed him sneaking out of Mr. Yates's room in the early hours of the morning, before the maids were even awake. But there was some unnamed instinct that told her this secret wasn't wrong like the others . . . just private.

"I forgot my sketchbook," she announced, suddenly remembering that it sat upstairs near her easel, and besides, she was desperate for a retreat that took her away from Tom and Mr. Yates, and didn't leave her having to face Edmund just yet. "I'll be right back."

She stomped back up the stairs, trying to leave behind Tom's knowing smirk. The worst part about it was that Tom was right. She *did* like Edmund. She'd never liked anyone but Edmund. He'd been the only one to be kind to her when she first arrived at Mansfield Park nine years earlier, and the two of them had become fast friends, bonding over being fellow outcasts. But then Edmund had followed Tom to school, because despite being an orphan he was still destined to be a gentleman.

He had only just returned home, and now Fanny was finding it harder to pick up where they'd left off at thirteen. There were moments when Edmund treated her just as he always had when they were children, but then he'd offer his arm and treat her like a true lady. . . .

Was he being courteous? Or was there something more to it?

Fanny had quite forgotten about Maria wanting to speak with Sir Thomas, until she caught the sound of Maria's voice, quick and insistent. "You cannot simply decide that!"

Fanny stopped abruptly, not wishing to intrude any further. She knew she ought to forget about her sketchbook, but something rooted her to the spot. The small part of her, perhaps, that hoped that Sir Thomas was putting his foot down for once. It was so rare that Maria got her comeuppance, and Fanny wouldn't mind witnessing it. It would surely keep her going for another six months, in fact.

She picked out some indiscernible whispering, and then Maria's voice rose again, laced with venom. "—will thwart everything!"

"You don't have a say!" Sir Thomas shot back, not much quieter.

Fanny crept forward a few more steps, allowing an elaborate wooden screen with mother-of-pearl inlay to shield her from sight. She peeked around it and spotted Maria and Sir Thomas about ten paces away. Maria certainly didn't appear to be chastised in any way—her hands were raised and one was curled in a fist. Her uncle's arms were folded, but his posture was slouched.

"I do," Maria insisted. "You have no idea what you're doing. You must let me—"

"It's not your place to question me. I'm your father, and I say we shall speak no more on this matter—"

"We *must*. He's expecting a response, and thanks to you I've kept him waiting for far too long!"

"And he'll keep waiting," Sir Thomas snapped, a note of finality in his tone. "I won't talk about this any longer."

"Father, we must—"

"I mean it, Maria, do not press me on this."

Sir Thomas's show of strength was not in the force of his voice but in his immovability. Her uncle was not a man who often sought out arguments or picked fights, especially not where his family was concerned. It was how Aunt Norris and Lady Bertram had convinced him to take on one of their sister's poor children and Fanny had come to live at Mansfield in the first place.

And he was clearly putting his foot down now.

"You'll regret this," Maria insisted.

"My dear, when you reach my age you'll see that regrets are inevitable. But this is one I can safely live with."

The creak of footsteps was the only warning that Fanny had before her uncle appeared around the screen, purposefully striding back to the front of the storehouse. He didn't notice Fanny's hiding spot, but Maria followed him just a moment later, and she did. "You sneak!" Maria hissed, reaching out to grab Fanny by the arm. "Father! Fanny's been eavesdropping again!"

Sir Thomas turned around wearily. "Maria, let go of your cousin. She's not harming anyone."

"But—" Maria protested at the same time Fanny said:

"I was just fetching my sketchbook—"

"Girls, can't a man have a moment of peace without being challenged?" His voice took on a jagged, aggravated edge. "Fanny, run along and see to your aunts. You've lingered here long enough. Maria, I don't want to hear another word of protest if you plan on staying."

Maria let her go, but not before getting in a savage little pinch at Fanny's inner arm. Fanny knew better than to rub at the spot while still in Maria's presence, and she knew better than to protest. "Yes, Uncle," she whispered, and she made for the door, sketchbook forgotten.

Sir Thomas closed himself in the little office at the top of the stairs, and Fanny didn't linger to see where Maria went. She hurried down the stairs, where Tom and Mr. Yates were still lounging about.

"I think the Grecian statues would do better with the likes of Doyle's social circles," Mr. Yates was saying as she reached the bottom of the stairs. She looked around for Edmund, not spotting him.

19

"Looking for your beau?" Tom asked.

"No!" Fanny replied hotly, but found herself unable to come up with the sort of searing retort that might have wiped the knowing grin off her cousin's face. She might have lingered a moment or two to figure it out, had she not heard Maria's steps on the stairs behind her.

"Who is Fanny's beau?" she demanded.

Egads, but she was being tested today! "No one!" Fanny proclaimed quite emphatically, and started to march toward the door. She tuned out the sound of Mr. Yates laughing and Tom's voice. Perhaps after all this, tending to Aunt Norris would be a mercy.

Well, probably not.

She'd made it almost to the door when she heard Edmund call out, "Fanny! Wait!"

Which was why she was perfectly poised to witness what unfolded next. Tom, Mr. Yates, and Maria were gathered near the workbench just a few strides from the bottom of the stairs, laughing at something, most likely at Fanny's expense. Edmund was on the other side of the open storeroom, emerging from between two large crates. It looked as though he'd been back in the receiving area beneath the second floor, where they stored packing materials and the workmen built and broke down crates to ship the wares.

Above them all was Sir Thomas, emerging from his office. He wasn't paying them any mind at all as he strode toward the stairs, but his feet caught on something unseen. He tripped, but this was no mere stumble—Sir Thomas fell headfirst.

If he'd been anywhere else, he might have fallen flat on his face and there would have been nothing more to say. But he was at the top of the stairs, and so he tumbled down with a loud crash that made Fanny shriek. His body seemed to go limp as he kept falling, finally coming to a slump at the bottom.

Fanny rushed toward him. Everyone else beat her to Sir Thomas, so at first all she could see were Tom, Mr. Yates, Maria, and Edmund huddling about. And then she saw his spectacles, cracked and lying on the rough-hewn floorboards. She picked them up, and her hands felt something wet.

Edmund looked up from where he was crouched beside Sir Thomas. "Fanny, you need to run for help!"

Fanny looked at her fingertips, eyes not quite believing what she was seeing. They were red.

"Fanny!"

She looked at Edmund. His face was white, and she'd never seen such panic before. "Fanny, *run!*"

TWO

In Which Fanny Uncovers Foul Play

FANNY RAN.

She lifted up her skirts to her shins, far above what Aunt
Norris would deem acceptable, and she took off for the main
house, the horrible image of her uncle falling replaying in her
mind, the shock of his blood spilling out making her pump her
legs faster. The storehouse for Mansfield Emporium was set a
ways back from the house, out of view of the main drive, so she
was quite out of breath by the time she burst through a side door
and into an entirely empty hall. It was just her luck that no one
was about, so she jogged down the hall, toward the front of the
house, desperately hoping for a footman or maid.

She finally emerged into the marble foyer of the front hall,
startling a footman carrying a silver tray. He looked at her in
alarm, his tray dipping in surprise, before righting himself.

"Accident!" Fanny gasped. "In the storehouse! Sir Thomas! Saddle a horse! We must . . ." She drew in a deep breath and finished, "Send for a doctor!"

Her presentation was alarming enough that the young man merely nodded and said, "I'll find Mr. Brooks."

As he disappeared to fetch the butler, the drawing room door opened behind her and Fanny spun around to find her aunt Norris standing in the door, her gray hair pulled back severely and her expression no more forgiving. "Fanny Price! Just look at the state of your skirts!"

Fanny had bunched them up in her fist as she ran and now she dropped them. "There's been an accident!"

"What on earth has gotten into you? Sit down! Running about like that—"

"It's Sir Thomas!"

Fanny did not usually interrupt Aunt Norris, but his well-being seemed a bit more important than the state of her skirts at the moment. However, Aunt Norris was the type of woman who did nothing unless her mind was made up about it, and Fanny could tell that she was unconvinced of the urgency of the situation.

"Get in here," she commanded, and Fanny followed her meekly into the drawing room. The drapes were drawn against the afternoon sun, and her other aunt, Lady Bertram, reclined against the sofa, her pug, uncreatively named Pug, nestled on her lap. Her cousin Julia sat near her, hopelessly squinting at a bit of sewing in the low light. They both looked up in alarm as Fanny entered.

"Now, you'll take a breath, and sit like a proper lady before going on with any nonsense," Aunt Norris ordered, pointing Fanny to a chair. "Honestly, running about and carrying on? At your age?"

"Yes, Fanny," Julia remarked in a bored tone, not bothering to look up from her needle and thread. "Honestly."

Lady Bertram opened her eyes at the sight of Fanny and, having slightly more empathy than her sister, said, "Oh my! What is it, Fanny?"

Fanny shocked them all by promptly bursting into tears.

Fanny was, by nature, not prone to dramatics, so this at least got the attention of both her aunts and her cousin. "You must send for a doctor. Sir Thomas fell, and . . . I fear he's seriously hurt. Tom, Maria, Edmund, and Mr. Yates are with him, but—"

"Oh dear," Lady Bertram said, looking to her sister. "What shall we do?"

"How bad?" Aunt Norris demanded. Her shrewd look made Fanny feel as though she didn't believe that Fanny wasn't exaggerating.

"*Bad*," Fanny insisted, closing her eyes against the memory. She needed to make them understand that haste was necessary. That was when she realized—she was still clutching her uncle's spectacles, smudged in blood. She held them up so Aunt Norris could see them.

It took the rest of the ladies a moment to realize what, exactly, they were looking at. But then Lady Bertram cried out and sagged back in her seat, clutching at Pug. Julia dropped her sewing. Aunt Norris merely narrowed her eyes and rang for a servant.

"All right now," she said, "let's all keep calm. Julia, go fetch Mrs. Donnelly. If it's as bad as that, we'll need water and bandages. Fanny, was Sir Thomas conscious?"

"I don't know," she said, remembering the stillness after the fall. "I don't think so?"

"Right," she said. "Fetch your aunt's smelling salts."

Lady Bertram had, quite predictably, fainted.

The butler himself arrived, looking slightly winded, and Aunt Norris launched a volley of questions. Had a doctor been sent for? Where was the housekeeper? Could Sir Thomas's valet be sent to help fetch him inside? Why was he still standing there?

Say what you will about her, but Aunt Norris is good to have in a crisis, Fanny thought as she retrieved the vial of salts and waved them under Lady Bertram's nose. She could do this without looking at this point. Lady Bertram came to with a snorting gasp, and then she looked up at Fanny and asked, "Will he be all right?"

He'd fallen headfirst. The hollow thud his body made when it first hit the stairs, the sound of him tumbling head over feet the rest of the way down, the moment of sudden stillness after, before someone had screamed—had that been her or Maria? Fanny shook her head, as if she could clear these horrible thoughts from her mind. "I'm sure he'll be fine," she said.

Lady Bertram frowned and pushed away the vial of smelling salts. "You're a terrible liar, Fanny Price."

Thus began the longest night of Fanny's life.

After what felt like an interminable wait, and a whole lot of bustling about by harried servants, she leapt to her feet when she heard a commotion in the front hall. All four ladies rushed out to find Mr. Yates, Tom, and Edmund carrying Sir Thomas's limp, bloodied body into the house under Maria's direction. Lady Bertram screamed at the sight and promptly fainted, and Fanny had to pull out the salts once more. She was still tending to the business of reviving her aunt when the doctor arrived, fending off shouted demands from multiple members of the Bertram family before he promptly kicked them all out of Sir Thomas's chamber. The entire family congregated in the drawing room, stewing like a soup gone bad.

While Tom and Maria had a whispered argument about how bad their father's condition truly was, Fanny sat next to Lady Bertram, rubbing her back. She looked across the way to Edmund. He sat near the fire, a cup of tea growing cold in his hands while he stared into the flames. Streaks of blood were smeared against his white shirt, but no one suggested he change. She mentally begged him to look her way, but he didn't stir until they all heard the front door open and another newcomer strutted into the room.

"I came as soon as I heard!" Mr. Rushworth proclaimed, as if hoping for applause. He looked about the room, noting the somber mood, and then added, "How is Sir Thomas?"

"You sent for *Rushworth*?" Tom asked, incredulous.

"He's my fiancé," Maria said a tad defensively, although she looked annoyed at Mr. Rushworth's insistence on kissing her hand. "Of course I sent for him."

"What can I do?" Mr. Rushworth asked, looking about the room. He blanched when his eyes fell on Edmund. "Should I . . . er, send for another doctor? Or . . ."

That seemed to be the sum total of all ideas that Mr. Rushworth had on the subject, and Tom rolled his eyes. "Nothing to do but wait, that's what the doctor said. Take a seat."

The kitchen maids had sent up endless pots of tea and a tray of cold cuts and biscuits, which Mr. Rushworth eagerly helped himself to.

"Nothing like a bite to settle the nerves, eh?" he asked, adding a third biscuit to his plate. Lady Bertram whimpered at his overly cheerful tone, but he just said, "Don't worry, Lady Bertram. I've never met a finer man than Sir Thomas, and I'm sure that doctor will patch him up in no time. Marlow, from the village, is it? Now, he lanced my mother's boil just last week, and she said she'd never had a more skillful attendant."

He looked around the room, beaming with what Fanny imagined he thought was a reassuring smile, and received no response. Fanny felt rather put off by her biscuit and set it down. When she looked up again, she caught Edmund's gaze, now alert and focused in her direction. His eyes widened and he tilted his head just slightly. It didn't take any special skill for her to decipher the meaning in his look: *This* was whom Maria had decided to marry?

But Mr. Rushworth had never met a quiet room he couldn't fill with inane chatter and was not so easily deterred by their silence. "So, what happened exactly?"

"Bugger if I know," Tom said forcefully. "He was upstairs one moment, and the next . . ."

"He fell," Maria clarified. "Down the stairs of the storehouse."

"Ouch!" Mr. Rushworth said around bites of cold ham, as if Sir Thomas had merely stubbed his toe. "A tumble down the stairs will put you out of sorts, all right."

The room shared a collective glance, but no one seemed willing to set Mr. Rushworth straight until Mr. Yates added, "He hit his head. Rather hard. Blood everywhere."

Lady Bertram hiccupped. Fanny reached for the smelling salts.

"Don't be crude, young man!" Aunt Norris commanded. "There are ladies present!"

"The doctor will patch him up," Edmund said, his attempt at confidence sounding more forceful than was necessary. "I'm sure of it."

He met Fanny's gaze again, and she offered him a weak smile. Perhaps he was trying to convince himself as much as anyone else. Fanny was no expert, but she'd never seen that much blood before. And it didn't seem like a good sign that Sir Thomas had not woken up yet.

"What I don't get," Tom said, "was how he fell."

"What do you mean?" Maria demanded. "He fell down the stairs. It seems straightforward to me."

"Yes, Tom, what do you mean?" Julia echoed.

"I mean, a man who goes up and down that staircase every single day doesn't just *fall*."

"Maybe he was distracted?" Julia asked.

"No, it's those stairs," Maria proclaimed. "They're steep and they're dangerous. They ought to be torn out and rebuilt."

"Perhaps Sir Thomas is just, ah, how to put it delicately . . . getting on in years?" Mr. Rushworth suggested.

"My father is not feeble!" Tom proclaimed.

Oh, honestly! Fanny couldn't stand this anymore. "He tripped over something."

All eyes turned to her, much to Fanny's chagrin. She so hated being the center of attention. She added, "I was standing

29

near the door, so I had a good view. He tripped over something, *before* he reached the stairs. At least . . . I'm pretty sure."

There was a moment of silence as everyone seemed to take it all in, and then Tom turned and said to no one in particular, "See, this is why Father is always on about cleaning up the clutter in the storehouse! Someone could get hurt!"

"Oh, do shut up, Tom!" Maria shook her head in disgust. "There's no possible way that Fanny could have seen Father trip over something from that distance."

"Aren't you nearsighted?" Julia asked her, even though it was in fact Julia who was nearsighted and pretended otherwise.

Her cousins carried on in this manner, and Fanny ignored them. The nice thing about their constant squabbles and impulses to diminish each other was that their conversations very rarely required any participation on Fanny's part. But as she looked about the room, she couldn't help but notice Edmund staring at her, a strange, intense look upon his face. She tilted her head slightly in question, and he shook his in return.

As the Bertram siblings' voices reached a fever pitch, Pug decided it was the perfect time to add her voice into the mix and began whining loudly. "Enough!" Aunt Norris declared. "Think of your poor mother! She deserves peace and quiet in this time of trouble, and you all are behaving like children."

None of them had the decency to look even the slightest bit abashed. Instead, Maria stared daggers in Fanny's direction and said, "Would you take that dog out, Fanny?"

Fanny knew her cue, and she was grateful for the escape. She stood and grabbed Pug's leash from the nearby table and clipped it to her collar. No one gave her a second glance as she gently tugged the dog, still snorting and whining in indignation, out of the room. Fanny was so used to slipping off with Pug so she could do her business that she was surprised to hear Edmund call out, "Fanny, wait!"

He slipped after her, taking her arm as they headed for the door. "It's getting dark," he observed. "You shouldn't go out alone."

"I do it every evening," she pointed out, although she wasn't upset to have the company. "But thank you for your concern."

"It's just . . ."

Fanny waited to hear what he would say, but when he didn't continue, she said, "You needed an excuse to leave?"

"That too."

They were quiet as they stepped outside, and Fanny found herself wishing that Edmund had slipped away to change out of his bloodstained shirt. It was hard to look at. It was hard to avoid it, too. But if he noticed her discomfort, he didn't give any indication. They let Pug nose about on the lawn for a little while in the fading light of evening, neither of them saying a word. When the dog had finished up her business, neither of them made any move to go back inside. Fanny tried desperately to think of something to say to break this odd tension between them, but she was at a loss. One moment they had been going about their days, seeing to normal things, and the next everything had changed.

But Fanny knew one thing for certain: if Sir Thomas hadn't fallen, she'd likely still be standing outside with Pug, dreading having to return to the drawing room.

"Do you really think you saw him trip?" Edmund asked suddenly.

"Yes," Fanny said. But already Maria's doubt was causing her memory to blur around the edges. "I mean, I'm fairly certain. I had turned back around because you called my name, and I had a clear view of everyone."

She could feel her cheeks heating up at the mere memory. She'd been fleeing the scene after Tom had teased her about Edmund, and in that moment she'd been afraid that Edmund had overheard. It all seemed so silly now, but she had to know. . . . "Did you hear what Tom said, before Uncle fell?"

"No," Edmund said. "Why, what did he say?"

"Never mind!" Fanny's cheeks were definitely pink now, she was sure of it. Thank goodness it was nearly dark. "Anyway, I'm certain I saw him trip before he even reached the stairs. And if that was the case, then he wouldn't have just stumbled over his own two feet. *Something* would have been in his way. . . ."

"Does it matter?" Edmund asked, although not unkindly. "What's done is done. There was nothing you or I could have done differently."

"I suppose not." Although now she wanted to know. If

Maria hadn't doubted her, hadn't been so quick to dismiss what she saw with her own eyes, maybe Fanny wouldn't have cared. "Come on," she said, tugging at Edmund's arm.

"Where?" he asked, but Fanny didn't answer. "Fanny, no. It's late. And nearly dark."

"It won't take long!"

Edmund followed reluctantly as Fanny traipsed across the dark lawn, toward the storehouse. The night air nipped at the exposed skin of Fanny's arms and neck, causing her to draw her shawl more tightly around her. The building loomed in the darkness, and Fanny shivered from both the cold and the strange sensation one feels when a place that had always seemed harmless suddenly holds a quiet menace.

"Maybe we shouldn't go in." Edmund stopped short of the door. "You only caught a glimpse of him, after. But there was a lot of blood. . . ."

"I have to," she said, voice stronger than she actually felt. "I just need to look around, and then . . ."

Then what? She wasn't sure. But before she could think about it anymore, she pushed the door in and stepped into the darkness, Edmund and Pug on her heels.

If it was dark outside, then it was very nearly pitch-black on the inside. Fanny blinked as the shapes of the shadows adjusted in her view, and she heard Edmund fumble with a lamp kept by the door. A sudden flare of light made the shadows dance, and Pug barked once. The sound carried throughout the wide space,

33

not quite an echo, and Fanny shivered.

"I want to see where it happened," she announced.

"Are you sure?"

She could hear the unease in his voice. "Yes."

Fanny couldn't explain this urge that rose up in her, other than the accident had been so shocking that it no longer felt quite real in her mind. But no, here was the base of the stairs, and here was the bloodstain soaking into the wooden floor. Sir Thomas's blood had congealed slightly as the pool had turned dark. *It looks like rot*, Fanny thought.

She was shivering, and Edmund could feel it. He wrapped his arm around her. "He'll be all right."

Fanny leaned into his embrace, grateful for the warmth and selfishly thrilled at the feel of Edmund's touch. What was wrong with her? Her uncle had been gravely injured, and here she was happy that Edmund was hugging her at the scene of the incident?

She hadn't realized she'd dropped Pug's leash until the dog trotted off, grunting happily to have her freedom. "Pug!" Fanny called. "Oh, dash it all! Pug, get back here!"

Edmund lifted the lamp to cast a wider circle of light around where they stood. "Here, boy!" he called.

"Girl," Fanny corrected.

"Really?"

"Yes!" She sighed in exasperation. "Come here, Puggy! Let's go back inside! Come!"

Pug, however, was not a trained hunting dog like the hounds kept in her uncle's kennels. She was a spoiled lapdog who rarely saw freedom from Lady Bertram's clutches, so she took her chances when she could. Fanny caught sight of her near the bottom of the stairs, dragging her leash perilously close to the pool of blood left by Sir Thomas's fall. "Pug, no." Fanny used her firmest tone. "Sit."

Pug did no such thing. Edmund advanced on her, and she took the opportunity to scamper up the stairs. "Pug!" Fanny cried out. "Very bad dog!"

Fanny made to follow her, but Edmund held up an arm. "Stay down here! It might not be safe."

"I can handle a few stairs," Fanny protested.

"We don't need you falling, too," Edmund called over his shoulder.

Well, that was a sobering thought. Fanny eyed the pool of blood with a shudder. "Fine, but that means you're not allowed to fall either!"

The light left with Edmund, and Fanny found herself standing in the dark, quite unsettled to be left alone. Above, she could hear Edmund's footsteps and his voice calling for the dog. He wasn't that far away, and yet the distance seemed to stretch out a full league.

This is silly, Fanny told herself, and with as much confidence as she could muster, she marched back over to the door, where she found a candle and lit it. Satisfied to have her own source of light, she walked back to the stairs. From the length of the shadows above, she could tell Edmund was deep among the stacks that made up the storage upstairs. "Any luck?" she shouted.

The only thing she heard back was a muffled reply that sounded an awful lot like "Damn dog!" to her.

"I'm coming up!" she called, and lifted her skirts. She eyed the rise of the steps. They were just stairs, for heaven's sake! She climbed countless sets about thirty times a day. She placed her foot on the first stair, then the next. They were solid. The candlelight revealed no tripping hazard. *This is fine*, she told herself.

When she got to the top of the stairs, she felt rather than saw something move in the darkness. "Edmund?" she asked. But then the sound of Pug's nails clicking on the wooden floor reached her ears, and the dog came trotting over.

"There you are!"

Fanny reached down to scratch Pug's ears, and the dog's entire back end wiggled in happiness. Pug was spoiled and very often naughty, but there was something to be appreciated about the one living creature in Mansfield Park who was ever excited to see Fanny. "Did you have a nice romp?"

Fanny leaned down to pick up the leash, calling out, "Edmund, I've got her," when something strange caught her eye.

The railing that separated the loft of the storehouse from

the open area below was held up by a tidy line of balustrades. They were nowhere near as ornate as the balustrades in the main house, but they had been smoothed into neat, long cylinders before being squared off at the bottom. The baluster closest to Fanny caught her attention, because the wood was gouged all the way around the smooth part of the baluster, right above where it squared off. There were even fresh splinters, somewhat attached to the groove.

Fanny crouched down and ran her finger over it, although she had no way of knowing if it was newly damaged or if it had been that way for months, if not years. However, one thing was for certain: there was no dust or grime built up in the groove.

Pug pushed her way between Fanny and the baluster, demanding attention. Fanny lifted the candle and looked around. It was as if her eyes knew what to look for before her mind could even process it all—almost exactly across from the damaged baluster was the end of a set of shelving. It was crudely designed but sturdy, nothing more than four wood planks secured vertically and three horizontal shelves attached at each corner. At the bottom of one of the planks, just above the floor, was a matching gouge in the wood, going all the way around the plank.

Fanny took a step back, drawing the line with her eyes. The gouges in the baluster and in the corner of the shelving . . . they lined up perfectly. As though something had tried to crudely saw about them in a circular fashion. Or . . .

Her gaze cast about, and she gasped.

Not ten paces from where she stood was a large spool of wire, used for hanging heavy frames. Fanny knew from experience that the wire was sturdy yet flexible, and it was almost exactly the width of the gouges. Her mind flashed to the split moment before the fall, and she looked down into the darkened first floor. Had it been about here that he'd stumbled? She eyed the stairway. It was just close enough. Anyone who might have fallen forward would have tumbled all the way down.

"Fanny?"

She spun around, hand flying to her heart. Edmund stood a few paces away, looking at her curiously. "You snuck up on me!"

"I wasn't trying to. Are you all right?"

Her mouth gaped open, then shut. Was it some kind of prank? If it was intended as such, it was a cruel one. One didn't have to be especially clever to know that if a person tripped near the top of some especially tall and steep stairs, the result wasn't going to be good.

"I'm a bit unnerved, actually," Fanny answered finally, her voice sounding strained to her own ears.

But Edmund just nodded in sympathy. "This place after dark is rather unsettling, and after this evening . . . well. Let's go back to the house. And after that, to bed. There's nothing more we can do tonight."

Fanny nodded, aware that her moment to point out what she'd seen was slipping, slipping, and then gone. She followed him, descending carefully down the stairs, followed by a reluctant Pug. She was at the bottom before the question struck her: Who would do such a thing?

Fanny, Edmund, Maria, and Sir Thomas had all been upstairs minutes before the fall, and they'd all made it down without noticing anything or tripping themselves. If someone had set up a trip wire, what were the chances that three people could have made it down just fine but a fourth would take a perilous fall? The numbers did not add up for her, and so she kept quiet and followed Edmund out into the night, away from the oppressive darkness of the storehouse and toward the beacons of light in the main house. They didn't speak on their way back, and Fanny was suddenly bone-weary, the events of the day catching up with her. *Things will be so much better in the morning,* she reassured herself. After she'd had a good night's sleep, a strong cup of tea, and the clear light of day to look at matters.

The house was eerily silent upon their return. So quiet, Fanny wondered if the rest of them had gone to bed after all, except there was light pouring from the drawing room. Of course, Lady Bertram wouldn't go to bed, not without seeing that Pug was safely returned. Fanny unclipped the leash and fixed a weak smile on her face. She stepped into the drawing room and announced, "Here's Pug, Lady Bertram—"

The room was quiet, but not empty. Everyone was there, right where she had left them, joined by the doctor. He stood before Lady Bertram, head bowed.

Fanny gulped back the rest of her words as Pug struggled to be let down. Behind her, Edmund stopped short and breathed a quiet, "Oh, no."

No one had to say it. Fanny just knew.

Her uncle was dead.

She felt her stomach drop and her throat close up, and for a terrifying moment it seemed as though her lungs had simply ceased their work. But then she drew in a harsh breath and her aunt let out a sob.

Maria's voice, then Tom's and the doctor's and Aunt Norris's floated around her, but Fanny didn't hear a word they said. She could only think, *He's dead*, and, *How can he be dead?* And then, like a lightning bolt, she realized something awful.

If what she had seen back in the storehouse was what she thought, then her uncle's fall had been no accident.

In fact, it was now a murder.

THREE

*In Which Fanny Makes the Acquaintance of
One Highly Unconventional Young Lady*

THE DAYS IMMEDIATELY FOLLOWING Sir
Thomas's death were some of the darkest Fanny had ever
known at Mansfield Park. Grief filled the house like heavy
smoke, choking all conversation and muffling all awareness of
the outside world.

The knowledge of what Fanny had found in the storehouse hung like a lead weight around her neck. Every time she
imagined telling someone about the gouges in the wood, the
implication of a trip wire, her throat would constrict. She could
just imagine how Tom would explain away the gouges, the way
Maria would declare her a hysterical fool while Julia giggled.
Lady Bertram's face would crumple even more in her grief, and
Aunt Norris would just shake her head.

As for Edmund . . . what if he didn't believe her?

Fanny could endure almost anything, but she couldn't stand it if Edmund thought she was silly, hysterical, or even worse . . . mad.

So instead, Fanny tried to do what she did best: keep busy. She helped the maids bring out the mourning gowns, focusing on letting out hems rather than the cause for letting them out. She assisted Maria and Aunt Norris with the funeral preparations and assumed all care of Pug, who had been unhappily abandoned when Lady Bertram took to her bed. Aunt Norris had taken this opportunity to move from her cottage into a spare bedroom, wresting control of the household from her sister and nieces. Maria was too busy asserting herself in Mansfield Emporium's affairs and conducting whispered arguments with Tom to mind the overstep.

Lady Bertram's one request had been that the funeral be kept private, so when the day finally dawned, Fanny was surprised when an unfamiliar gentleman and two ladies arrived for the small service and attended the graveside. As they greeted Lady Bertram, Tom, Maria, and Julia with solemnity and respect, Fanny whispered to Edmund, "Who are they?"

"I'm not sure." A faint line appeared on his forehead as he watched the newcomers. "They must be business associates of Uncle."

Fanny's curiosity waned as the funeral got underway. The service was short and solemn, but Fanny didn't hear a word the clergyman spoke. She wore a borrowed black wool dress that was too heavy for the warm spring day, and it itched terribly. Aunt Norris glared whenever Fanny wiggled her shoulder blades for a bit of relief. After the last rites had been performed, each member of the funeral party dropped a handful of sun-warmed dirt over Sir Thomas's casket. Fanny was last, even behind the mysterious trio of guests, and so she lingered over the open grave. Her fistful of earth felt surprisingly light in her hand, insubstantial.

"Goodbye, Uncle," she whispered as she let the dirt slip through her fingers. She imagined him as he was on the last day of his life. His approving nod as he took in her painting. He'd thought it was good—that she was good. He'd believed that if she applied herself, she might become a true artist. No one else at Mansfield Park had had as much faith in her. Her aunts believed that she would spend the rest of her days as a companion, a glorified servant. Her cousins barely thought of her at all. But Sir Thomas . . . he'd seen her.

And now he was gone, and she hadn't even had the courage to speak up about the suspicious circumstances of his death.

As the last of the dust settled over his casket, she whispered, "I'm sorry."

When she looked up from the grave, she found Edmund lingering at a respectful distance. He offered her a tiny smile, which she returned with a small stirring of excitement in her chest, loosening the tight ache of grief. Edmund offered her his arm and she took it gratefully. "Thank you for waiting," she whispered.

"Of course." They began the long walk back to the house. If not for the sad occasion, it would have been a lovely day for a stroll. "I'm sorry no one else was willing to wait."

Fanny shrugged. "They've all got more important things to worry about than me."

"The problem is that they don't ever seem to remember you at all, even in the best of times."

"True," she acknowledged. "But allow me to let you in on a secret—sometimes, I don't mind. Especially if it allows me to take walks where I can hear my own thoughts."

"You always seem to find the bright side of any situation," Edmund said, shaking his head with either wonder or exasperation—Fanny couldn't tell which.

"Yes, well, it helps to maintain perspective," she acknowledged. Because otherwise she'd just be the sad, hurt little church mouse she was when she first arrived at Mansfield, and Fanny couldn't be that person all the time. It was, in a word, depressing.

"And what is your perspective on this circumstance we find ourselves in?"

Fanny looked ahead to their relatives—it was difficult to think of them as family. They were well out of earshot. "Not good," she admitted.

"I fear . . ." Edmund's voice trailed off. Her stomach fluttered with nerves—perhaps Edmund had the same suspicions? If he also thought their uncle's death might be foul play, then she needn't worry about being believed, and more to the point, Edmund might know what to do!

"You fear what, exactly?" Fanny probed, trying to make her voice sound as gentle as possible.

"Fanny! Edmund! Hurry up!" Julia's voice broke through Fanny's swirling thoughts, and they both started, turning toward the house where their youngest cousin stood framed by the door. "We can't read the will without you."

She looked at Edmund and asked, "Does that mean . . . we're named in the will?"

Edmund's expression was a mix of surprise and confusion. "It must. I doubt they'd wait for us otherwise."

They picked up their pace and found everyone inside Sir Thomas's study, which was blessedly cool after the warmth of the morning sunshine. Mr. Yates was nowhere to be seen, but Mr. Rushworth was settled in a chair next to Maria. Aunt Norris resolutely shut the door, as if needing to keep out prying eyes and ears.

Fanny and Edmund took a seat on a chaise longue in the back of the room, and Fanny expected to fulfill her normal role: to be seen and not heard. But when she looked up from arranging her skirts, she saw the green eyes of one of the young ladies firmly fixed upon her. Fanny offered a weak smile but quickly dropped her gaze back to the floor. It seemed most odd that a solicitor should be accompanied to a funeral by two young ladies—how did they know her uncle?

She peered through her lashes at the trio assembled at the front of the study. The green-eyed young lady spread out a sheath of documents on the large surface. She surveyed the entire room with a glance that felt shrewd but not unkind. The young man was tall, with a proud expression, and Fanny got the distinct impression that reading the final will and testament of Sir Thomas Bertrand of Mansfield Park was on his schedule, but it was not the only thing he hoped to accomplish that day. However, he didn't try to hurry along the proceedings and took a position off to the side.

The other young lady unpacked a portable writing box with brisk efficiency and set herself up near the gentleman. While her companions were pale skinned, her complexion was a rich brown, and her fingers were long and nimble as she sharpened a quill. She dipped the tip in her inkpot, then looked to the other young lady.

"Is everyone present?" the green-eyed young lady asked, but Fanny had the impression she already knew the answer.

"Yes," Tom answered, his response snappish. "All accounted for. Now, do you mind explaining to me what happened to my father's last solicitor? Collins?"

"Mr. Collins is no longer employed by Longbourn and

Sons," the young lady replied, her crisp tone offering no room for questions. "I am Miss Elizabeth Bennet, and I have been overseeing your father's account for the past nine months."

"You?" Tom asked. "Not him?"

The *him* in question, the proud-looking young man, wore an expression of faint amusement. He shook his head but didn't interrupt.

"This is Mr. Darcy. He often accompanies me when I travel. And this is Miss Lucas, head secretary at Longbourn. Now, if I may—"

"My father never said anything about a lady seeing to his affairs," Tom cut in. "It's absurd. Are you a solicitor?"

He addressed Mr. Darcy, who inclined his head slightly.

"Then you ought to be explaining this, not her—"

"I beg your pardon," Mr. Darcy cut in, "but you seem to have difficulty grasping the situation. Miss Bennet is *your* solicitor. I wouldn't have the faintest idea of where to begin with settling your father's estate."

Fanny's shock at this revelation came to her in a mix of delight and confusion. A young lady solicitor? Who would have thought? "Did you know?" she whispered to Edmund, and he shook his head briefly.

"It is true, I'm afraid," Miss Bennet said with a winning smile. "I have all the details of your father's will, and Miss Lucas keeps impeccable notes, so I assure you everything is in order. Now, we have a great deal to go over before we must catch the next coach back to London, so if you will—"

Tom whirled on his family. "We aren't about to listen to some strange woman and a foreigner tell us how Father left things."

"Oh, Tom, do shut up!" Maria snapped. "Do you want to know what's in the will or not?"

"Thank you," Miss Bennet said, her disarming smile never wavering. Fanny noted that the other young lady also kept a cool, professional expression, and her hand was steady as she took notes. "Now, I'll read the will and then we'll go over the particulars and tend to outstanding matters. I'll have plenty of time to address concerns at the end."

Concerns? What might be concerning? Fanny and Edmund exchanged worried looks.

Miss Bennet picked up a document and began reading in a clear, loud voice. "I, Sir Thomas Bertram of Mansfield Park, being of sound mind—"

"Cut to the chase!" Tom demanded.

The only sign of annoyance Miss Bennet displayed was a quick flick of her gaze upward. Fanny was beginning to think that she would not like to be on the lady solicitor's bad side.

"To my wife, Lady Bertram," Miss Bennet continued, "I bequeath a sum of five thousand pounds, and give her use of Mansfield Park for the remainder of her days. To my son, Thomas Bertram, I leave the sum of ten thousand pounds, and the property of Mansfield Park, with all the fixtures and furnishings within, bar the exceptions listed in this will."

"Ha," Tom said, looking insufferably smug as he grinned at Maria. She rolled her eyes.

"To my daughter Maria Bertram, I leave a sum of five thousand pounds to be held in trust until the time of her marriage, or age twenty-five, whichever event occurs first."

"Twenty-five?" Maria exclaimed. "But I'll be so old!"

"To my daughter Julia Bertram, I leave the same."

"I have to wait longer than anyone else to get my money?" Julia asked. "How is that fair?"

Miss Bennet soldiered on, earning Fanny's admiration if not respect. "To my wife's sister Mrs. Norris, I leave a sum of five hundred pounds and the use of Mansfield Cottage for the duration of her lifetime."

"Oh well, that's quite generous," Aunt Norris said. "Sir Thomas was always thinking of others."

"To my niece Frances Price, I leave a sum of twenty pounds."

Fanny gasped, her fidgeting fingers finding stillness. *Twenty pounds?* It was no fortune or dowry, but that much money . . . why, Fanny could scarcely fathom it. She'd never had even two shillings to her own name before.

"To my nephew Edmund Bertram, I leave the cherry viola, which has been on loan to him for these past five years."

Miss Bennet paused, as if anticipating protest. Fanny looked to Edmund, whose expression was arranged in consternation, but he didn't protest. Instead, it was Tom who let out a small huff of nervous laughter. "Tough break, chap."

Next to her, Fanny could feel Edmund's hand curl into a fist, and she placed one of her own over it. Otherwise, he showed no other reaction.

"Well, I hardly think that Edmund has cause to be upset," Maria said, voice disapproving. "Don't you have your own trust?"

"That's right," Aunt Norris agreed. "I'm sure Sir Thomas didn't leave you much because your father left you everything he had." In a voice that wasn't quite an undertone, she added, "Although, if you ask me, his money ought to have gone back to the family estate."

"The viola is very fine," Julia added. "You could probably sell it."

"I won't," Edmund said crisply. "And I am very grateful to have it."

Fanny squeezed his hand, which he slowly unclenched. They were very nearly holding hands now! Fanny quickly withdrew her own hand, not liking the way Aunt Norris tracked the motion with her own sharp gaze.

"Moving on," Miss Bennet said, but Fanny wasn't paying attention anymore.

"Are you all right?" she whispered.

Edmund shook his head slightly. "I'm fine. I don't need an inheritance from Sir Thomas, and besides, the viola is worth a great deal," he told her in a low undertone.

Fanny felt her brow crease. "Even so—"

"What?!" Maria screeched, yanking Fanny's attention back to the front of the room.

"Now, see here—" Tom was saying.

"Both of you, sit down and let Miss Bennet speak!" Aunt Norris snapped.

"I shall repeat myself once more," Miss Bennet said, her voice calm but with a core of iron to it. "In regards to Mansfield Emporium, it was your late father's wish that equal shares of the business be split between his son and oldest daughter."

"Split?" Maria reiterated.

"But she can't—she's a girl!"

"I'm a woman, thank you very much. And I'm perfectly capable of running a whole business, let alone half."

"I can't run Mansfield Emporium with *her*." Tom looked to Miss Bennet with fire in his eyes. "Give me that! I need to see for myself."

He advanced on Miss Bennet, but before he had gone two steps, Mr. Darcy was between them, and his expression was no longer bored—it was dangerous. He didn't gesture or make threats, he simply stood between Tom and Miss Bennet like a marble pillar and quietly said, "You may inspect the documents when she has concluded the reading."

Tom looked as though he meant to argue, but Mr. Darcy's stony expression made him reconsider. Instead, he turned on his sister. "You're going to be married soon and you can't own half a business then. And there's no way that my father meant to hand over half of it to Mr. Rushworth."

Mr. Rushworth did not seem to register the insult, for he simply nodded amicably and said, "Quite right."

"You'll have to work it out," Miss Bennet said. "But the will is very clear."

"Besides," Maria said, crossing her arms, "you assume I would surrender my property upon marriage."

"Maria!" Lady Bertram exclaimed. So she was paying attention after all. "Do you mean to say that you don't wish to marry Mr. Rushworth?"

"No, of course not," Maria said, casting a furtive glance at Mr. Rushworth.

"Now's the chance to break it off," Edmund muttered.

Fanny leaned in closer to whisper, "Do you think she will?"

"Why not?" Edmund asked. "Uncle never gave his blessing for them to marry. And now that she's independently wealthy, she can marry anyone."

He had a point. Fanny looked to Mr. Rushworth, who was not so subtly loosening his cravat. His face was pink despite the coolness of the room, but conflict seemed to make him sweat. Fanny had no doubt that Maria would find a way to have her cake and eat it, too, and the likelihood of her sharing seemed slim.

"But surely there must be some provision that allows me to maintain my share of *my* inheritance." She turned to glare at Miss Bennet, as if the solicitor herself were at fault for the unjust women's property law.

But before Miss Bennet could respond, Tom was already thinking aloud. "Of course! You can place your shares in a trust before you marry, so Rushworth can't control them. Then if he dies, they'd revert back to you. Father must have meant for you to place them in trust with *me*."

"As if I'd entrust *anything* to you!"

"This is about to get interesting," Edmund muttered.

Tom sputtered with fury, "What—but—I mean, who else would you place them with? As far as I'm concerned, Father meant to protect you in case you were ever left in a vulnerable situation, but he knew that you'd marry and that I'd control the business anyway. I can't say as it's what I was expecting, but we can work with it."

"He didn't leave anything to Julia!"

"That's because Julia—"

"Sir Thomas left no stipulations or conditions regarding Miss Bertram's shares," Miss Bennet hastened to interrupt, and Fanny had a moment to appreciate the young lady's foresight and quick thinking. She'd spent barely ten minutes with them and yet she knew to curtail an argument between Tom and Maria before the situation devolved even further. "What Miss Bertram chooses to do with her shares is her business, but there are more pressing matters we must discuss."

"What could be more pressing than the future of Sir

Thomas's legacy?" Aunt Norris demanded.

"I'm very sorry to have to tell you this," Miss Bennet said, casting an earnest gaze about the room. "But I'm afraid that Sir Thomas was overdrawn in all of his accounts, and he owes a considerable sum to various creditors. Many have heard news of his death and started to call in his debts, and I imagine more will do so by the end of the month."

"Overdrawn," Tom repeated.

"Debts?" Aunt Norris asked, aghast.

Maria said nothing. Of all of them, she seemed the least shocked.

Fanny bit her lip. It wasn't often that her relatives were stunned into near silence, so this couldn't be good.

"Oh, dear," Mr. Rushworth said finally, never one to leave an awkward silence well enough alone. "Well, try not to look so glum, everyone. Every estate has debts. You'll bounce back in no time."

"Not now, James," Maria hissed.

"You seem like a clever enough girl," Aunt Norris said to Miss Bennet, but her tone indicated she thought otherwise. "But I've been helping my poor sister during this trying time, even going so far as to help with the ledgers. There is most certainly money in the accounts."

"The numbers are forged, then," Miss Bennet said, not backing down. "All of Sir Thomas's own bank accounts were drained months ago, and to keep his business and this household afloat, he borrowed money."

"From whom?" Maria asked, and Fanny noted that her voice barely hid a tremble.

Miss Bennet looked straight at Fanny—wait, no. At *Edmund*.

"Wait," Edmund said. "*My* trust?"

"Indeed," the solicitor confirmed with an apologetic wince. "At the time of his death, Sir Thomas held about thirty pounds in a household account for day-to-day expenses. Every other account was empty, and more than half of Mr. Edmund Bertram's trust has been spent. It goes without saying, of course, that it and all of your creditors must be repaid."

No one responded for the longest time, until finally Julia said, "So . . . we're poor?"

"Of course not," Aunt Norris said. "Look at this house. Look at the dress you're wearing. Silly girl."

"But she just said—"

"Aunt Norris is right," Maria said. "The accounts might be empty, but we have a storehouse full of goods, all waiting for sale."

"We'll need to get a good price on them," Tom said, biting his thumbnail.

"*Obviously.*" Maria shook her head, making clear she thought her brother was a first-rate idiot.

"See, there's nothing to worry about," Aunt Norris said, sending Julia a sharp look.

"I wouldn't quite say that," Miss Bennet interrupted, earning a sour look from Aunt Norris. "Your creditors have been conspiring together, and they believe they have just cause to call in your debts. I don't think I need to warn you of the consequences should these bills not be paid in absolute haste?"

When no one spoke, she sighed, the first sign that her professional patience was slipping. "If these creditors aren't paid quickly, they'll send bailiffs to take up residence in Mansfield Park, and those men will garnish any funds they see until the bills have been paid in full."

"That's absurd!" Aunt Norris proclaimed.

Lady Bertram looked to Miss Bennet. "They can't really do that, can they?"

"They can," Tom confirmed grimly. "I've seen it happen before, to a schoolmate's father."

"But . . . Sir Thomas was a gentleman. A baronet!"

"And that is precisely why they shall simply send a bailiff rather than take your son to debtors' prison, Lady Bertram."

Miss Bennet's frank response set off a flurry of conversation. Fanny picked out, "The scandal!" and, "We simply must not—" and, "They wouldn't really?" Above it all came Julia's plaintive question, "So we *are* poor, then?"

"I have a question," Edmund said, and everyone quieted as they turned to him. "When did Sir Thomas start spending my trust?"

Miss Bennet consulted a document. "It looks as though the

account was first drawn upon two years ago, and the last withdrawal was a month ago."

"Don't worry, chap!" Tom clapped his shoulder and plastered on an unconvincing smile. "We'll get it all straightened out."

"As soon as we take care of immediate needs," Maria added.

"Quite right," Tom agreed.

"Was *this* why he wouldn't let me have a London season?" Julia demanded.

"No, he wouldn't let you have a London season because you're silly and reckless," Maria snapped, which started another round of bickering.

"But what happened to all of his money, do you think?" Fanny posed the question in a low undertone to Edmund, meant as a quiet aside. Unfortunately, she just so happened to speak at the precise moment that everyone else stopped, and so her words were heard by the entire room. They all turned to stare at her. Fanny couldn't help but wonder why they seemed so surprised: Was it because she had asked a completely reasonable question or because they'd forgotten she was there?

"Never you mind," Aunt Norris snapped. "It's not your place to pry into the business of your uncle."

"Running a business takes a lot of capital," Tom added, a defensive tone creeping into his voice.

Maria rolled her eyes. "Why are you bothering to explain that to her?"

"I meant no offense. It wasn't like Uncle to be . . . careless."

What Fanny wasn't able to ask was, *Why are none of you skeptical about this turn of events?* Did they truly not think it odd that Sir Thomas should die, revealing an estate in financial ruin and embezzlement?

Or was Fanny merely suspicious because she was the only one who suspected Sir Thomas's accident was no accident?

Miss Bennet's face softened into sympathy. "I can't speak to exactly where the money was all going, I'm afraid. That shall be up to you all to sort out. Of course, if I can offer any assistance, I am happy to do so."

"You can keep the bloody bailiffs from coming," Tom muttered, but not quietly enough.

"I'm afraid that it's beyond even my capabilities," she said, tossing out a charming smile that made Fanny wonder what exactly Miss Bennet was capable of.

The reading devolved from there into a flurry of paperwork, signatures, and barbed jabs as Maria and Tom bickered about what was to be done, while Julia and the aunts bemoaned what was to become of them. But Fanny watched Edmund out of the corner of her eye. He wore a stunned expression, eyes staring at seemingly nothing.

He had no money. He was just as beholden to Mansfield Park and their cousins as she.

Fanny had had nine years to reconcile herself to this fact,

but she felt a wave of empathy nonetheless. At least she'd never had a fortune to be lost—she'd always been poor, so she'd never know that grief. Perhaps that explained why she felt strangely calm in the face of this storm. In this moment, she wasn't thinking about fortunes lost or gained. Instead, she was thinking of the gouges in the balusters.

She surveilled the room yet again. Who would have wanted Sir Thomas gravely injured, if not dead? Who would have wanted it to look like an accident? Perhaps Tom, for complete control of the business? But Maria . . . she had been arguing with Sir Thomas minutes before the accident. Her gaze flicked to Edmund, who still wore an expression of shock.

No, not Edmund. Besides, Edmund had gone down the stairs before Fanny, and he hadn't gone back up them. And he was totally reliant on their uncle until he came of age later in the fall. He had more motivation now, after learning about his trust being spent, than he'd had when Sir Thomas was alive.

And he was not the only one who'd been in the storehouse that afternoon. Aunt Norris had been there, too. And Mr. Yates, with Tom. And Julia and Lady Bertram would have had equal access.

Any one of them could have done it. All Fanny knew with absolutely certainty was that it hadn't been *her*.

Miss Bennet and her associates rose to take their leave when it was apparent that they could shed no more light on the sad situation. None of the family made any move to see them to the door, and they didn't notice Fanny get to her feet to follow them out.

The hall was blessedly quiet after the ruckus in the study. Miss Bennet turned and noted Fanny's presence with a small smile. "Did you have any further questions?" she asked.

"No, I . . ." Fanny tried to swallow, but her mouth was completely dry. She'd followed them out on an impulse and hadn't planned what to say. "I apologize for my family. They're . . ." *Greedy, selfish beings* seemed to put too fine a point on the matter, so she ended with, "Overwrought."

"Hmph," said Mr. Darcy, and Fanny caught the warning look Miss Bennet gave him. But the glance was full of fondness, too.

"Unfortunately, wills bring out the worst in even the best people," Miss Bennet reassured her.

Fanny nearly laughed but smothered it with a fake cough. The idea that this was her family at their worst was almost charming. "The thing is . . . what if . . ."

She looked around. The housekeeper and butler were nowhere in sight, although one of them couldn't be far away if guests were still in the house. Besides, what if Miss Bennet thought her mad?

"What is it, Miss Price?" Miss Bennet asked. Her eyes held no judgment or even a hint of impatience. But there was a bright spark of something there—curiosity, perhaps?

"What would happen if my uncle's death weren't an accident?" she asked.

Miss Bennet's eyebrows rose, and she slowly turned to look at Mr. Darcy. He heaved a sigh with the air of someone who was long-suffering. "I knew we should have booked tomorrow's coach instead."

Miss Bennet patted his arm fondly. "And next time, I shall listen." To Fanny, she said, "Come along, and tell me *everything*."

FOUR

*In Which Fanny Learns More Than She Cares
to Know About the Nature of Murder*

FANNY WAS UNUSED TO being listened to when she spoke up, so when Miss Bennet whisked her away to the private sitting room in the village inn and all three Londoners turned their attention to her, she found herself tongue-tied.

"I don't quite know where to start," she said.

"Start wherever you want," Miss Bennet encouraged. Unlike back at Mansfield, here at the inn Miss Lucas wasn't poised to take notes, and Mr. Darcy wore a look of interest.

"Well . . . I don't think my uncle's death was an accident," she said. "But perhaps I'm just being silly."

She waited for them to agree and send her packing, but they merely waited for her to say more. Their silence was unnerving, so Fanny kept talking.

"It doesn't make any sense that he'd be . . . murdered." The word seemed so harsh, so unforgiving. "But where he died, there were these . . . marks near the stairs."

"Tell me about them," Miss Bennet said, leaning forward.

Fanny found that it was rather easy to unburden herself, once she'd started. She told them about that afternoon, tucked away on the second floor of the study. Who all had been there, and Maria's heated conversation. How she'd turned and looked back at precisely the right moment to see him trip—"He stumbled before he reached the steps, I'm sure of it!"—and what she'd found when she and Edmund had returned later.

It was easier telling them about the circumstances and events surrounding the accident. She didn't have to think about the moment he fell, the glimpse of his body after. She skipped right over that unpleasant business and described the gouges in the wood in great detail—what they looked like and their precise position. "I think that someone strung picture wire between the two points," she explained. "There was a whole spool of it sitting not five paces away."

"And have you told anyone else of your suspicions?" Mr. Darcy asked.

"No, because it doesn't make *sense*." She looked between the three of them, expecting them to agree with her. When they didn't, she added, "We were all going up and down those stairs. If someone had planted a trip wire, why didn't anyone else trip?"

"But didn't you say Maria was the last one down, before

63

your uncle?" Miss Bennet prompted.

"Yes, but—"

"And she was arguing with your uncle," Miss Lucas added, speaking for the first time.

"Motive, means, opportunity," Mr. Darcy muttered.

"Perhaps she set it up beforehand, and then seeing that Sir Thomas was the only one left upstairs, she pulled the wire taut?" Miss Bennet suggested. "Unless . . ." She turned back to Fanny. "Could there have been anyone else in the storehouse?"

Fanny shook her head, then paused. "Perhaps. If there was, I neither heard nor saw them."

"But you're certain the death is foul play?" Mr. Darcy asked.

"No!" Fanny started to stand. Maybe she'd made a mistake coming here. "I'm not certain of anything, really, and maybe this is all just silly and I—"

Miss Bennet sprang to her feet as if to block Fanny. "No, no, Miss Price! Please stay. He didn't mean it like that." She gave Mr. Darcy a look that seemed to say, *Apologize!*

Fanny hesitated, but then Mr. Darcy stood and said, "Please, Miss Price. Sit. I meant no offense. Miss Bennet tells me I can be rather . . . brusque."

"Blunt," Miss Bennet corrected cheerfully.

He nodded at Miss Bennet, acknowledging that her description was correct. "You know what you saw, and I agree that the evidence does suggest some sort of malicious intent. Whether the intent was to do him harm, or worse, well, who's to say?

But you would not willingly pursue our input if you weren't, on some subconscious level, certain of your own instincts."

Fanny considered that. It wasn't often that someone else had confidence in her opinions. These Londoners had never met her before today and yet they were listening to her. Perhaps she wasn't mad.

"The whole situation feels wrong," Fanny admitted. "Sir Thomas was not a reckless spender. I know of no vice or extravagance that could have bankrupted the family. If anything, Aunt Norris complains he is too stingy. And it seems so unlike him to take money from Edmund's inheritance."

"There's no doubt that your uncle was the one who withdrew the money from the trust," Miss Bennet confirmed. "But perhaps he had reason to. Reasons that led to his death."

"But it's also possible that there is a simple explanation," Mr. Darcy added. "An innocent one."

"He means a legal one," Miss Bennet said. "Charlotte, what do you think?"

The legal secretary had been mostly quiet throughout the conversation, but she'd paid close attention to Fanny's words. "What puzzles me the most is the absence of the trip wire, despite the evidence that it had been set."

"But if picture-hanging wire was used, I suppose it could have been discarded into any corner and no one would think anything of it," Fanny acknowledged. "We use so much of it, it's hardly out of place."

"But that would imply . . ."

Miss Bennet seemed to show signs of uncertainty for the first time since Fanny had met her. Even Mr. Darcy and Miss Lucas looked grim at the prospect of this question.

"What?" Fanny asked.

"It would imply that someone must have cleaned up the scene," she continued. "Who might have done that?"

It felt like a kinder way of asking which one of her family members might have wanted Sir Thomas dead. And despite Fanny's suspicions and her speculations about each and every member of the household, she found herself unable to speak. "I . . . I don't know."

"It's an unpleasant thought, I know." Miss Bennet seemed genuine, at least. "But in my experience, murders usually fall into two categories: crimes of passion, or crimes of opportunity. Passionate murders are spontaneous things—people lose their tempers, or find themselves suddenly desperate, and they . . ." Miss Bennet snapped her fingers.

"But the crimes of opportunity are different altogether. They might be premeditated—either months in advance, or maybe just hours or minutes. But the person responsible makes a choice, you see. They decide how they are going to kill someone, and how to get away with it, if possible. And then they execute the plan."

"Oh." Fanny had never given so much thought to murder before—she assumed a crime was a crime. But Miss Bennet's voice had taken on an animated edge, which indicated that she'd given it *much* thought indeed. "And the difference is significant?"

"When trying a case in court, the difference is crucial," Miss Bennet confirmed. "And oftentimes when investigating the crime, too. If you can think like the killer—"

"Here," Miss Lucas said, placing a fresh cup of tea in Fanny's hands. "Not everyone is quite so accustomed to speaking frankly about murder, Lizzie."

"I'm sorry," Miss Bennet said, not sounding sorry in the least. "But this case—it sounds like a crime of opportunity to me. Placing a trip wire takes planning. Even placing it at the top of the stairs, near a known tripping hazard, seems to speak to a clever person who wanted to conceal his crime."

"Or hers," Mr. Darcy added.

"Or hers," Miss Bennet conceded. "They would have to have motive, of course, and that could be anything. It could be related to your uncle's business, or his financial woes. It's too soon to say. So I suggest we focus on who had opportunity."

Miss Bennet spent the next few minutes interrogating Fanny as to whether or not the storehouse was locked, who had access throughout the day, and who was familiar with the space. She asked Fanny to repeat all she knew about everyone's whereabouts on the day of the incident, even going so far as to ask her to estimate how long after the accident it was before Mr. Rushworth arrived at Mansfield Park.

"Not terribly long," Fanny answered, baffled. "A half hour? Three-quarters of an hour at most?"

"And is that fast?"

"I don't know!" Fanny felt a headache coming on. "Maybe? Maybe not if he was already out riding."

"And no one left the drawing room after the doctor arrived and you all gathered there? Not even to run to the privy for ten minutes?"

The mere mention of the privy made Fanny blush, but Miss Bennet didn't notice. "No, we were all there until Edmund and I took Pug out. Then we went straight to the storehouse, and we didn't see anyone else there."

"And did Edmund leave you at any point while you were out there? Before you stumbled upon the evidence?"

"No! I mean, yes. He ran after Pug. . . ." Fanny slowed, not liking the direction this was taking. "He went up the stairs before me, but he was running after the dog. I would have noticed if he'd taken the time to undo a trip wire!"

"You're certain?"

"Yes," Fanny said, more forcefully this time. She couldn't imagine Edmund doing this, let alone having the audacity to clean up evidence under her nose. "Besides, if he'd been the one to do it and he wanted to clean up after himself, then he would have found a way to keep me from returning to the storehouse. It was my idea to go back there."

"It still doesn't explain how the wire was set up without

anyone else in the storehouse tripping," Mr. Darcy added in a low tone.

"Hmm, I suppose you're right." But Miss Bennet didn't sound very happy about that fact. "Well, there's only one thing to do, I suppose."

"Take the case before the magistrate?" Fanny asked with a bit too much eagerness.

"You could do that," Miss Bennet said carefully, but her tone implied it would not be advisable. "However, the magistrate will want evidence. At the very least, he'll want a suspect. Who is the magistrate for this county?"

Fanny's mouth went dry. "Oh. It's, well . . . Mr. Rushworth."

"Your cousin's fiancé," Miss Bennet said, nodding as if all the pieces were falling into place. "Well, that does complicate things."

"Can we go elsewhere?"

Miss Bennet looked apologetic as she shook her head. "Even if we approached someone in London, they'd still want evidence. Especially for a crime such as murder."

"Or manslaughter," Mr. Darcy added.

"Both are serious charges. And one does not make them without a suspect. Preferably a confession. Confessions are awfully handy in such circumstances."

"You would know," Mr. Darcy muttered.

"You must find out more," Miss Bennet told Fanny.

"I can't! I mean . . . I'm just . . ." Fanny wasn't certain how to finish her sentence. All her life she'd only ever been a girl in the way. Expendable to her parents. Only so useful to her relatives.

"You can do this," Miss Bennet assured her. "In fact, you might be the only one who can."

That was a sobering thought.

When she had followed Miss Bennet out of the study back at Mansfield Park, she had thought that if she could only tell someone—someone very responsible—then perhaps they could take matters in hand and solve this problem for her. But that wasn't the case. The decision to investigate or not, to find the truth or not, to seek justice or not, was entirely in her hands.

Which was quite a terrifying prospect.

"I don't have the faintest clue how to go about investigating a crime," she protested weakly. Even now she struggled to say the word *murder*.

"We could always provide a referral to Norland and Company," Miss Lucas said.

"True," Miss Bennet agreed. "They're an investigation firm we've worked with in the past."

"Are they run by ladies as well?" Fanny asked, mostly in jest.

"Yes, actually."

Fanny was starting to believe that London was indeed the place of great opportunity that Julia claimed, but for altogether different reasons. "I'm afraid I don't have any money to pay a private investigator," she admitted. "I doubt I shall ever see my inheritance either, after today's announcement."

"Don't worry," Miss Bennet said with far more confidence than Fanny felt. "You have a tremendous advantage. Why, I'd venture that you're in a much stronger position to catch this killer than even Miss Dashwood herself."

Fanny had no clue who Miss Dashwood was, but the praise warmed her. "Really?"

"You live at Mansfield Park. You have a sensible mind. And, I hope you aren't offended by me saying so, but it would appear that you have the advantage of being tragically overlooked."

Fanny didn't mind. Much.

"Use it to your advantage," Miss Bennet advised.

"To do what, exactly?"

"Poke about. Find out what it was your uncle was hiding. I would start by following the money."

"And what if I'm wrong?" Fanny wanted to be wrong, but the problem was that she didn't believe in her heart that she was. "What if it truly was an accident?"

Miss Bennet gave her a significant look. "Then you'll have intelligence about the household. And Miss Price, take it from me—when you are a young lady, especially one without her own fortune, it is never a bad thing to know precisely what is happening behind closed doors."

Fanny should have been shocked by Miss Bennet's candor, but she found instead she was grateful. No one had ever been so blunt with her, but she found herself responding well to the young lady's words. Fanny *did* possess a few handy secrets about Mansfield Park and her family. Perhaps now was the time to utilize what she knew and do some digging. As terrifying as it felt, she had to admit that the prospect was better than sitting around, cleaning up after Pug, and wondering what Tom and Maria would do next.

"All right," she agreed, nodding in part to convince herself. "I shall do it."

Miss Bennet gave Fanny her card. Miss Lucas clasped her hand and wished her good luck. Mr. Darcy gave her a courteous bow, but his parting words chilled her to the bone.

"Do be careful, Miss Price. In all likelihood, you're living under the same roof as a killer."

FIVE

In Which Fanny Finds Her Resolve

MR. DARCY'S WARNING ECHOED in her mind on the long walk back to Mansfield Park.

She didn't want to believe anyone in her family capable of murder, but she could see why Miss Bennet had come to that conclusion. If Sir Thomas had indeed been murdered, the killer would have needed intimate knowledge of the family, their habits, and the estate. No outsider, save perhaps Mr. Yates or Mr. Rushworth, would have that.

"What am I thinking?" Fanny muttered to herself. "And the staff, of course."

No, she decided. It was highly unlikely anyone who worked for Mansfield was responsible. Sir Thomas was admired as an employer, and he treated those who worked for him well. In fact, the servants all understood that with the loss of Sir Thomas, they would find themselves in a much worse position having to answer to the whims of Aunt Norris and Tom. And if the conflict was over money, why go to great lengths to injure Sir Thomas rather than just steal one of the valuable pieces from the house or Mansfield Emporium storehouse?

Fanny shook her head deliberately, as if she could loosen these disturbing thoughts. This was all the fault of Miss Bennet and her probing questions and macabre insights into the art of murder.

The marble halls of the house were silent when she crept back inside. There was no barking Pug or scolding Aunt Norris demanding to know where she'd been. Likely they all had more important matters to attend to than watching her every move, and while Fanny didn't mind the freedom, it left her feeling strangely adrift, as if Sir Thomas's death had upset the house's natural order.

Outside the study, she heard muffled voices and pressed her ear to the door.

"—such a trifling sum," Tom was saying. "Surely it can wait until we're on better footing."

"If you truly believe that, then you'll pace yourself with that port," Maria snapped.

"Our father just died. I can have one glass."

"Oh, you and I both know that is not your first nor your last."

"I think we should all just calm down," Mr. Yates cut in.

"Oh, shut up! I can't believe I'm left running a business with my idiot brother and his—"

"Excuse me. You get half the business, *and* a dowry!"

"Don't pretend that this entire estate isn't worth more than my dowry, which I don't even have unless we can turn the business around."

"Oh, I'm supposed to feel sorry for you when you're the future mistress of Sotherton?"

"Fanny," a voice said, startling her. She jumped and pulled back from the door, unable to hide her guilty expression. She found Julia standing behind her. "Are they still at it?"

She didn't have to guess at what Julia meant. "Yes."

Julia sighed. "Is it scary? Being poor?"

Fanny blinked at her but found she had no words. She opened her mouth to—respond? Reassure? But in the end, nothing came out.

"Oh dear," Julia said. "I suppose that means we'll just have to send you back to where you came from."

And she swept past Fanny, opening the door to the study so she could slip inside. Fanny did not miss the small, vicious smile that Julia wore as she shut the door in her face.

"Oh," Fanny said, the word coming out small and hollow.

She hadn't ever considered that would be an option. After all, what was there for her to go back to? A cramped flat in

Portsmouth, a father who drank, a harried mother with too many children, a family business that could scarcely provide for them all?

She closed her eyes and imagined writing to William, her older brother. *Bad news: Sir Thomas is dead. Good news: I'm returning home.*

Home. Portsmouth wasn't home. It hadn't been home for nine years. And as happy as William would be to welcome her back, her homecoming could only be more bad news for her already struggling family. They'd barely made ends meet with her family's circulating library, her father's penchant for the bottle, and her mother's insistence on not going without a housekeeper.

Besides, if she was sent back to Portsmouth, who would investigate Sir Thomas's death?

Fanny turned on her heel and went in search of Edmund. It wasn't hard—she merely had to wander upstairs and follow the mournful strains of his viola.

The sweet, rich tones of the instrument swelled throughout the second floor as she drew closer to the music room, which looked out over the east gardens. The door was open like an invitation, but Fanny approached on cautious, quiet footsteps. As always, the tumult in her chest seemed to still a little when she heard Edmund play. He sat in the center of the room, back to her as he drew his bow across the strings of the viola. The music was beautiful and loving, but the pace was sedate. A mourning song.

Just as the tune seemed to draw to a close, Edmund's posture shifted slightly as he seemed to sit up straighter. He plucked at the strings and abruptly shifted into an upbeat melody. It wasn't pleasant, exactly, but it was a beautiful shift into rising and falling notes that would seem almost gleeful, if not for the melancholy music he'd been playing just moments earlier. Fanny furrowed her brow, trying to place the music, but she couldn't. And yet, something about it felt familiar.

Edmund stopped playing abruptly just as Fanny realized what the music reminded her of: the rise and fall of Maria's and Tom's arguing voices.

"How long have you been standing there?" he asked, turning to face her.

"Sorry. The door was open."

Edmund's face was heavy with exhaustion, but he smiled. "It's all right, Fanny. I thought you were Aunt Norris at first. Come in."

"What was that?" she asked, nodding at his instrument.

"Oh, just a little something I've been working on."

"Truly? You wrote that yourself?"

"You sound surprised," he remarked. "I can write music as well as play, you know."

"I'm impressed, is all. It was so good I thought that perhaps one of the masters composed it."

He smiled at the praise. "Well, I wouldn't go so far as that. . . ."

She sat in one of the spindle-armed chairs across from him. "You are talented," she insisted.

"Not that it will do me any good. Did you hear the news? Aunt Norris thinks I ought to become a clergyman, and that way Tom can give me a living here when old Dr. Grant finally succumbs to old age, which, according to Maria's estimates, should be soon enough."

Fanny wasn't sure what startled her more: the suggestion that Edmund devote his life to the Lord or his dark tone. "And your trust?"

"He insisted it would be paid back—in time. But this would be a way to keep me 'preoccupied' until then. More like he hopes that if he gives me a good living, I won't complain about our uncle's misdeeds."

"Surely you have some other option?"

"None." The word came out with a bitter snap. "Unless I wish to hire a solicitor of my own and press the matter. But then Tom and Maria will be forced to sell off parcels of the estate, and the family is already in a precarious enough position. They're down there arguing about what can be sold and how to economize."

She let out a mirthless laugh. "That makes sense, then. Julia said something about sending me back just now." Edmund's brow furrowed in confusion, so Fanny added, "To Portsmouth."

"They wouldn't!" Edmund set his viola down with a musical *thump*. "They can't."

"They certainly could," she said, and she wondered why the prospect didn't feel more . . . shocking. Perhaps one could take only so many life-changing revelations in a single day before becoming inured.

"But they rely on you so much! And what would people say?"

Fanny shrugged. "They'll say they're grief-stricken and they need time to themselves, or that my parents called me back because they couldn't do without me. My mother has had three more children since I've been gone."

Three siblings that Fanny had never met, only heard about in letters from William. She couldn't remember the little ones so well anymore. Her memories of Portsmouth were not wholly unpleasant—she knew there had been laughter and games—but it was not as easy to recall them as it was to dwell on the nights when they'd had no fire to warm them and the ache in her belly when there'd not been enough to eat.

"But it's preposterous," Edmund insisted. "What would you even do?"

"Help with the children," she said despondently. Just the thought of it sent an ache throughout her entire body. It wasn't merely that she was always fed and kept reasonably warm and comfortable at Mansfield Park. Mansfield Park had Mansfield Emporium. Artwork. Paints and canvases. Opportunity for her to dedicate herself to her craft. She thought back to some of the last words Sir Thomas had spoken to her. *You have some measure of talent. . . . If you apply yourself, who knows. . . .*

But there would be none of that if she returned to Portsmouth.

"Don't even think about it," Edmund implored her. "We'll find a way for you to stay. You belong in Mansfield."

"Perhaps," she said. She wasn't sure why the word slipped out, but it gave Edmund pause.

"What do you mean by that?"

"It's just . . . I love this place, you know I do. But lately, I've wondered if home was actually less of a place, and more about whom one makes it with." She felt a flush rise in her cheeks. This was as close to admitting her feelings to Edmund as she'd ever gotten.

"I know what you mean," he said, and her heart leapt in wild hope as he met her gaze. "With Sir Thomas gone, Tom and Maria will run unchecked, and make life here miserable. But surely not so miserable as you'd contemplate returning to *Portsmouth*?"

Disappointment dashed her hopes. "Of course not," she murmured.

"Besides," Edmund continued, "this doesn't have to be our lives."

"What do you mean?"

Edmund's features were composed, but a fire burned in his eyes. "I can't stay here, Fanny. I can't join the clergy, and take Dr. Grant's living, and jump to obey every order Tom gives me for the rest of my days. I'm not an heir."

"There are other considerations for second sons," Fanny began to say, but Edmund shook his head.

"That may be true, but I hardly think it a universal practice to give considerations to nephews."

"But what will you do?"

"Go to London." His response was immediate, and it made Fanny think he'd given it a great deal of thought. "Make my way as a musician. Do you remember when we were children, and we talked about doing that? You'd be a painter, I'd play at sold-out concerts, and we'd live in a town house all to ourselves and read about ourselves in the society papers."

Fanny's cheeks flushed at the memory, which had been innocent when they were children but now seemed rather suggestive. "Yes, but it doesn't seem very realistic now."

"You're right," he agreed. "You don't read the society papers."

"I would if you were mentioned," she said, and she felt her composure slip as her voice broke on the last word.

"Don't cry!" Edmund reached out and took her hands in

his. Then he said, "Come with me."

"*What?*" Shock dried her tears quicker than anything else he might have said. "Edmund, I can't."

"Why not? What life do you have here? Especially now that our uncle is gone?"

She understood what he meant, but she still felt vaguely insulted by the question. "I do have a life here. A very comfortable one, too." Then she added, "For now."

"That's just it—you do for *now*. But the future we could have, the freedom we could have—think about it. You could be more than a lady's companion."

Fanny wanted all of this, of course. If Edmund was going to leave Mansfield, she wanted to follow him. But what exactly was he asking? For her to marry him? They may have been raised like cousins, but they weren't related by blood. There was no way that Fanny could be a respectable painter if anyone found out she'd run away from her family to live with Edmund in London.

"How would it work? How would we live?" She hesitated, then added, "People will talk."

She waited, hopeful that he'd laugh and say, *Of course we'll get married. Did I forget to mention that? Silly me!* And then she could laugh at him and say, *Yes, you did forget to mention it, but never mind, I accept.*

"I don't have all the details quite figured out," Edmund

said. "And there is the matter of money. It would be easier if I had my trust for us to live off of, but I have friends from school who live in London. Perhaps I start modestly and can send for you as soon as I've found a respectable place. Maybe we'll both find patrons!"

Fanny stared at him for several beats, letting his words sink in. No marriage proposal. Not even a *hint* of one. And no acknowledgment of what it would do to her reputation, to her future, if she moved with him to London. No one would hire her to paint their daughters' portraits if they thought her a fallen woman. She'd rather stay in Mansfield than mar her reputation in that way! No, she'd rather go back to *Portsmouth*.

"I can't," she said.

Edmund's face fell. "What? Why not?"

She almost told him her exact thoughts, but the disappointment and concern on his face made her hesitate. Perhaps he wasn't thinking sensibly. This was Edmund, of course he cared for her. She just didn't know if he cared for her in *that* way. And what if he might come to do so, but admitting her true thoughts on the matter made him feel pressured to propose and ruined her one chance at them finding happiness in their own time?

She couldn't tell him the truth.

So instead, she inhaled deeply and told him the second-best reason she could think of for staying at Mansfield Park: "Because, I think our uncle might have been . . . murdered."

The word landed with all the grace of a sledgehammer between them. Edmund dropped her hands abruptly. "What? Fanny, that's . . . don't even joke about that."

Fanny had thought her greatest fear in sharing her suspicions was in not being believed, but now she realized that not being taken seriously was even worse than doubt. "I'm deadly serious, Edmund."

She didn't realize the irony of her word choice until Edmund's face sobered. "But . . . what? How?"

Fanny got up from her chair and went to the music room door and shut it firmly, but not before making certain that no one was out in the hallway. Then she marched back to Edmund and dragged her chair closer to him. Edmund watched her with a baffled expression as Fanny sat and told him everything, beginning with overhearing Maria and Sir Thomas argue the day of his death and ending with Miss Bennet's advice.

When she was finally done, Fanny sat back with a sigh and waited for him to speak.

"I . . . Fanny. I can't believe this."

"I'm not exaggerating or lying," she insisted.

"No, no—I know you would never. But I think I'm in shock."

"I know it's a lot to take in," she said. "But you must understand the urgency of the situation. And why I can't simply leave Mansfield Park until . . ." She swallowed, feeling vaguely guilty about this twisting of the truth. But Edmund didn't seem to notice.

"The urgency?" he repeated.

"Yes. We must figure out who, and why, and get proof."

She didn't think it was possible for him to appear even more shocked, but she was wrong. "Are you *mad*?" he said in a whisper that somehow managed to sound like a shout. "If one of our relatives killed Sir Thomas, then the last thing we ought to do is *confront* any of them."

"Even if a crime has been committed?" she asked.

"Especially then!" Edmund leapt to his feet and began pacing. "Sir Thomas was a peer of the realm. Tom is now very powerful, and Maria is poised to marry the magistrate of our county. Not to mention that the Bertram name is highly respected. It would be social death to us both if we were to accuse Tom or Maria or Julia of murder."

"Well, it probably isn't Julia," Fanny admitted, striving for levity.

But Edmund didn't laugh. "This isn't funny. If Sir Thomas was murdered, the safest place for us is *away* from Mansfield Park. If they even think you suspect them . . ."

Fanny was not too principled to admit that it felt good to see Edmund fret about her safety and well-being, but now that she'd divulged her secret, she found she couldn't simply let the issue drop.

"We can't let them get away with it. There's no one left to hold them accountable. You can't really believe that Tom will simply restore your trust if there's no reason for him to? If we were to reveal the truth of Sir Thomas's death and bring the perpetrator to justice, then . . ."

"Then what?" Edmund asked, sounding almost belligerent. It scared Fanny, for a moment, to hear the roughness in his tone. But she steadied herself. Edmund was just scared, as was she.

"Then the truth would be known. They would have to restore your trust. And perhaps they'd stop seeing us as pawns for their own personal amusement. Perhaps whoever was left would be grateful that we revealed the truth, and we'd have the freedom to live our lives."

"So much is riding on *perhaps*," Edmund noted.

"Perhaps," Fanny agreed. "But think of this: Of all the people in this house, who has treated us the best since we were children?"

"Sir Thomas," Edmund said without hesitation.

"Precisely. The rest of them can fritter away their lives and fortunes for all I care, but if our uncle was killed, then I want to experience the moment of looking into the killer's eyes when they've been caught. And I want to ask them *why*."

Fanny surprised herself with the strength of her own conviction, but her words were convincing. Edmund sighed. "I suppose there's no talking you out of this?"

"No," she replied. If only Miss Bennet could see her now!

"We must see that our uncle's killer is brought to justice."

Edmund's jaw was set, and his chest rose and fell with heavy breaths, but Fanny knew her words had taken hold within him. Finally, he looked up and met her gaze. "All right," he said. "Where do we begin?"

SIX

*In Which Fanny's Amateur Sleuthing
Yields Mixed Results*

WITH EDMUND CONSCRIPTED TO her cause—
albeit somewhat reluctantly—Fanny found herself feeling rather
optimistic the next morning. Accepting Miss Bennet's advice
about following the money, Fanny decided the first place they
ought to look was the household ledgers for any clues as to what,
exactly, had caused the Bertram family's financial downfall.

However, given that no one was likely to open the pages
and invite Fanny to peruse them, a certain amount of stealth
was required.

Fanny was no lady solicitor like Miss Bennet or a professional investigator like the alluded-to Miss Dashwood, but
she was certain that half a lifetime spent in Mansfield Park

qualified her for this task, especially with her relatives so distracted by their state of affairs. The trouble was finding the right opportunity.

Fanny spent the morning skulking about the hallway outside of Sir Thomas's study, trying to find the ideal time to slip in unnoticed. Unfortunately, Aunt Norris and her cousins had taken over the study, sorting out business matters in between pointed arguments about how best to earn back their lost fortune, showing no signs of leaving things be. As a result, it took half the morning before Fanny overheard that Mr. Rushworth was coming to call after luncheon, at which time they'd have a "family" discussion to determine their next steps.

"How nice of them to invite us," Edmund muttered when Fanny breathlessly relayed the news.

"Be glad they didn't," Fanny said, even though she felt the same twist of the metaphorical knife. There was no doubt about it—they were being pushed out most deliberately. "This is our chance."

Fanny would slip into the study while Edmund would serve as her lookout. Simple enough. But Fanny hadn't accounted for just how reluctant Edmund proved to be. "Don't you think I should be the one to search the study?" he asked. "And you can be my lookout? Or better yet, go to luncheon, act oblivious, and if they decide to head to the study, stall them."

Fanny winced, and not just because this was a terrible idea.

"Do you think I'm not capable of searching for the proper evidence? Besides, I wouldn't be able to stall Maria—she's never listened to a word I've said."

"And she'll listen to me?"

"They at least look in your general direction every now and then." Fanny sucked in a deep breath and tried to remain calm and collected. Edmund was taking his fall in status rather hard, and she had to remind herself this was all new to him. "Besides, you've been away to school for the last five years. I have a better sense of household matters."

Edmund sighed, but after a hefty pause he said, "Fine. But don't get caught."

It took a great deal of fortitude for Fanny not to roll her eyes.

A half hour before luncheon, Fanny headed downstairs at a sedate pace, keeping an eye out for any of the staff. She had to duck into an alcove when a footman came around the corner unexpectedly, but she breathed a sigh of relief when he continued on his path without pause. She slipped down the hall and into the library, which was fortuitously empty. Then, just to be on the safe side, she crouched behind an armchair out of sight of the doorway, feeling completely foolish. There was moving about the manor inconspicuously, and then there was sneaking about, and sneaking was new to her.

The doors to the study were sturdy, but not so thick that she couldn't hear her cousins murmuring from the other side. They were discussing outstanding correspondence when she heard the muffled sound of the butler announcing luncheon. There was the rustling of paper and then Maria's voice saying, "Thank you, Brooks. Have one of the maids tidy up in here, would you? Mr. Rushworth is coming directly after luncheon."

"Of course, Miss Bertram," he said, and Fanny bit back a sigh.

Fanny kept an eye on the grandfather clock in the corner as she waited for her cousins to retire to the dining room and for the maids to tidy. If she didn't get into the drawing room within half an hour, she'd have hardly any time to do a proper search. Finally, the door to the hall clicked shut and the maids' footsteps faded away. Fanny counted to thirty and then rose to her feet, wincing as her legs tingled in protest. She carefully unlatched the door to the study and peered inside. Empty. On the desk sat a stack of ledgers.

Perfect.

Like her cousins, Fanny had been taught the essentials of how to manage household accounts. Unlike her cousins, she'd never been granted access to Mansfield's books. Usually the housekeeper kept them under lock and key and brought them out once per week for Lady Bertram's inspection and approval, with input from Maria when her mother's headaches interfered. This was the first chance Fanny had to look at the actual numbers.

What she found was nothing particularly unusual when it

came to household expenses. She pored over charges from the greengrocer, the butcher, the candlemaker, looking for anything that might be amiss. She inspected tallies from the London shops, where her cousins often sent for goods they couldn't get from the village. The numbers made her swallow, but as she paged back through the ledgers, comparing charges that went back months and years, she noted that the Bertrams' spending was fairly consistent.

She flipped through accounts of household expenses, estate improvements, and staff wages. She was searching for an increase in spending, an obscene bill, or perhaps some hidden vice. But all she found was an orderly account of household expenses that, for some reason, started to go unpaid around six months earlier. It was as if the money coming in from Mansfield Emporium had simply dried up.

She searched the desk but didn't find a ledger for Mansfield Emporium's business accounts. Why wasn't it here? Was it in the storehouse or locked in a drawer? Fanny let out a frustrated sigh. Following the money was a lot less straightforward than she thought.

Just then, Fanny heard voices in the hall. She quickly began to straighten up the mess of ledgers and paperwork, hastily closing the books and stacking bills. She was just about to step away from the desk when the door opened and she went still.

But her luck had held—it was only Edmund. "You have to go!" he hissed. "They're coming!"

There was no time to be grateful that she wasn't caught yet. Fanny picked up her skirts and ran as quietly as she could to the adjoining library, Edmund on her heels. They'd just slid the door shut behind them when they heard voices enter the study.

"—don't understand why we need to have this conversation with *him*," Tom said as Fanny sagged against the sturdy oak, heart still galloping.

"If you insist on including Yates in important business decisions, then I can have my fiancé here," came Maria's response.

"Yates and I are business partners."

"And that makes him more important than my fiancé?"

Edmund tried to pull her away, but Fanny shook her head. *I want to listen*, she mouthed.

"We'll all be family," Mr. Rushworth added. "And I think I ought to know what my wife is doing with her assets in the meantime."

"I'm not your wife yet," Maria reminded him. "And they're still my assets."

"Apologies, future wife," Mr. Rushworth corrected.

Edmund rolled his eyes, and Fanny had to stifle her laugh.

"You're really going to go through with the wedding, what with Father barely cold in his grave?" Tom asked.

"It's what Father would have wanted. After an appropriate period of mourning has passed, we'll have a small ceremony."

Tom snorted. "Define *appropriate*."

"I think that sounds more than reasonable," Aunt Norris

intervened. "A wedding will bring us all some much-needed cheer."

Fanny shouldn't have been surprised to hear her aunt's voice—she always needed to have a say on anything that went on at Mansfield.

Tom scoffed. "You know what I think? I think that if Father truly was pleased with this match, he would have given you his blessing months ago."

"Now see here—" Mr. Rushworth began.

"Sit down," Maria snapped, presumably at her fiancé. "Tom, quit speculating on business that doesn't concern you. We have to work together whether we like it or not. Now are we going to get ourselves out of this mess, or bicker like children?"

There were some murmurings and mutters that Fanny couldn't quite make out, and then Tom said, "Fine. Right now, we need to make some significant sales by the end of the month, or we won't have money to pay the servants' wages."

"Rushworth and I have a list of clients we can write to immediately," Maria said.

"That won't be enough. No selling a painting here or there, hoping a big score will last us until some old biddy in Cornwall wants to redecorate her drawing room. We need to move most of our stock."

"You think I don't know that?" Maria shot back. "Rushworth has his own network of buyers, and I can think of three people who'd want the Millbrook that Father has been hanging on to for some inane reason."

Fanny inhaled sharply. Her favorite painting. The thought of it being sold off before she had a chance to finish her replica was nearly as upsetting as the prospect of being sent back to Portsmouth.

"That's all well and good, but we can't just make sales to all our contacts," Tom continued. "Otherwise we'll end up in the same predicament next month, or three months from now. We need to find new buyers, expand our network. Father never wanted to consider this, but I think it's high time we at least consider, or explore, the idea of . . . well, the option of—"

"Just spit it out, Tom." Maria's annoyance made her sound bored, although Fanny was sure she was anything but.

"We propose changing up the business model," Mr. Yates announced.

Fanny raised her eyebrows at Edmund, who was now just as rapt as she. He gave a tiny shrug.

"Oh, I can hardly wait to hear what harebrained scheme you two have cooked up," Maria said.

"Listen to him," Tom urged. "He knows a fellow—"

"Heaven help us."

"—who is an expert in setting up fine-art auctions. He mostly deals with estate sales and the like, but he's well-known in the art world. He could help us out."

"In what capacity?" Aunt Norris asked. "Surely you don't mean to sell off Mansfield Emporium?"

"No, of course not," Tom said. "But this man is an expert in finding new ways to sell art—he could help us with an auction ball."

"An auction ball?" Maria repeated, the horror dripping from her voice.

"Oh, a ball! Father never let us have one of those," Julia said.

"It would be indecent," Aunt Norris cut in, and for once Fanny found that she agreed with her aunt, which was a very unpleasant sensation. "Your father hasn't even been dead a week."

"It wouldn't happen next week," Tom said. "But let's invite this fellow to Mansfield, have him evaluate the collection, and get his expert opinion. Maria, you can continue to work your connections and try to make private sales, but we need to get the best possible prices and drum up interest in our collection. It wouldn't hurt to gain some new clients as well."

Silence followed, and Fanny imagined that the idea of large profits was enough to entice them into considering Tom's proposal.

"If I agree to this," Maria said finally, "then I would want your assurance that we could continue to deal with Mr. Rushworth's contact in Scotland."

"Stewart? Well, as long as you don't go giving him our best pieces. . . ."

"I'll give him whatever pieces he wants."

"But the expense—Maria, be reasonable. It costs enough to ship to London."

"You know my terms." A dangerous silence followed, and Fanny could very well imagine Tom grimacing at Maria's steely reserves.

"Fine. Now, if you want to keep Rushworth's fellow happy with a few sales here and there, all right. But you're not sending him the Millbrook, it'll fetch a much better sum with the London crowd—"

This launched a round of raucous arguments that drew in Mr. Rushworth, Julia, and Aunt Norris. Even Mr. Yates tried ineffectually to clear his throat and say, "May I?" several times, but the Bertrams were not ones to stop and offer permission when arguing, so the shouting continued.

Edmund winced and whispered, "Aren't you glad you aren't in there?"

Fanny nodded her head ever so slightly. They really were quite close, she noticed. He had the loveliest eyelashes she'd ever seen, long and dark and enchanting. She'd never considered eyelashes a trait to admire in a gentleman before, but Edmund's were really making her reconsider this.

"Enough!" Aunt Norris roared.

The room fell silent on the other side of the door, and Fanny flinched, causing Edmund to grab hold of her hand.

"Now, I don't know what the best course of action is.

Never been much for business, myself, nor have I ever shown an interest."

At that blatant lie, Fanny very nearly burst out laughing.

"But bickering won't solve anything," Aunt Norris continued. "Not when there very well may be bailiffs on their way from London as we speak. You both need to compromise."

Fanny strained her ears for any sound, but the room was silent on the other side of the door. She saw Edmund swallow hard at the mention of bailiffs. If the bailiffs turned up, would they send Fanny away? What would they do to Edmund?

Would he continue their search for the truth, if Fanny was no longer around?

Finally, Julia spoke up. "I really don't want to be poor."

There was some muttering, and Fanny would have bet her twenty pounds that Tom would be the first to crack.

She was right.

"Look, we need to make money quickly. Maria, how about you offer Stewart five pieces in the storehouse—wait, let me finish. We sell the rest here in England, for as much as we can get. Then moving forward, we can talk about offering him more. But we can't have too much of our money tied up in haggling with him. Aunt Norris is right—those bailiffs could come calling any day now."

"*Fine.*" Maria spat out the word as though it offended her. "Five for now, but if you don't let me offer him more business later on, I'll find literally any other man in England to entrust my shares of the business to when I marry."

Tom scoffed, and Fanny could sense another argument brewing like a thunderstorm. But Aunt Norris cleared her throat and said, "Speaking of the possibility of bailiffs . . . we ought to have a plan for if they take up residence."

"What do you mean?" Tom asked.

Fanny could envision her aunt clearly: she was likely wearing a demure expression that did nothing to hide the cunning in her eyes—Aunt Norris was never as subtle as she believed herself to be. "It seems awfully unfair that every ha'penny that comes into this house must be turned over to them once they take up residence," she said. "The family ought to have a little something to live on. Just in case. What if your mother takes ill, or we need something from the village?"

Fanny nearly betrayed her hiding spot by laughing. No one in the village would dare turn down business from Mansfield Park, and the doctor would attend to Lady Bertram without even considering the possibility that the family couldn't afford to pay. But Aunt Norris was smart to appeal to her cousins' greed.

"What do you suggest?" Tom asked.

"Nothing untoward," Aunt Norris assured him. "Just that perhaps Maria's business with Mr. Stewart ought to be conducted through my cottage. That way whatever proceeds come from the sale are kept out of the bailiffs' hands. And the family has some money set aside for . . . incidentals."

What Aunt Norris described sounded very untoward indeed to Fanny's ears. She turned an incredulous look at Edmund and saw her own shock mirrored in his expression.

"That sounds . . . prudent," Tom admitted. "If you'd be willing to allow the business to intrude upon your home, that is."

"No intrusion," Aunt Norris insisted. "I'm here so often, I shouldn't notice it at all."

Fanny shook her head in disbelief. Not only were her cousins planning on opening Mansfield Emporium, and the estate itself, to the public, but now they were openly discussing scamming their creditors?

"Capital," Tom exclaimed. "I'm glad that's settled. You'll see, by the end of the month we'll be back on track."

"That's rather optimistic," Maria said. "Don't forget we have to pay back the artists and dealers, settle all outstanding household and business debts, and there's the small matter of Edmund's trust. . . ."

Someone made a disparaging sound, and Tom said, "How much is it exactly?"

A rustle of paper and a long pause, and then Maria said, "Just under two thousand pounds."

Someone whistled, low and long. Likely Mr. Yates. Then Tom said, "Oh well, that's rather . . . a lot."

Fanny saw Edmund's jaw tighten, and she reached out and placed a hand on his shoulder. He didn't acknowledge it.

"It won't be paid back overnight." Maria sighed. "Father

started borrowing against the sum a few years ago. I spent all evening with the ledger, and as far as I could tell, he tried to hide it, funneling small amounts from the trust into the business coffers. He would label it as sales to a Mrs. Frere. But then last year, 'Mrs. Frere' made an awfully large purchase of . . . six hundred pounds."

Mr. Yates chuckled. "Mrs. Frere. Hardly subtle."

"How so?" Julia asked, and Fanny rolled her eyes. Had she forgotten all of their French lessons?

"Frère is 'brother' en le française," Mr. Yates said.

"Mrs. . . . oh, I get it! He was labeling the purchases from Mrs. *Brother*, because it was his brother's trust."

Her incredulity would have been funny, if Edmund weren't standing right before her with anger storming in his eyes.

"Yes, well . . . we'll chip away at it," Tom said. "And let's hope that Edmund doesn't want the full amount at his birthday."

"He's entitled to it," Maria reminded her brother. "And if we can't pay it, then he could take us to court."

Fanny shook her head. "You'd never," she whispered to Edmund. It never ceased to amaze her the way her cousins assumed the worst in people just because they had no scruples whatsoever. But strangely, Edmund didn't agree with her. He just tilted his head, expression expectant, as he waited for a response from Tom.

But when it came, it shocked Fanny.

"That wouldn't be wise of him," Tom said. "I mean, when you think about it objectively . . . well, Father dies in an accident in the warehouse, and Edmund was there mere moments before. . . ."

Fanny gasped, no longer caring whether or not she could be heard.

"Come now," Tom said into the silence that followed. "I'm not saying he pushed Father or anything, but just that if he decided to get solicitors involved, things could get very nasty."

"It wouldn't hold up," Fanny whispered to Edmund. "You weren't anywhere near Sir Thomas. *Maria* was the one—"

"Hush, Fanny," he whispered, silencing her with a harsh look.

"I've never known him to be a vindictive boy—disobedient, yes," Aunt Norris said. "But who knows how boys change when they're sent away to school?"

"He has been awfully broody since he returned," Julia added.

"And he was upset when Father wouldn't let him go to London . . . ," Maria mused.

Fanny looked at Edmund and raised her eyebrows. When had he asked Sir Thomas to go to London? But Edmund merely shook his head.

"See?" Tom said. "You all looked at me like I was mad to suggest it, but I'd say that's our defense if Edmund tries to do anything rash. He's a reasonable sort, he just needs to be patient."

"But think of the scandal," Maria hissed. "The business would be ruined. We would be the topic of gossip for months!"

"I'm not saying we should accuse him. I'm merely pointing out that we have a handy method of persuasion if he insists on being paid money we don't have."

Fanny was, by nature, soft-spoken and slow to anger. She didn't like speaking up for herself, and she dreaded causing any kind of scene, but hearing her cousins malign Edmund in such a way was too much. They didn't care about the truth, only money. And it turned out that hearing malicious lies and rumors about someone she loved was the one thing that would induce her to act.

Edmund seemed to know what Fanny was about to do before she did. "Fanny, no—"

But it was no use. She was already throwing open the door.

Tom and Maria were standing, and Mr. Rushworth was lounging with his odious boots on a footstool, rubbing black polish into the upholstery. Aunt Norris sat in the corner next to Julia, and Mr. Yates looked up from a letter he was writing at the side table.

"What on earth—" Aunt Norris began, but for the first time in her life, Fanny interrupted her.

"How dare you accuse Edmund of such a thing? Your own

family?" Her anger, usually tamped down tightly, came pouring out now, turning her voice shrill.

"You ought to know better than to listen at doors at your age," Aunt Norris snapped. She rose and came to take Fanny's elbow, not bothering to be gentle about it.

"No one is accusing anyone of anything," Tom insisted, as if Fanny simply hadn't heard correctly.

"Edmund was nowhere near the stairs when Uncle fell! And Maria was the last person upstairs with Sir Thomas before he fell!"

"Are you accusing me of something?" Maria asked, her voice deadly.

Fanny's mouth went dry. "No, but—"

"Good," Maria interrupted. "Because I would hate to have to tell everyone that my poor cousin from Portsmouth is tragically afflicted with a hysterical condition, and she's not a reliable witness at all."

"That would indeed be a hardship," Aunt Norris agreed. "Think of your cousins, Fanny. Their reputations would be marred."

The anger that had propelled Fanny into a confrontation ebbed away as she looked from Maria to Aunt Norris to Tom. Mr. Yates and Mr. Rushworth looked away from her, as if she were an embarrassing thing, beneath their recognition. Julia watched her with a squint and a slight smirk.

"You ought to be careful with idle accusations, Fanny," Maria continued.

"Edmund wouldn't dare hurt Uncle," she said, her words a whisper. It was a weak stance, but she took it nonetheless, because she believed in her heart that it was true.

"That's enough from you," Aunt Norris said, tightening her grasp on Fanny so that her fingers dug into the bruise that Maria had left days earlier." Come along."

"No," Fanny said, wrenching her arm away from Aunt Norris. It was partly a reflex to save her poor neglected skin, but she was done being hauled away like Pug when she soiled the carpet. She turned to find Edmund, to take a stand.

But he was no longer behind her.

Where had he gone? She thought he'd been with her when she threw open the doors to the study, but no one had acknowledged his presence—they'd all been focused on her. Had he retreated from view and left her to face the wolves alone?

"You are on thin ice, Fanny Price," Aunt Norris warned, and steered her out of the room. This time, Fanny didn't resist. She let herself be dragged up the stairs to her chamber, which was the former nursery on the third floor. Aunt Norris shoved her inside. Before she closed the door, she said, "You've tried my patience for nearly ten years now, and don't think that because you're my sister's child that I will continue to make allowances for you. Sir Thomas is dead, God rest his soul, and things are going to change around here. You can either be a good girl and make yourself useful to the family, or so help me, I'll send you back to the hovel you came from! Do I make myself clear?"

"Yes," Fanny said dutifully, although her heart rebelled.

"Good."

Then she slammed the door.

Fanny slumped down on her narrow bed. This was why she shouldn't trust her anger toward her relatives—it felt powerful and good to give in to it in the moment, to challenge their awful words, but they always found a way to outsmart her. And they had all the power, which meant she was usually left alone, worse off than she was before. It was better to just swallow it and stay out of everyone's way.

Maybe Edmund was right, and it was no use fighting back. That was why he'd probably stepped back while Fanny had charged ahead. What hope did Fanny have of correcting things when no one seemed to notice or care about propriety or legality? Why, even Aunt Norris's suggestion that they go so far as to illegally conceal business dealings . . .

Wait. Fanny sat up on her thin mattress, hand to her mouth.

Aunt Norris has seemed very *prepared* to make that offer.

And Maria was awfully keen to support the idea.

Almost as if they'd planned it.

Follow the money, Miss Bennet had suggested. What if the money she ought to be following wasn't in any household ledger? What if she needed to pay more attention to the shady dealings *outside* of Mansfield Emporium?

Aunt Norris hadn't been inside the storehouse at the time of Sir Thomas's fall, but that didn't mean she was innocent. Maria had always been Aunt Norris's favorite niece, so if there was even the slightest chance that Maria had done anything to cause her own father's death, well, then . . .

There was a good chance that Aunt Norris was in on it.

SEVEN

In Which Fanny Engages in Some Light Trespassing

UNDER NORMAL CIRCUMSTANCES, FANNY wouldn't dare enter Aunt Norris's cottage without an invitation, and even then she would be reluctant to step into her lair. But she couldn't shake the feeling that there was something more to be discovered there. Naturally, it was a source of great frustration when Fanny couldn't immediately go poking about.

"You can't simply sashay in," Edmund told her when Fanny divulged her suspicions. "You have no reason to go there, and she'll know that you're investigating, or worse. . . ."

"Worse?" Fanny wasn't sure what was worse.

"If you discover something, and she discovers you . . . do you think that she'll be content to send you back to Portsmouth? If you're right and she and Maria are responsible, then, well . . . we know that they're capable of causing accidents."

The words sent a shiver down Fanny's spine, but strangely, she wasn't deterred. "I'll be careful. No more wild accusations or angry confrontations. I'll let her think she's subdued me with her threats, but I can't let this go, Edmund."

He hadn't liked that, she could tell. He shook his head, and for half a moment Fanny was afraid that he'd do something silly and forbid her from further investigation. Instead, he caught one of her hands in his, sending a shock of warmth up her spine.

"Edmund?" she whispered.

"I just don't want you to do anything rash," he said, squeezing her hand gently.

She peered at him, hoping his eyes would meet hers. What if they did? Would she find the strength to confess her feelings? And if Edmund asked her to marry him, and leave Mansfield Park behind, would she go?

No. She had to find the truth.

She returned the squeeze, then gently withdrew her hand from his. "Nothing rash," she promised.

She repeated those words to herself nearly a week later, while out walking Pug. "Nothing rash," she told the dog, who sniffed about happily in the grass. "Nothing rash about taking a stroll. And if we happen to end up at Aunt Norris's cottage on a day when her housekeeper goes to the village, well. That would just be coincidence."

Pug seemed to grunt in agreement.

The walk wasn't overly long—Mansfield Cottage sat on the

lane that led to the rest of the estate, separated from the main house by a swath of dense woods. The path was sheltered from the sun thanks to the new foliage on the trees, and the dirt of the path was dark and wet. As a consequence, by the time she emerged into the clearing where Mansfield Cottage sat, her boots were caked with black mud . . . and Fanny didn't even have to look at the bottom of Pug's paws to know that they were also filthy.

"How likely is it that you will sit here quietly while I pop inside?" Fanny asked the dog.

Pug cocked her head at Fanny in a manner that she took to mean, *Not very.*

"Fine," Fanny said with a sigh. "But you must be very good."

She knocked on the back door of the cottage and listened intently for any sound of life within. Aunt Norris's housekeeper was a middle-aged woman named Anna, who no doubt was enjoying a well-deserved reprieve from Aunt Norris's constant oversight. Fanny knew that Anna had a sister in the village whom she often visited when her aunt wasn't around, and she hoped that this afternoon would be one of those occasions.

After waiting and knocking once more, Fanny opened the kitchen door. "Hello?" she called out. But the cottage was still and quiet.

Pug trotted right in, leaving muddy paw prints on the swept and polished floor. "Pug!" Fanny hissed, and the dog stopped and turned back to look at her as if to say, *Well? What are you waiting for?*

Fanny hovered at the threshold. Thinking about investigating Aunt Norris's cottage and doing it were two very different things, as it turned out. Now, she couldn't help but wonder—was she taking this task a bit too far? Was she being *rash*?

Then she thought of Miss Bennet. What would she do?

Fanny stepped inside and removed her shoes before shutting the door behind her.

A hallway extended from the kitchen to the front of the cottage, and Fanny crept along, leading Pug by her leash, and peeked in on an empty dining room, a pristine parlor, and a slightly shabbier and more lived-in sitting room. There was a closed door between the kitchen and the dining room she'd never once seen open, but when she peeked inside she saw a storeroom filled with the normal wares of a small household—sacks of flour and sugar, canned goods, candles, and linens stacked neatly on shelves.

Fanny stood in the middle of the hall and let out a short sigh. Nothing.

But then again . . . if Aunt Norris were truly hiding something here, she would hardly stash it in her spare sitting room, where any visitor might walk in by chance. She headed for the stairs.

Four doors branched off from a landing at the top, and all

were firmly shut. She turned right and very quietly opened a door onto a spare bedchamber, made up for guests. There was a bed with a blue coverlet, a neat washstand, a chest of drawers, and a rag rug on the bare floor. The walls were plain and Fanny could spot nothing suspicious.

The next room was nearly identical, but this one had a lavender bedspread. Both rooms were so stripped of any sort of personal items—books, a stray handkerchief, a packet of letters—that Fanny wondered if Aunt Norris had ever had visitors. She closed the second door behind her and crossed the hall to the third room.

The other two rooms faced the afternoon sun, but the first was dim, with drapes drawn tightly against the sunlight. Fanny blinked, waiting for her eyes to adjust. On first glance the room appeared to be a private sitting room, with a desk and writing chair pushed against one wall and a settee before the cold, empty fireplace. But then the details began to emerge, and Fanny stepped inside with a small gasp.

There were paintings everywhere.

Not on the walls, but on the floor in frames, leaning against the walls. The perimeter of the room was ringed with stacks of paintings—there must have been at least fifty. Far more than the five pieces that Tom had promised Maria could sell.

She walked over to the nearest stack and flipped through them, inspecting the contents of each frame. The art varied in size, subject, artist, and style, but they all looked vaguely familiar. Fanny's eyes snagged on one painting she knew for a fact she'd seen before: the painting was medium-sized and the portrait was nearly—but not quite—to scale. It depicted a man with dark, graying hair and sideburns, and he was looking off to the right of the frame. He looked worn down, almost melancholy, but in his blue eyes blazed a spirited light that wouldn't be defeated.

Fanny sucked in a breath. It was a self-portrait of George Rasmussen, a painter whose work her uncle had bought and sold often. And she remembered this picture. It had been purchased in a lot of artwork two seasons ago and her uncle had sold it quickly, before the artist died. She was certain of this, because Sir Thomas had complained that the value of the portrait had surely doubled upon his death.

What was it doing in Aunt Norris's upstairs sitting room?

Then there was a creak behind her, and Fanny turned, expecting to see Pug. A figure stood in the doorway, and Fanny screamed.

"Good heavens, miss!"

Fanny's hand flew to her chest. "Anna! I'm so sorry. I didn't hear you."

"Clearly," the older woman said, glancing between Fanny and Pug, who was sitting in the hall. Some watch dog she was. Anna's expression was hard and unreadable. "You shouldn't be in here, miss."

"Of course," Fanny agreed, and then wanted to kick herself

for saying so. "It's just . . . Aunt Norris sent me to see if, um, a painting was still here? So I just came over to find it, and now that I've, uh, found it . . . I'll go."

The lie fell flat between the two of them, and judging from Anna's dubious expression, she wasn't convinced. "Mrs. Norris doesn't allow anyone in here."

And for good reason, Fanny thought. There had to be a small fortune in fine art here. What sort of scheme was Aunt Norris running? And had Sir Thomas known?

Anna took a few steps into the room and made to steer Fanny out, forcing her to do some quick mental calculations. Anna was a good housekeeper, and she needed her job. She would not likely want to jeopardize her position, especially if lately she'd been given the freedom to come and go as she pleased. Besides, Fanny had already implied that she was here with Aunt Norris's knowledge and consent, and even if Anna wasn't convinced, Fanny knew that admitting her trespassing wouldn't gain her any traction.

"I know what Aunt Norris is doing," she announced.

Anna pulled her out of the room and shut the door firmly behind her. "Oh?"

"Yes," Fanny said, heart racing faster than her churning thoughts. "She . . . is in on it with Maria."

Anna had no reaction, so Fanny took it as a confirmation. "It's Maria's contact, isn't it?"

"If you know what Mrs. Norris is doing, then surely you

don't need me to comment on any of that," came the house-keeper's reply.

She looked behind her at the closed door and thought of Aunt Norris's suggestion that the family sell pieces from Mansfield Emporium to Mr. Rushworth's Scottish contacts through her cottage, out from under the nose of any bailiffs who might install themselves in the house. That suggestion had been so calculated that Fanny hadn't thought it out of character . . . but it was a very keen suggestion. Almost as if . . . she'd already been doing it.

"How long have those paintings been in there?" Fanny asked.

Anna sighed and shook her head. "It's not my place, miss."

"Please," she said, her tone pleading. "I didn't mean to be a snoop, exactly. It's just that Aunt Norris and Maria have been whispering an awful lot, and I had to know if they were planning something. Tom doesn't exactly inspire confidence in the future."

A look of uncertainty flashed across Anna's face as she shifted from one foot to the other.

"Please understand, I have no wish to get anyone in trouble," Fanny continued. "But my own situation is tenuous, and I don't want to be surprised by a sudden change in circumstances."

Anna sighed, and Fanny held her breath as she waited for the other woman to speak.

"Don't ask me exactly what is going on, because I don't

know," she said finally, her voice barely more than a whisper. "Mrs. Norris just stores the paintings. She doesn't explain, and I don't ask. About once a month, a man in a covered wagon comes and takes a few paintings and leaves some others. No one else from the big house is involved, and Mrs. Norris says she's doing the household a favor."

Incredulity made Fanny snort. "How is it that she's doing the household a favor, exactly?"

"Because these deliveries only ever happen at night, and she says that they'd wake the whole household."

Fanny's lips formed an *oh*, but no sound came out. Anna noted her surprise and seemed to grow more unsettled. She looked about the landing, as if Aunt Norris might appear at any moment. "You should go," she said.

"Wait." Fanny tightened her hold on Pug's leash. "The day of my uncle's accident. Did the man come then?"

"I told you, he only ever comes at night," Anna said.

"But when did he last come?" Fanny asked, trying not to let desperation creep into her tone.

"Later that night," Anna finally said. "I think you should go now."

Fanny allowed herself to be propelled down the stairs, but all the while her mind was turning. She recalled the words that Maria had spoken minutes before the accident—something about a response and keeping him waiting? Him. At the time, Fanny had assumed that Maria was pestering Sir Thomas about when he'd give his blessing for her to be married to Mr. Rushworth. But what if Maria had instead been speaking of someone else?

The mysterious man who picked up paintings from Aunt Norris's cottage in the middle of the night? Who was he?

"The man who picks up the paintings," Fanny said. "Do you know him?"

"He's not from around here," Anna said shortly. "And next time you decide to go snooping through other people's things, don't let that ridiculous dog track mud all over my clean floors!"

Fanny looked down at the stairs. Muddy paw prints led all the way upstairs, like a fairy-tale trail of bread crumbs to where she'd been poking about. "I'm sorry," she said. "I'll clean them up."

"No, it's high time you go," Anna insisted. Once they were in the kitchen, she oversaw Fanny pulling on her muddy shoes and she added, "I don't need to let Mrs. Norris know you stopped by to visit, do I? It would look awfully awkward if it was known you came by and I wasn't here to receive you."

It took Fanny a beat to realize the agreement that Anna was offering. *You don't tell your aunt I was gone, I won't tell her you were snooping.*

"Of course," she said, gathering her shawl around her. "It would be silly to bring it up."

"Very good," Anna said, and she opened the door for Fanny. Pug was all too happy to dart back outside, and as she tugged at her leash, something else tugged at Fanny's mind.

"Wait!" she called out, turning around to catch Anna before she could close the door behind her. "You said that the man who comes at night for the paintings isn't from around here. How can you be certain?"

"Because," Anna said, voice finally cracking with impatience, "he has a Scottish accent."

EIGHT

*In Which Fanny Is Nearly Run
Down by a Rogue Barouche*

FANNY HAD TO ADMIT one thing as she left Aunt Norris's cottage: it felt good when one's hunch proved to be right. She could understand now why people like Maria became so preoccupied with being correct all the time. It made one feel positively invincible.

Of course, that didn't mean she was any closer to figuring out who might have wanted Sir Thomas dead.

She made the decision to walk home along the lane rather than the forest path to avoid getting more mud on her shoes, although a bath for Pug was likely inevitable at this point. This way was also longer, which gave her time to think.

What would Miss Bennet do if presented with this new information? Fanny hardly knew the other young lady, so it wasn't exactly an easy question to answer. All she could imagine her saying was, *It's all well and good that you've discovered that your aunt is likely in cahoots with your odious cousin and dealing art under the cover of night without your uncle's knowledge or consent, but it doesn't* prove *a thing.* Fanny sighed. Her inner Miss Bennet was right, unfortunately.

But, she did know more than she had earlier this morning. The man with the Scottish accent—he had to be connected to Mr. Rushworth's contact. Why keep it from the family? Why try to convince Tom that they should start dealing with him when Maria had been secretly dealing with him before Sir Thomas's death?

And was Mr. Rushworth involved?

He had to be, she decided. He must have told Maria about this contact of his, someone who wanted in on the artwork that Mansfield Emporium could provide. And it must be shady in some way, if Sir Thomas wouldn't deal with him. So when rebuffed by her father, Maria must have gone to Aunt Norris to help her make the deal anyway.

But how did she expect to get away with it?

Or maybe she hadn't expected to get away with it. Maybe she'd just needed to manipulate an "accident" in the storehouse to incapacitate her father.

Had she meant to kill him? Fanny shook her head. She still didn't know enough.

Fanny was so consumed with these speculations that she

hardly noticed the sound of an approaching carriage until it was quite loud and impossible to ignore. Pug yanked on the leash to get away from it. She looked over her right shoulder and gasped: a barouche pulled by a pair of gray horses was bearing down upon her, and the driver showed no signs of reining them in.

Somehow, instinct kicked in and Fanny leapt for the ditch after the dog, tumbling through the brush as the barouche swept past her. She lost her grip on the leash as she landed hard on her knees. Small branches scratched at her face and hands as she struggled to her feet. In the distance, she heard a man's voice call out, "Whoa!"

Splendid. They had caused her to fall, and now they were stopping to witness her humiliation. Fanny made a grab for Pug's leash before the dog could dart over to the newcomers, but Pug preferred to berate them from afar, yapping at them from the ditch.

"Hush," Fanny ordered, and the dog got in one more bark before stopping. Fanny tried to straighten her skirts and brush off the dirt, feeling more than a little frazzled about her disheveled state. It didn't immediately occur to her to be upset that *they* had nearly run her over with their rig, because it was hard to feel indignant when one's short and uneventful life has just flashed before one's eyes.

But all of that slipped from Fanny's mind when she looked up and saw the young lady.

She was still seated in the barouche, but she'd turned to

look back at Fanny. Fanny could hear her voice, although she couldn't make out her words. It sounded as though she were scolding her partner, but when she caught a glimpse of Fanny her attention turned and she called out, "Are you all right?"

Fanny was certain she'd not seen anyone more beautiful. She was pale, with dark hair and full pink lips that reminded Fanny of the painting of Athena in Mansfield's portrait gallery. Her nose was strong and perhaps a bit longer than would be considered conventionally attractive, and she had piercing blue eyes that pinned Fanny in place.

"Um, yes," Fanny managed to say after a prolonged pause. "Quite fine, thank you."

"I didn't see you until we'd rounded the bend," the striking young lady's companion called out.

"It's all right," Fanny replied, although it didn't escape her notice that the driver's words weren't exactly an apology.

She got a better look at them both as she cautiously approached on wobbly legs, Pug trotting after her. The young lady's companion was the male reflection of her features: they shared the same dark hair, the same pale complexion, and even the same long sloped nose. Siblings, they had to be. Fanny's fingers twitched with the desire to sketch them. Their barouche was best suited for short pleasure drives, but Fanny didn't recognize it as belonging to anyone in the county . . . and she certainly didn't recognize this pair.

"We're on our way to Mansfield Park," the young lady said,

and as Fanny took a few steps closer she realized that this Athena was not as old as she initially assumed—perhaps only nineteen or twenty. She wore a wide, eager smile. "Do you know it?"

"We don't need directions, Mary," the gentleman grumbled. "The letter gave perfectly clear instructions."

"Don't be rude," the young woman—*Mary*, Fanny thought—muttered.

The gentleman sighed, but when he turned to face Fanny he wore an affable expression. "As my sister said, we're headed to Mansfield Park. It's just up ahead, correct?"

She looked upon them in surprise, for she didn't recognize this pair as any acquaintances of the family. But if they were social guests, surely they'd know exactly where they were going. Were they potential buyers? "Yes. You can't miss it."

"See?" he said to his sister. "I told you I knew where we were going."

Before she had the chance to respond, he flicked his reins and the horses started up once more. The young lady was still turned toward Fanny and dismay colored her expression as she reached out a hand to steady herself. "Thank you!" she called out, but soon enough they were out of earshot, and so Fanny didn't bother with more than a small wave in response.

They were just out of sight when Fanny realized who they must be: the business contact of Mr. Yates, come to Mansfield a day early. The one who would orchestrate an auction sale in the hope of saving them all from financial ruin.

No one had said anything about a sister, though.

Fanny quickened her pace, eager to get back. It was another half hour before the house was in sight, and Fanny was quite winded as she ascended the front steps. A footman came forward to collect her cloak, and she asked him, "Is the family receiving visitors? I saw a rig in the lane."

"Yes, miss. A Mr. Crawford and his sister, Miss Crawford. They're in the drawing room, taking refreshments."

"Thank you," Fanny said, and the footman retreated with a small bow.

Normally, Fanny disliked socializing with her family's acquaintances. No one quite seemed to understand what her role was within the house, and her relatives hardly made any attempt to include her in conversations and outings, so as a result she was usually ignored. This suited Fanny just fine—if one was to be ignored in social settings, why bother engaging in them at all? Usually, she would gladly sneak away upstairs and use this time to write to William or paint, but curiosity over the striking Miss Crawford overtook her.

Snatches of conversation drifted out of the open drawing room door, and Fanny approached slowly. She could hear the smooth purr of the voice Maria used on guests and Tom's overly congenial laugh. It was followed by a response too low for her to make out, but Fanny knew it was her—Mary Crawford. She'd remember her voice anywhere. Fanny looked down at her skirts, and at Pug, and realized with horror that they were both covered in mud and her skirts were streaked with grass stains. She couldn't go in there!

She intended to march Pug and herself straight to the wash-tub, but when she cast one last look into the drawing room, her eyes met Miss Crawford's. The other young lady's expression shifted suddenly and it was enough to garner the attention of Aunt Norris, who looked up and said, "Fanny? Don't lurk in the doorway, girl. Come and greet our guests."

The room went silent and Fanny reluctantly entered, pink-faced. She'd no sooner taken in the scene—Miss Crawford at the center of the room, sitting next to Edmund, while Tom, Maria, and Mr. Crawford stood admiring a painting—than Aunt Norris's expression shifted. "Heavens, look at you! What happened?"

Edmund's eyes widened and he mouthed, *Are you all right?* The trio before the painting turned to look at her, and Fanny had the small satisfaction of watching Mr. Crawford's expression slacken in surprise as he took her in.

"My apologies," she said. "I've just come in from a walk. I didn't wish to be rude."

Pug let out a bark and ran for Lady Bertram, who was seated next to Miss Crawford. Fanny let the leash fall from her fingers as the dog made a beeline for her mistress, and Lady Bertram smiled. "Oh, there's my Puggy!"

Pug, having no sense of how dirty she was, launched herself at Lady Bertram, who let out a small shriek of horror when the dog tracked mud all over her dress. "Fanny! She's *filthy!*"

"If you didn't wish to be rude, you ought to have cleaned up before greeting our guests," Aunt Norris scolded. She let out a long sigh that seemed to rather delight Julia and Maria, who were wearing twin smug expressions. "Mr. Crawford, Miss Crawford, please forgive this most unusual display. This is Fanny Price, our niece."

Somehow, being introduced in such a disparaging manner felt worse than nearly getting run down by a carriage. But Miss Crawford surprised her by standing and approaching to shake Fanny's hand. "I'm afraid this is our second encounter of the day, and we are quite at fault for the state she's in—our barouche ran her off the lane. I am so very sorry, Miss Price."

Miss Crawford's hands were warm and soft, her fingers long and nimble. Fanny could scarcely formulate thoughts, let alone a response, as she gently shook the other lady's hand.

Miss Crawford smiled at her, then turned to her brother and said, "See, Henry, I told you we ought to have stopped to offer her a ride."

"My apologies again," Mr. Crawford said, giving her the courtesy of a full bow. "I had no idea you lived at Mansfield. You should have said."

Fanny glanced down at her plain brown skirt, streaked with mud. She hadn't looked like a lady, let alone a respectable young lady. She'd looked . . . common. They had probably taken her for a servant or village girl, walking her dog. "It's all right," she said, hating all the attention upon her. "I'm happy to see you've found the place without any trouble."

It was the right thing to say, for the tension in the room seemed to ease. At least until Maria said, "What on earth were you doing walking down the middle of the lane?"

"I . . ."

"Oh, never mind that, Maria," Edmund said. "Hardly anyone comes down our little lane. We're so out of the way, out here in the country."

"But it's such a marvelous setting," Miss Crawford said, returning to her seat next to Edmund. "Why, I can't remember the last time I saw such a pretty landscape—the gardens and lawns alone are glorious."

She seemed to say this directly at Fanny, but Julia quickly cut in. "But you've come from London! Certainly you've seen nicer and more exciting places."

"None quite so fine as this, I think," Miss Crawford said, and by her smile Fanny couldn't tell if she was teasing Julia or being completely sincere.

Either way, Fanny took this as her cue to retreat to the outskirts of the party, taking a seat out of the line of Aunt Norris's disapproving gaze. Lady Bertram seemed to have forgotten about the mud on her skirts as Pug settled happily in her lap, tongue lolling.

"The beauty of the countryside is no match to the artwork within, though," Mr. Crawford added. "This piece is truly brilliant, and you know how to display it so well, Lady Bertram.

A painting such as this should not be crowded upon the wall."

Fanny supposed he meant to be complimentary, but considering the reason for his arrival, she found his comment distasteful.

Lady Bertram looked up from where she'd been cooing over Pug. "I am afraid that was all my late husband's doing. He insisted it be hung there."

Mentioning Sir Thomas was like draping a veil over the room, muting everything slightly.

"I'm very sorry for your loss," Mr. Crawford said, and his words did indeed seem genuine. "I know it must be a difficult time for you."

Aunt Norris cut in. "Yes, we must all bravely carry on."

"That is admirable, especially considering the legacy he left." Mr. Crawford turned away from the painting and took the nearest seat. Fanny watched him, trying to form an opinion of him that was not colored by the fact that he'd nearly run her down not an hour earlier. She glanced at Edmund, wondering if he was as impressed with Mr. Crawford's attempts at flattery, but Edmund appeared rapt.

"Yes, and it's a legacy we take very seriously," Maria said, rushing to take the chair across from him. "The business was Father's pride and joy. We want to see that it flourishes, for his sake."

"And not their own?" Fanny muttered to Edmund, but he didn't respond.

"I completely understand," Mr. Crawford assured Maria, his gaze lingering on her chest before rising to meet her eyes. Fanny felt her brow furrow as she glanced about the room. Did no one else notice? "I inherited my business from my late father, and I consider it both an honor and responsibility."

Maria's smile was catlike. "Exactly."

Mr. Crawford turned to Tom, which was just as well because the way he was looking at Maria was mere moments away from becoming indecent. "I hope that you'll consider my presence a help rather than a burden. I understand that Mansfield Emporium is used to doing things a certain way, and I wouldn't dream of intruding where I'm not welcome. But times are changing, and certain London trends might be slow to reach the countryside."

"What trends?" Julia asked, nearly falling out of her seat in her eagerness to hear more.

"Oh, well . . . I'm not sure if we should get into business at the moment," he demurred. "I wouldn't want to offend your hospitality, Lady Bertram."

"Oh, don't worry yourself about us," Aunt Norris insisted. "We are quite curious as to your methods, Mr. Crawford, and how they might apply here at Mansfield."

Mr. Crawford looked to Lady Bertram for reassurance, and she nodded. "Please, enlighten us."

"Well, only if you insist," Mr. Crawford said.

Oh, he was good. But if there was one thing that life at

Mansfield had taught Fanny, it was that people with two very different sides to them were seldom to be trusted.

"I'm a dealer, of course," Mr. Crawford said, then leaned forward and faux-whispered, "But not a conventional sort."

"Certainly, a conventional art dealer wouldn't have the fine reputation you do," Tom agreed.

"Thank you, sir. I inherited this trade from my father, who spent decades building his clientele list. While we never operated on the level that Sir Thomas did, we had a good business acting as intermediaries between artists and potential buyers. Are you acquainted with many artists?" he asked the room.

"Father knew a few," Maria said, waving her hand. "But they're a prickly sort to deal with, are they not?"

Being an artist herself, Fanny let out a tiny huff of indignation and looked to Edmund, but he was watching Mr. Crawford.

"They can be," Mr. Crawford agreed. "So many artists don't want to sell their work, or they attach all sorts of conditions. But I'm able to convince them to part ways with their work by placing them in the most desirable houses and establishments. You see, not everyone understands art. But most people understand that owning art, *good* art, is desirable. My business is about connecting the right pieces with the right people, and creating the allure of exclusivity."

Fanny had to actively work to keep her distaste hidden. Art had nothing to do with society or who had a more expensive painting on their drawing room wall. Art was about emotion, feeling, capturing specific moments in time. It was about conveying what could not be said or described, delighting the senses.

"And how do you go about creating that exclusivity differently from other dealers?" Aunt Norris asked.

"Ah, that's where I look to my lovely sister for her help." Miss Crawford smiled on cue, and Fanny wondered how often the Crawfords had given this little sales pitch. "The bulk of my father's clients were art collectors with their own unique set of tastes. But my sister and I discovered that when one of my art collectors throws a social event, say a dinner party, they tend to invite friends who are, if not art collectors, then art appreciators. And inevitably these art appreciators will flock to me, asking for advice on how to build up their own collection. Which led me to conceive of an idea that allows my friend, the collector, and all of his friends, the appreciators, to benefit."

He paused for dramatic effect, and Fanny could see Tom and Mr. Yates lean toward him. *Please, sir*, Fanny wanted to say. *Do go on and let us know how you plan to benefit.*

"My client assembles all of their art-loving friends, and we create a social event. It could be a dinner or house party, but we've even thrown balls, garden tea parties, and special auctions. The client invites their social circle, and they are given the opportunity to appreciate the art. We stage it in the client's home, to make it seem as if it belongs there. Then, when all of my client's guests are swooning over this painting and that sculpture, when they can see the possibilities of how it could be displayed in their own homes, we tell them that every piece is for sale."

Mr. Crawford said the last bit rather smugly. Fanny merely stared in shock, but the others looked on in wonder.

"And do you have many clients who are willing to open their homes in such a way?" Maria's voice dripped with skepticism.

"Oh yes," said Mr. Crawford. He paused and then added, "It doesn't hurt that they receive a modest honorarium for their part."

Everyone around the room went "Ahhh," except for Fanny. Her skin prickled in horror. Was Mr. Crawford seriously suggesting that the family use their social clout and standing to entice their friends and connections to Mansfield for a party, only to sell them art? It was . . . deceptive.

"Didn't I tell you he was a genius?" Mr. Yates whispered to Tom.

Tom leaned so far forward Fanny feared he might fall on his face. "How many pieces do you think you could move at Mansfield? We have quite the collection, as you can imagine."

"In your case we might have to negotiate something slightly different," Mr. Crawford said with a flash of that charming smile. "You're far from London, and you'd be providing all of the artwork. A collection this size, with the reputation of your family . . . I think buyers will make the trip, if we give them good reason to."

"A reason such as . . ." Maria let her words dangle rather suggestively, but Mr. Crawford smiled affably.

"Oh, Miss Bertram," he said, "I fear that I have overstepped on your good mother's patience by talking enough business for this evening."

"Hm?" Lady Bertram asked, clearly distracted by Pug.

"Quite right," Tom asserted. "We shall have a proper meeting in the morning, once we've given you a tour and you've seen what we have to offer."

The talk in the drawing room tilted back toward polite nothings as Julia offered to take Miss Crawford for a turn about the room to admire the family's more precious artwork. Fanny sat still in her seat while the others shifted about, but she watched Miss Crawford as she followed Julia from painting to tapestry. She had kept quiet while her brother spoke, her smile sweet and perfectly polite, but Fanny sensed there was something more to her by the determined set of her jaw and the way she never seemed to miss a cue. But that smile faltered just a tiny bit when she happened to glance Fanny's way and saw her staring with a fixed intensity that made Fanny's eyes squint just slightly.

"She's quite beautiful, is she not?" Edmund whispered, causing Fanny to break her gaze.

"What?"

Edmund sat next to her, keeping his voice low. "Miss Craw-ford. She and her brother make a striking pair. And honestly, this scheme of theirs is the only one I can see actually saving our necks."

Of all the things Fanny expected to come out of Edmund's mouth, that was the last. "Excuse me?"

He turned and got a good look at her expression. "Oh, come on, Fanny . . . you have to admit, it's a clever business."

"Clever business or not, you support turning them loose on Mansfield?" she hissed.

"Support? Not exactly. But I don't see any way out of it, and if we get to the point where . . . certain other parties take up residence . . . then we don't stand a chance of righting this ship."

"But . . ." She floundered for words. She wanted to protest that the type of art her uncle had spent his life collecting and dealing deserved more respect than that. But any arguments died from her lips when she truly thought about Edmund's words. Had it really come down to this, then? Inviting oppor-tunistic strangers into the drawing room, selling things for the highest price, scheming for ways to maximize profit?

And then a darker thought: Sir Thomas had left them in this position. And while it could certainly be argued that he didn't plan on dying, they were in this mess nonetheless.

What were you involved in, Uncle? she thought.

"What are you two whispering about?" Julia demanded.

"Nothing," Edmund said. "Except we were wondering—Miss Crawford, do you enjoy riding?"

"I do," she said, smiling with obvious delight. "Although I've not had the opportunity in quite a long time."

"Well, we've got plenty of horses here," Edmund assured her. "We shall have to ensure that you get all the chances you desire to see the grounds. Fanny rides, and I'm sure she'd be happy for the company, right, Fanny?"

Fanny merely blinked at him in shock. This was why she was horrid at social interactions. She could not separate the shock of what Mr. Crawford had proposed, and her family's complacency with the idea, from the mundane talk about riding. But Miss Crawford had already turned her striking blue eyes on Fanny, and she graced her with an eager smile that Fanny suspected had little to do with wanting to go riding with her and everything to do with ingratiating herself within the household.

"Certainly," she said, her words coming out crisp. "That is, if Miss Crawford will have the time. It sounds like everyone will be busy preparing the entire bulk of Sir Thomas's legacy for sale."

That startled the smile right off Miss Crawford's face. Fanny thought she'd feel triumph at watching her expression shutter, but instead she just felt mean-spirited.

"Of course," Miss Crawford said. "And I shouldn't wish to impose on your time, Miss Price."

Edmund was quick to come to her defense with assurances that it would be no such imposition, and they would find the time. Fanny watched him closely and then remembered his words from a few moments earlier. *She's quite beautiful, is she not?*

She was. Very beautiful. There were some things that money just couldn't buy. Like beauty. And grace. And a position in society. And . . . good sense, apparently.

Fanny was suddenly overwhelmed with an impulse to run away as fast as she could. She didn't want any part of this. "You must please excuse me," she said as she rose. "I ought to freshen up, and see that Pug is bathed."

She didn't risk a backward glance as she fled, forgetting the dog, because she wasn't sure what precisely she was running away from: the people determined to destroy the business her uncle had built or the way that Miss Crawford and Edmund looked at each other.

NINE

In Which Fanny Is Thwarted,
in More Ways than One

DESPITE THEIR RATHER INAUSPICIOUS meeting, Fanny had to admit that the Crawfords' arrival had its uses: Tom and Maria were going to open up the storehouse once more.

It had been locked up tightly since the morning after Sir Thomas's death, and only Tom and Maria held keys. Fanny was itching for more information about the artwork in Aunt Norris's cottage, and she was certain if she could just find some trace of paperwork—ledgers, invoices, even a bill of lading—she could piece together the mystery.

But she had to willingly spend time with her cousins in order to achieve this.

"Here's the plan," she said to Edmund over breakfast.

"We'll tag along to the storehouse when they give the Crawfords a tour."

"They won't want to include us," he protested around bites of bacon.

But Fanny had thought of a way around that. "Usually, no. But they've got guests. They won't want to seem impolite in front of them—especially Maria. She's working awfully hard to impress Mr. Crawford."

"Rushworth better watch out."

"She'll be tolerable to us, so all we have to do is engage one of them—Miss Crawford—in conversation. She'll naturally assume we're coming along, and no one will contradict a guest."

Edmund nodded slowly, and Fanny's heartbeat sped up. Did he notice the strange, breathless way she mentioned Miss Crawford? Despite her distrust of the young lady's intentions, perhaps there was a part of her, a small part, that was intrigued, too.

"How do you expect to do any sort of sleuthing with a whole party in the storehouse?" Edmund asked. "And what exactly are you hoping to find?"

Fanny tried her best not to sigh in impatience. "Paperwork. Anything that provides a bit of context to what I saw."

"Are you sure you're not mistaken about the art? Perhaps—"

"I know what I saw," Fanny said, giving Edmund a withering look.

Fanny tried not to let Edmund's doubt rub at her as they

left the breakfast table and made their way down the hall to the foyer, where the party was to assemble before walking out to the storehouse. Why was he always second-guessing her and trying to sway her from investigating? Did he not believe her capable? Fanny was so lost in her thoughts that she wasn't paying attention until Edmund laid a hand on her shoulder, stopping her just out of sight of the foyer.

Mr. Crawford was speaking, and she heard him say, "I'm just trying to discern what Miss Price's position might be. Is she out?"

She heard Tom laugh, and a trickle of dread ran down her spine. What would he say? "No, she's not been introduced to society. I suppose Aunt Norris and Mother intend to keep her on indefinitely as a companion."

"How curious," said Mr. Crawford. "But she doesn't strike me as the sort who would be suited as a lady's companion."

What was that *supposed to mean?*

"Well, we could hardly *pay* her," Maria said, whispering the word *pay* as if it were an insult. "She is family, after all. But trust me, she'd be much happier here than where she came from."

Fanny's skin prickled in indignation. Was that what Maria truly thought or what she wanted to believe?

"Oh?" Mr. Crawford asked, tone suddenly much more interested. "Why is that?"

"Her family is quite poor," Maria said dismissively. "She's got, oh, just gobs of siblings, I can't keep track of them all.

Her mother married quite beneath her, so Mother and Aunt Norris refused to have anything to do with her. But they eased the burden by taking on Fanny. It was a very generous thought at the time, but now I have to wonder if it's almost cruel, plucking up someone so unsuited for this life and trying to make her fit in."

Fanny sagged against the wall, hardly noticing Edmund's hand on her shoulder. She wasn't surprised to hear that Maria thought so little of her. She'd known in under a week at Mansfield that Maria saw herself quite above Fanny, and she'd been a mere child then. But to hear Maria voice these opinions *aloud*. In front of *guests*.

It wasn't just mean-spirited, it was *improper*.

Julia spoke up then. "Maria! Someone might overhear."

Someone. Not Fanny. Of course not. Because no one cared what she thought.

"Come on," Edmund whispered. "Hold your head up high."

She nodded once and then took his proffered arm and followed him into the foyer.

"Good morning," Edmund said pleasantly. "Are you all about to go out to the storehouse?"

"Good morning," Miss Crawford said, her voice just slightly too loud and slightly too eager. It was the only sign she gave of . . . embarrassment? Fanny wasn't certain. She didn't know the young lady well enough to get a sense of if she was guilty or merely abashed at nearly being caught out gossiping.

"What are you two—"

Tom started to speak at the same time Miss Crawford rushed to ask, "Will you both be joining us?"

"We'd love to," Edmund said, inclining his head slightly toward Miss Crawford. Fanny managed a faint smile, and despite the sting she felt at Maria's insult just moments earlier, she got a small twist of satisfaction at the look Maria and Tom exchanged—equal parts baffled and annoyed.

But her plan worked—no one challenged them, and so Edmund and Fanny were able to tag along as Tom and Mr. Yates, Maria and Julia, and the Crawfords led the way out of the house.

"I am so glad to see you recovered from your fall, Miss Price," Miss Crawford said once they were out in the sunshine. "I felt absolutely horrible about the whole ordeal."

Fanny was momentarily tongue-tied, both at Miss Crawford's concern and by how pretty and innocent she looked, lit by the morning sun. "It was nothing, really. Thank you for your concern."

"You must be made of hardier stuff than me, to say that what we put you through was nothing!" Miss Crawford's smile wasn't unkind, but it still took Fanny a moment to realize that the other young lady was teasing her.

It wasn't often that someone teased her without meaning to put her down, so Fanny merely smiled, but it felt more like a grimace.

"Fanny is very familiar with the grounds, and all the paths and trails of the estate," Edmund cut in. "She's an avid outdoorswoman."

"Well, that might be a stretch," Fanny hastened to add, lest Miss Crawford get the wrong idea about her. "I simply enjoy nature. And walks."

I simply enjoy nature and walks? What a positively inane response!

But it did the trick of taking Miss Crawford's full attention off of her, for something in her tone must have put off the other young lady. She and Edmund began speaking of riding—which Fanny quite enjoyed, actually, but her rudeness the previous evening had put an end to the possibility of joining them—and Fanny found herself a quiet tagalong to the conversation until they reached the storehouse.

The party was full of oohs and aahs as Tom ceremoniously unlocked the storehouse and threw open the double doors to usher them all inside. "Ladies and gentlemen," he announced, "welcome to Mansfield Emporium!"

"Oh my," Miss Crawford breathed as they stepped inside. "It's larger than I imagined."

Fanny wondered exactly what Miss Crawford had imagined. Piles of money, perhaps?

"I must admit, I am impressed," Mr. Crawford agreed.

"Come," Maria said, gesturing broadly toward the aisles on the first floor. "Let's begin our tour over here."

Mr. Crawford obliged by offering her his arm, and Fanny glanced at Edmund to see if he noticed. He was pointing out the piano to Miss Crawford, telling her how he'd tuned it himself. Julia noticed, though. She fell back with Fanny and muttered, "It's not *fair*. She's already engaged."

The last person she wanted to discuss the matter of equality with was Julia, so she offered a limp smile and was satisfied when her cousin followed after Maria and Mr. Crawford with a huff. Fanny lingered behind, glancing toward the stairs. Sir Thomas had kept an office upstairs, which was where the business ledgers and invoices must also be kept. She wasn't certain what she was looking for, precisely, but she knew that if answers were to be had, she must start there.

The problem was in slipping away unnoticed.

Fanny trailed behind the rest of the group as Tom and Maria jockeyed for the position of tour guide. They'd scarcely gone down two aisles before her cousins devolved into squabbling over provenances.

"That's not the Templeton, it's the Temple*worth*," Maria corrected her brother.

"It's Templeton, I'm sure of it. I just read the provenance letter—"

"Oh, well, if you read the letter!" Maria shot back.

Fanny wanted to cover her ears, but she was surprised when Miss Crawford fell back beside her and said, "You seem restless, Miss Price. This tour must be boring you."

"Oh no," Fanny said, striving for a polite smile but not quite managing it. "I enjoy spending time here. Although I haven't been since . . ."

An awkwardness settled between them, and Miss Crawford swallowed hard. "Right, of course. I'm sorry, I wasn't thinking."

Edmund also fell back to join them, having heard the exchange. "I assure you, we have more happy memories here than unhappy ones. Fanny especially. She's quite the artist. She's too modest to say so, but she's always sketching and painting in her free time."

"It's merely a hobby," Fanny rushed to say, not trusting the keen interest in Miss Crawford's eyes. "I'm no professional."

"You should let us be the judge of that," Edmund said, to Fanny's horror.

"Oh yes, I would love to see your work sometime," Miss Crawford added.

"Really, there is no need." Fanny looked pointedly at Edmund, hoping he'd drop the subject. "It is just something I do to keep myself occupied."

Her tone was just an edge too sharp to still be considered polite, but it did the trick of bringing Edmund and Miss Crawford into momentary silence.

But horror upon horrors, she'd garnered the attention of the others. Mr. Crawford had turned to look at them, evidently having heard Edmund's praise. "As an appreciator of art and an artist yourself, Miss Price, you must approve of our plans for Mansfield Emporium."

"Proposed plans," Maria corrected, but there was no force behind her words. In fact, they sounded almost playful, as if she were putting up an opposition for the sake of argument alone.

Fanny decided to dodge the question. "It's not my place to say how the business dealings ought to proceed."

"Oh dear, that rather sounds like disapproval to me," Mr. Crawford replied, but he was smiling as though he expected this. "Truly, you think it's a poor idea? Please, be honest. I'm curious to know what the average art appreciator thinks of our model."

She hoped Tom or Maria would intervene with a cutting comment at her expense—she'd take it if it meant getting out of saying what she truly thought. But they all awaited her response. "I admire that you wish to make art, and owning art, more accessible. Surely everyone comes out the better for it—the artist who benefits from the sale and the new patron who benefits from owning artwork." *And Mr. Crawford and his host or hostess*, but she didn't dare say that. "But I find the notion of arranging social gatherings for the sole purpose of tricking one's acquaintances into a business dealing for personal gain . . . rather off-putting. I don't think Sir Thomas would have approved."

"Well, it's a very good thing that my father didn't will the business to you, then!" Maria said, trying to make a joke of it. But her voice was as tart as a fresh lemon.

"I'm sorry if my words offend," she said. "But Mr. Crawford asked my opinion."

"Indeed I did," he said with a laugh that seemed to indicate he'd taken no offense whatsoever. "And I appreciate your candor, Miss Price."

"May I ask," Miss Crawford cut in, delicately, as if she were hoping to change the course of the conversation, "have you sold any pieces of your work?"

"Oh no." Fanny felt embarrassed by the question and, strangely, by her response. "My uncle gifted one of my paintings to a patron once, as a gesture of goodwill. But as I said, I am not a true artist."

Then why did she feel a strange wave of shame for wishing that she could be? For wishing that her artwork could be sold— not in one of Crawford's horrid social gatherings, but maybe in a gallery one day or a private sale?

"You create, therefore you are an artist, are you not?" Miss Crawford asked. "Or do you think that because your work hasn't sold, it is not true art?"

All of this attention was going to cause Fanny to break out into hives. "Of course not. I am just saying that what I do . . . it's not the same as all of this!"

"Why not?" Miss Crawford asked.

As Fanny gazed into her blue eyes, as striking as they were

probing, she found that she couldn't come up with a coherent answer. Her pulse quickened and she was overcome with a feeling so big, so overwhelming, she couldn't begin to find the words to describe it. It was as if a maelstrom of thoughts and emotions were swirling inside of her, and she wasn't sure if she should laugh or cry, stand her ground or flee.

Mr. Crawford broke the silence when it became clear that Fanny was unable to respond.

"This is why artists need us!" His tone was light, almost playful. "They must eat, they must be clothed, and they need a roof over their heads. Not to mention, they need the tools of their trade. And unless they are independently wealthy or have a patron, they must sell their artwork. I just don't see how a healthy, thriving economy is a bad thing."

"Hear, hear!" Tom agreed.

But Mr. Crawford wasn't finished. "And with so many artists hoping to make their way in the world, well . . . they can't all be masters fit for kings and nobility. Perhaps they are merely good, and perhaps someone is willing to part with their hard-earned money for a pretty painting on their wall. We help ensure a smooth transaction, and elevate new artists."

Fanny couldn't stand his self-assured tone, but this was an argument she'd had no wish to engage in in the first place. "Of course, Mr. Crawford. You know your business far better than I."

"I am glad to hear you think so," he said with an affable

smile that got a laugh out of everyone—everyone but Miss Crawford, curiously. "What we do is good for artists. Those who might otherwise languish in poverty or obscurity or who give up their craft altogether are benefited by what we do."

And so are you, Fanny thought. Just how much of a sale went to the artist and how much went to the Crawfords and their party hosts? And when they held auctions, did they do so in the hope of getting the most money for the artist . . . or lining their own pockets? And besides, what did he know about poverty? Had he ever feared being a burden on society and his family?

Surprisingly, it was Miss Crawford who interrupted him. "All right, Henry, you've made your point. I am sorry for my brother, Miss Price. He can be rather dogged about his passions."

Fanny acknowledged this with a nod, but Mr. Crawford made no such apologies. Luckily, he seemed to grow tired of arguing with her, and Mr. Yates took this opportunity to inquire about Mr. Crawford's opinion on some O'Rourke sculptures. They soon concluded their tour of the lower level and turned toward the stairs.

Fanny lingered at the bottom, but only a moment. Someone had cleaned up the blood that had fallen on the wood floors, scrubbed it away so neatly it was as though it had never been there. But Fanny had seen it. She could remember it, clear as day.

Stay the course, she reminded herself. *Do it for Sir Thomas.*

But once she was at the top of the stairs, something horrifying occurred to her: her replica of the Millbrook painting was still at the back of the storehouse, sitting on its easel just as she'd left it that fateful day. The thought of her cousins and the Crawfords seeing it, *judging* it, after all they'd just said, made her feel ill. And what would they think about her replicating someone else's work? Likely that she was getting above herself.

As Tom said, "Down here we have quite the collection of Swiss figurines—perhaps not quite in fashion, but surely valuable to the right buyer," Fanny lingered at the back of the group.

They all went ahead of her, even Edmund, and Fanny wavered. The door to her uncle's office was just a few paces away. In the opposite direction was her replication. Did she choose self-preservation or her investigation?

She wasn't proud of it, but self-preservation won out.

Tiptoeing past the group, she slipped down an aisle on the far side of the storehouse and made her way to the back of the building, hoping no one would notice her absence.

Her painting, all her tools, everything was exactly where she'd left it more than a week earlier. Her own replication was tilted on its easel, but it wasn't enough to merely cover it with a drop cloth—that would just pique the Crawfords' curiosity. As quietly as she could, she picked up the painting and looked about for a hiding place. It wasn't heavy, but the size of the canvas was awkward, and she didn't wish to damage her work. She slid it carefully behind a dusty crate and arranged a drop

149

cloth around it, hoping that would do the trick of concealing it. Tom's voice drew closer, so she dashed down an empty aisle and circled back to rejoin the group from behind, just as they came before the Millbrook.

"My word, Bertram," Mr. Crawford declared, "you didn't tell me that you had a Millbrook!"

"You recognize the artist?" Fanny asked in surprise, slightly out of breath.

"Yes," he said, striding forward to inspect the painting. "No one paints quite like him. This must be an early piece—I've never seen it."

"Father bought it from the artist himself a couple of months ago now, I think?" Maria said, following Mr. Crawford to stand right behind him. "He's been holding on to it for some inane reason."

"Fanny was—" Edmund began to say, but Fanny elbowed him hard.

Mr. Crawford didn't seem to notice. "Your father met Millbrook? He's notoriously reclusive. Lives on some country estate in York, I think."

"I heard Sussex," Mr. Yates added.

"No matter. He's quite the sensation in London right now. Six months ago, a portrait of his was purchased by Lady Wilkshire, and it became the talk of the town when she displayed it in her ballroom. Now people are clamoring for Millbrooks, but the man can't paint fast enough to satisfy the ton. Why, this . . .

this is just the thing we need to make an auction ball at Mansfield a success."

Fanny distrusted the gleam in Mr. Crawford's eye, but his excitement was infectious.

"Truly?" Maria asked. "I had no idea we were sitting on such a gem. I assumed it was a silly domestic painting that Father paid more than he ought to, and was waiting in the vain hope its value would increase."

"If so, the gamble paid off," Mr. Crawford said, stepping back to better behold the entire picture. "Mary, what do you think?"

"It's beautiful," she said, stepping closer. "It doesn't have the sophistication of the paintings we saw in London last month, but an early work will certainly be of interest. And this one has such exquisite layers."

Fanny felt a burning sensation right below her heart.

"How much do you think something like this might go for?" Tom asked.

"I know at least three people who'd offer you two hundred pounds on the spot," Mr. Crawford said. "But I'd advise you not to take it."

"Oh?" Maria's voice was coy.

"If it went to auction, we could easily sell it for three hundred. Likely more. Maybe even as much as five hundred."

"And five hundred pounds is a lot of money?" Julia asked.

Fanny nearly fainted. *Of course* it was a lot of money. It was

151

a nearly unheard-of sum for a single painting.

"It's enough," Tom said, and she could hazard a guess at what he was thinking: it would wipe out a sizeable chunk of their debt.

"But—" Fanny said, though she stopped herself before she could say more. Sir Thomas had kept the painting because it intrigued her, because she had loved it. And then he'd given her the task of painting it because he saw that she had talent. She'd never forget the day that he looked upon her efforts and deemed her worthy of lessons. Worthy of more than just an existence doing meaningless, endless tasks to make her aunts happy and comfortable.

Fanny had felt whole in that moment.

No, she'd felt like a *real* artist.

"Are you all right, Miss Price?" Miss Crawford asked in a hushed tone. She'd sidled up to Fanny without her noticing. "You've gone a bit pale."

Before Fanny could respond, they were interrupted by the arrival of a footman, who appeared suddenly behind Fanny, out of breath. "Begging your pardon," he said with a gasp, addressing Tom. "You're needed in the house, sir."

"Good God, man, did you run here?" Tom asked. "Surely whatever it is can wait until we're finished."

"I'm afraid not," the poor footman said, looking very much as though it pained him to contradict Tom. "You have two . . . visitors awaiting you."

"Tell them we aren't accepting callers today," Maria instructed. "If it's urgent they'll leave their card."

"I'm afraid it's not that simple, miss," the footman said. "They won't leave. They're bailiffs, and they say they've come to take up residence at Mansfield Park."

TEN

In Which Fanny Uncovers an Alarming Betrayal

THE BAILIFFS WERE TALL, burly-looking fellows who didn't seem to be any happier to be standing in the Bertrams' foyer than the family was to see them.

"What is the meaning of this?" Tom shouted, making a good show of seeming indignant as he stormed back into the house.

A bailiff with faded red hair and a graying beard stepped forward and handed Tom a sealed letter. "The son of the late Sir Thomas Bertram, I presume?"

"Yes," Tom said, and Fanny could see him swallow hard.

"I'm Weston, my colleague is Briggs. Per this letter, your father's debts are being called in. Can you arrange to pay the creditors listed?"

"My family have been loyal customers for years, and never

saw such mistreatment!" Tom kept darting frantic little glances at the Crawfords, making it clear this performance was for their sake.

"And for many years our clients always received prompt payment, but that seems to have changed in recent months," Weston continued. "If you can pay, we are happy to take our leave."

"I don't have that kind of money just sitting around." Tom's voice had dropped to a harsh whisper, but it echoed throughout the foyer nonetheless.

"And you know exactly how much is being called in, do you?" Weston asked, tone bored.

Tom seemed to realize his mistake instantly, for he hadn't opened the envelope to inspect the amount. The Crawfords had the decency to look away, and Tom's face turned red. Maria's eyes closed for a brief moment.

It was an excruciatingly long moment before Weston said, "Then I am afraid we must install ourselves on the premises until payment can be arranged."

"But . . . that's absurd. You cannot—"

"I assure you we can. The law is on our side."

"Be reasonable," Maria said, cutting in with a smooth, authoritative tone. "Why, look about you. Does this look like the home of someone who cannot pay their debts? My father might have missed a few invoices here and there, but we have considerable assets. Is this really necessary?"

155

"It does indeed appear that you are capable of paying your debts," Briggs said, his dark eyes roving over the vases on display and fine furnishings in the foyer. "So I suggest you do, and we'll be on our way."

An awkward silence followed while Tom gaped like a fish and Maria's eyes turned stormy. Fanny feared she was on the brink of making a bad situation much worse through her stubborn refusal to acknowledge what Miss Bennet had tried to make them see the day of the funeral: they had debts, and they must be paid.

But then Mr. Crawford spoke up. "Allow me to introduce myself—I'm Henry Crawford, and I've just come up from London to discuss business with the Bertram family. I believe that we've only just come up with a business arrangement that shall be favorable for all parties, including your clients. Should we step into the study and discuss it?"

The bailiffs looked unimpressed, but they allowed themselves to be convinced, and soon the Bertrams and Aunt Norris were swept into the study, leaving Edmund, Fanny, and Miss Crawford behind. Fanny felt quite at a loss for words.

"Tea," Miss Crawford finally said. "I do believe we should order tea, should we not?"

And with that, she ushered them into the drawing room, where Fanny had the presence of mind to ring for a maid and order tea.

Miss Crawford's blue eyes were probing Fanny, and she

156

wasn't sure what the other young lady was looking for. "How . . . fortunate your brother was here," Fanny finally managed to say, although what she really wanted to say was *opportunistic*.

Miss Crawford looked uneasy, likely because Fanny's tone was none too warm. "I am no expert, but I hope my brother can help."

"But don't you assist your brother in his business?" Fanny asked. "Surely you know art."

"Yes, and I enjoy spending time with artists," she said, and Fanny noticed that she said artists and not collectors. "But my true passion is music."

Edmund lit up with delight, and Fanny felt faintly sick to her stomach to see his eager reaction as he asked, "Truly? And do you play?"

"I do," Miss Crawford confirmed. "The piano, of course, but my great love is the harp. I have one in our residence in London, and I already miss it."

"We have a harp," Edmund proclaimed. "It's upstairs, in the music room. We would be happy to show you, and you ought to play it whenever you like. Why, maybe we could even give a performance."

"Really?" Miss Crawford set her tea down in her excitement. "What do you play?"

"The viola, piano, and harpsichord, but the viola is my first love."

All this talk of love! Fanny was going to be ill.

"I know just the duet for a harp and viola," Miss Crawford said. "I heard it in London a few months ago!"

"Sampietro?" Edmund asked. "I've heard of it, but not played it."

"I have the sheet music!"

Fanny was left in the dust as the two chattered on about music and composers and performances. They made a striking pair—Miss Crawford with her pale skin and dark hair, and Edmund's golden tan and warm green eyes. She felt as if she were watching the beginning of something, and she ought to feel happy for them. Instead, she felt herself shrinking, so much so that she doubted they'd notice if she were to stand up and slip away.

It was tempting.

"Are you coming, Miss Price?" Miss Crawford asked.

Fanny shook herself out of her gloomy thoughts. Edmund and Miss Crawford were standing.

"I'm going to show Miss Crawford the music room," Edmund explained.

"Now?"

"I am not made to sit still and do nothing," Miss Crawford said with a smile. "Please, come along."

Fanny rose, because she was asked and she was agreeable, and also because it would be quite improper for Miss Crawford and Edmund to go alone. Upstairs, Edmund threw open the door to the music room and Miss Crawford gasped at the sight of the harp. She ran her hands over the wooden frame and plucked at the strings experimentally. "What a lovely instrument," she proclaimed.

"Please, play it for us," Fanny said, trying to sound polite. "No one in the house plays, and I'm sure such a nice instrument deserves to be appreciated."

"Indeed," Miss Crawford agreed, flashing Fanny a brilliant smile that made her feel quite disoriented. "Thank you."

Edmund helped her position the harp in the center of the room while Fanny took a seat off to the side, watching the pair of them work. Edmund procured a stool and Mary began tuning the instrument, making small adjustments here and there, her mouth quirking to the side and her head tilting slightly as she listened to the notes. When it was tuned to her satisfaction, she launched into a beautiful, lilting piece that filled the room with heavenly music.

"Isn't she just remarkable?" Edmund whispered to Fanny.

Fanny didn't trust herself to answer that question. She thought of the deal that was being hashed out downstairs, of the way that Miss Crawford had just so happened to find herself on the same side of the closed study door as Edmund and Fanny. Had that been deliberate?

"Edmund," she whispered, hoping he'd look at her.

But he didn't tear his gaze away from Miss Crawford for a single moment. There would be no pulling him away anytime soon. Was his attention so easily diverted by a pretty face? Did he not care about what Henry Crawford might be negotiating just downstairs?

And why was it that he didn't seem to remember they were supposed to be figuring out how Sir Thomas had died?

Fanny would just have to keep moving forward with her investigation—with or without him.

In the end, Tom and Mr. Yates got their way: that evening, the party toasted the new business arrangement between Mansfield Emporium and the Crawfords, and everyone looked quite satisfied about the partnership, including Maria. The bailiffs were satisfied to hear of the plans to sell most of Mansfield Emporium's collection, and once things were decided upon, there seemed to be no point in waiting—and so it was decided that the Bertrams would auction off the bulk of their artwork a week hence, and to soften the blow, there would be a ball for the occasion.

Fanny was aghast to learn of the plans, and to see her relatives so quickly abandon decorum in favor of a ball and a chance to sell off her uncle's entire store of artwork, but she held her tongue. It was no use trying to persuade them to wait once the plans were set, and so she spent an excruciating three days helping her aunts and cousins prepare for the party. Everything was exactly to Mr. Crawford's specifications, from the menu to the guest list, and Fanny suspected this was due to the fact that he was paying for the event. In between assisting with writing invitations and opening up little-used rooms for the onslaught of guests, Fanny kept her eyes open—even if it meant that she had to endure the way that Edmund stared at Miss Crawford.

Stymied, she wrote to Miss Bennet and updated her on all that she'd discovered thus far, but she knew it wasn't enough. She still needed to figure out what Sir Thomas might have known, or suspected, about Maria's cover-of-night dealings, and she had a hunch that the only way she'd figure it out was by getting a good look at the business accounts.

Opportunity presented itself the day before the auction when she spied Tom and Mr. Yates walking through the front hall, arms laden with documents and exchanging whispers. She lingered in the hall, despite Pug pulling at the leash, and watched them disappear into the study.

Interesting.

Were they also suspicious of Maria? Or—and this was an angle she hadn't given much weight to—did they have their own scheme cooking? They had both been in the storehouse that day, and Tom had been awfully quick to propose bringing Mr. Crawford in, on Mr. Yates's recommendation.

Pug whined, but Fanny was immovable as she pondered the possibilities.

Tom had wanted to expand the business now for a while, but Sir Thomas wouldn't give credence to any of Mr. Yates's ideas. What if Tom had grown impatient? Maybe he'd even known that the business was floundering and the estate was falling into debt, and he thought he could run it better. Maybe he hadn't meant for his father to die—an accident would put him out of commission long enough to get his hands on the business.

Fanny had to see what those documents contained.

Later, during luncheon, Edmund asked, "Fanny, will you come riding with us? I promised Miss Crawford I would show her the grounds."

"Oh, I . . ." Fanny nearly finished with *would love to*, but at the last moment she caught herself. "I'm feeling rather unwell. But thank you anyway."

"Oh, rotten luck," Edmund said without real feeling.

"I hope it's nothing serious?" Miss Crawford asked, her earnest gaze making Fanny's chest flutter. Why did this beautiful, worldly young lady seem to care so much about her?

"Just a headache," Fanny assured her.

"Well, I hope you don't object to my boring company," Edmund interjected.

"Come now. You are anything but boring."

Fanny's headache was a story, but it might become real if they persisted in flirting.

"Fanny, you don't mind if Mary rides your horse, do you?"

Fanny nearly spit out her lemonade. *Mary?* Were they truly at the point of exchanging first names? "Not at all!" Her voice sounded unnaturally high.

"Oh, I would hate to impose," Miss Crawford said.

"It's no imposition," Fanny assured her. "After all, Patience isn't truly my mare. She belongs to Mansfield." Just like everything else Fanny "owned."

She found an excuse to look anywhere else but at Edmund and Miss Crawford for the rest of the meal and didn't have to wait long after for everyone to disperse—Edmund and Miss Crawford out riding, with a reluctant Julia tagging along to make things proper, Lady Bertram to her rooms for her afternoon respite, and Aunt Norris and Maria to the sewing room to inspect the progress on Maria's dress. Tom, Mr. Yates, and Mr. Crawford were cataloging the art to be put up for sale in the storehouse, under the supervision of the bailiffs, and so Fanny merely walked through the study door and shut it behind her.

The pile of papers sat in stacks on her uncle's—now Tom's—oak desk. Fanny's fingers twitched in her eagerness to rifle through them, but she forced herself to pause and observe first, memorizing the haphazard angle they were strewn about on the desk and skimming the dates and content.

The invoice on top was dated two years ago. She quickly read the sales summary—a painting by an artist she barely remembered—and looked at the totals. Nothing seemed amiss. But what interest did Tom have in old invoices?

With trembling hands, she picked up the topmost invoice and scanned the one below it. It was from around the same time, and again nothing struck her as strange. She carefully began to wade through the pile, resisting the urge to tidy up the stack as she went along. Tom might not notice if someone had paged through the stack, but he'd certainly pay attention if it had been straightened.

Minutes passed and Fanny found her eyes blurring at the sight of so many numbers—dates, amounts, invoice numbers. She began to doubt herself and her suspicions. Perhaps Tom was merely updating records. Maybe he was researching the value of past pieces in order to price the current inventory. There could be any number of logical reasons that he and Mr. Yates had whisked these papers inside. But then she saw it: an invoice she very nearly passed over, dated last October . . . for the Rasmussen self-portrait.

It had sold to a Mr. Colin Stewart, for ninety-seven pounds.

Stewart. Surely it was no coincidence that Mr. Rushworth's Scottish contact shared the same surname.

Excited at the connection, she rummaged through the invoices once more, this time searching desperately for his name. But she didn't find anything more. What she did notice was that her uncle had been pulling in quite a bit of money. She was no expert, but twenty pounds here and thirty-five there were common enough figures. A few notable sums over fifty pounds made her raise her eyebrows, but overall there had been money coming in and with great frequency, enough to cover the expenses she'd seen in the household ledgers. How had it been eaten up so quickly?

Something must have changed about her uncle's financial

status between Maria entering society and his death, and whatever it was didn't appear to include a decrease in earnings. By all appearances, Sir Thomas had a profitable business.

So why had he taken from Edmund's trust, if not to bail out the business?

The obvious answer was that he was in some sort of trouble outside of Mansfield Emporium. Fanny's own father had many vices, and although it had been years since she lived with her parents, she recalled the smell of drink and the late nights spent gambling. Sir Thomas had shown no signs of any of that.

Then another thought struck her: What if her uncle hadn't been the one with the expensive vice?

Fanny recalled the way that she had listed her relations' secrets to Edmund just a few weeks ago: Lady Bertram drank, Aunt Norris was constantly helping herself to Mansfield Park's amenities, and Julia was light-fingered. But was any of that enough to bankrupt an otherwise thriving business?

And then there was Maria: ambitious, and she'd pushed Sir Thomas to expand and bring in Mr. Rushworth's contacts. But Tom . . . he was reckless with money, and he showed very little self-governance. And Sir Thomas had never fully trusted Mr. Yates's influence on his son.

Had her uncle been covering for any one of them? And to his own peril?

Fanny found herself looking at more recent invoices, unsure of what to think. Her attention snagged on one with

Lord Marbury's name, as the name was familiar. His wife had admired Fanny's painting of Mansfield's lilies from last spring, and her uncle had gifted it to Lady Marbury. Fanny had been happy to let it go, especially when Sir Thomas had explained this gesture of goodwill would go a long way in sealing the deal of a much larger and more valuable painting to Lord Marbury—a boring piece that depicted some old battle or another. Fanny skimmed it, curious to see what it had gone for. Nearly a hundred and fifty pounds! But then she read the next line of the invoice.

Lilies, by F. Price. Provenance: Mansfield Park, 181_.
Sold for 25 pounds.

Her eyes widened, and she went over the memory in her mind. Had she gotten it wrong? Had he actually sold the painting, and she had misunderstood? That must be it. Surely she had misheard him.

But . . . Fanny could lie to herself about a great many things. This was not one of them. If she closed her eyes, she could remember the feeling of pride when her uncle had asked her if it was all right to gift the painting to this very important customer. The thrill in her veins as she'd consented, and the euphoria that had carried her for weeks, knowing that something she had created was good enough to hang in a countess's house.

That Sir Thomas had thought her art good enough to be beneficial to him.

But Sir Thomas had lied.

Fanny threw the invoices down on the desk to cover up the offending one that proved what she didn't want to accept. Sir Thomas had sold her work and pocketed the profits. Would it have made a difference if he'd asked to sell her work? Even if Fanny hadn't asked for a single penny of the sale in return?

Yes, she decided. Because for so long, she'd known that her position in the household was always contingent on how useful she might be. And even if no one had threatened to send her back to Portsmouth while her uncle was alive, she might have been able to relax her shoulders slightly, knowing that she had value in this house. She'd been happy to gift the painting to Lady Marbury because it had allowed her to feel that she was finally contributing to the many pounds that her uncle had spent on her over the years, but somehow knowing that he'd also sold the painting felt like a betrayal.

Another thought struck her: Had he truly wanted to offer her painting lessons because he thought she was good? Or had it been part of a larger plan, to use her artwork to continue to bolster his sales?

Tears flooded her eyes, quickly and with a force that surprised her. She tried to get hold of herself—it wasn't as though Sir Thomas weren't justified in trying to recoup the money he'd spent on her. And it wasn't as though she wasn't willing to work for her keep. She'd enjoyed the fine hand-me-downs, the good food, warm blankets, and sturdy boots. The French and drawing lessons from the governess, and the long afternoons spent in the storehouse studying great works of art. The canvases, the sketchbooks, the charcoal pencils, the expensive paint.

It wasn't about the money. It was that she had been so obviously used, and Sir Thomas had lied.

And if he had lied to her about the sale of her painting, then Fanny finally had to admit that perhaps there were other things he'd lied about. Other deceits she had yet to uncover.

And perhaps they were the reason someone had set a trap for him in his own storehouse.

The sound of voices from the hall made her stiffen for a moment. Someone was coming. She swiped at the tears clouding her eyes and frantically cast her gaze about the room for a hiding spot. She didn't have enough time to cross the study and retreat into the library, which left her with under the desk or behind the drapes. Fanny chose the drapes and had no sooner settled them around her when the door opened and Tom and Mr. Yates could be heard entering.

". . . it'll be a success," Mr. Yates said, his voice laden with reassurance. "I told you that Crawford fellow knows what he's about, even if his methods might be a little unorthodox."

"You're right, per usual," Tom said. Fanny heard them step into the room and the door click shut behind them. She closed her eyes. "Thank God Maria finally came around. I thought she'd refuse out of spite."

"Yes, well, Crawford does have his charms. I suspect it's all part of his success."

Tom chuckled. "I almost feel bad for Rushworth."

"For a man so concerned about the tie of his cravat, you'd think he could see what is literally happening under his nose." There was the sound of footsteps coming closer and the clink of the crystal decanter followed by a splash as he poured out a drink. "If it wasn't Crawford, it would have been some other dandy with a half-decent personality."

Ah, so Fanny wasn't the only one who believed Maria was showing an inappropriate interest in Mr. Crawford.

"I don't care that she marries for money," Tom said, and there was a pause as if he were taking a sip. "But it really irks me, the thought of that man having any say in our business. We must convince her to sign over her shares before she marries that fool."

Fanny heard the squeak of the chair behind the desk. She was grateful she hadn't chosen it as a hiding spot now, even if she was rather conspicuously pressed against the window. "And I don't believe for a single moment that she doesn't know where those missing documents are. She probably has them stashed away somewhere."

Fanny's interest piqued. Missing documents?

"She might," Mr. Yates allowed. "Or your father could have hidden them."

"I suppose, but why?"

"Don't think about it now," Mr. Yates said, his tone soothing. Another creak of the chair. "Soon you'll have money again, and we can get back to sorting Maria once and for all."

Sorting Maria? What exactly did *that* mean?

"What would I do without you?" Tom asked.

The chair creaked once more. There was a noticeable pause, before Fanny heard Mr. Yates respond, "I suppose you'd be beholden to your sister."

"Anything but that," Tom joked. "I won't be tied down to any woman."

"Definitely not," Mr. Yates responded, and then Fanny heard the sound of what she could only imagine was kissing—all inhalations and the smacking of lips. Fanny shuddered—she was not opposed to kissing on principle, but this was *private*.

She was just weighing the advantages and disadvantages of making her presence known (there were a frightful number of reasons not to, but the singular reason of ending this agony was very appealing) when she heard one of the men groan and Tom say, "We ought to get back. I don't trust Crawford with Maria for an instant."

"Because you don't trust his intentions, or you don't trust her?" Mr. Yates asked.

"Both," Tom said darkly.

There was a squeak of relief from the chair and the sound of straightening of limbs and clothing. Fanny felt her face flush in relief.

"You have to admit," Mr. Yates added, "it's all working out quite well."

"Better than I expected, that's for certain," Tom said.

"Just a little while longer and you'll be free," Mr. Yates promised, and there was the sound of one last lingering kiss.

"Do I look decent?" Tom asked.

There was a smirk in Mr. Yates's voice as he said, "Decent enough," and then the door opened and the room fell silent as it closed behind them.

But even though the coast was clear, Fanny was immobile, playing over their conversation in her mind.

You have to admit, it's all working out quite well.

Better than I expected.

Sorting Maria once and for all.

This entire time Fanny has been suspicious of Maria. She was the one caught arguing with Sir Thomas before his death, and it only stood to reason that she should be behind dealing art out of Aunt Norris's cottage to a Scottish man that had to be Mr. Rushworth's associate Mr. Stewart. If she was doing something illegal, and she had been caught by her father, then maybe she'd decided to do something drastic. To take her father out of the picture . . . or just leave him injured and unable to work for a while.

But if Tom and Mr. Yates were running their own scheme . . . then they couldn't be discounted.

It was too big to consider here, and she suddenly needed to get out of this room. The room was empty, so Fanny moved to step out from behind the drapes . . . but not before she caught a figure in her peripheral vision, on the other side of the glass, not twenty paces away.

Fanny turned and found Mary Crawford, dressed in a smart navy riding habit, staring straight at her.

ELEVEN

In Which Fanny Finds Consolation and
Inspiration in a Surprising Source

FANNY FLED, NATURALLY.

She knew, distantly, that doing this only made her look guiltier, but she had never been very good at playing off awkward situations. She ran up to the old nursery, feeling a certain sense of relief when the door closed behind her.

This room was where her relatives had stuck Fanny when she first arrived all those years ago. Back then, all of the children still slept in the long, narrow room, but curiously they all seemed to move out within months of Fanny's arrival. The old cribs and playthings were packed away and stacked at one end of the room, and the other end was filled with Fanny's narrow, utilitarian bed, a straight-backed chair, a scratched writing desk, and a small round table laden with drawings and art supplies. Her easel stood near the windows, positioned to catch the best of the sunlight. The nursery might be out of the way, and the fireplace was always cold and empty, even in winter, but it was Fanny's own space, an escape from the outside world and the one place where she felt herself truly relax.

But she couldn't calm her racing heart now. Miss Crawford had seen her hiding, had proof that Fanny had lied about her headache, and then had seen her flee the scene. Perhaps she'd be too polite to ever bring up this strange behavior? But if she did . . . well, Fanny would have to come up with some kind of explanation.

A knock sounded at the door and Fanny started, then sat absolutely still. Aunt Norris didn't knock, the maids never even bothered to clean the old nursery, and even Edmund wasn't inclined to ever venture upstairs. Another knock sounded and a feminine voice called out, "Miss Price?"

Fanny's eyes widened in horror. It was *Miss Crawford*.

She stood out of some impulse to flee, but there was nowhere else for her to go, and she knocked over her chair in the process. She winced, and Miss Crawford called out again. "Miss Price, are you all right?"

"One moment!" Fanny called out, and then looked about her room, imagining how it might appear to Miss Crawford. Maybe she ought to just try climbing out the window? Would a fall from three stories cause grievous injury? Likely, but it was more appealing than answering the door.

Nonetheless, she picked up her chair, smoothed out her skirts, and tried to steady her breathing. When she opened the door, Miss Crawford stood in the hall, wearing a look of concern mixed with uncertainty. She had changed out of her riding habit and now wore a dove-gray day dress with pink ribbons, so pretty and delicate that Fanny instinctively began to imagine which paints she might mix to capture the colors.

"I'm sorry to intrude," Miss Crawford began. "But I wanted to see how you were."

"I . . . beg your pardon?"

She stepped inside, while asking, "May I come in? It's just, I realized that I might have caught you at an awkward moment earlier, and I didn't want you to think that I was prying or being nosy. What you do is none of my business."

Then why are you here? Fanny wanted to ask, but she decided to play ignorant. "I don't know what you're talking about."

Miss Crawford tilted her head, as if questioning Fanny, but she chose not to clarify. "What a lovely room you have up here. It must get the nicest morning light."

It did, in fact, but Fanny wasn't about to admit that. Miss Crawford continued to prattle on. "I know you object to what is to be done with your late uncle's collection. Please don't hold it against Henry or me. We're orphaned too, you know. And you understand that orphans—well, we must make our way in the world the best we can."

It took Fanny another moment to realize what Miss Crawford was implying. "But I'm not an orphan," she protested.

Miss Crawford's smile slipped. "I beg your pardon?"

"Sir Thomas and Lady Bertram are my guardians," she explained. "But I'm not an orphan. My family is from Portsmouth."

"Oh, I didn't realize," Miss Crawford.

"Didn't you?" Fanny waited a moment and then added, "I thought my cousins might have explained the situation between my mother and aunts."

She enjoyed seeing the moment that Miss Crawford realized Fanny had overheard their gossip. "I beg your pardon, I assumed and I . . . I'm so sorry."

She turned to go, and something inside of Fanny twisted when she saw Miss Crawford's embarrassed flush. Did it really matter that she'd caught Miss Crawford in a tiny deception, if she'd been trying to be kind to Fanny? What was it about this young lady that enchanted her so?

"Wait."

Miss Crawford stopped and turned slowly. Fanny gestured to her sole chair. "Please, sit."

Fanny sat at the foot of her bed while Miss Crawford took the proffered chair and took her time arranging her skirts. Good manners dictated Fanny, as de facto hostess, come up with some small topic of polite conversation, but Miss Crawford had sought Fanny out. And Fanny had deep reserves of patience. She could wait out Miss Crawford any day of the week.

Miss Crawford's gaze swept across the room, landing on a collection of canvases leaning against the long wall opposite the windows. "You are quite talented," she said, taking in Fanny's work. The paintings in view were mostly landscapes of Mansfield Park's grounds or cascades of the flowers that bloomed in summer. "How fortunate to be born into such an artistic family."

Fanny let out a sharp bray of laughter, then quite surprised herself when it turned into a hiccup and the hiccup turned into a sob. And then she was crying messy tears and gulping down great breaths and it was all too much and she buried her face into her hands and hoped that Miss Crawford would just *go away*.

But Miss Crawford did not. She plopped down next to Fanny on her thin, hard mattress and pressed a lilac-scented handkerchief in her palm. A reassuring warm hand rubbed circles on her back, and Fanny began to feel faint. She finally managed to get her tears under control and pressed the linen handkerchief into her eyes until it was damp.

"Now, I've made quite a lot of assumptions, and I don't dare make any more until you tell me why it is you're so upset," Miss Crawford said. "I'd be happy to listen, if you like."

There were a hundred reasons not to confide in her, but

Fanny was sick of bottling everything up. "My uncle sold a painting."

"All right," Miss Crawford said, voice tentative but encouraging.

"One of *my* paintings."

Miss Crawford waited.

"It was one I was quite proud of, actually. And he sold it." Fanny hiccupped. "For a lot of money—well, a lot of money to *me*. And he said that he merely gave it away, to one of our clients."

"Oh." Miss Crawford's hand ceased drawing circles on her back. *"Oh."*

"I shouldn't be mad at a dead man," Fanny continued in a trembling voice. "But . . ."

"You're allowed to be angry."

Emotion bubbled up inside her. And at first, Fanny couldn't identify it because she was so used to pushing it down, masking it with a smile, or pushing it aside. Girls like Fanny were expected to be grateful. They were not allowed to question their circumstances, because Sir Thomas had done her a favor, and her aunts would be quick to remind her how much worse her life could be. But the anger was there, running deep in her veins, showing up at inopportune times. No one had ever given her permission to *feel* it before. Now, Fanny did. Fanny was heartbroken and disappointed, but the anger surged in her veins and it made her want to scream.

"Let it out," Miss Crawford encouraged. "What you say won't go beyond this room."

"How dare he!" Fanny spat out the words, knowing that this was her only chance to do so. "I was proud of that painting! He turned it into a commodity, and lied about giving it away. I wouldn't have even cared had I known he'd sold it—I would have painted him a dozen more to sell, to pay back my debt. But he lied! I hate a liar, Miss Crawford."

"Mary, please," she murmured. "I feel like we are far past formalities."

"Then you must call me Fanny," Fanny said, and then, feeling a little reckless, she asked, "How do you stand it? The deception?"

She was referring, of course, to the whole conceit of social gatherings turned into business affairs and thought at first Mary wouldn't respond, or she'd fall back on the same defenses that her brother had deployed.

But Mary merely shrugged. "Because we must. I don't relish trickery, but neither do I relish sleeping on the streets or going hungry. Of all the terrible lies in the world, it is a small enough trick. We're orphans, and what little family we have has no interest in us. Henry does what he does in order to make money. And I . . ."

"What?"

"I think that if I had someone to take me in, and give me a home such as this, I wouldn't ever want to leave." Mary's voice was fervent, and her gaze swept about the room in appreciation. Fanny wasn't sure if she meant the room itself or all of Mansfield.

"Is it truly home if it's not yours, though?"

Mary's shoulders slumped. "Maybe not."

"That's what I want," Fanny said, her voice barely a whisper. "I want a home that's mine and mine alone. It doesn't have to be grand, but I want my own bed and my own four walls, and perhaps a garden. Enough set aside for painting supplies. And I'll never have to ask anyone for bare necessities or feel as though I must constantly be singing my thanks. I want something no one can take away from me at a moment's notice."

"It sounds lovely," Mary murmured.

Fanny felt she'd done quite enough soul bearing and went silent for a long while. Mary stared at her collection of work. "Why do you think your uncle did it?"

"That is the question of the hour," she said, surprising herself with the bitterness in her tone. "If I had to hazard a guess, I'd say it's because I'm not a Bertram."

"But you're *family*," Mary protested.

"Perhaps," Fanny allowed. "But I've never seen it like that. There are relatives, and there is family. And as far as I'm concerned, family is about far more than blood or the bonds of marriage. I used to hope . . ."

Mary didn't prod her, but Fanny felt the weight of her expectant gaze.

"I used to hope they'd see me, accept me as family. But they only see duty. I may be artistic, but that doesn't mean I belong with them, or that they care about my well-being. I've always known their true feelings. But my uncle's death has forced me to face it."

"I'm so sorry for your loss," Mary said, placing a hand over Fanny's. Fanny looked up and into her eyes. The brilliant blue was much more stunning this close up. "But that doesn't mean you can't still be a successful artist and sell your own paintings."

If only that were the extent of it. But Fanny didn't need to burden her with any more of her woes. "Thank you. I'm sorry to have been such a wet blanket."

"You're not," Mary insisted, and she leaned forward just a breath, making Fanny's own breathing turn shallow. "You've had quite the shock these past weeks. But I do hope that you'll consider me a friend."

"Of course," Fanny said quickly, and she abruptly looked down at her lap. Her presence, the sweet lilac scent of her, it was all too much. When was the last time someone had comforted Fanny when she cried? "I'm grateful for your kindness."

Mary stood suddenly. "I'll not intrude any longer."

Her exit was nearly as abrupt, and Fanny watched her go, perplexed. Had she said or done something to scare her off? Fanny stood and closed the door to the nursery and turned to survey the room. The only sign that Mary had ever been there at all was her handkerchief, still clutched between Fanny's fingers, and the lingering scent of lilac.

That was when Fanny realized two things: First, Mary hadn't said a word about seeing Fanny lurking suspiciously behind the drapes.

Second, Fanny had a good idea where her uncle might have hidden those missing documents.

TWELVE

In Which Fanny Takes an Inadvisable Risk

THE LAST TIME THAT anyone had ever comforted Fanny as she cried was when she was nine years old.

Fanny was newly arrived to Mansfield Park, and the size of the estate and the opulence of the furnishings astounded her every day. She had to remind herself not to stuff her mouth at every meal, and at night she relished her small, narrow cot that she didn't have to share with a single sibling. Her new dresses were hand-me-downs, but they weren't patched like her old gowns, and every day there was something new to learn about etiquette or rules or how things were done at Mansfield. And for a moment in time, she'd thought that she and Maria and Julia could be friends.

She knew they were different, of course—her cousins wore pretty pastel dresses and ribbons in their hair, and their faces were never smudged. They curtsied properly and giggled whenever Fanny used the incorrect utensil at a meal. But growing up in a large family where her parents argued about money and the cost of everything was dear had instilled in Fanny a deep desire to please, to make herself small and agreeable. She believed that if she simply worked hard enough, paid enough attention, and applied herself, she could be transformed into the type of girl that her cousins would like.

The day that Fanny realized it was all for naught was hot and stifling, the kind where the air felt like soup and her aunts wilted in the dimmed parlor, too listless to pay close attention to the children. Tom and Edmund were at their riding lessons, and the girls had been turned out into the gardens to amuse themselves while their governess flirted with a footman. Fanny was delighted to bring along her brand-new sketchbook and scout for subjects, but the moment they stepped outside Maria announced, "I'm bored!"

"Me too," Julia said.

Fanny set aside her drawing. "Should we play a game?"

"What game?" Maria asked, suspicious of whatever Fanny had to suggest.

"We could get the hoops," she said. "Or play with ribbons?" But she suggested these things only because she knew that they were what the girls would normally do.

"That's boring," Julia complained. "What games do you play with your brothers?"

"We don't want to play her games," Maria was quick to say. "She plays in dirty streets."

Fanny's cheeks felt flushed. "We play lots of games, like hide-and-go-seek."

Maria was curious, but she didn't relent in her challenging stare. "How do we play it?"

Fanny explained the rules, and the game was deemed acceptable. Secretly, Fanny was thrilled—the gardens were expansive and full of tall, swaying flowers, densely packed bushes, and all sorts of nooks and crannies. And best of all, there was no one around to yell at them to get out of their garden or cart or go back home to their mothers—just the gardener, and he was clipping the front hedges. This would be the best game of hide-and-go-seek *ever*.

"I want to hide!" Julia announced. "And Fanny, you find us."

"No, I'll be the seeker," Maria corrected. "And that way I'll know if the game is any good."

"All right, but don't forget to count all the way to one hundred!" Fanny reminded Maria, who rolled her eyes.

Fanny took off the moment Maria started counting, not even waiting to see if Julia also rushed off to find her own hiding spot. She knew where she wanted to hide—behind the topiary hedges at the back garden, near the drive that separated the gardens from her uncle's great storehouse, where he spent many hours of his day. The sound of Maria's voice faded away the farther she got, and she nestled herself behind the topiaries, tucked quite out of sight. Her giddiness at her hiding spot grew the more time that passed. Surely Maria was done counting by now? Well, it would take her time to make her way to Fanny. She settled in, imagining her victory at being the winner.

But as the afternoon stretched on and her legs began to cramp, she worried that perhaps she'd been *too* good at hiding. What if Maria couldn't find her? Fanny would win, but then Maria would be cross and she wouldn't ever want to play the game again, not even with Edmund and Tom, and everyone knew that it was much better to have as many people as possible when playing hide-and-go-seek.

She was there another half hour more and still Maria didn't come—and there was no sound of her searching, either. That was when the fear began to set in. What if they forgot about her? Her skinny arms were turning pink from the sun, so she scooted even deeper in the shade, uncertain of what to do.

Finally, she heard the sound of her own name being called out. Relief and excitement leapt in her chest until she realized it wasn't her cousins or even the governess: it was Aunt Norris. "Fannyyyyyyyyyy! Fanny Price! Where are you, girl?"

Fanny didn't dare move. Aunt Norris wouldn't care if she was playing a game. Aunt Norris was full of cross words and sharp scoldings, and Fanny would be in trouble if she gave herself up now. Perhaps if she waited a little longer, Maria and Julia would find her and they'd explain that it was a game and Fanny had won it. Aunt Norris would believe them.

She made herself very small and still until she saw Aunt Norris's skirts swish through the shrubbery, muttering as she went and barking out Fanny's name. She was nearly past when a deeper voice asked, "Have you lost something?"

Fanny gave out a tiny gasp. It was Sir Thomas!

"The girl," Aunt Norris said, voice sour. "Maria and Julia came in saying she's run off."

Fanny nearly gave herself away then—she hadn't run off! They were playing a game!

"Oh my," her uncle remarked, unperturbed. "Well, I do hope she turns up."

"Do you? I fear that taking on the child is far more trouble than she's worth."

"Mrs. Norris!" Sir Thomas's voice was sharp and shocked.

"Begging your pardon, sir, but she's proving to be quite the corrupting influence, and I worry about your girls. You have to take naughty children in hand when they're young. Otherwise they're too spoiled and it's no good. They're bad through and through."

"I don't believe that," her uncle responded. "I believe that a child just needs a bit of care and attention—and yes, discipline, I won't argue with you there. But she's far from spoiled."

"If you say so," Aunt Norris said, in such a way that suggested she didn't believe it. "I'll be going now."

"Good luck," her uncle replied. "I'm sure she'll turn up."

Fanny waited until her aunt's skirts swished out of sight, and then she let out a big, hiccupping sob. Maria and Julia had never intended to truly play the game—they just wanted to get her in trouble. And Aunt Norris thought she was bad, and she'd likely send her home for good. Her heart ached to see William and her siblings again, but Mama would be so disappointed and Papa would lose his temper—

"Hello, there," Sir Thomas said, startling Fanny. She looked up to see her uncle peering down into the hedges, a look of curious concern on his face. "I'm happy to see you're not lost to the fairies. What's the matter?"

His kindness only made Fanny cry harder, until her uncle offered her a hand and pulled her out of the hedges. She expected him to march her back to the house to meet her fate, but instead he handed her his handkerchief and led her to the storehouse. She'd never been inside but knew vaguely that it was full of old things that her uncle sold. She was surprised to find that it wasn't full of dust motes and grime, but very clean and filled with natural light, and every wall and surface held art. Art like what she saw in the great house, but different.

Her cries settled into hiccups, and she quickly cleaned up her tears as her uncle beckoned her up the stairs to a loft above. He didn't say anything, and fear made any questions die on Fanny's tongue. He ushered her into what appeared to be a small office and indicated that she should take a seat in a chair in the corner. Her heart was pounding now—what sort of punishment awaited her? But her uncle didn't seem upset.

"I know that life here is strange for you," he said. "But you mustn't let Aunt Norris get under your skin."

He turned his back on her and was rustling about with something behind his desk. Her curiosity got the better of her, and Fanny peered around him to see him push aside a stack of documents on the shelf behind the desk. He pushed against the board of the back wall and with a loud squeak, it popped out.

Fanny gasped. Her uncle turned his head, saw her watching, and gave her a wink. She saw his hand disappear into the secret hole in the wall. There was the clinking of glass, and then he withdrew a small, slender box. He lifted the lid off and presented the contents to Fanny.

It was full of small squares in every color of the flowers in the gardens, from dazzling bottle green to the lightest blush pink.

"Go ahead," her uncle said. "Take a few. They're quite delicious."

Not wanting to seem greedy, Fanny took two—a daffodil-yellow square and one the color of blue-purple hydrangeas. She was uncertain what to do with them at first—but Sir Thomas had said they were delicious. She bit into the yellow one and was surprised when a rich, sweet flavor melted against her tongue. She immediately regretted not taking more.

"There you go," her uncle said, smiling. It was perhaps the first time that Fanny had ever seen him smile at her. "This will be our little secret, eh?"

And it was.

What would Miss Bennet think if she saw me now? Fanny wondered as she got dressed in the quiet of her nursery room the night of the auction. Fanny had gotten quite adept at sneaking about and poking through files and private rooms since her uncle's death. Granted, she had gotten caught nearly every time, but neither Anna nor Mary had given her away to the people who'd really care about her nosing about. She'd like to think Miss Bennet would be pleased by her plans for that evening. She only had to make sure she was seen by Aunt Norris, then give her the slip, then sneak back into the storehouse. . . .

But first, she'd have to figure out how to tie the laces of her new gown.

"Dash it all!" Fanny exclaimed, reaching behind her back with little luck. She could grab hold of the dress's laces but not properly tighten and tie them. It was a pretty, midnight-blue gown that Julia and Maria had passed off as too plain for their own wardrobes, and while it was finer than anything Fanny owned, the dress did her no favors. Not only was it impossible to lace up without the aid of a sister or maid, but it made her skin look too pale and her brown hair too dull. Nonetheless, Maria had decreed that none of them save Lady Bertram were to wear black that evening, so as not to remind their guests of the tragedy and spoil the mood.

A knock came from her door, startling her from her attempts at pulling the bodice on straight. "One moment!" she called out, voice tinged with desperation.

There was no way she could answer the door like this! The dress was on, and it properly covered everything it was supposed to, but it was loose and the opening at the back gaped. Another knock sounded, and Fanny realized she'd just have to undress and pull on a plain gown she could do up on her own, just to see who was knocking.

"I need just a few minutes!" she called out.

"Fanny? Do you need help?"

Fanny stilled. It was Mary Crawford's voice. "I just—um, well . . ."

"I'm coming in, all right? It's just me."

And to Fanny's surprise, Mary Crawford opened her bedroom door and slipped in, clicking the door shut behind her. She was dressed in a dazzling sapphire gown and her hair was carefully pinned so that perfect ringlets fell, framing her face. Fanny clutched at the back of her gown, but the only sound that fell out of her mouth was a shocked, "Oh, it's you!"

Mary and Fanny hadn't really spoken since Fanny abruptly started bawling over Mary the previous day, but the tears hadn't seemed to put her off in any way. Fanny still found her nearly impossible to read, but something subtle had shifted between them. She now got the sense that there was some unspoken understanding between them, as though they might be friends.

But they were not so close that Fanny didn't feel a vague, buzzing sense of panic at greeting Mary in a state of undress.

Mary didn't seem to notice. "I'm sorry for being so forward, but I only just finished dressing when it occurred to me . . . you don't have a maid to help you, do you?"

It was a silly enough question, not least because of the way Fanny was desperately gripping the back of her dress. "Heavens, no. I usually can manage just fine on my own."

"That's what I thought," Mary said, smiling at Fanny in a way that made her pulse quicken. "But these party gowns aren't the sensible, everyday wear we're used to. They require some strapping into. May I?"

Fanny pursed her lips. The idea of turning her back to Mary was more difficult than she might have imagined. But what were her options? She slowly turned.

Mary stepped forward and said, "Oh, these are tricky!" and then Fanny felt her grab hold of the laces and begin to work at tightening them. "Too much?" she asked.

Fanny pressed her hands to her stomach to hide their trembling and reminded herself to breathe. "No, that's just right."

"Good. We don't want any swooning tonight."

Fanny let out a small scoff. "Do women actually do that outside of novels?"

"Oh yes," Mary said pleasantly, her hands working quickly

and efficiently. "Although, I think that most of them exaggerate for attention. Even so, if you overheat in a warm ballroom and find yourself out of breath from dancing, and your dress is a bit tight . . . well. A little swooning does the job of getting you a seat, a fan, and a cool drink rather efficiently." She paused, then added, "Not to mention the attention of numerous young men."

"Oh, well, I wouldn't want *that*," Fanny said, not even thinking about her words. She felt the tickle of Mary's small laugh on the back of her neck.

"There you are," Mary said, tying off the laces and letting her hands fall away slowly, but not before grazing Fanny's waist. Fanny struggled for breath as she turned and met Mary's gaze. She didn't know what to say. She didn't know what to *think* about Mary Crawford.

"Thank you," she said finally.

"Don't think of it."

Flustered by the memory of Mary's touch, Fanny asked, "Should we go down?"

"Wait a moment," Mary said, touching her arm. "I have something to give you."

"Me?"

Mary pulled a small velvet bag from her reticule. "I'm sorry if this is gauche to say, but I've noticed the way that your family treats you, and it pains me. You deserve . . . well, you deserve better. I hope I haven't embarrassed you by saying so. I want you to have this."

Fanny's hands came up automatically to receive the small pouch, and she drew it open with trembling fingers. A necklace fell into her palm. A chain of luminous pearls glowed in the candlelight, and at the center was a round pendant of black jet. It was understated yet beautiful, and it was without a doubt the prettiest thing that Fanny had ever been given.

"I can't—Mary. Miss Crawford. I can't accept this."

"Nonsense," Mary said. "And I'm Mary, not Miss Crawford. Let's not go backsliding now. You need something beautiful to go with this lovely dress."

She plucked the necklace from Fanny's hands, and before Fanny realized what she was doing, Mary draped it around her neck and stepped behind Fanny to clasp it.

"It's too fine of a gift," Fanny tried again, but less forcefully. "What will people say?"

"My dear, one of the delightful things about being at a party such as this is imagining what people will say. And besides, it's fun to give them all something innocuous to talk about." Her breath whispered against Fanny's neck, and she shivered.

"But I don't like it when people are looking at me," Fanny whispered.

Mary drew Fanny into the candlelight, giving her a once-over that made Fanny want to squirm. "I don't see why not. You really must get used to the idea that you're worth looking at, you know."

And before Fanny had the time to process that, Mary

was blowing out the candles and pulling at Fanny's arm. She allowed herself to be led downstairs, where dozens of guests milled about in the main hall leading into the ballroom. Candles on nearly every surface made the house glow with rosy light, and the murmur of polite chatter filled Fanny's ears. It was profoundly strange to see so many people in the halls that usually stood so empty.

"It's a very good turnout already," Mary whispered to her as they slowly descended the main stairs. "Everyone wants to see what the legendary Mansfield Emporium has to offer."

"I didn't know that we knew so many people," Fanny responded.

"Oh, well . . . you don't. Many of these people are my brother's contacts, too. Like, right there—that's Sir John Allerton, he'll come to any event my brother throws." Mary subtly pointed out a middle-aged man with dark, curly hair wearing a plain black evening coat, making his way to the ballroom. "He's likely one to watch tonight. And I see Mr. and Mrs. Parkins. They're nouveau riche, but they love art. Henry wasn't sure if they'd come all this way."

And speaking of Henry Crawford, he stood near the front door in the receiving line next to Maria, Tom, and Lady Bertram, greeting guests as they arrived.

He looked to the stairs and watched as Fanny and Mary descended. Fanny was glad Mary had her by the elbow because Mr. Crawford's gaze made her want to turn on her heel and run right back upstairs. He was appraising her like a painting, and she didn't want to know what he perceived as her value.

Luckily, by the time they reached the bottom Mr. Rushworth was making his grand entrance. If Fanny had been hoping for a ridiculous display in order to distract attention away from her, he did not disappoint. His evening jacket was a deep emerald and his shirt and cravat a crisp white. A riotous red-and-gold-paisley vest clashed with the jacket, but they were tame compared to his black-and-gold-checked breeches. He was, naturally, wearing those obnoxious high-heeled boots he always went on about.

"Maria, my love!" he proclaimed rather loudly upon entering. "You're a vision!"

Maria turned at the sound of her fiancé's voice, and even from a distance of thirty paces Fanny could see her cheeks heat with embarrassment. "Mr. Rushworth!" Her tone was scandalized, but he didn't appear to notice.

"And Tom, hello, Lady Bertram, an honor." He bowed to each of them, completely ignoring Mr. Crawford. "Isn't our Maria lovely? One of our artists ought to paint her. It would sell for hundreds of pounds."

"James," Maria hissed.

"I don't disagree with you," Mr. Crawford said, pretending to ignore Mr. Rushworth's slight. "But I don't think that any artist is up to the task."

Maria preened, while Mr. Rushworth gaped back at Mr.

Crawford, clearly at a loss for words. "Quite right," he managed, and then offered Maria his arm. She refused, choosing to stay in the receiving line, and Mr. Rushworth was forced to continue into the ballroom without her.

"Poor man," Edmund whispered behind them. "You know he likely spent the entire drive here coming up with that one line, only for Mr. Crawford to one-up him in a moment."

Fanny and Mary turned to find that he'd quite sneaked up on them. "Oh, don't tease him," Fanny said. "It really isn't his fault if Maria seems to have thrown him over in favor of . . . well."

"I'm afraid my brother can be overly charming," Mary said. "But I assure you, he'd never stand in the way of an engagement."

"Oh, I don't think your brother is the one anyone needs to worry about," Edmund said, then abruptly changed topics. "You both look quite lovely this evening."

"Thank you," Mary replied, while Fanny's tongue seemed to swell in her mouth. Edmund thought she was lovely? Mary continued, "And you clean up rather well yourself."

"Yes," Fanny managed in agreement. Why couldn't she think of anything more to say?

"May I escort you to the ballroom?"

Fanny looked from Edmund to Mary. Which one of them was he asking? But before she could figure it out, Mary accepted his offered arm, and Edmund extended his other arm to Fanny.

Oh. Well, this was certainly better than being left behind.

He escorted them between neighbors and strangers in equal fashion, until they came to the large double doors leading into the ballroom. Fanny gasped at the sight of it. She had helped with the setup and decorations, but that quite paled to how the room looked now, transformed into an art gallery of sorts, with paintings on every wall and tables laden with sculptures, vases, and trinkets. The Millbrook painting took a place of honor in the center of the room, and space was left around it so a crowd could gather and admire it. Each piece boasted a small, cream-colored placard with a carefully written number, and Mr. Yates and Tom made certain that every numbered piece matched their list of records for the auction portion of the evening. But it wasn't just the effect of seeing the art displayed that took Fanny's breath away: never before had she seen music, candlelight, art, and people fill the space. It was even more surreal than coming down the staircase had been.

Fanny almost wished she didn't plan on leaving early. *Almost.*

"Do you approve?" Mary asked eagerly.

"I . . ." Fanny didn't exactly approve, but she also couldn't think of a single sour thing to say. Instead, she responded with, "I can hardly believe this is the same place where we used to slide around on the floor in our stockings."

Edmund laughed. "You know, I'd forgotten about that."

"I would have liked to see it," Mary teased. "Although I

confess I have a hard time imagining you both as children."

"Who said we were children when we did it?" Edmund asked.

Mary laughed, and just like that Fanny went back to feeling like a drab impostor in the pretty dress while the two of them shared a joke. She struggled to think of something to say as they moved into the ballroom, but before she had the chance, she felt a sharp pinch at her free elbow.

"There you are!" Aunt Norris whispered. Fanny dropped Edmund's arm in surprise.

"Please excuse me," Fanny said to Edmund and Mary, who hardly seemed to notice, and then allowed herself to be yanked away. Aunt Norris propelled Fanny to the edge of the room and proceeded to scold her.

"I was against you attending, but I was overruled. Therefore, if you must be here, you'll follow some basic rules. No parading yourself about. No speaking to anyone you've not been formally introduced to. No dancing. You let the guests have a seat before you take one yourself. You're to be seen, not heard. Understand?"

Fanny nodded and made her eyes wide, hoping she looked convincing. *Don't worry, Aunt, I have no intention of sticking around*, she thought. "Yes, Aunt Norris."

Aunt Norris studied her suspiciously, then said, "Stay close. I'll be watching you."

Which was how she found herself being dragged along by

her aunt around the room, smiling vaguely and being introduced only when absolutely necessary. It was clear that Aunt Norris cared more about the people in the room than the artwork. Just when she was beginning to despair at ever giving her aunt the slip, she caught sight of a young lady in spruce green standing with a tall gentleman on her arm, examining a painting of yellow roses that always made her feel slightly queasy to look at. The young lady turned and gave Fanny a wink.

She gasped. It was Miss Bennet!

Mr. Darcy was on her arm, naturally, and it seemed as though they'd both spotted her but had the good sense not to approach. Fanny subtly tilted her head to her aunt. Miss Bennet understood immediately and whispered something to the rather unhappy-looking Mr. Darcy.

Fanny took a tiny step back, then another. Aunt Norris didn't seem to notice, so she kept creeping toward her uncle's solicitor until they appeared to be studying the same sickly-looking roses, but not together. "Sorry," she whispered, just loud enough to be heard over the noise of the party. "Aunt Norris is watching me very closely tonight."

"It's all right," Miss Bennet whispered back. "Are you safe?"

Fanny shrugged one shoulder very lightly. "As safe as I am anywhere, I suppose."

"And have you discovered anything?"

Fanny quickly shared what she'd discovered since her last letter—Tom and Mr. Yates's suspicions and suspicious conversation, and her suspicion that she might yet find something in the storehouse office. "I know it's not proof, but . . ."

"You're on the right path," Miss Bennet assured her. "Can you get away yet this evening to check your uncle's office?"

Fanny cast a furtive glance over her shoulder. Aunt Norris was talking to a middle-aged woman who looked as though she were casting about for her own escape. "As soon as I give my aunt the slip."

"The dour one?" Miss Bennet asked. "Allow me."

"She's very curt," Fanny warned, but Miss Bennet merely winked.

"Don't worry, you'd be surprised at how charming Darcy can be when it matters."

"Dour aunts are a specialty of mine," Mr. Darcy deadpanned.

"Be prepared to make your move!"

And faster than Fanny could have thought possible, Miss Bennet and Mr. Darcy glided over to Aunt Norris, allowing the lady she'd been conversing with to slip away gratefully. Fanny slowly edged out of Aunt Norris's line of sight, and when Miss Bennet caught her aunt's attention, Fanny began her retreat. In the hall, Fanny turned her back on the stragglers and went farther into the house, straight out the back door into the gardens, cutting across the lawn to the warehouse under the cover of night.

When she arrived at the storehouse, she was afraid that

perhaps she'd judged wrong and it would be locked up tight, empty as it was. But the side doorknob turned easily under her touch, and she slipped into the still building. There was a moment or two of groping and fumbling with a flint and candle near the entrance. Then Fanny had a weak light that made the shadows inside dance.

The structure felt oddly empty, even if she couldn't see beyond her light. She hurried for the steps, wincing as each one seemed rather noisy. She'd never before been in the storehouse alone, and her thoughts flashed to that fateful day. How had the culprit managed to set the trip wire without anyone noticing?

And what other dangers might be hidden in the shadows?

She shook the thought off as she began climbing the stairs. Whoever was responsible had targeted Sir Thomas. No one else knew she was there, and as long as she was quick, no one would ever know.

The office door was unlocked as well, and once inside she closed the door behind her, not liking the thought of her candlelight serving as a beacon for whoever might be lurking in the dark. (*Don't be daft*, she reminded herself. *There was no one there!*) She set the candle on her uncle's desk and tried to remember the day he'd revealed his hiding place, nearly a decade ago. The shelves on the walls were empty, their contents either boxed up or splayed across the study back inside the house. She couldn't remember which board had been the one to slide away. She started by pressing against the shelves, then the boards behind them. She knocked and rattled, and nothing gave way until her fingertips grazed a panel while her other hand pressed against a shelf. She felt a wobble.

Fanny bit back a smile.

It took another minute or two of pushing and wiggling, but finally one of the boards came loose, revealing a very dark gap. She brought the candle closer, scarcely able to breathe.

Inside was a cubby full of an odd collection of items—a half-full bottle of spirits, a small box, and a packet of letters tied together with string. She left the bottle and withdrew the other items. The letters she stuffed into her bodice—as much as it pained her to wait to read them, she knew she ought to return to the party before her absence was noticed. She pried open the small wooden box and felt her breath catch in her throat.

Chocolates. Small, colorful chocolates. The box was half-full of them—not the same box from years earlier, blessedly. The thought of her uncle keeping a box of chocolates hidden away in his office all these years . . . it made something inside of her crack. Sir Thomas had been a complicated man. He had agreed to take on the responsibility of his wife's sister's child but had rarely said anything when her aunts had used and mistreated her. He'd recognized her artistic ability, fostered it, even profited from it, but hadn't given her a say in the sale of her own work. He had been supportive and generous, but at times distant and indifferent to her. All of the anger she'd been carrying like a burning ember began to abate, and she was left feeling cold, empty, and just *sad*.

Then she heard the distant but unmistakable sound of a door opening.

Fanny didn't think—she just blew out her light. She clutched the box of chocolates and the candle, with its hot wax slowly congealing, and listened hard.

The sound was coming from below and in the direction of the smaller side entrance. Fanny crept to the exit as silently as she could and very carefully unlatched the door. It glided open on well-oiled hinges, and she was glad of that when she realized—the rest of the storehouse was pitch dark.

Had they gone?

Fanny strained her ears, not quite willing to give away her position.

Creeeeeeak.

Her eyes had yet to adjust to the sudden darkness, but she knew the sound had come much closer, not quite directly below her. Whoever this person was, they were creeping through the bottom level of the storehouse and they were taking as much care to keep quiet as she.

Fanny struggled to control her breathing. She was half tempted to go back into the office and attempt to barricade the door . . . but with what? A flimsy chair? And besides, if she did that, then she'd be cornered, quite literally, until the door was battered down or her awful relatives remembered she existed, which could be *days*. No, her best bet would be to hope to evade this intruder and make a run for it when she could. But if she was going to succeed at that, then she needed to move away from the office and away from the stairs.

Abandoning the candle and chocolate box, she gathered her skirts in one hand and listened once more. She could now make out the shape of the shelves upstairs, and the only way to avoid detection was to go down those shadowy aisles. If she could find a hiding nook, and the intruder were to come upstairs and get past her, she could run for it. Fanny had practically grown up in this building—she could outrun someone in the dark any day, with or without skirts.

She carefully eased her weight on her right foot and stepped back with her left. It was slow going, moving this carefully. Stopping to listen for sounds of the intruder coming up the steps. But she kept at it, trying not to imagine what would happen if she were caught.

Creak!

She went completely still.

But it was undeniable: that creak had been from the floorboard beneath her. And now she could hear the footsteps from below changing direction, not taking as much care. The intruder was coming upstairs, and she had to hide, now!

Still trying to keep quiet, Fanny turned down one of the aisles of shelving. Although most of the art had been removed from the storehouse for the party, some crates and frames were strewn about on the shelves, and Fanny hoped it would be enough to conceal her. She crouched down behind a particularly large crate as the intruder reached the top of the stairs.

The figure seemed to linger there, uncertain of which direction to take. Fanny was certain it was a man, judging by the lack of skirts. After a long moment of no movement, she wondered if he was having second thoughts. But then he began to move very carefully toward the aisles.

Please don't come down this one, she thought desperately, and got the first turn of good fortune when the figure started down the aisle just before hers. It was darker back here, so she hoped that she could stay hidden. All the same, her legs screamed at her for being dropped into an uncomfortable crouch. He drew up alongside her in the next aisle, and Fanny held her breath. He was moving slowly, deliberately, and she could hear his light breaths.

He was now mere feet away. The only thing that separated them was the crate and the open storage shelving. He took one step beyond her, then another . . . and stopped.

There was no room left in Fanny for hesitation. She launched into motion, running down the end of the aisle, headed for the stairs. She could hear the figure behind her spin around and give a quiet cry of surprise, but then she was hurtling down the stairs, and his steps thundered after her. She was halfway across the storehouse, then three-quarters of the way. The door was so close, then within reach, and then—

A rough hand clamped down on her shoulder, jerking

Fanny back. She screamed as loud as she could, not caring about keeping quiet anymore. She flailed against her captor's grasp, trying to throw off his weight, but then his other arm came up around her and grabbed her free hand and she was caught.

"Fanny!" the intruder said in an all-too-familiar voice. "Fanny, shhhh! It's me! Damn it, it's just me!"

Fanny stilled, but her heart was still galloping and her breath came in ragged hiccups. She twisted around in her captor's arms. "Ed-Edmund?"

THIRTEEN

*In Which Fanny Finds Herself
Caught between Two Impulses*

"YOU SCARED ME TO death!"

Fanny was glad to have Edmund's arms around her, for she felt unsteady on her feet. Adrenaline pounded in her veins, demanding release, and it was easier to channel it into outrage.

"What on earth were you thinking?" she demanded. "You nearly tackled me!"

"I thought you were . . . Fanny, I'm so sorry. Hold on, let me . . ." Edmund fumbled in the dark and found the flint and another candle. "What are you doing here?"

The light was a welcome relief, but Fanny still felt shivery at the sight of those leaping shadows. "What are *you* doing here? I thought you'd be performing with Mary?"

"Not for a while yet," he said. "I saw you give Aunt Norris the slip. It took me a little while to figure out where you'd gone, but I should have known you'd be here. Did you get it?"

"Get what?" Fanny asked, heart skipping a beat. How did he know about her uncle's hiding spot?

"Your painting, of course. Isn't that why you're here?"

"Oh."

Her replication of the Millbrook painting. It felt like an age since she'd hidden it away in that nook upstairs, and even longer since she'd actually thought about it. She'd been distracted as of late, to say the least. She wasn't sure if she should feel happy that Edmund had thought of her painting or annoyed that he seemed to have forgotten his promise to help her find their uncle's killer.

"No," Fanny finally said, her chin jutting out a little. "I was actually searching for evidence."

Even in the flickering light, Fanny could see the surprise on Edmund's face. "Really? But I thought . . ."

"You thought that I'd what? Given up? No, actually. While you've been entertaining Miss Crawford, I've been looking for clues."

Edmund rubbed at his temples. "Fanny, I know you're upset about Uncle, but what good will come of this? Do you actually *want* to be sent away?"

"Of course not! But . . ." She tried to find the words that

matched her complicated roil of feelings. "They might send me away anyway, Edmund. If they do, I want to have at least discovered the truth. And if I can solve this mystery, then perhaps whoever is left standing will . . ."

She wasn't quite sure how to finish that sentence.

"Be so grateful that they'll keep you on?" Edmund asked, and the sarcasm in his tone stung. "Fanny, you're being far too idealistic! The family wants nothing more than to move on. If there was foul play, one of them is probably responsible and I doubt the others would relish you inviting scandal to Mansfield by bringing this all to light."

"But don't you care about the truth?"

"I can't help you if I have no money!"

Fanny's anger evaporated, leaving her feeling deflated. "Of course. I'm sorry, I wasn't thinking."

Edmund shook his head. She'd never seen him so frustrated. "I'm sorry, too. It's not that I don't care . . . I just care a little bit more about the future than I do the past. If they turn you out, you have a home to return to in Portsmouth. I'll have no one, and hardly any money besides."

Fanny didn't think it was possible for her to feel any worse, but Edmund proved her wrong. "I . . . wasn't thinking of it that way," she admitted softly. She'd always seen her position and Edmund's as the same, but now she could see that they weren't the same thing at all. If they were both turned out, Edmund would only have as much money as the Bertrams were able to give him, and nowhere to turn. Who would have considered that *she* was the one with slightly more security? Certainly not Fanny.

"I'm sorry for yelling," he said finally. "And for giving you quite the shock."

"I thought you were the murderer," Fanny admitted.

"Good for you I was not."

"Do you truly have no place to go if Tom wipes his hands of you?" she asked. The thought of Edmund being alone in the world was heartbreaking.

"No decent options," he admitted. "My schoolmate Percy has let some rooms in London, and he'd likely take me in. But he's worse off than me. Either way, I need the money from my trust or I need a way to make a living."

Fanny nodded. She could respect that. At the same time . . . "I don't know if I can just give up on this, Edmund. If I don't find the truth, no one else will."

"Why does it matter so much?" he asked. "I'm not saying you shouldn't, but why?"

Fanny thought of Mary's words earlier that evening. *I've noticed the way that your family treats you, and it pains me.* Julia's gleeful implication that her removal from the house would be a matter of saving money. Her uncle . . . he had promised her a lot of things. Given her a lot of things, too. He deserved better than the ending he got, she was certain. He might not have been perfect, or even great. But no one deserved to be killed in their own home.

Which led her to an epiphany that was quite uncharacteristic: *I want them to be held accountable.*

The thought seemed to spring from nowhere, but Fanny knew where it stemmed from. It was born of years of teasing, neglect, belittling her talents and worth, and assuming that because she had nothing they could take everything from her and she would be *grateful* to them for it.

"Because," Fanny said simply, "whoever is responsible for our uncle's death should face judgment. And if no one else will find the truth, it's up to those who care to at least try."

Edmund took this news stoically but eventually nodded. "You realize that if they don't like the outcome, they could take it out on you?"

"Yes," she said. "But they take everything else out on me, so how much worse can it really get?"

That earned her a small quirk of the lips. Before Edmund could think of any reason to try to talk her out of it, she added, "I might have found something, you know."

With a small bit of fumbling and a great deal of embarrassment, she pulled the sheath of papers from her bodice and held them aloft in the candlelight. "These were hidden in the office upstairs."

Edmund's shock was almost amusing: his eyes widened and his mouth dropped open. "Wha-what is it?"

"Don't act so surprised. I've become capable while you're entertaining the Crawfords."

"I shall never doubt your capabilities," Edmund assured her, so seriously she wasn't actually sure if he was teasing or not. But rather than dwell on it, she focused her attention on the small bundle of letters. She undid the string and shuffled through them, pulse racing with anticipation.

They appeared to be letters, but they weren't addressed and had no other markings. Perhaps they were unsent? But why have so many of them? Fanny unfolded the top one with trembling fingers and Edmund held up the candle so they could both read the spiky, masculine writing:

"'Sir,'" Fanny read, then cleared her throat and started again. "'Sir, your daughter is engaged in illicit business dealings that, if known, would be injurious to her reputation and her future. I think we can both agree that the details of her activities should not be made known to your business associates, as it would reflect poorly on the good name of Mansfield Emporium and result in a loss of business. Therefore, I am prepared to offer you a significant bargain: Please enclose twenty pounds . . .'"

She trailed off, too shocked to believe her own eyes.

"Good God," Edmund whispered. "Are they all blackmail notices?"

Fanny opened the next one. "'Sir, I thank you for your prompt attention on the matter of our last correspondence. I was quite disappointed to see that your daughter is still engaging in these less-than-acceptable activities. Perhaps it's time to cut off her dress allowance? I'm afraid that I must request yet another payment, this time in the sum of twenty-five pounds. A trifling sum, I assure you. . . .'"

She stopped reading aloud and paged through the rest of the missives. They weren't dated or addressed, and they all seemed quite solicitous in tone, but there was an undercurrent of mockery that made Fanny shiver. Whoever the blackmailer was, he knew things about the family that outsiders would not.

Sir, I am beginning to fret about the well-being of your family. You seem to have trouble controlling your daughter. I would hate for her influence to extend to other members of the family.

Sir, I admit I find your action—or inaction—rather curious. Why do you not let your eldest daughter marry, when my sources tell me she's been engaged to a wealthy gentleman for many months now? Do you fear what would happen if you were to make her his problem?

Sir, I would hate to think of what the scandal might do to your family. Is your son truly prepared to face the consequences and steer the family through rough storms, or will he flounce off to London and join Mr. Yates in his lowly theater troupe? Whatever will your youngest daughter do if she cannot find a respectable husband?

"This is horrid," Fanny announced as she got to the end. There were nearly twenty of them, and judging by the mocking commentary about Maria's engagement and Tom's activities, Fanny could guess that they'd been delivered over the course of the last two years. "Each time, the blackmailer asks for more funds. And it looks like he paid him."

"Well, that would explain what happened to the trust," Edmund said grimly.

"It would," Fanny agreed. Her uncle hadn't bankrupted the family on a whim or some bad business venture or vice. He'd been trying to protect his children's reputations. "So Sir Thomas knew what Maria was up to. . . ."

"What was Maria up to, exactly?" Edmund asked. "I'm fuzzy on the details."

"Me too," Fanny said. "But whatever it was, I think that's what they argued about right before he died. At first, I assumed they were talking about her engagement. But I think our uncle was trying to get her to stop her business dealings with Mr. Stewart, and Maria said she wouldn't."

"Or couldn't," Edmund suggested. "If the dealings were illegal, and Maria was entangled with them, then perhaps it was impossible for her to stop."

"But he was blackmailed for ages before he ever said anything."

"Perhaps he didn't believe the blackmailer at first. I'm sure no father wants to believe his child is using his own business in such a way."

"And he would have paid anyway," Fanny said, searching for a note in the middle. There was a line she recalled: *I sense now you believe my intelligence about your daughter's activities. Well, what shall you do about them?* "He thought he was preserving Maria's reputation, and then at some point he must have realized his blackmailer wasn't lying. But why wouldn't he have reported it?"

Edmund gave her a look. "Because, once one's honor is sullied, it's difficult to restore. And Maria doesn't even have the high ground of being falsely accused."

"But surely he could have taken these letters to the authorities. He would have wanted to discover who was behind this. I doubt he'd have sat to the side, waiting for his coffers to be entirely drained while some mysterious figure taunts him."

"The same magistrate who was engaged to his daughter?" Edmund asked.

"Oh."

Mr. Rushworth was, it must be said, not the most sensible of men. But he was one of the few landed gentry of good and elevated standing in their county. Sir Thomas always said one must be incredibly noble or incredibly foolish to want to take on the unpaid position of magistrate in the area, and well . . . Mr. Rushworth was certainly one of those things.

"But wouldn't Mr. Rushworth want to help clear Maria's name? The man is curiously devoted to her."

"Unless . . ." Edmund didn't finish his sentence.

"Unless?"

"Unless . . . Sir Thomas feared that Mr. Rushworth was the blackmailer."

"What?" Fanny could scarcely believe the man capable of something so cunning. "Why?"

"It would explain how this person knows so much about the family, and about our uncle's business affairs. And these letters . . . there's no address or postage. Someone must have hand-delivered them." Edmund was starting to sound excited.

"But he demands payment to a box in London."

"Anyone can open one of those boxes at the mail-sorting stations," he said. "And they're so busy, it would be nearly impossible to keep watch for who retrieved funds from that specific box. Besides, you could always pay a man to do it for you."

Mr. Rushworth. Fanny could scarcely imagine it. Quite honestly, he didn't seem intelligent enough for it.

"And think on it, Fanny," Edmund continued. "He's been doing an awful lot of improvements on his estate. *Costly* improvements."

217

"Do you think Maria knows?"

Edmund paused a moment before saying, "She might be in on it."

That was a chilling thought. But . . . . "Why kill her father, if he was giving them what she wanted?"

"Maybe she knew the money was running out. Maybe *because* he discovered that she was in on it. I don't know. But Fanny, this is your proof."

Fanny gathered the letters up once more and thought of what Miss Bennet said. They needed proof, but a confession was better. "It's proof of blackmail, but not proof of who is responsible, or who killed our uncle. We must keep digging."

Edmund looked upon her with surprise. "But . . . surely presented with these letters . . ."

The idea of approaching Maria and accusing her fiancé without solid evidence made Fanny shake her head. "They could easily deny it. I won't gamble away our evidence unless we're certain."

Edmund looked intently at the packet of letters. "What should we do with the notes?"

It was a fair question. They couldn't put them back, and besides, Fanny was loath to let them out of her sight. Perhaps there was some clue to them, to the box in London, that could connect them definitively to Mr. Rushworth. How to investigate that, though? She could hardly pop down to London and stake out the box. . . .

"I know! I'll give them to Miss Bennet!"

Fanny could tell by the look on Edmund's face that he wasn't keen on the idea. "Are you sure that's wise?"

"I trust her. She's not steered me wrong yet."

Edmund sighed. "I could stash them away someplace safe?"

But the more Fanny thought about it, the more resolute she became. "No. We need Miss Bennet and her connections in London to trace where the money was deposited. And besides, I think I'd feel better if they weren't left on the estate."

Edmund didn't have to ask what she meant by that. They were all too aware of the fact that whoever had written them knew far too much about the family than was comfortable. Being that Edmund didn't appear to have any better ideas, he nodded. "Fine. We better get back—Mary and I are supposed to perform at midnight, and it has to be quarter to already." Edmund blew out his candle, and they made their way back to the ball in the dark. The walk was mostly silent, and Fanny felt the weight of all they'd discovered settle on her shoulders. She needed a nap. Investigating crime was such *work*.

On the darkened terrace, Edmund laid his hand on Fanny's arm. "Before we go in, I have something to say."

She looked up at him. His face was pained. "What's the matter?"

"I don't want you to think that I don't take you seriously, or that I've been dismissing your concerns. Tonight scared me. The moment when I realized that you were all alone in the

219

storehouse, and anything could have happened to you . . ."

"But nothing did," Fanny rushed to reassure him.

"But something *could*." He clasped her hands in his and stared into her eyes. She'd never seen such misery there. "I could never live with myself if someone harmed you."

"Oh, Edmund," Fanny whispered. She couldn't reassure him that nothing would happen to her—tonight's fears still lingered, but to have him looking at her as if she were the most precious thing in the world had been all she'd ever wanted.

Edmund seemed to lean in closer, and Fanny thought for a fleeting moment that this was it. The moment she'd dreamed of for years. But strangely, she didn't feel like herself, and Edmund didn't feel like . . . Edmund. Instead, all she could think of was how they must look from the outside: a young gentleman leaning in to kiss a young lady in the dark of night. How would she paint it?

"Edmund! There you are. Everyone is looking for you. . . . Oh! I'm sorry, am I interrupting?"

To Fanny's horror, Mary Crawford stood on the edge of the terrace. Fanny took an instinctive step back, hoping to preserve a shred of propriety, but when she saw the abashed look on Mary's face, she knew she wasn't fooling anyone.

"You're not interrupting at all," Edmund said, smiling and releasing Fanny's hands gently. "I'm sorry, I didn't mean to keep anyone waiting."

"It's all right," Mary murmured, carefully avoiding looking

too closely at Fanny. "We still have time."

"Of course, if you'll excuse me." Edmund gave Fanny a small, regretful smile that seemed to say, *Foiled yet again.* He walked inside without a backward glance.

Mary didn't follow him. Instead, she was peering at Fanny with open curiosity—not the contempt or condemnation that she might have expected. "Don't worry," she said. "I won't tell anyone."

Relief made Fanny sigh. "It wasn't what you think."

"It doesn't matter what I think." Mary was smiling, but there was something brittle about her expression. "It's none of my business."

She had to be upset, Fanny thought. For a week, Edmund had practically been courting her in front of everyone, only for her to find him about to kiss another young lady. Fanny knew all too well the sense of betrayal and disappointment that Mary must be feeling. It made her feel awful in turn, and she thought, wildly, *I'd take it back if I could.*

But why did she care so much about what Mary Crawford thought?

Mary had turned to go, and Fanny called out, "Wait!"

"I have to get back inside," Mary explained. "Our duet."

But she lingered, as if Fanny might say more. Fanny wanted to say more. She wanted to say, *I've loved Edmund half my life.* And, *Nothing happened.* And, *Why are you friendly with me?* And, *Why did you give me a necklace?*

Instead, she said, "Do you spot that young lady in green, near the refreshment table? Could you possibly tell her I am here, and I wish to speak with her?"

It was an unfair thing to ask, but Fanny wasn't ready to go back inside. "Of course," Mary said. She lingered a moment longer and added, "I hope that you and I can be friends, no matter what."

And then she rushed inside, leaving Fanny feeling rather guilty and quite confused.

Fortunately, Fanny didn't have to wait long for Miss Bennet to slip outside, searching the darkness for her. "Over here," she whispered, and the young lady quickly approached.

"Did you find anything? You were gone so long I was beginning to worry. I'm afraid we could only keep your aunt preoccupied for so long, but she's definitely noticed your absence."

"No matter," Fanny said, withdrawing the blackmail letters from her bodice. "I found something. These are letters blackmailing my uncle. They're related to Maria's business dealings. Can you read them, and see what more you can find out?"

Miss Bennet took the letters and pocketed them swiftly. "Of course. Blackmail! Sir Thomas never said . . . Is there any indication of who might be responsible?"

Briefly, Fanny thought about sharing Edmund's theory with her. But she swiftly decided against it. It wasn't that she had any great love for Mr. Rushworth. It was that Fanny wasn't yet convinced, she was unwilling to color Miss Bennet's opinion—although it had to be said that Miss Bennet's professional conduct seemed to be above such things.

"None. The money was deposited in a box in London. Perhaps you, or Mr. Darcy, could . . ."

"Consider it done," Miss Bennet assured her. Then her brow furrowed. "Edmund knows of the letters?"

"He followed me," she explained. "And I showed him what I found. Don't worry, we can trust him."

"All right," she said. "Tell no one else, though. We don't want to give the blackmailer reason to empty or close the box before Mr. Darcy and I get back to London. Will you wait for my letter?"

Fanny nodded. "I don't know what else I can do here. Except, observe."

"Observations are good, just be careful that you don't put yourself in any more danger."

Fanny promised, and Miss Bennet went back inside. She was grateful to them, strangers that they may be. When Miss Bennet came up behind Mr. Darcy, all she had to do was take him by the elbow, and he turned and bestowed a smile upon her. It surprised her, for Fanny couldn't recall ever noticing the gentleman smile before. But he did when he saw Miss Bennet.

She was wistful for things that she couldn't even fully articulate, but there was only so long she could lurk on the terrace before Aunt Norris discovered her. Besides, it was an *auction* after all. The pieces would all be shipped off early the next day.

This might be her last chance to glimpse her favorite works, and suddenly Fanny couldn't stand going to bed without seeing the Millbrook painting one last time.

When she slipped back inside, the harmonious melody of Edmund and Mary's duet had already begun, riveting most of the audience. They were positioned at the opposite end of the ballroom, so it was easy enough for Fanny to edge her way through the crowd until she found herself before the Millbrook once more.

Under the candlelight, the painting seemed to glow, and she felt as though she could sense new depths to the line work and colors. Her glance lingered over the second sister, the only figure she'd not finished before everything had unraveled. Her brown eyes didn't offer any more clarity in this setting, though, and even if Fanny could return to her own replica, hidden away in the storehouse, she wasn't sure she could begin to re-create the strange longing in her eyes. But now, in this wide and crowded space, Fanny felt as though she could also sense a fierceness in her gaze that she hadn't picked up on before.

She was so enamored of the painting, and overcome by the thought that this would be her last chance to view it, that she was unaware of those around her until she felt someone stumble into her.

"I beg your pardon," she gasped as a gentleman's hand came to her elbow to steady her.

But her mouth dried when the gentleman's grip tightened

painfully. She lifted her gaze and found Mr. Rushworth staring down at her, an intense expression transforming his otherwise jovial face into something that immediately clanged a warning in her chest.

"I must speak with you." And without giving her a chance to respond, he yanked her toward the door.

FOURTEEN

In Which Fanny Resolves to Take
Matters into Her Own Hands

PANIC CLOSED AROUND FANNY'S throat like a vise as Mr. Rushworth steered her out of the ballroom and down the hall, away from any observers . . . or help.

There was one part of her that screamed, *Run!* Another part, the one that was apparently in control of her faculties, simply went immobile with fear. *What does he know?* Had he followed Fanny to the storehouse and observed what she discovered, or overheard the conversation with Edmund? Was Edmund right, and he was the mastermind all along?

And what did he have planned for her?

He made to retreat up the main staircase of the hall, and Fanny let out an involuntary whimper of protest, remembering

226

how her uncle had looked at the bottom of the steps after his fall.

Mr. Rushworth released her immediately and came to a halt. The absence of his hand on her arm startled her so much, Fanny didn't think to run. She just looked up at him, bewildered.

And that's when she got a true look at his expression. It was desperate and distraught, but *not* enraged or murderous. He was breathing heavily and visibly shaken, but when he scrunched up his face, Fanny realized it wasn't because he was about to hurt her.

Mr. Rushworth was . . . trying not to cry?

"Mr. Rushworth?" she asked, voice wobbling just slightly. Her own heart had yet to recover from the shock of fear. "Are you all right?"

"I'm sorry for alarming you. I don't mean to be untoward."

"What's the matter?" she asked.

"It's . . . you must be frank with me, Miss Price." He looked almost frantic but dropped his voice to a loud whisper. "What are Mr. Crawford's intentions?"

"Mr. Crawford?" Fanny echoed. There was a part of her that was still suspicious, but she felt her guard come down. Was that what this was about? But why come to her about Mr. Crawford?

"Yes, Crawford! The charming bloke that Maria can't seem to tear her gaze from!"

His anger made Fanny take a tiny step back. "Well. He is incredibly charismatic."

Mr. Rushworth's face fell.

"But a gentleman," Fanny hastened to add. "And he knows that Maria is engaged to you, and as a gentleman he would never take liberties."

Fanny wasn't actually certain this was the case, but she hoped it was. At best, Mr. Crawford was a flirt and a cad. At worst . . . well, Fanny didn't want to think about what his worst would mean for Maria.

For Mary.

Mr. Rushworth must have had similar doubts, for he was not so easily convinced. "I know that I am not the . . . gentleman he is. He's well traveled and he knows a great deal about art. But there are things I can offer Maria that he can't. An estate, a position."

It was as though he were trying to convince Fanny, when she was not the one who needed to be told. "Maria is . . . passionate about her father's legacy," Fanny said, choosing her words carefully. "If she seems preoccupied with Mr. Crawford, I'm sure it's only because she wants to see the auction be a success."

"I suppose," he relented, looking beyond her toward the ballroom. "I know there are things I cannot give her, but I do try. She can still deal in art after we're married. I've gone to great lengths to ensure . . ."

He trailed off, and Fanny held herself very still in the hope that he would share more. He'd gone to great lengths to ensure what, exactly? That she would inherit her father's business? That she had dealings with his Scottish contact?

When it became clear that Mr. Rushworth wouldn't expand upon what he'd ensured, Fanny went fishing for more information. "It's not every fiancé who would take so much care in securing his future wife's interests."

If Mr. Rushworth thought that Fanny was poking too close to any secrets, he didn't show it. Instead, he simply sighed and his shoulders slumped into a defeated posture. "I would do anything she asked of me," he admitted.

Well, then.

But before Fanny could register what was happening, Mr. Rushworth gave her a half-hearted little bow and went back to the party.

Fanny watched him leave, the lurid green of his jacket so absurd in a sea of men's black jackets.

Was that truly the face of a man who had manipulated his future father-in-law into draining his fortune, only to engineer his death?

Fanny wasn't convinced.

Fanny awoke early the next morning, despite her unusually late night, to the sound of a team of laborers packing up all the artwork that had sold the previous night. By the time she dressed and came downstairs, half of it was already carted off, including the Millbrook, which had sold to the wealthy Lord Allerton, whom Mary had pointed out the evening before.

There was little for Fanny to do but wait until Miss Bennet wrote to her with the results of her investigation into the postbox in London and watch everyone carefully. The days stretched by painfully, until three days after the auction when Tom was able to send the bailiffs from Mansfield Park, their debts settled. To celebrate, Maria suggested a small garden party to toast their success. The only guest outside of the current residents of Mansfield Park in attendance was Mr. Rushworth, for their financial troubles were not yet so far behind them that they ought to go all-out, but everyone seemed determined to make it a festive affair.

"Perhaps they've an announcement to make," Edmund murmured to her as she donned a bonnet and prepared to head out into the garden. He was shifting nervously in the hall. "You know that Tom and Maria must have made a small fortune. They've enough to pay back my trust, I should think."

"I hope so." The longer Tom took to pay back Edmund's inheritance, the more frayed the family bonds would become. "And if he makes you wait for it? Will you still go to London?"

"Probably," Edmund admitted. "My mate Percy wouldn't mind sharing the rent with someone. But I don't want to go until I can get a promise from the Crawfords that they'll introduce me to London society."

"Fanny!" Aunt Norris called from outside. "Stop dawdling,

and come along! Someone needs to hold Pug's leash."

Fanny sighed as she tied the ribbon of her bonnet under her chin. "How is it that I am the one dawdling when you are the one who pulled me aside to chat?" she asked.

Edmund looked surprised at her outburst, and Fanny marched outside before he could respond.

Although the concept of a garden party with the same people they'd all see at dinner that evening felt a little superfluous, Fanny had to admit the day was particularly lovely and the gardens were vibrant and bursting with spring blooms. Cakes and tea and lemonade were served, and even Lady Bertram cracked a smile at the sight of Pug racing across the lawn in a circle, grunting with joy. Fanny withdrew her sketchbook and made quick drawings of the gardens, of the dog, and, almost without thinking, of Mary, looking lovely in her mint-green dress and straw bonnet.

But beside her, Edmund simmered with dark energy and there was a strained quality that didn't quite hide under the genteel surface. When he caught sight of Fanny's sketches, he raised a single eyebrow, and Fanny had to resist the urge to clutch the drawing to her chest.

"I really ought to go to London and see about acquiring new pieces," Tom announced suddenly. "Yates and I can go make our visits to the artists and talk to some overseas traders."

"That sounds an awful lot like something I should be involved in," Maria said.

Tom seemed to have anticipated this, for he replied, "I'm not planning on opening up the house in London. Yates and I will stay at the club. It'll be far more economical that way."

Before Maria could offer a rebuttal, Mr. Rushworth cut in. "Should you really be going all the way to London anyway? I was hoping that we could refocus our attentions on the *future*."

His heavy-handed emphasis on the word left no doubt as to what was on his mind.

"Oh, it would be wonderful to have a wedding to look forward to," Lady Bertram remarked. Since her husband's death, she always sounded dreamy and far away. "Planning it will be a lovely distraction."

"But is it proper that I should get married this year?" Maria asked. "While we're still in mourning?"

"Are you still in mourning?" Mr. Rushworth asked, which was about as close to argumentative as Fanny had ever seen the man. Maria was wearing not a single stitch of black, but instead a white-and-blue lawn frock.

"I don't think your father would want you to wait on his account," Lady Bertram replied, as if he'd simply gone on a trip overseas.

"Then why did he put off giving his blessing until it was too late?"

Fanny's gaze met Edmund's, and she had to school her features into careful nonchalance. Was Maria playing the innocent, or was she merely trying to wiggle out of an engagement? It was difficult to tell, but for the first time Fanny wondered—if Mr. Rushworth was responsible for Sir Thomas's death, and Maria hadn't asked him to do it, what might he do if Maria broke off the engagement?

The thought sent a shiver down her spine, despite the heat of the afternoon.

"Speaking of the future," Mr. Crawford said, trying to sound natural and failing miserably. "I've actually had a letter this morning of an exciting new opportunity."

That got everyone's attention.

"A business partner of mine has written, and he's managed to book the Pantheon for a private event. We've long hoped to host an auction party, like the one we did here, but at a much larger venue. We intend to throw a masquerade ball there in two weeks. We'll be showcasing the best art that our artists and dealers have to offer."

The party congratulated Mr. Crawford, but Fanny's gaze went immediately to Mary, who wore a brittle smile.

"So you'll be leaving us, then?" Maria asked.

"I'm afraid so. We'll depart the day after tomorrow. Lady Bertram, you've been such a gracious hostess."

"Say, you wouldn't be looking for pieces for the show?" Tom asked.

Mr. Crawford looked surprised, and Fanny had to admire

233

his acting skills. "My good man, I wouldn't dream of asking you to contribute, not when you've just turned out your entire collection for the ball."

"Well, we might have a few pieces that we've kept back," Tom replied, his gaze sliding to Maria. "Right, Maria?"

"But I thought—" Julia began, only to be cut off by Maria.

"I think we have sold everything of substance, Tom."

"Are you absolutely certain, Maria? Perhaps we ought to do a sweep of the storehouse and make certain that there's nothing we missed."

Their words were laden with unspoken meaning, and Crawford was practically drooling, watching them speak. But then Mr. Rushworth said, "Yes, Maria—you should give Mr. Crawford the pieces you've been holding back."

"I haven't been holding back anything," Maria said forcefully, turning a sharp look on her fiancé. "You must be mistaken."

"I thought I saw—"

"They were some of Fanny's silly paintings, that's all," Maria snapped. "I held them back because they weren't of the quality we wanted to showcase."

Maria could have slapped her and the party wouldn't have been more shocked. Fanny, however, was not. Mr. Rushworth knew about the paintings that Maria sold to his Scottish contact. And Fanny would wager that Mr. Rushworth knew there were more than the five paintings Tom had agreed to spare sitting in Aunt Norris's cottage, but Maria didn't want anyone *else* to know that.

Fanny knew better than to expect an apology, so it was up to her to break the awkward silence. "Thank you, Maria. I daresay you've done me a favor. I wouldn't want to be embarrassed in front of all your fine guests, Mr. Crawford."

"That's not fair!"

To Fanny's surprise, it wasn't Edmund protesting her self-deprecating words—it was Mary.

"I've seen Fanny's work, and she's quite good. She's a natural talent, and she has an eye for color and light that I think rivals many of the artists working today."

Everyone looked to her with surprise, Fanny included.

And then, almost as if he didn't want to be outdone, Edmund rushed to add his compliments. "It's true, I've always said Fanny was talented, and so did Sir Thomas. Why, Fanny—tell them about what you were working on, replicating that painting."

Her work on the Millbrook wasn't exactly a secret, but it wasn't at all anything she wanted to discuss. Fanny shook her head, but Edmund didn't pay her any heed.

"It was the Millbrook. Sir Thomas saw it right before he died. He said that if Fanny kept up the good work, she could really be a true artist one day. He promised her lessons."

A slight stretch of the truth, but Edmund glowed with

pride to tell their relatives this bit.

"The Millbrook?" Mr. Crawford asked, and now he seemed very interested. "Where is this replication?"

"I can't imagine Father would have *actually* gotten Fanny lessons," Maria said.

Tom nodded. "And with what money?"

"I didn't know, at the time, about the finances," Fanny said, but it felt like a weak defense. "I didn't ask for them. I thought . . ."

She had thought that her uncle had finally seen her value. But had he, really, if he knew at the time he couldn't have afforded the lessons? Had he made her empty promises for the sake of making her feel better about her abilities?

"Well, this is an exciting turn of events," said Mr. Crawford. "We must have our own private showing."

"Oh no," Fanny protested almost desperately. "I never finished it."

"Well, finish it up and show us tomorrow," Aunt Norris said, as if it were that simple.

"I couldn't possibly—"

"Certainly you could," Edmund said, with what she supposed was meant to be an encouraging smile. "You don't have that many more details to see to."

"Is that true?" Aunt Norris demanded.

"Well," Fanny hedged, "it depends on what you consider details. . . ."

"Do not worry yourself," Mr. Crawford rushed to say. "I am sure that imitating someone as technically complex as Millbrook is no small feat, but no one here expects you to match the man perfectly. Just add your final dabs of paint and let us be the judges."

But that was precisely the problem: Fanny had no desire to let them judge anything. When she looked to Mary, she found a silent apology written across her face. Fanny shook her head. Mary couldn't have known what she would unleash, and Fanny knew it was no use refusing. They'd only badger her to death over it.

"All right," she muttered.

This was met with a round of tepid enthusiasm and some interest before Tom brought matters back around to business and Mr. Crawford's upcoming London event, but Fanny found herself quietly seething. How long must she endure their jokes and abuse, their demands couched as favors? Until her uncle's murderer was caught? Until she could establish herself as an artist?

For the rest of her life?

Fanny wasn't sure, but her skin suddenly felt like a too-tight dress that she ached to shed. And a fleeting thought crossed her mind: *I cannot live like this forever.*

But what were her options? Stay, or go home to Portsmouth, where there would be no paintings and no time for artistic expression? Gamble her reputation by following Edmund to

London? Or was there some other path, something she wasn't seeing?

Fanny was still dwelling on the corner she found herself backed into when the party retired inside, and as was her habit these last few days, she made a point of walking by the hall table to inspect the correspondence that had arrived. This time, she was rewarded by the presence of a letter with her name on it, and she snatched it up, not waiting for a private spot to tear it open.

> *Longbourn & Sons*
> *London*
> *Dear Miss Price,*
> *Since our return to London, Darcy and I have visited the location of the blackmailer's box. A source tells us the box was reserved two years ago and is paid up through the end of the year. No one has collected anything from it, although deposits have been made—likely by your uncle. We've got eyes on it, and will follow whoever collects. If not now, then before the lease is up at the end of the year. Have patience, stay safe.*
> *Sincerely,*
> *Miss Elizabeth Bennet*

Fanny must have made some small sound of distress, for Mary was at her side in an instant. "Is it bad news?"

"No," Fanny said, quickly folding the letter. "Just a note from my brother William."

"Is your family well?" Edmund asked.

"Yes," Fanny said, trying to smile.

Aunt Norris gave her a suspicious look, but as a rule she did not make a habit of inquiring about her youngest sister or her family. "Then why do you look so distressed?"

She said the first thing she could think of. "It just occurred to me how much I miss William. I haven't seen him in so long."

"Hmph," Aunt Norris said, and continued down the hall. "I don't see as that's any reason to carry on. You have frequent letters, that should be enough."

Mary's polite demeanor could not hide her shock at Aunt Norris's callous words. "I should think that letters are no substitute for being able to talk to and embrace one's own sibling."

"If you say so," Aunt Norris threw over her shoulder.

"Don't mind her," Edmund said in a low tone. "She's beastly to the two sisters she has."

"Really? She seems rather attentive to Lady Bertram."

"Like I said." Edmund shrugged. "Beastly."

"Are you truly all right?" Mary asked Fanny.

She offered Mary a tight smile and tried not to feel too guilty about her deception. "I will be. Thank you."

While Mary continued up to her room to change, Fanny pulled Edmund aside and showed him Miss Bennet's letter.

The lines in his forehead deepened as he read. "The end of the year? But that's still months away. Surely she doesn't expect us to wait when we know who is responsible."

"We *think* we know who is responsible," Fanny corrected, although she wasn't fully convinced of Mr. Rushworth's guilt. "And I don't like it any more than you."

"We should have it all out," Edmund said. "You know how he is—he'll likely become so overwrought that he'll confess the whole scheme."

"You're assuming he isn't cunning," Fanny countered. "I think someone would have to be rather clever to figure out a way to make our uncle's death look an accident and leave behind very little evidence. How did he set it up? How did he get rid of the trip wire? I don't think we should underestimate him, if he's indeed responsible. The clueless persona may very well be a very clever act."

Edmund sighed. "Fanny . . . we can't wait on Miss Bennet indefinitely."

"I know." Fanny looked past him, up the curving staircase to the second floor.

A plan was already forming.

FIFTEEN

*In Which Funny Inadvertently
Makes Matters Much Worse*

FANNY DIDN'T COME TO the decision to break into Maria's room lightly. She enjoyed living, after all.

But Fanny knew in her bones that she couldn't wait months and months for a lead on the case. And no matter how dogged Miss Bennet's source might be, what happened if whoever came to collect skirted past their notice? Fanny would be right back where she started, suspicious of everyone and without evidence.

But if she could just find proof that Maria and Mr. Rushworth were engaged in illegal business dealings together—some letter or missive about Mr. Stewart, perhaps a longing letter in which Mr. Rushworth pledged to do whatever it took to win her over . . . then Miss Bennet could build her case from there.

Besides, if Maria married Mr. Rushworth and left Mansfield Park for Sotherton, it would become even more impossible to get the evidence she needed.

These were all the things that Fanny told herself as she lurked about the second-story hallway, biding her time until Tom and Mr. Yates enticed Maria and the Crawfords out to the nearly empty storehouse to salvage any appropriate pieces to send down to London. Tom was absolutely gutted at the possibility of not participating in the masquerade at the Pantheon, so Fanny expected them to linger for at least a half hour, if not more. It would be plenty of time.

The hall containing the family's bedchambers was silent, but she tiptoed anyway, not wishing to disturb a napping Lady Bertram. The door to Maria's room opened silently, and she quickly slipped inside. It was an ornate space: the carpets and the wallpaper were a rich plum color, and the room was impeccably tidy. A lady's writing desk sat in the corner, but Fanny knew it was unlikely that Maria would keep important documents regarding shady activities there. Her gaze slid to the wardrobe, and a memory jostled loose.

She'd been twelve, and Julia had told Fanny she knew where Maria kept her sweets hidden—in a false bottom in her wardrobe. She'd tried to convince Fanny to sneak into Maria's room with her so they could help themselves . . . but Fanny knew better than to be fooled by any of her cousins. Julia didn't want a coconspirator—she wanted someone to take the fall if they got caught. In the end, Julia had stolen them herself, and when Maria went to Aunt Norris to report the theft, Julia blamed Fanny. She'd been hurt by the betrayal, but now she was glad of it. She carefully slid open the drawers of the wardrobe and pushed aside silk chemises and beribboned undergarments, running her hands along the bottom, fingers searching for any catch or latch. In the end, she wasn't sure what she did exactly, but something caught with a tiny *snick*, and the bottom lifted up to reveal a trove of papers.

Fanny picked up the entire sheath. She was tempted to steal them, but if Maria noticed the theft, she would be alerted that someone was on to her, and who knew what she would do. Instead, Fanny lifted them up to the light and began to read.

Invoices. They were all invoices for the art she'd seen at Aunt Norris's cottage . . . but not exactly. There were bills of sale and then resale back to Maria. It seemed as though Maria were selling the art to Mr. Stewart . . . and then several months later buying it right back.

But *why*?

Frustration welled up in her, threatening to overflow in some kind of dramatic display of emotion. She was too old to stamp her feet or slam things, and screaming seemed rather overdramatic. Tears were messy. But she was just so tired of not being able to see the entire picture. It was like a great unfinished portrait, and her fingers itched to fill in the blank spaces, to draw connections between one disparate element and another. What was she missing?

Fanny was left with a dilemma: keep snooping or replace the paperwork and sneak back out? There was nothing in the invoices that incriminated Maria or implicated Mr. Rushworth—everything looked very aboveboard, actually, even if it made little sense. And even if the more skeptical of magistrates would want to know what on earth Maria was playing at, Fanny could already imagine Maria batting her eyelashes and saying, *Why, is it against any law to sell a painting and then buy it back?*

Fanny was pretty sure it wasn't, but that didn't make her activities any less suspicious.

Unlike the last time she'd gone snooping, Fanny received no warning that someone was just outside. The door to Maria's room merely opened, and Fanny heard her say, "I'll explain how it all works, but not where we might be over—"

Fanny went very still, because there was nothing else to do. She was in plain sight of the doorway—no chance of dropping behind the bed or stepping in the shadows of a bureau. But Maria and her guest were so single-mindedly focused on each other that they closed the door and took a few steps into the room, arms tangled around each other, stealing kisses, before Henry Crawford looked up and spotted Fanny, standing miserably in the corner.

"Good God, woman!" he shouted.

"What now?" Maria asked, then followed Henry's gaze to Fanny. Her face went completely white. Fanny thought it might have been rather satisfying to see Maria in such a state, but then just as quickly Maria's expression lit with fury.

"What do you think you're doing?"

Fanny swallowed. She tried to muster up words, but nothing came to her.

Maria's eyes dropped to the papers clutched in Fanny's hands. "Give me those! Were you stealing? You ungrateful little weasel!"

She crossed the room quickly and snatched the papers from Fanny, ripping them in the process. She raised her hand and Fanny knew the slap was coming and yet she still didn't move.

But Mr. Crawford caught her hand before it had a chance to strike. "Maria, shhh! If you cause a scene, someone might come running."

Maria went still as the logic of that settled. If anyone were to discover them, even a maid, they'd see Henry Crawford there and . . . well, it didn't matter if Fanny was there, too. Mr. Crawford had no business in Maria's private bedchamber.

"I demand an explanation!" Maria hissed, her voice quieter but no less deadly.

"I . . ." Fanny flicked her gaze to Mr. Crawford, but he would be of no help, of course. And Fanny couldn't even think of a halfway decent lie. No, she was caught. She could accept Maria's rage or try to brazen her way through.

But Fanny was not the brazen-her-way-through-*anything* type of girl. She was usually the type to take the abuse and roll

245

her eyes about it later. Except . . . those papers now in Maria's hands were proof of something.

"Well? What do you have to say for yourself?"

"You're running some sort of scheme," Fanny said simply, her calm tone belying the racing of her heart. "You're selling artwork to a man in Scotland out of Aunt Norris's cottage, and he sells it back to you for exactly what he paid. Why?"

"You're a stupid girl and you don't know what you are talking about!"

"I may be quiet, but I'm not blind." Fanny said the words quietly but firmly. No one spent nearly ten years in this house without learning a thing or two, and Fanny knew that made her reasonably intelligent. "I've seen the paintings in Aunt Norris's cottage, and I know that you and Sir Thomas argued about them the day he died."

Maria's face was twisted in fury. "That's business, and you know nothing about it."

"If it's regular business, then why did you remove all of these invoices from the storehouse? Is it to hide your dealings from Tom?"

Mr. Crawford placed a hand on Maria's shoulder. "Maria, maybe we should—"

But Maria slapped his hand away, not taking her eyes from Fanny for a second. "If you're ready to fling about wild accusations, then you better be able to back them up."

"I haven't accused you of anything that can't be proven,"

Fanny said, but felt a warble in her voice at the vicious look on Maria's face.

"Oh really?" Maria suddenly lunged for the fireplace and tossed the invoices at the center. Fanny let out a cry and leapt to stop her, but Mr. Crawford blocked her, quicker than she could have imagined, as Maria struck a flint and touched it to the pile of paperwork. Flames curled around the edges of the invoices greedily.

Fanny stood still, numb with shock.

"You have wild ideas and mad speculations," Maria said, turning to face her once more. There was cruel satisfaction in her tone as she continued, "No proof, no evidence. And no sense, apparently. Now get *out*."

Fanny didn't need to be told twice. She turned on her heel and ran. She didn't stop until she'd reached the third floor and entered her room. She slumped against the door as her heart hammered in her chest.

What had she been thinking?

Why had Maria and Crawford returned to the house so quickly?

How could she have found evidence, only to see it destroyed so quickly right in front of her?

And worst of all, what would Maria's retribution be like?

Fanny didn't have to wait very long to find out.

That evening, Fanny followed Edmund and Mary down to

the drawing room early. It would be another quarter hour before the rest of the family came down before dinner, but they had fetched her from her room, acting rather . . . cagey.

"We want you to inspect the painting presentation before the rest of the family comes down," Edmund said by way of explanation.

"But I already know what the painting looks like," Fanny told them, registering the complaint in her tone and not caring. "I'm sure wherever you set it up is just fine."

"You're the artist," Mary said. "You have to approve of it before anyone else comes in."

"If you insist," Fanny said, because it seemed easier to allow herself to be led than belabor the point. It hardly mattered, anyway. Given how angry Maria had been only a few hours earlier, Fanny could hardly imagine how any of it mattered anymore.

They opened the door to the drawing room and ushered her in with no less fanfare than if she'd been a princess. Fanny was too preoccupied wondering what all this fuss was about to notice the contents of the room at first. It wasn't until Edmund said, "Well, what do you think?" that she took a proper look around the drawing room.

The replica of the Millbrook stood, nearly finished, at the center. It was positioned in the best light, with a wide enough space before it that viewers could gather and observe it. But that wasn't all—a dozen of Fanny's other paintings sat around the room, displayed cleverly on tables and easels. Her other work mainly consisted of landscapes and scenes of Mansfield's natural beauty. The rose garden, the fishpond in autumn, a wintry view of the lane. There was even a small painting of Pug that Fanny had given Aunt Bertram at her last birthday.

Fanny just stood there, overcome. "Where . . . how?"

"It was Edmund's idea," Mary said, taking Fanny's arm in her own. "He wanted it to be like your own little gallery show, and I remembered all of your wonderful pieces in your room . . ."

"And so we decided to showcase some of the best work!" Edmund finished.

They had gone into her room and taken her paintings. And in her distress following her entanglement with Maria, she hadn't even noticed that they'd been missing.

Fanny wasn't sure if she should be grateful that they'd thought to do this for her or upset at the violation of privacy. She was left grasping for words, but none came.

"Oh dear," Mary murmured. "Do you hate it? Is it too much?"

Before Fanny could reassure her otherwise, Edmund jumped in. "Don't be silly! Fanny, you are talented! You deserve all of the recognition. Think of this as practice—one day, when you're attending gallery showings of your own work in London, you won't be able to hide in the corner!"

That very well might be the case, but Fanny hardly thought that was valid enough reason to present her work without her permission! Mary bit her bottom lip while Edmund stared at her with something that looked like . . . impatience? As always, her eagerness to please superseded her true feelings in the moment, and Fanny pasted on a smile. "I was just surprised. This is incredibly thoughtful. I've never seen my work in such a fine setting before."

"It'll appear in finer rooms yet," Edmund promised, ushering her farther into the room.

"Are you sure it's all right?" Mary whispered, but Fanny just nodded. What was done was done.

Nonetheless, she couldn't help but feel vaguely ill as Mr. Rushworth arrived and the rest of the family entered the drawing room. There were exclamations of surprise all around, and Lady Bertram beamed to see her painting of Pug positioned near her seat. "It looks just like her, does it not?" she asked each and every one of them.

But not all were amused—Aunt Norris kept casting her suspicious looks and Maria's face was pinched, as if something somewhere in the room smelled. Julia kept squinting at her work, as if searching for something. Fanny felt as though she herself were on display along with her artwork and at any moment she might be expected to perform a cheap parlor trick.

"I say, isn't this just a surprise," Mr. Rushworth exclaimed as he settled into the settee next to Maria. "I hadn't the faintest clue Miss Price painted so much."

"Yes, well, there is a great deal you do not know about Fanny," Edmund said.

No one reprimanded him for his rudeness, but Fanny winced at it nonetheless.

"I think they're quite good," Mr. Rushworth continued, oblivious. "Clearly this family has been quite the positive influence."

"Well, let us be the judge of that," Maria said, not looking at Fanny. The only thing worse than facing Maria's direct wrath was perhaps realizing that she would do her level best to destroy you without a sideways glance.

"Come now, Maria," Mr. Crawford said. "There's no need to be so harsh. How could anyone not be influenced by your family's appreciation for art?"

A thick stillness settled in the room following Mr. Crawford's words, but he seemed oblivious to his mistake. Fanny held herself very still and watched Mr. Rushworth to see if he'd noticed that Mr. Crawford had addressed Maria by her first name.

Given that his cheeks were growing pinker by the second, he most certainly had.

It hadn't escaped the notice of anyone else in the room, either, but Maria was determined to act as if it hadn't happened.

"Influence is one thing, talent is another. I will allow that these pieces are good, but they aren't the sort we deal in. What say you, *Mr. Crawford*? Is there a market for work like Fanny's in London?"

Ah, now Mr. Crawford realized his misstep. He swallowed visibly but recovered quickly. "I believe with the right guidance and the right audience, yes."

Murmurs of surprise came from the aunts and Julia, and Tom even looked questioningly at Mr. Crawford. "Are you serious? You're not humoring her?"

"I don't need humoring," Fanny rushed to say.

"Hush, Fanny," Maria snapped. "Mr. Crawford is the expert."

"You've implied on multiple occasions that you're not much of an artist, Miss Price, but I feel as though you sell yourself short." He struck a contemplative pose as he beheld her replica. "Aside from the fact that it's incomplete, I can't see much of a difference."

"I assure you, sir, there are many differences." Fanny looked to Mary, but she was also studying her brother with an unreadable expression—something that wasn't quite surprise, but more akin to curiosity.

"Well, to be certain, you are no Millbrook," Mr. Crawford agreed. He pivoted from her replica and pointed out the painting of Pug. "But you do know how to capture a likeness, even if the subject is merely a dog."

And then he went to her painting of the gardens. "And these are pretty—your perspective is good, and you have a knack for capturing your subject at interesting angles. Ladies of the ton want something attractive but not mundane. However, they don't want to venture too far afield of convention. If you can do more like these, then you'll have quite the business."

Tom certainly perked up at the word *business*. "You're saying that these paintings are marketable?"

Mr. Crawford cast a meaningful look around at all of her work, displayed for the entire room to see. If someone had hung out all of her underthings, Fanny would have been just as mortified. "Yes," he pronounced. "I am."

He wielded a smirk at her then, as if he'd just made her a very generous offer.

"I'm sorry," Fanny said. "I don't—"

"Don't be silly," Maria snapped. "Mr. Crawford is offering to represent your work! To *sell* it."

"I think we ought to start you out with leaning into what you're successful at," Mr. Crawford continued, heedless of her shock. "These florals will build your reputation amongst the ladies. Do you think you could replicate them?"

The room was overly warm, and Fanny's head felt perilously light. What had Mary said about fainting—that it was an awfully effective way to get one a seat and a cool drink? She wondered if swooning right now would get her out of this room. "Please," she said. "I think you mistake my wishes."

"Is your wish not to be an artist?" Maria asked. When Fanny met her gaze, she saw more than just the typical impatience or outright dismissal that Maria usually felt toward her. "To be successful? To not be a burden to this family?"

And that was when Fanny understood: this was Maria's punishment. Maria was trying to buy Fanny's silence. Whether she was afraid of Fanny revealing her tryst with Mr. Crawford or her suspicions about her underhanded business, Fanny wasn't certain. But she had decided to use the one thing that Fanny held dear against her: her own passion.

"My, this is a generous offer," Aunt Norris said, a tad too dramatically for Fanny to believe she wasn't in on the scheme. "Are you certain that you are willing to do this for our Fanny? We wouldn't want you to go out of your way."

"I am a businessman," Mr. Crawford assured her, "and I would not make the offer if I didn't think it would benefit everyone involved."

"Say, do you think that her work would be a good fit for the Pantheon?" Tom asked. Fanny cast a shocked look at him, but she could tell he was thinking only of pounds and profits.

"I think so," Mr. Crawford said. "It would be a good debut. Her work would likely be in one of the adjacent galleries, but the point of these events is that we have a range of artwork that is affordable—"

"I didn't say yes!"

Fanny's voice rang out, halting the conversation. Mr. Crawford and her relation turned to look at her, bemusement in their expressions. "Of course," Mr. Crawford said smoothly, almost apologetically. "You'll want to hear terms. I'll retain forty percent of whatever you sell, and I'll have the exclusive right to represent you—that's standard, you understand. In return, I am happy to pay for any supplies you might need against your first sale. And we'll have to find better frames for these—that will come out of your commission, too, I'm afraid. But showcasing is everything."

Fanny summoned all of her strength and grace and managed to grit out, "You're too kind, Mr. Crawford, but I cannot accept."

He kept smiling, which worried her. "Don't be silly. Of course you can—your family already approves. I can make your work quite successful. I can make *you* quite successful."

At the price of her silence. By sacrificing her morals. The idea of giving up on finding the truth about what was going on at Mansfield made her blood rush. She might have started poking about because of her suspicions about her uncle's death, but this investigation had become so much more than simply finding out the truth about that one night. It had pulled back the curtain on so many messy, scandalous, and morally indecent behaviors that Fanny found she couldn't let the curtain close once more, not without shining a light on it all. Not even if it

255

cost her a chance at selling her work, earning her own money, and finding a shred of independence.

"No," she said, letting the bluntness of the word speak for her.

Nervous titters filled the room. Aunt Norris snorted in disbelief. "Don't be daft, girl! This is a generous offer!"

"Fanny, think of the money," Tom said. "Think of our reputation—Mansfield Emporium needs this."

"Just say yes," Maria snapped, her eyes flashing a warning.

Fanny looked to Mary and Edmund, sitting in stunned silence by her painting of the weeping willow at an old grotto on the grounds. Mary looked absolutely anguished, as if she hadn't seen this coming. Maybe she hadn't. Fanny couldn't be sure. Edmund, however, wore a pleading expression.

He wanted her to accept.

Of course he did. Accepting meant that they could be one step closer to their goal of leaving behind Mansfield, of being the masters of their own fates. She had an offer that he wanted but hadn't yet achieved.

Fanny almost wavered then. But then she closed her eyes and breathed deeply.

She wouldn't go against her morals. Not even for Edmund.

"I'm flattered," she said when she opened her eyes once more. It was a lie, but some instincts for politeness could not be fought. "But I am afraid we have very different visions of my work, and my career."

There was a shocked silence, and Fanny couldn't resist adding, "Besides, I don't trust you."

Pandemonium broke out then—the aunts cried out their shock at Fanny's rudeness, her cousins began berating her, and Mr. Rushworth was chuckling to himself, likely pleased to see Mr. Crawford thwarted in some way. Finally, Aunt Norris cried out, "What will make you see sense, girl? Edmund, she listens to you—tell her to accept if she knows what's good for her!"

"It's not a matter of sense," Fanny protested. "But a matter of my own morals. I must follow my own course."

She looked to Edmund, who wore a dismayed expression. She couldn't tell if he was upset to be singled out by Aunt Norris or upset by Fanny's refusal to consider Mr. Crawford's offer. He met her gaze and she tried her best to impart a silent message to him: *Please have my back. I will not be manipulated.*

"I cannot persuade Fanny to do anything she doesn't want to," Edmund said. "And I know for a fact that she will not budge on this matter."

Fanny felt weak-kneed with relief. He understood.

"What is this nonsense about not trusting Mr. Crawford?" Aunt Norris demanded. "I cannot believe the two of you—were you not raised better? I am grateful that Sir Thomas did not live to see the day you ungrateful children spat in the face of his family's generosity!"

"Generosity?" Edmund echoed, his tone incensed. He stood swiftly. "What you call generosity is manipulation! And how dare you use Sir Thomas against us when in fact someone in this very room murdered him!"

The room went utterly still for five long, painful beats. Fanny could do little more than gape at Edmund in horror. Had he lost his mind? This wasn't part of their plan!

"What are you talking about?" Maria asked, her voice quiet and coiled with venom.

Edmund did not back down. "The day of Sir Thomas's death, someone set up a trip wire. Fanny found the evidence. And there are other things to suggest that he might have been in danger. He was being blackmailed—"

"What!" Tom shouted.

"Fanny found proof!" Edmund turned to look at her, entreating her to back him up. But she was immobile with shock.

"And where is this proof?" Maria demanded.

"With the solicitor." Fanny's voice was faint.

"Miss Bennet?" Maria snapped. "That minx."

"If she thinks she'll have business with us after this . . . ," Tom declared.

"Where did you find it?" Maria demanded.

"I found the blackmail letters in his office in the storehouse," said Fanny, meeting Maria's murderous glare.

"Impossible!" Tom was fuming. "We would have found it."

"It was hidden well," she continued. "And it explains why

the estate was in debt. Why Sir Thomas took from Edmund's trust."

"But why?" Lady Bertram asked. "Why would anyone want to blackmail him?"

Fanny turned to look at her cousins, who suddenly looked very nervous. All three had secrets, secrets worth blackmailing their father over. But Fanny wasn't sure if she should voice them, even now.

In the space of Fanny's hesitation, Maria launched her own accusation. "How do we know it wasn't you and Edmund all along? You've always been a pair of jealous leeches!"

No one leapt to their defense. Fanny stared down her cousin and found that, curiously, she wasn't afraid of Maria's wrath anymore. She'd been toeing the edge of the precipice and occasionally peeking over into the abyss, but now she was tumbling, free-falling, and very little mattered anymore.

"I have gained nothing by Sir Thomas's death," she said with a calm she didn't feel within. "And neither has Edmund. If anything, we've lost our security and our hope for the future because Sir Thomas was the only one in this family who cared about our well-being."

"He wasn't obligated to do any more than that," Aunt Norris snapped.

"Perhaps not, but he was kind to us, which is more than any of you can say!" She stared down Aunt Norris and found that her bravery extended to facing her aunt as well. "He gave Edmund the viola that led to his passion, he encouraged my painting—"

"Fat lot of good that did, considering you won't even do anything with your work," Mr. Crawford grumbled.

"Henry, please. I think this is a family matter," Mary tried to placate him. "We should excuse ourselves." But no one paid her any attention.

"Sir Thomas was being blackmailed because Maria is running some kind of scheme out of Aunt Norris's cottage," Edmund announced. Fanny's eyes went wide. "Tom, you might have allowed Maria to sell a few pieces to Mr. Rushworth's contact, but there are at least fifty paintings squirreled away in Aunt Norris's spare room."

Fanny had the sensation of a speeding carriage careening out of control. This was not how she wanted to present Maria's misdeeds. "Edmund," she said, her voice a warning.

But Tom turned to Maria. "Is this true? Where did you get those pieces?"

At any other time, Fanny might have enjoyed seeing Maria squirm, but Edmund continued to divulge everything. "Of course, this began with Maria's engagement to Mr. Rushworth," he continued. "Mr. Rushworth introduced Maria and Mr. Stewart, did you not?"

Mr. Rushworth looked as though he were having trouble

keeping up. He looked between Maria and Edmund and said, "Er . . . yes?"

"Don't say anything more!" Maria snapped, and it was unclear if she was speaking to Edmund or her fiancé.

"You've turned it into quite the flourishing little enterprise, haven't you?" Edmund goaded. "How much money have you been making, and withholding for yourself? Perhaps you've been passing it on to Mr. Rushworth?"

"Don't be ridiculous, of course I haven't!"

"But then Sir Thomas began to receive blackmail threats, demanding that he shut down your operation," he continued, a mocking edge to his tone.

"I was opening up another line of business, which was perfectly legal. Honestly, I don't need to sit here and be subjected to such baseless accusations!"

She stood as if to flee, and Fanny finally saw her opening. "You were selling the paintings, and then buying them back from Mr. Stewart. I saw the invoices. It was going on for months. If it was perfectly legal, why hide the paperwork and then burn it once I discovered it?"

"You have no proof of anything." Maria's objections were becoming more and more frantic sounding.

"No thanks to you," Fanny conceded. "But I know what I saw."

"The thing is, Maria, I don't actually care what you get up

261

to," Edmund said. "But Fanny and I couldn't help but wonder . . . why didn't Sir Thomas report the blackmail attempts? Why keep paying until his business and estate were nearly bankrupt rather than go to the local magistrate?"

"Did he?" Lady Bertram asked, turning to Mr. Rushworth. "Did my husband bring this matter to you?"

"He certainly did not!" Mr. Rushworth exclaimed. "I wish he had, because I would have put a stop to anyone who accused my fiancée of a crime."

"Would you?" Edmund asked.

The question, posed casually, seemed to cast a stillness over the room. "Of course!" Mr. Rushworth protested.

"Because then I began to wonder . . . it would seem that Sir Thomas would be happy to enlist your help. He wouldn't want any blackmail or even a whisper of wrongdoing to mar her reputation. So there must have been a very good reason as to why he never approached you."

"Such as?" Mr. Rushworth asked.

"Such as . . . he suspected you were responsible."

Maria's face went white and gasps were heard around the room. Fanny reached out to take Edmund's arm, but he shook her off as if she were a fly.

"How do you figure?" Tom demanded angrily.

"Mr. Rushworth introduced Maria to this Mr. Stewart, and she was clearly in deep with some kind of suspicious business dealing—no one sells artwork and then buys it back at the same price months later. Whatever the scheme was, it was likely illegal, given that when Sir Thomas told her to stop, she claimed she couldn't simply back out." He turned to Maria and asked, "Was it very lucrative? Did your fiancé balk at the idea of you making your own money? Or were you simply holding onto those paintings and waiting for the right moment to sell them yet again?"

Maria's hard-edged anger had disappeared. She was merely shaking her head, as if she could make Edmund stop by denying it.

But he didn't stop. He was unleashing his own torrent of anger, and unfortunately Fanny knew all too well what it was like to be caught up in that tide of powerful emotion, to let it all out. There was no stopping him now. "Did you refuse to share the earnings, perhaps? Or did you get cold feet and decide you didn't want to marry Rushworth after all? Is that what induced him to start blackmailing your father? He thought that if Sir Thomas knew what you were up to, he'd put a stop to it. Force the marriage to proceed, and that would be that. But he didn't. He didn't believe his own daughter capable of all the things that were said, and maybe after a while he began to suspect who the blackmailer might be. Reporting the blackmail to the authorities was out of the question, not without sacrificing your—and Julia's—reputation. So he paid. And paid, and paid. Until there

263

was nothing left. And when he realized that you *were* involved in something nefarious, he begged you to stop. But you refused."

"I couldn't stop," Maria whispered. "You don't understand."

"Was that when you arranged for his death?" Edmund asked, and it was unclear whom he was addressing. "Make it look like an accident, so no one would investigate too closely?"

"Edmund, enough!" Fanny cried.

Mr. Rushworth laughed, a high and nervous sound. He looked about the room at the still, shocked faces of the Bertrams and Crawfords. "Well, that's absurd, of course. I knew Maria was selling pieces to Stewart, but I certainly didn't blackmail anyone."

"Didn't you?" Edmund asked. "The letters were hand-delivered, and you had opportunity. Means. Motive."

"You've had me place letters on his desk on occasion," Maria said, turning her gaze to her fiancé. Fanny was afraid of the fury she saw in her cousin's face, but at least she wasn't the target. "And I gave you my key to the warehouse."

"Those letters were nothing more than reports about potential clients. And you let me borrow it *once*, to retrieve my hat. That was weeks ago."

"It took you two days to return it," she retorted. "I don't suppose you made a wax cast of it and had your own key made?"

Tom stood up. "That's it! I've heard enough. We'll be taking this matter to a judge."

"Please, Maria. My love. I didn't do this!" Mr. Rushworth

had gone from confused to panicked. "You must believe me, I love you! I would never—"

"I am not your love or your fiancée any longer!" Maria cried. "You rotten, horrible, lying, murderous—"

Aunt Norris clapped her hands briskly. "All right, enough of that."

Maria was openly weeping now. "You used me. I meant nothing to you!"

"That's not true! I thought we agreed, you said this was a good opportunity for us. If anyone ought to be arrested or questioned, it's that blasted Stewart."

"Get him out of my sight!" Maria screamed.

"Come on," Tom said, pulling Mr. Rushworth away. The man barely struggled, he only had eyes for Maria. "Yates, Edmund, help me out. We're going to lock you in the study, and then you'll come with us to London."

"Maria, it's not true! I've never killed anyone in my life. I love you! Maria!"

The four men swept out of the room, leaving Maria sobbing and the rest of them stunned. Mr. Crawford, ever the opportunist, offered Maria an arm and she threw herself on him. He led her to a chair while Julia followed, attempting to pat her sister on the back.

Fanny plopped into the nearest chair, stunned. She couldn't believe Edmund had taken such a risk by divulging everything they knew and accusing Mr. Rushworth in the heat of the moment. Had they truly done it? She thought she'd feel triumphant at the moment of discovery, but instead she just felt shaky, hollow.

"Are you satisfied now, Fanny?" Maria demanded, having collected herself enough to glare over at her. "You've destroyed my happiness, and all for what? I was only moving the art for Rushworth! He threatened to ruin me if I didn't."

Fanny knew that Maria Bertram didn't do anything she didn't want to do. But it seemed crass to argue with her now. "I *am* sorry, but wouldn't you rather know the truth than marry someone who might have killed your father?"

It seemed like a reasonable question to Fanny, but it just enraged Maria. "I never want to see you ever again!" she screamed.

Fanny opened her mouth to protest . . . but what, exactly? Maria was perfectly justified in her anger. Fanny had uncovered her illegal dealings and implicated her rich fiancé in the murder of her father. What could Fanny even say to that?

"Right, then," Aunt Norris said, standing. "I warned you, Fanny. Go upstairs, pack a bag."

"What?" Fanny asked, looking to both aunts. Lady Bertram was hugging Pug, but she didn't intervene. Aunt Norris glowered.

"There's only one way you would have known about what I was doing to help your poor cousin. You trespassed upon my cottage. You've broken our trust. You will return to Portsmouth immediately."

"But I—"

"Do not argue with me, Fanny Price!" Aunt Norris thundered. "We wash our hands of you!"

Only then did Maria smile, and Fanny realized that she'd forgotten something very important about life at Mansfield Park:

Maria Bertram always got what she wanted.

SIXTEEN

In Which Fanny Says Farewell to Mansfield

FANNY PACKED THE SAME well-worn valise that she'd arrived with nine years earlier. It was heavier now, and yet she felt as if half her heart were being left behind. Her paintings, her canvases and easel, and all of the framed artwork downstairs in the drawing room would have to stay. In the end, she had just her watercolors and sketchbooks.

She looked around her bare little room. It wasn't much, but it had been hers . . . sort of. She'd dreamed of what it would be like to one day say goodbye, but not like this. A tear slipped down her cheek and she brushed it aside.

A knock came at the half-open door, quiet and tentative. Mary Crawford was standing on the threshold and she was holding a large canvas.

"What on earth?" Fanny asked.

Mary didn't waste time with silly questions, like asking her if she was all right. Instead, she set the painting down on the easel in Fanny's room, placed her hands on her hips, and said, "Well. That was an unmitigated disaster."

It was her unfinished Millbrook replica.

For some reason, a small giggle erupted from deep inside of Fanny, startling them both. But then Mary joined in, and they were both laughing. "It's not funny," Fanny gasped. "And yet, I can't stop."

"Let it out," Mary encouraged. "It does no good to bottle your feelings in. Laugh, cry, yell if you must. I myself have enjoyed the invigorating scream every now and then."

"Really? But doesn't it alarm others?"

"Yes," Mary agreed. "That's the best part."

Mary guided Fanny to the bed and pushed her to sit down, then she sat in the hard chair across from Fanny.

"My dear," Mary said, and the endearment warmed Fanny's chest, "I'm so sorry. About your uncle, the circumstances . . . everything."

"Thank you," Fanny said, and she felt as though Mary truly meant it. "And I'm sorry for causing such a scene."

"Think nothing of it." But the look on Mary's face was troubled. "So, you're leaving tomorrow. Are you . . . happy about going back home?"

Fanny sighed, for her feelings on the matter felt as muddied as all her paints running together, turning into a brownish-gray mess. "I suppose. I've often longed to see my brother William again. But I didn't want to be exiled from the Bertrams and this life, either. I had hoped that no matter where I went, it was on my own terms."

"Everybody likes to go their own way," Mary agreed. "And to choose their own manner of devotion, and how to spend their time. Are you certain . . . you won't change your mind?"

Fanny thought at first she was asking her to change her mind about leaving, but then she realized by Mary's sideways glance at her replica painting, she meant about her brother representing her work. "No, I won't," she said, her words coming out hard and clipped.

"If I may ask . . . why not?"

The question seemed earnest enough, which was why Fanny didn't want to admit the truth: she didn't trust Henry Crawford. Not his intentions, not his business practice, and certainly not his honor as a gentleman.

Instead, she said, "If I decide to share my art with the world, I want it to be my own decision, not influenced by any person or feeling of desperation. I don't get to decide where I live or how I spend my days. Painting, for me, has always represented freedom. I refuse to allow that freedom to be taken from me."

Mary nodded. "I can't claim to fully understand that. I am of the mindset that a large income is the best recipe for happiness that I've ever heard of, and I wish that for you."

"Maybe so," Fanny said. "But I have always been poor, and

there are worse things in life than having to work hard for a small wage. I am willing to do that, with my dignity intact."

"My brother doesn't deserve an artist like you," Mary said, leaning closer. "You are kind, and quiet, yes. But you hold fast to your convictions. I appreciate the way you share your view of the world, but you don't take offense if anyone has differing opinions. You don't try and convince anyone of anything."

Mary was so close now, her sweet lilac scent flooded Fanny's senses. She wondered if Mary's dark hair smelled of lilac, too. If it curled when pulled out of its pins. Fanny had never had a friend like Mary before, and she couldn't decide if she wanted to sketch Mary or *be* Mary.

Mary leaned in and took her hands, setting Fanny's heart racing. What was this sensation, and why did Fanny suddenly feel warm all over? "I don't think my brother has ever met an artist who didn't desperately want something from him," Mary murmured, almost as if distracted. "It confuses him when people don't want something."

"I want many things," Fanny whispered. "Just none that your brother can give me."

Mary's blue eyes flashed as they met Fanny's, and she saw in them both apprehension and a challenge. "What do you want?"

Rather than tell her, Fanny acted. She leaned in, keenly aware that if Mary withdrew or even so much as flinched, she would stop immediately. But Mary did none of those things, and Fanny kissed her. Their lips met and Fanny didn't have time to agonize over the fact that she had no idea what she was doing. Mary was soft and sweet, and before Fanny had a chance to worry that she was making a colossal mistake, Mary kissed her back.

And then she pulled away.

When Fanny opened her eyes, she found that Mary's gaze was unfocused and she wore a slight frown.

"I'm sorry." Fanny stood so that Mary had to let go of her hands. "I don't know what came over me. You've been nothing but kind to me, and I . . . I . . ."

"Fanny," Mary said, but Fanny had already turned her back on Mary and she clutched her hands into her stomach, muscles clenched so tight she was afraid she'd break into a thousand pieces. *What have I done?*

"Please, let's not speak of it. I am so tired, and I have a long journey tomorrow. It's probably for the best that we say goodbye now, isn't it? We can pretend this never happened and part . . . friends. I hope."

The floor creaked behind her as Mary stood. Fanny didn't dare turn around and face her. Why had she done that? Why had she ruined the first friendship she'd ever had? Maybe Aunt Norris was right, and she was useless. Useless and a burden to all who knew her. It was just as well that she was being sent away.

After a very long pause, Fanny heard Mary's footsteps as

she retreated. The door opened, and Mary asked, "May I write you?"

Fanny said the most hurtful thing she could think of in the moment. "I don't think it wise, do you?"

Her ears strained for a response, and Fanny desperately wished that Mary would argue with her. But the only response Fanny received was the sharp click of the door closing behind her.

Fanny was now truly alone, left to sink into her bed and cry herself to sleep.

But Fanny didn't sleep that night.

She paced her room until she heard the distant sound of a carriage taking Mr. Rushworth away—to London or to the neighboring magistrate, she wasn't certain, but his indignant protests could be heard, faintly, even from the old nursery. Not long after, she dressed for bed and tried to go to sleep, but every time she closed her eyes, she saw Mary's surprised expression when she kissed her. She tossed and turned over the sound of Mary walking away.

When the clock struck one, Fanny rose and lit every lamp and candle in her room. She faced the Millbrook replica, knowing this would be her last chance to attempt to finish it. It seemed like months ago that she had stood in the storehouse, contemplating the eyes of the middle sister. Now, Fanny reached for a palette and paints without stopping to second-guess herself. Instead of trying to paint from her memory of the original painting, she simply painted by instinct, not questioning if it was good or bad. She painted because she wanted to finish, and because she needed the distraction, and because she'd forgotten that creating art had always been an escape, a release, and a refuge. And she needed all three now more than ever.

By the time the bells tolled five o'clock, she had finished. The sister's face was complete, her blue eyes now holding all of the angst that Fanny felt in her heart. She allowed herself to step back and take in the entire work. She had done this. It was not an original work, but it was an accomplishment nonetheless. At one time, Fanny thought she might take pride in all she learned and achieved while copying out this painting, but now she felt hollow. She turned her back on her work, dressed, and wrote a quick note to Miss Bennet, explaining the circumstances of her removal from Mansfield Park. She'd just sealed it when Aunt Norris rapped on her door at half-past.

Neither her cousins nor Lady Bertram woke to bid her goodbye. Not that she truly expected Maria to kiss her cheek and wish her well—in fact, if she did so, Fanny would worry that Maria had something nefarious planned for her.

But Edmund hadn't even bothered to come see her to say goodbye.

"This will be better for you, really," Aunt Norris told her once they reached the first floor. "We've tried our best for you, but a bird cannot change its feathers. You are a Price, not a Bertram."

"And you are a Norris, so I suppose that makes the pair of us family outcasts," Fanny said without thinking. Aunt Norris stopped abruptly and looked at her with unadulterated shock. Fanny steeled herself for the anger, but Aunt Norris merely shook her head wearily.

"This is for the best, girl. You don't see that now, but trust me."

Before Fanny could question her, she heard footsteps from above and Edmund called out, "Fanny! Wait!"

He thundered down the stairs, agony on his face. Fanny was surprised when the first emotion to flare up in her was anger—it was his fault she was leaving. Aunt Norris sighed and said, "I'll give you a moment. But don't keep the carriage waiting."

And with that, Aunt Norris swept outside.

Fanny turned to Edmund, who was slightly out of breath. "I'll find a way to bring you back. Things are just . . ."

Fanny scrounged up a half-hearted smile. "I don't think you'll have much luck."

"Oh, Fanny." Edmund wasn't normally the type to show his true emotions—living with the Bertrams had a way of stamping that out of a person. "When I told everyone everything, I didn't expect . . ."

What *had* he expected? That everyone would thank them and then throw a party in their honor? "You were right about one thing, at least—we were foolish to think they'd be glad to know the truth."

"I was trying to emulate you," he said. "You always see the good in people."

At that, the lingering anger she felt at him for upending everything faded into a sadness so big it threatened to swallow her up. "I struggle to find it now." She tried to redirect the conversation, before she burst into tears. "Will you write?"

"As often as I can," he promised, and enveloped her in a hug. They hadn't touched much as children aside from an occasional shove or grabbing each other's hands to play a game. As they grew older, the most they'd ever done was shake hands or take each other's arms. This hug was different, though. This was the Edmund she loved. He smelled of pine and she felt the tickle of his breath on her ear as he whispered, "I'll find a way to London, and then you can follow me. I promise."

He withdrew before Fanny could respond, and she looked up as he pulled away. How nice to know that there was at least one person who wouldn't hate her upon her departure. She had no sooner thought this when Edmund leaned forward and kissed her.

It was . . . not unpleasant. His mouth was warm and the haze of pine that filled her nose was all fine. The kiss was chaste and rather too brief for her to react to—as soon as she realized his lips were upon hers, it seemed that he was drawing away. Fanny could do nothing but stare at Edmund in shock, well and truly speechless.

"Ahem." A quiet, polite female voice startled them both.

Edmund stepped neatly away, giving Fanny the appropriate polite distance, and Fanny saw, with horror, that Mary Crawford stood on the stairs behind him.

Had she seen the kiss? *Of course* she had seen it. How could she have not?

"I wanted to wish you safe travels," Mary said. Her tentative smile seemed forced. "I am very sorry to see you go, Miss Price."

Calling her Miss Price was a skewer right in Fanny's heart, and she swallowed the lump of hurt in her throat. "Thank you," she said, unable to revert to calling her Miss Crawford. "It was very kind of you to wake up early to say goodbye."

"Of course," Mary said, so softly that the words might have been lost in the distance between them, had Fanny not been paying such close attention.

Then Mary held out a small slip of paper. "My address in London. I hope you'll think of writing me there."

"Of course," Fanny said, stepping forward and reaching out to take the slip of paper. Mary was careful to pass it to her in such a way so that their hands never touched. "And my address in Portsmouth—"

"I'll see that Mary gets it," Edmund cut in.

Fanny nodded, but she felt as though her head were wrapped in thick cotton and she couldn't quite make sense of the awkward scene she'd found herself in. But before she could dwell on it much longer, the front door opened and Aunt Norris called out, "Fanny! Come along. The driver is eager to get off."

"I must go," she said, looking between Edmund and Mary, unsure of whether or not to shake hands or try to hug them both.

"Safe travels," Mary said, and Edmund nodded in agreement.

"Write the second you arrive," Edmund added.

"I will," she promised, and she lingered in the hall a moment more before Aunt Norris barked out her name. She turned and walked away from them both, managed a perfunctory goodbye to Aunt Norris, then climbed into the carriage, head full of too many swirling thoughts and heart full of too much sadness and confusion to pay much notice as Mansfield Park slid past her window.

SEVENTEEN

In Which Fanny Faces a Homecoming, of a Sort

TWO MISERABLE DAYS LATER, Fanny's carriage rolled to a stop in front of a shabby town house in Portsmouth. The air felt different here, salty and cool, but it was invigorating after Fanny's long travels, most of which were spent wallowing in her decisions and their consequences.

Her legs felt unsteady after sitting folded in the cramped carriage, but maybe it was nerves as well. She'd left in such a hurry, there'd been no way of sending word ahead. When she'd imagined reuniting with her family, it wasn't like *this*.

The door opened and a middle-aged woman stepped out of the house, suspicion weighing down her features. Fanny's heart skipped a beat at the thought, *Mother?* But no, this woman wasn't her mother. She must be the housekeeper. "Can I help you?" she asked, voice sharp.

A blond boy of nine or ten dashed out of the open door, and Fanny gasped in recognition. "Tom!" she exclaimed, for the little boy had to be the baby Tom she had once carried everywhere, changing nappies and rocking to sleep.

The boy had been intent on running down the street for some misadventure or other, but he turned at the sound of his name and squinted. "Who're you?" he asked, not suspicious like the housekeeper, but wary.

Fanny couldn't find her voice. He didn't recognize her. Well, of course not. He had been a baby crawling about on the rug the last time he'd laid eyes on her. But the housekeeper seemed alarmed that this apparent stranger knew Tom, and she said, "I don't know what you're about—"

But she was interrupted by a male voice saying, "Rebecca? Is there someone at the door?"

"Some lady," Rebecca sniffed as she stepped aside, and there was William.

"William!" Fanny cried at the sight of her brother.

He was tall and the blond curls of his youth had given way to lighter brown hair, the same shade as Fanny's, which he wore closely cut, and his brown eyes were framed by gold-rimmed spectacles. His mouth went round in shock, but then he broke into an enormous smile, revealing the slightly gapped front teeth she remembered from their childhood. "Fanny!" he shouted without any hesitation, and swept her up in a fierce hug.

Fanny was so relieved to be welcomed that tears leaked from

the corners of her eyes. They were absorbed into her brother's coat as she buried her face in his shoulder and inhaled the forgotten scent of home—woodsmoke, paper, and the hint of salt from the sea.

"Fanny Price, as I live and breathe," William said when they finally pulled apart. He glanced at her valise. "Have you come for a visit?"

"Something like that," she said, withdrawing a handkerchief from her pocket and wiping at her eyes.

"I'll be off, miss," the driver said.

Fanny turned and said, "Thank you very much. Please give everyone at Mansfield my best."

The driver tipped his hat and then was gone, and when Fanny turned back William was staring at her with something like wonder, as if she were a very rare book. "I imagine you have a lot to tell me, but first, the family will be glad to see you."

Then he turned and shouted into the open doorway, "Mother! I've a surprise for you!"

Two more little blond heads peeked around Rebecca, whose scowl had relaxed somewhat only at William's recognition of Fanny, and Fanny caught her breath. These must be her younger siblings, born after her departure. How did one introduce oneself to a sibling they'd never met? But before she had a chance to think about it, Mrs. Price was coming to the door, saying, "I don't know what you're on about, William, I don't need any more surprises at my age."

"Not even if they're your long-lost daughter?" Fanny found herself saying, and then had the pleasure of seeing her mother's jaw drop open in shock.

"Fanny!" she whispered, clutching at her chest. "Oh, my dear girl!"

She was hugged and kissed upon each cheek, and her mother exclaimed over everything from how tall she'd grown to how lovely her complexion was to how fine her dress appeared. As a child, Fanny hadn't found her mother to be particularly affectionate—but she'd had four other children, so really, Fanny couldn't have blamed her for rationing out hugs and kisses. Now, Fanny delighted in her mother's embrace and attention, like the neglected child she'd once been. Or, she realized, like the neglected child she'd *always* been.

Perhaps the strangest shock Fanny received was in realizing first how much older her mother appeared after nine years, and second just how much she looked like Lady Bertram and Aunt Norris. Granted, premature age made her appear to be their older sister and not the youngest, but beholding her reminded Fanny of Mansfield, which she found oddly comforting.

Mrs. Price drew her inside and took care of introducing Fanny to Charles, who was seven, and Betsey, five. They gaped at the sister they'd heard of but never before laid eyes upon, and Fanny crouched down to say hello, but neither was inclined to hug her as she'd hoped. Then Fanny was ushered into a room so small that at first she mistook it for a passageway. She stood awkwardly, trying to find the door to the parlor, when she realized that this dingy room, with its one settee and worn armchair, was in fact the parlor.

"Sit!" her mother ordered, and then turned to the hallway and said, "Rebecca, tea! Fanny will be terribly hungry after her long journey—have you come all the way from Mansfield? Never mind, we'll get to that in a moment. We can dress a steak, if you like . . . although, we've not much meat at the moment. It's a terrible hassle, you know, not having a butcher on the street anymore. The Browns closed their shop up on the road last winter, and it's been an awful inconvenience. Rebecca, what do we have to offer Fanny?"

"I would prefer a good cup of tea to anything," Fanny said, not wanting Rebecca or her mother to go to any trouble on her account.

Just then, another head peeked into the parlor. Fanny looked up and gasped in delight—it was Susan, her younger sister. Susan's hair hadn't dulled to brown like Fanny's and William's. It shone golden in the weak lamplight, and she wore a shy smile. "Susan," Fanny said, rising to greet her.

"Is it really you?" Susan asked, stepping into the room carefully.

"It really is," Fanny reassured her, and Susan was happy to embrace her, even if their younger siblings were still wary.

When they finally drew apart, Susan asked the question that was surely on everyone's mind. "But what are you doing here? If we'd known you were coming . . ."

"Not that we aren't happy to see you," their mother rushed to add, but Fanny could see the gleam of curiosity in her eyes.

"I know it's unexpected, and I don't mean to put you out in any way," Fanny began. She'd had two full days to explain her sudden presence in Portsmouth, and yet the excuse that she'd come up with felt suddenly flimsy. "With the household at Mansfield in such a disarray since Sir Thomas's death, my aunts thought that I ought to return for a visit, since it's been so long."

Fanny hoped her mother would buy the lie, but one glance told her that she wasn't fooled. Her face had fallen into a frown. "They've abdicated all responsibility, then?"

She winced. "I wouldn't say that, exactly. . . ."

"How long shall you stay?" her mother asked. "Or did they not say?"

Her second question was laced with sarcasm, and Fanny felt disappointment wash over her heart. Of course, her presence here would be quite the inconvenience. But if there was anything that Fanny didn't want to do at the moment, it was beg. So she lied. "A few weeks," she said, hating how relieved her mother looked at this news. "The family will be in London for a month or two for business. I didn't want to go, and my aunts didn't think it appropriate that I should stay behind at Mansfield with no one but the servants for company."

"No one but the servants indeed," her mother said sarcastically.

Luckily, William stepped in. "No matter how long we have you, I'm glad you've finally come home. I've missed you, Fanny."

"And I you," she said.

"All right, enough with the sentiments," their mother said. "Tell us the news from Mansfield. How're they all holding up after Sir Thomas's death?"

Fanny was peppered with questions, and she did her best to answer honestly and to her family's satisfaction. The little ones soon lost interest in their oldest sister and ran off. They could be heard running up and down the stairs, in and out the front door, and down the hallway. Fanny was regularly startled from her conversation by their sudden outbursts and arguments, but her mother didn't appear perturbed by the roughhousing or the noise.

After Fanny had drunk her tea and told her mother everything she could possibly think of about the household at Mansfield without giving away the true troubles there, Susan was sent upstairs to prepare a place for Fanny to sleep. Mother added, "And take care to be quiet so as not to disturb your father."

Fanny had nearly forgotten about her father in all the ruckus and excitement, and she thought there was nothing that quiet, gentle Susan could do to disturb him that her younger siblings hadn't already done in the past ten minutes. Nonetheless, she asked, "Is Father well?"

"Your father has been poorly," Mother responded tersely.

Fanny looked at William, and the tightening of his smile clearly said, *I'll tell you later.* "But I should go look in on him and see if he's up to receiving you. He'll be happy to hear you're home."

Fanny had never been particularly noticed by her father as a child, so she wasn't sure if she believed he'd be happy, but she smiled anyway and said, "Yes, I'd love to see him."

Susan and Mother left the parlor, leaving Fanny alone with William. She turned to him and whispered, "Is he bedbound?"

William sighed. "For a few weeks now, yes."

Fanny puzzled over that response. "You never mentioned that in any of your letters."

A pained expression flashed across William's face, and then it was gone. "Illness comes and goes in fits, where Father is concerned." Then with a quick glance around, he added, "It's the sort that's unlikely to improve."

"You mean . . ."

"Let's talk later. Little pitchers have big ears." And he nodded to the hallway, where Fanny caught a flash of one of her younger siblings, gone too quickly to discern which one.

"Right," she said.

"Besides," William added, "I believe you have some things to share, too."

Fanny bit her lip, feeling guilty at how easily William could see right through her. "I'll tell you the whole story," she promised.

Just then Betsey walked in the room to announce that "Papa

will see Fanny now!" and she rose, giving William a nervous look before following her youngest sister up the old staircase, which was far narrower and steeper than she recollected.

The landing at the top boasted three doors: one led to her parents' bedroom, and the other two led to bedchambers for the boys and girls. How small this house was! Her spacious yet cozy nursery room back at Mansfield felt like a luxury in comparison. She knocked lightly and entered her parents' bedchamber, lit by the light of a single candle. Her mother sat at the foot of the bed, and her father was in bed, coverlet pulled up to his chin.

Fanny approached nervously, glancing at her mother for reassurance but finding little. "Hello, Father," she said. "It's me, Fanny."

The man in the bed looked decades older than she remembered. His gray whiskers were badly in need of shaving, and his hair was tangled and greasy. His eyes fluttered open, and Fanny was shocked at how bloodshot they appeared.

"Fanny," he rasped out.

"Yes, Father," she confirmed, then stepped forward to kiss his cheek. It seemed like the right thing to do. Expected, even.

His whiskers were itchy against her lips, and as she drew close she could smell the tang of spirits on his breath. She withdrew quickly and resisted the urge to rub at her mouth. "How wonderful to see you."

He surveyed her with watery eyes and grunted. "You've grown," he proclaimed.

"Yes, I suppose I have," she said.

"Have you a husband?"

She forced a smile. "No, I don't."

Another grunt. "A grown woman like you will be wanting a husband."

Fanny didn't know what to say to that. His words reminded her of a kiss—not Edmund's kiss, but the other one. A kiss from a person who could never be her husband.

When her father said nothing more, and with Fanny at a loss for words, her mother turned and said, "Your father is very tired, dear. It's his illness. He'll be more himself tomorrow."

Fanny nodded. "Good night, Father."

As she slipped out the door, she heard her father's voice rasp once more before the door latched. "How long is she staying?"

EIGHTEEN

In Which Fanny Finally Unburdens Herself

FANNY SHARED A BED with Susan in the tiny, cramped corner of the girls' bedroom. As soon as her head hit the flat pillow, she fell into an exhausted sleep and didn't wake until the following morning, when the slam of a door and thunderous steps on the stairs woke her. As she stirred, she realized that both Susan and Betsey were gone and scurried out of bed. She dressed in a plain, olive-green day gown that always appeared drab at Mansfield but was very nearly fine here.

Downstairs, her family crowded around the dining room table, save for Father.

"There you are," her mother said, a note of disapproval in her voice. "Thought you might sleep the morning away."

"Apologies," Fanny said, looking about for a seat and finding none. "I'm afraid I was even more tired than I realized."

"I was hoping that was the case, and not that you expected breakfast in bed like some fine lady."

Fanny couldn't tell if her mother was teasing or not. She was attempting to braid Betsey's hair, but the child was squirming and making the job difficult.

"Oh, Mother, Fanny isn't like that," William said, mercifully coming to her rescue. "She was tired—she had to travel two full days to get here."

Fanny smiled her thanks. "I'm quite restored now. I haven't slept so soundly in a long time."

Her mother scoffed a tiny bit, and Fanny bit her lip. But then Mrs. Price slapped the table and said, "Betsy, stand still or I shall cut off your pretty curls and sell them to the wigmaker!"

Betsey wasn't so much chastised as she was mildly subdued by this threat, which made Fanny wonder about the manner of discipline in her parents' house. But before she had a chance to dwell on it further, William stood. "Here, Fanny. Take a seat. Breakfast is a casual affair here."

She smiled her gratitude and procured a plate and a cup of tea. She'd no sooner settled down when William said, "I know you've only just arrived, but would you like to come with me to the lending library today?"

Fanny had just taken a sip of tea, sparing her from having to respond immediately. She wanted to, desperately. Something about the closeness of the small house and the chaos wrought by her bickering, misbehaving younger siblings made her want to flee, and that made her feel terribly guilty. She *should* stay and help her mother, restore the connection between them. Surely she didn't mean to sound so short-tempered. It couldn't be easy, wrangling so many children and a sick husband. Another set of hands would go a long way toward earning her mother's good-will.

But she was spared from any decision-making when her mother said, "Oh, go on. Always thick as thieves, you two. Besides, I've managed this long without you, I can manage a day more."

This was not altogether the reassuring response Fanny might have hoped for, but she was too happy to care. She had questions that could be put to William only when they were alone.

After breakfast, Fanny met William at the door, sketch-book in hand. The younger children followed them down the street, but when they got to the corner, William stopped and shouted, "All right, you lot—back home now!" There was a chorus of displeasure among them, but they trotted obediently, if reluctantly, back down the road.

"I daresay they listen to you more than Mother," Fanny said.

"Oh, they most certainly do. Drives her mad. But they know when to take me seriously, and when I'm joking with them."

He offered her his arm and they crossed the street, and Fanny whispered, almost under her breath, "I've missed you so much."

William heard—she could tell by the way his grip tightened on her elbow. She wondered if he could hear the guilt in her voice, too. The truth was, she'd given very little thought to what day-to-day life might have looked like for them all these years. Her mother had written at first, but those letters became fewer and fewer as the new babies took up more of her time, until William became her only point of contact. And his letters were always relentlessly cheerful, encouraging her to learn all she could and take every advantage offered her at Mansfield. He was happy to share funny and amusing stories and good news, but now Fanny saw he'd shielded her, too.

Just as Fanny had taken care to conceal her true position at Mansfield.

"How long has Father been . . . ill?" she ventured to ask.

William sighed heavily. "Father's been ill our whole lives, Fanny. He *was* sick . . . but now he's just a drunk who's too weak to get out of bed."

It was the first note of impatience, or perhaps frustration, that Fanny had picked up from her brother. He didn't say any more as they turned onto the high street and William withdrew a key to their family's lending library. The shop front looked much the same as she remembered, with its paned windows and the simple, demure wooden "Circulating Library" sign that had been commissioned back in their grandfather's day, when the library had first opened. But there was a newer wooden sign, posted next to the door, that read "Personal and Family Subscriptions Available."

They stepped inside and William immediately set to work lighting lamps. The old familiar smell of paper and ink filled Fanny's heart as she inhaled deeply and looked around the reading area, which was a small but tidy space with one large table and six straight-backed chairs at the center, surrounded by a collection of gently shabby armchairs and settees. She followed her brother around the table to the long counter, which boasted catalogs of the books the library owned, and was satisfied that even after nine years away, she still felt a thrill at being allowed to step behind the counter.

"It hasn't changed a bit," she breathed.

William harrumphed. "Trust me, a great deal has changed. I slip Susan a bit of pocket money to come and clean twice a week, which Mother and Father don't know, so mum's the word. And you'll find our clientele has shifted somewhat."

"Oh?" Fanny asked. Her memories of the place were certainly dingier, but also of middle-aged gentlemen clustered around the table, of debates and arguments. Their father's father had fancied himself a bit of a scholar, although he possessed no formal training, and used the last of a modest inheritance to start his business before Fanny and William had been born. He'd died when Fanny was an infant, leaving it to their Father. Mr. Price, who'd had little interest in books or philosophical debates, had taken over rather reluctantly. Fanny could easily recall him standing behind the counter, furtively swigging from a bottle of spirits stashed between books while snapping his fingers impatiently anytime he wanted a young William to fetch a book.

"When Father took ill, I cleaned the place up a bit," he admitted. "And then when it became clear that Father's recovery would not be . . . quick . . . well, I started to take liberties with the collection."

Now that the circulating library was better lit, Fanny began glancing around at the books on display on the counter. "Are those *novels*?"

"Yes," William reported sheepishly.

"And the sign about the family rate?"

"Also new," he confirmed. "We needed more customers. And it turns out that when you offer a family rate, gentlemen tell their wives and daughters, and they like reading novels."

"I am certain the appeal of a novel is not limited to ladies," Fanny countered. "But that sounds very prudent of you."

William's shy smile was the same as she remembered from their childhood. He eagerly showed off all the little changes and improvements he'd made to the place, and he looked to her with hope for her approval, which she readily gave. Fanny's pride swelled seeing her brother so in his element. He didn't just love books—he loved sharing books with others. And William understood the way books could unite people across all divides, and that was what motivated him to come to work each day, not the pay. William, Fanny realized, had a purpose.

"And who knows, maybe one day we might expand into the shop next door," he said.

"William, this is incredible." Fanny shook her head in wonder. "I am so amazed."

"Yes, well . . . I know you've been up to all sorts of exciting things too," he added.

Nothing as incredible as expanding their family's circulating library. How useful. How proactive! But she had to ask . . . "What does Father think of all this?"

Fanny immediately felt it was the wrong thing to say, because William's happy face fell into a wince. "Well."

Fanny laughed. "He doesn't know!"

"Fanny. I don't think Father will ever return here."

"You mean . . . ?"

"Each week he gets worse."

Shock rushed through her, followed by alarm. "Should we call a doctor?"

He shook his head. "It's no use. I had one come around two months ago. He said that Father would improve if Mother stopped giving him drink, which she refuses to do. He becomes mean without it. But I can look after the library. It won't make us rich, but it makes enough."

Fanny looked around for a place to sit and her eyes landed on a low stool. She plopped down abruptly, and William said, "Fanny?"

"I'm all right," she said, but she wasn't. Not in the slightest. "It's just . . . a shock."

"I know," William said, coming to stand by her. He hovered awkwardly, as if unsure what to do. "It's quite sad, the idea of losing Father."

Inappropriate laughter bubbled up in Fanny, but she gulped it down. "William. I don't give two figs for our father. He's never cared much for me—don't look at me like that! He let me go off to Mansfield because it would be one fewer mouth to feed, and he wasn't at all pleased to see me last night. I care about you. All you've had to do . . . and you never told me."

"I didn't want to worry you," William said softly.

Unfortunately, Fanny understood all too well.

"And besides, what would you have done? Come back? Fanny, it may have been harsh, but you going off to Mansfield . . . well, it was a relief. I never had to worry about you going hungry, the way I did the others. You were spared that, at least."

This did little to comfort Fanny, because she hated the idea of any of her siblings going hungry. "How you all must have resented me."

"No," William insisted, and if anyone else were to say so, she wouldn't have believed them. But William was William.

296

So pure and empathetic. "It used to get me through the bad times, knowing you were free from all this. I never wanted you to come back here, Fanny. Although, don't get me wrong, having you for a visit is probably the best thing to happen in ages."

Fanny wiped a stray tear from the corner of her eye, hoping that it wasn't a sign of more to come. "Yes. Well. About that."

She looked up at William, who waited patiently as the truth came pouring out of her. She told him everything, from Uncle's death to her discovery, from Maria's schemes to their money worries. She told him of the Crawfords, the plans to open Mansfield, the auction ball. Her suspicions that someone in the family might be responsible, directly or indirectly, for her uncle's death. The offer of representation, and finally, how Edmund's accusation caused her to be sent away.

When she was done, she felt more spent than she had the previous evening. William let out a noisy breath, puffing out his cheeks, and Fanny felt a surge of affection for him. She'd forgotten how he always did that when he was stressed or thinking.

"Well, that sounds like a right mess," he said finally, meeting her gaze. But then he smiled and added, "You've let it all out now, and that has to feel good, hm?"

Of course, that only reminded her of Mary and how she encouraged Fanny to release her feelings. "I suppose," she said miserably.

He stood and placed his hand on her shoulder, squeezing gently. "I'm glad you've told me all of it. And we'll sort through it, too. But for now, I have to open the front door."

Fanny looked up and was surprised to see that a small throng of readers was queued up at the door, peering in with curiosity or impatience. "Of course," she said.

Guilt picked at her, though, because she hadn't exactly told William *everything*.

Such as how Edmund had kissed her. Which overwhelmed her with doubt, not joy. Because it wasn't her first kiss.

And, this was the hardest to admit of all:

She was certain she'd preferred her first kiss to Edmund's.

NINETEEN

*In Which Fanny Struggles to Find
Her Place in Portsmouth*

FANNY TRIED TO THINK of being sent to Portsmouth as a reprieve. She no longer had to worry about the Bertrams' money woes, what Maria was up to, or if anyone had taken Pug for a walk that day. She didn't even need to worry about the outcome of the case against Mr. Rushworth.

But not knowing, she found, was almost worse.

She thought at first that she might distract herself by helping with the children and household chores. Her mother spent much of her time caring for her father, and Rebecca, the housekeeper, cooked and cleaned—if what she did could be called cleaning. Rebecca was more interested in gossip on the street corner and taking many (many) breaks for tea in the kitchen than actually working. But when her mother caught Fanny sweeping out the parlor, she was hauled away by her elbow as her mother hissed, "What do you think I pay Rebecca to do?"

"But that's rather the point, I'm afraid," Fanny whispered. "I don't think Rebecca sweeps."

"Regardless," her mother scolded. "I can't have you doing her job. She might be offended and leave. Do you know how difficult it is to find good help?"

Fanny had left it, but later she said to William, "It's not that I aspire to be a housemaid, but it seems to me if Susan and I were organized about it and we wrangled the children and gave them some tasks, we wouldn't need Rebecca. And then wouldn't we be saving quite a bit of money?"

"I've already tried that," William told her with a sigh. "But Mother is quite set on keeping her. It's a point of pride, you see. No maid is worse than a bad maid in her mind."

So household work was quite out of the question.

She did find an ally in Susan, who, although quiet and shy, proved eager to gain Fanny's respect. She seemed just as bothered by the chaos of the household, although she never complained. (Aunt Norris would undoubtedly think *her* a marvelous companion.) She was the one who attempted to teach the little ones how to read and do their figures, and Fanny thought if she couldn't so much as sweep without getting a scolding, she might as well try to help with her siblings' education. But the children had no use for Fanny's lessons and, furthermore, no respect for Fanny as their oldest sister. On a day during which

Betsey blew raspberries every time Fanny attempted to speak, and Tom purposefully broke a charcoal pencil when she tried to show him how to multiply, and all four of them burst into a rather indecent and rowdy sea shanty when she began lecturing on history, Fanny was near tears and about ready to give up.

"Don't pay them any mind," Susan reassured her, sensing that Fanny was on the brink. "They're incorrigible. Go take William his lunch, and then see if you can help him there."

Fanny had begun to suspect that William left his lunch at home on purpose, in order to give her an escape. She was glad of it. Fanny felt stifled at home, where the children were always yelling, arguing, and thundering up and down the stairs. Where if Mrs. Price wasn't complaining, it was Rebecca. Where her bedridden father shouted obscenities through the closed bedroom door when he wanted quiet, and where she sometimes caught her mother looking at her as if she were another mouth to feed and not her long-lost daughter.

Fanny had finally, truly, become what she'd feared the most at Mansfield Park: a burden.

But at the lending library, she was at least able to pretend she was useful. She fetched books, helped with the accounts, and sketched absently during lulls in business. It was during these quiet moments, while William read or responded to correspondence, that she tried desperately to think of ways to earn her keep.

It was a slow hour when the bell above the door rang, and

301

she felt more than saw William suddenly stand to attention, brimming with nervous energy. When she looked up, she saw he wore an eager smile, and his trembling hands were clasped behind his back.

"Good day," he said, and Fanny looked up to see a young lady approaching the counter.

She was petite, with blond curls that were nearly bursting out of her bonnet, which was a becoming shade of cornflower blue. Her matching blue dress was understated and modest, but clearly of very good quality, and she had a sweet smile and a spray of freckles across her nose and cheeks that Fanny knew some ladies would find horrifying but she found to be quite endearing. Her overall demeanor was of a country shepherdess in many of the wholesome paintings that every matron wanted to hang on the wall of her young daughter's bedchamber.

"Hello, Mr. Price," the young lady said, already blushing. "I've come for the second volume."

She held a small book aloft and then carefully placed it on the counter before William.

William cleared his throat and looked down at the book, nodding enthusiastically. "Excellent. What did you think?"

"I loved it," the young woman said. "It was just like you said—funny, wise, and not dull in the least. I couldn't wait a second longer to see how it continues."

"I'm glad," William responded, and he seemed to make no move to replace the book or retrieve the next volume.

Fanny stood, garnering the attention of William and the young lady. Fanny saw the young lady's face twist in dismay, but only for a moment before it was replaced with a perfectly cordial expression. "Hello," Fanny said. "William, should I go fetch the next volume?"

"Um, oh, yes, please?" William looked between Fanny and the young lady. "This is, erm, Fanny, I mean . . ."

"Miss Fanny Price," Fanny clarified, lest William work himself up into a nervous fit. "His *sister*," she added.

The relief on the young lady's face told Fanny that she was not imagining things in the slightest. She gave out a small, tinkling laugh and said, "Oh, how marvelous. I am Miss Sophia Rogerson."

She gave a little curtsy that Fanny felt was wholly unnecessary, but she liked this Miss Sophia Rogerson even more for it. "Wonderful to meet you. I'm just helping William—no, let me go get it. I must learn where all the books are shelved."

Fanny skipped off, whisking the book away from William's grasp. She took her sweet time following the cataloging system that William had implemented, swapping out cards between the library's catalog and the book, then double-checking the placement of the next volume on the shelf. Fanny took a few moments to flip through the books, flick a speck of dust from one of the shelves, and push all the volumes neatly together so not a single space was left between them. She could hear the soft murmur of her brother's voice and the clear bell of Miss

Rogerson's laugh, and she smiled to herself before finally making her way back to the front of the library.

"Did you find it?" William asked.

"Yes, yes," Fanny said, placing the book before Miss Rogerson. "Don't mind me, I'm not as quick as William at this, but I'm learning."

"How wonderful to see you have help," Miss Rogerson said. "I've often told him he ought to hire a clerk." She said this bit for Fanny's sake, then seemed to realize the implication of her words and rushed to add, "Which isn't to say that you are a clerk, Miss Price."

"No, I quite understand," Fanny said. "And I'm pleased to help out any way I can. I know how hard my brother works."

William blushed at the compliment and said, "It's no hassle whatsoever. Keeps me busy."

But Fanny knew William couldn't afford to hire a clerk. Though there were hours when hardly a person would come in, there were plenty of times when multiple book dealers and patrons would come in, all demanding William's attention. Perhaps this was the best she could offer: alleviating the burden for William to earn a living for the family. Still, it was a far cry from contributing in any meaningful way.

As Miss Rogerson paid for her next volume, her gaze fell upon Fanny's abandoned sketchbook, which was open to a sketch of the street outside. "Oh, what a lovely drawing—is this yours, Miss Price?"

"Fanny is quite the talented artist," William boasted. "And she paints, too."

"You flatter me," Fanny said, but her cheeks warmed at the praise. "Thank you, Miss Rogerson."

"May I?" she asked, indicating she'd like to see more. Fanny nodded, although she felt nervous watching this fine young lady page through her sketchbook. At least she was fairly certain there was nothing embarrassing in this sketchbook—just sketches of the streets of Portsmouth, of the ocean and the ships in harbor, little portraits of William and Susan, and oh . . .

"Who is this?" William asked.

"Oh . . . um. Her name is Miss Crawford," Fanny said. She was certainly blushing now. "She was an acquaintance of mine, back at Mansfield Park."

She feared that they would pry some more, but Miss Rogerson looked up and said, "You have talent, Miss Price. Did you do this from memory?"

"Yes," she said simply, trying to keep her emotions under control.

"And you paint as well?"

"One of her paintings sold to a countess," William boasted.

Miss Rogerson looked impressed. "Well, if you ever take commissions, I know a few ladies who would be interested in sketches or paintings of their sons and husbands, before they go to sea," she said. "My father captains the *Vestal*, and his sailors are often gone months if not years. My mother regularly socializes with the wives and mothers of his lieutenants."

"Oh." Fanny looked to William to gauge his reaction. He stared at Miss Rogerson with a mix of awe and admiration. "I would indeed be interested."

Miss Rogerson gave Fanny her calling card and extracted a promise from Fanny that she'd call in two days' time. She made her goodbyes, and as soon as she was gone, Fanny turned to William. "She seems very sweet."

"Yes, it was very kind of her to offer to introduce you to her circle," he said, face still pink.

"Hm, yes. I'm sure it had nothing to do with the fact that I'm *your* sister."

"Nothing at all," he agreed. "Your talent speaks for itself."

Fanny couldn't tell if William was being exceptionally dense or putting her off. She tried once more. "So her father—"

"Is a ship's captain, yes. Which means whatever notions you have right now ought to be stopped immediately."

"Notions?" Fanny asked. "*I* have no notions. But she seems to have plenty."

"She's merely an acquaintance," William emphasized. "Just as your Miss Crawford is an acquaintance."

"She's not my—I mean . . ." Fanny was so taken aback, her words came in a jumbled heap. "I beg your pardon?"

"Mmhmm," was all William would say, before walking off to help another patron.

Properly chastised, Fanny flipped to her sketch of Mary.

She would be in London by now, helping her brother prepare for the masquerade. Did she think of Fanny at all, or had their parting soured Mary's memory of her altogether? She thought about writing in her snatches of spare moments, but nothing ever felt right. *I had never had a friend before*, she thought about writing, *and then I met you. The force of my feelings confused me. Please forgive me. Don't hate me.*

She shook loose these stray thoughts. It was no use. She would not send that letter, because the truth was, she could not bring herself to regret kissing Mary.

And now she'd never see her again.

Fanny had just come home from a successful second sitting sketching out the profile of a first lieutenant for his new wife. She had a spring in her step, coin in her pocket, and the day was uncommonly lovely. It was late April, but the warm air and softness of the wind suggested May was not far off. The sun was bright as it slid toward the horizon, more leisurely now that it was spring, and everything looked beautiful when the shadows played with the light as they did today.

She was thinking optimistically of the future and how she might expand her little business when she found Mrs. Price sitting in the parlor, a letter clutched in her fist.

"Hello, Mother," Fanny greeted, but the coldness in her mother's gaze when she looked up stopped her abruptly.

"When were you going to tell me that you were banished

from my sister's house?" Mrs. Price demanded.

Fear, but also terrible shame, washed over her. "I'm not sure if I'd say *banished*," she said, words coming out faintly.

"I would. And so would my sister—she wrote the word out here. See!" Mrs. Price thrust the letter into Fanny's face, and she caught a glimpse of Aunt Norris's hand before her mother whisked away the letter. "What do you have to say for yourself?"

She sat in the hard chair across from her mother and said, "It wasn't that I wanted to keep things from you."

"Then why did you?"

"I didn't know how to tell you," she answered truthfully. "I didn't know what to say."

"My sister says that you shamed the entire family with your hysterics!" Her mother's voice rose and she shook the letter in Fanny's face. "Destroying an engagement? Distressing my poor sisters to the brink of breakdown?"

That last bit was a stretch. Fanny stopped herself from rolling her eyes just in time. "That's hardly what happened. Did Aunt Norris also explain she was engaged in a shady business scheme with Maria, and that someone conspired to have Sir Thomas killed?"

"Why on earth would you say such things?" Mrs. Price demanded. "They are your family. You were a guest in their home. It is not up to you to question their personal business."

"But it was wrong!" Fanny didn't know what else to say. "Did

308

you expect me to turn the other way and pretend I hadn't seen?"

"*Yes!*"

The force of her mother's response stunned Fanny into silence. Mrs. Price didn't care to know Fanny's side of things, she realized. Fanny had failed in her mother's eyes. She felt a spike of anger—at herself, for growing impatient and getting caught by Maria. At her mother, for sending her away in the first place. At the Bertrams, for caring so little about the circumstances of Sir Thomas's death. And at Edmund, for accusing Mr. Rushworth without consulting her.

As she tried to get her breathing—and her riotous emotions—under control, Mrs. Price dropped the letter next to a cooling cup of tea and said, "So you're here for good now, are you?"

The abrupt switch of topic threw Fanny off guard. "Well . . . it would certainly seem so."

"There are no friends you can visit, or acquaintances for you to call on? No suitors in the wings, or anyone of class who can elevate your position?"

Fanny shook her head.

"Well, some things certainly must change around here," Mother said. "We cannot afford to support you forever. That was the whole point of sending you to my sisters."

"I know that," she said, and she withdrew the coins from her pocket and placed them on the small table between them.

"I earned these today, drawing a portrait. I hope this will lead to more opportunities."

Her mother eyed the coins, then swiped them up quickly and tucked them into her own pocket with a sniff. "Just be sure that you don't go dishonoring this family's good name."

Fanny's cheeks flamed at that implication. "I won't, Mother. Never."

With nothing more to argue, her mother seemed to deflate. She withdrew a letter from her apron pocket and held it out to Fanny. "This came for you."

Hope and fear surged through Fanny as she accepted the letter. She looked at her name written on the outside of the folded sheet and felt a peculiar plummeting sensation.

It was from Edmund. Not Mary.

"Well, are you going to read it?" her mother demanded. "It's from that other Bertram boy, isn't it? The one they took in and who didn't get himself booted from the estate?"

"Yes, Mother," Fanny said, letting her impatience show in her voice. Edmund hadn't gotten himself banished because he was a Bertram, and a boy, but there was nothing Fanny could do about that. "I'm going to take a short walk."

"But you just got in and tea should be on soon," Mrs. Price protested. Fanny ignored her and headed straight back outside, for both their sakes.

Once back outside, Fanny itched to walk and keep walking. She wound through the streets until she drew closer and closer to the ocean, then climbed the steps to the ramparts, which offered a glorious view of the sea. The waves dashed against the stone in a way that suggested a merry dance, and when she inhaled deeply the salt air was both bracing and clarifying. She broke open the seal and began to read, holding tight to the paper fluttering in the wind.

Bertram House, London

Dear Fanny,

Forgive me for not writing sooner. The household has undergone many changes since you departed, and I've scarcely had a moment to think. After we said farewell to the Crawfords, Maria became determined to travel to London with all possible haste. Whether this was out of a lingering affection for Mr. Rushworth or a desire to be near Mr. Crawford, I cannot say but I'm sure you can draw your own conclusions. Of course, that led to Aunt Norris declaring she needed to chaperone, and not to be left out, Julia demanded to join. Aunt Bertram was very resolute that she ought not to come to London, being in mourning, so it would seem that she would be quite alone at Mansfield. I believe that's when they began to regret sending you away.

Of course they'd miss her once they realized how useful she was to them. Fanny scoffed into the wind, needing a few moments before reading on.

Julia kicked up quite a fuss about being left behind, so it was decided that as long as Aunt Bertram could bring Pug, and as long as she wasn't expected to attend any social gatherings, she would rather come than stay. We all set out in two carriages, with Tom, Yates, and myself riding alongside so that we could travel as quickly and as lightly as possible. Our plans for expediency were thwarted, however, because along the way Tom's horse spooked and he was thrown.

Fanny gasped.

He suffered a broken leg, and ended up riding in the carriage—I don't envy him that journey, poor fellow. The doctor was able to set the bone and believes that he'll eventually regain full function of his leg, but it could be weeks if not months. He'll be staying at the London house in the meantime, and he's quite cross about not being able to attend the masquerade, but better his leg than his neck.

Because I know you must be wondering, Aunt Bertram expressed a desire to invite you back now that we are in town, but I'm afraid Aunt Norris put an end to that notion, as there is no time for any of us to come fetch you from Portsmouth. (At least, I think that's the main reason. Maria is still quite upset, but I believe she'll come around.)

What else? I've seen the Pantheon Bazaar, when I went with Maria and Mr. Yates to see how Mr. Crawford has set up the space, and it'll be a fine performance hall for my London debut. Did I forget to mention that? Yes—the Crawfords have invited me to play during the masquerade, my own introduction into the music scene. I hope that it is a success and the first step to a brighter future. Just know that I think of you often, especially since our parting, and I look forward to putting this dreadful business behind us. I would like to visit you in Portsmouth later this year, if you would welcome me. I do miss your sensible approach and calm demeanor.

Yours sincerely,
Edmund

Fanny lowered the letter, disappointment curdling in her stomach. She hadn't realized until that moment that a small part of her harbored hope that her aunts would realize they made a grave mistake and send for her. Or that Edmund would tell them all they were wrong and send for her himself. She'd been the one to notice that her uncle's accident had looked suspicious, she'd done the lion's share of investigative work, and she'd been the one to consult with Miss Bennet. But Edmund . . . he'd revealed all against her wishes. He hadn't even wanted her to investigate in the first place! And somehow, Fanny had been the one to be sent away while Edmund got to go to London and pursue his dreams.

Fanny was not one to expect fairness out of life, but this really was too much.

Frustration welled up in her as fragments of memory and miscellaneous thoughts rushed through her. Maria's triumphant expression. The artwork in Aunt Norris's cottage. Mr. Rushworth's protests as he was grabbed by Tom and Mr. Yates. Her uncle admiring her painting. The Millbrook, sold for an ungodly sum. The lilac scent of Mary leaning close. The sound of her younger siblings all shouting in a too-small house.

What was it that Mary had said? *It does no good to bottle your feelings in.* At the time, sitting in her nursery room, the thought of bellowing her anger and yearning and disappointment seemed silly. But the crashing waves seemed to welcome such wild displays of emotion. She pocketed the letter and looked about, not seeing anyone. Then she glanced back out to sea. She drew in a deep breath and cried out, "Ahhhh!"

She sounded meek, scared. Like a gull that might be injured.

She resolved to try again, drawing breath up from her diaphragm. "Ahhhhhhhhhhhhhh!"

Good, but could be better. She thought of her uncle in a heap at the bottom of the stairs, of the invoice detailing the sale of her lily painting, of every injustice, big or small, that she had experienced in the last two months, the last nine years. Then she opened her mouth once more. *"Ahhhhhhhhhhh!"*

She screamed until she was breathless, and that first gulp of cool air afterward felt like a rebirth of sorts. The gulls swirled ahead, as if startled by her. And why shouldn't they be? She was no powerless mouse.

"Fanny?" a voice called out, buffeted by the wind.

She spun around to see William, climbing the steps of the rampart, puffing slightly. "Are you hurt?" he called out. "I heard shouting!"

"I'm fine!" she called back, turning to meet him. He wore an anxious, almost fearful expression. "Has Mother sent you to find me? She knows about my banishment. Aunt Norris wrote to her."

"No," he gasped, "although yes, I had heard about that. I ran all the way home to fetch you, only for Mother to say you'd gone for a walk to read a letter in peace. I've been looking every-where for you."

"What's the matter?" Fanny asked, alarm rising in her chest.

"Nothing," he said. "At least, I don't think anything's the matter. But you better come to the library, quick. There's a lady come up from London to see you. She says her name is Miss Bennet."

TWENTY

In Which Fanny Makes an Impulsive Decision

FANNY HAD HOPED FOR a letter. She hardly expected to see Miss Bennet in her family's library, wearing a hunter-green traveling dress and perusing the shelves.

"Miss Bennet!" she exclaimed, slightly out of breath. She had all but run from the ramparts. "Whatever are you doing in Portsmouth?"

"Oh, just taking in the sea air," she said, her smile bright.

Disappointment plummeted in Fanny's chest. "Oh."

The other young lady laughed, but not unkindly. "No, silly. We've come to see you."

"We?" Fanny asked, looking about. "Is Mr. Darcy here as well?"

"No," Miss Bennet said, slowly and suddenly uncertain.

"It's me," said a voice to Fanny's left, mostly concealed by one of the wingback chairs.

Fanny turned slowly, scarcely believing her ears. "Mary."

She stood, looking like a skittish cat in a navy traveling dress, her dark hair somewhat windblown and her cheeks pink. "Hello."

"But . . . what . . . why?" Fanny looked between the two of them. She wanted to throw her arms around Mary, but she doubted that such a greeting would be appreciated given how they had parted. "I don't understand."

"We've come with news," Mary said, face grim.

"Bad news?" she asked. "Is it Tom? I had a letter from Edmund just this morning that he broke his leg."

"Nothing to do with your family," Miss Bennet confirmed. She exchanged an inscrutable look with Mary. "Shall we sit?"

"I'll bring you some tea," William said, flipping the sign on the door from "Open" to "Closed." He nudged Fanny in their direction, whispering, "So this is your hardly worth mentioning acquaintance Miss Crawford?"

"Shush!" she whispered, thwacking him on the back as he retreated.

When she turned, Mary smiled shyly at her. "I like your brother."

That pleased Fanny immensely. "I do too," she agreed, then turned to the topic at hand. "But please, tell me why you came all this way. I'm imagining the worst."

Miss Bennet sat across from Fanny. "Did Edmund write of the case?"

Fanny's heartbeat quickened. "No . . . is there news already?"

Something shifted in Miss Bennet's expression. "I shall be blunt—Mr. Rushworth was released."

"What?" Fanny looked between the two of them. They were equally grim-faced. "But how?"

"He maintains his innocence, and there's nothing but circumstantial speculation and Maria's word to implicate him. I don't like bringing cases of he said, she said in a court of law. Ladies, in general, have a habit of not being taken seriously in those halls. Mr. Rushworth has engaged very good, very expensive legal counsel, and they will relentlessly attack Maria's character to cast their client as the innocent. They've already said that Maria accused him so as to wiggle out of the engagement, in order to attach herself to someone else."

Fanny didn't need to guess at who that someone else might be. "So because he has expensive solicitors, you can't accuse him in a court of law?"

"No," Miss Bennet said firmly. "Because I don't have evidence."

Fanny felt as though she'd been pushed down a flight of stairs herself, only she had no idea when or where she'd land. "This is all my fault," she whispered. "I'm sorry, Miss Bennet."

"It's all right," Miss Bennet said, and the hardness in her

voice a moment earlier dissipated.

"No, you don't understand. I was a horrid investigator. I got caught *every* time."

A tiny smile flickered on her lips, and then Miss Bennet said, "But you were the one who uncovered your cousin's suspicious dealings with Mr. Rushworth's business contact."

"Yes," she acknowledged.

"And you discerned that there were missing invoices from Mansfield Emporium's records."

"Only because I overheard Tom say so."

"But you also found the blackmail notes."

"Well, yes." Fanny recalled then what they had led to. "The postbox! Has anyone come to collect the money?"

"Not yet," she said. "But don't worry, I have someone watching around the clock."

"Well, at least that's something," she said with a sigh. "But surely you both didn't come all this way to tell me that Mr. Rushworth has been released?" That could have been a letter.

"Not exactly," Miss Bennet said. "After the judge dismissed the case against Mr. Rushworth, I went to inform your relatives. And that's when I ran into Miss Crawford."

"Henry has been working with Miss Bertram," Mary said. "Rather closely."

"I'm sure they have," Fanny muttered.

"They were together when Miss Bennet informed them of Mr. Rushworth's release. And she asked after you, and that's when they said you missed your family so much, you'd gone to visit them in Portsmouth. Indefinitely."

"They wish!" Fanny said.

"Yes, Miss Crawford was all too happy to enlighten me otherwise. She also had another tidbit that we thought might be of immediate interest to you."

Fanny turned to look at Mary. She seemed to suck in a steadying breath, but her next question was most unexpected. "Am I correct in assuming that your feelings about selling your artwork haven't changed since . . . the last time we spoke?"

The words *the last time we spoke* conjured up images of Mary's hurt expression, of the kiss. And it reminded her how much she still wanted to kiss Mary, even after everything. It took her another moment to process the question before those words. "No, they haven't changed. Why?"

Mary winced. "Then I am very sorry to be the one to tell you this, but . . . your cousins have entered five of your paintings into the showing."

"What?" The pressure that Fanny had released on the ramparts by screaming into the wind returned in a rush.

William arrived with the tea just then and set the tray down. "They can't do that, can they?"

"Henry has been known to take a loose view of what he can and cannot do when it comes to business," Mary said haltingly. She looked at her lap and added, "You are probably wise not to trust him."

Fanny's anger dissipated in the face of Mary's distress. She reached and took Mary's hand, and Mary looked up at her in surprise. Fanny never regretted pushing Mary away more than she did in that moment. The kiss had been impulsive, reckless even. Never had Fanny heard of a lady kissing another lady the way she wanted to kiss a gentleman. Ladies weren't supposed to want to kiss *anyone* according to society's rules.

But . . . Fanny also knew that society rarely accounted for the desires of the heart. And if Tom and Mr. Yates cared for each other the way a couple might, why not Fanny and Mary? The possibility filled her with a surge of hope. But she needed to focus on the matter at hand.

"I'm sorry about how we parted. I was not in my right mind. I'm so glad you've come."

Mary's smile was enough to make hope bloom in her heart again.

"So, my cousins have proven themselves to be dishonest beasts once again. But I'll ask again, Miss Bennet: Why come all this way to tell me this?"

Miss Bennet and Mary once again exchanged significant looks, which made Fanny feel like a bit of a fool. But it was William who spoke up next.

"They came all this way because you must return with them to London, Fanny."

He said the words quite casually, as if he were remarking upon the weather.

"You can't be serious—you didn't really come all this way for that?"

"Yes, we did," Miss Bennet confirmed.

"But . . . what could I possibly do that I haven't managed in all this time?"

"I don't know if you realize this," Miss Bennet said, "but I've had to spend a fair amount of time in court the past few days with Mr. Rushworth."

"And?"

"And . . . tell me honestly, Miss Price. Do you think him capable of the crime of which he stands accused?"

It felt like a trick question. Miss Bennet clearly had her own opinion, but Fanny wasn't quite certain what she was expected to say. "I suppose . . . I believe that he would do anything that Maria asked of him."

"Even kill her father?"

That was the elusive question, wasn't it? Fanny considered it carefully. She thought of the ostentatious way he dressed, how he fawned over Maria and the family, his boastful stories of renovations and grounds upkeep. She tried to picture him sneaking about, setting traps. All she could think was . . . he wasn't the type to get his hands dirty.

But then again, neither was Maria.

"I don't know," she said finally.

"Fair enough," Miss Bennet said. "It's hardly ideal that he was accused prematurely, but Miss Crawford told me that was a heated discussion. But if there is more to this case, then I'm not ready to give in yet."

Fanny looked to Mary, who grimaced. "I don't like to admit it, but there's something going on between my brother and your cousin. They have something planned."

"And you really think that I'm the one to help you find out what that is?"

"Of course!" Miss Bennet said. "You're the one who started this all. You have to see it through."

"You're the only one who can," Mary confirmed.

Fanny looked to William, not for permission but with an apology on her lips. She was afraid that she'd find disappointment or anger in his gaze. But he had been the one to put to words what she must do, and so he was the last one to hold her back. "Go," he insisted.

"But I just got here. And now you want me to say goodbye?"

He just kept shaking his head, smiling in that unbothered way of his. "I'd rather say goodbye as you head to a future you want than see you stay here and be miserable."

"I'm not miserable here," Fanny protested.

"That's because you haven't had time to grow bored yet."

A tiny huff of a laugh escaped her. "But what about you?"

"What about me? I have this library. And my patrons."

Fanny raised an eyebrow. She was fairly certain by "patrons" he meant a particular young lady who seemed to fancy him a lot. "And if I leave, will the company of your patrons be sufficient?"

"What will be sufficient for me is the knowledge that my beloved sister, who will write me often, will be chasing her own happiness."

Fanny couldn't help it. She launched to her feet and threw her arms around William.

Fanny hid her tears with a smile as she released him. Then she turned to Mary and Miss Bennet.

"All right, let's go."

TWENTY-ONE

In Which Fanny Finds Bravery
in an Unexpected Moment

THEY SET OFF FOR London in a large black coach that gleamed with the Pemberley crest. Miss Bennet made a big show of rolling her eyes when Fanny beheld it.

"I know, it's quite ostentatious. But Darcy worries terribly when I travel outside of London, and he insisted." She paused as she watched the driver load Fanny's bags, then conceded, "However, his influence does have its uses."

"Is Mr. Darcy her . . . fiancé?" Mary whispered.

Fanny shrugged. She wasn't quite sure how to explain who Mr. Darcy was to Miss Bennet, because she wasn't entirely certain herself. "Something like that?"

"Whatever they are to each other, we shall be traveling in

style," Mary confirmed. "It was by far the most comfortable journey I've ever undertaken."

The drive passed quickly as the three of them discussed their next steps. Miss Bennet determined the best thing to do was to attend the masquerade ball and try to discern what exactly Henry and Maria had planned. She didn't come out and say she suspected that Maria's business dealings had gotten Sir Thomas killed, but she didn't have to—Fanny shared the suspicion and was all too willing to investigate once more in the hope of finally finding evidence that would stick.

That evening they spent the night at an inn, where they shared a meal in a private sitting room and then a room for the night. Fanny was desperate to pull Mary aside and apologize in more exact words for what had occurred between them, but it felt quite impossible with Lizzie never more than a few paces away. Mary and Fanny shared the wider of the two beds in the room, and as she climbed beneath the covers, trying not to sneak peeks at Mary in her billowing nightgown and dark hair tumbling down in a messy plait, Fanny felt as though it would be a very long night.

She held herself as stiff as a board, careful not to edge too close to the center of the bed as she felt Mary shift and settle. Everyone was silent after their quick murmured good-nights. Fanny's heart was racing. Did Mary feel the same tension? Was she nervous that Fanny might force herself onto her once more? She couldn't help but relive that kiss over and over, wondering what exactly Mary thought about it.

Gradually, she heard the sound of breathing give way to a loud snore. It was Lizzie, she was certain. *At least one of us should get our rest*, Fanny thought grimly, carefully moving to shift into a more comfortable position.

"Are you awake?" came Mary's soft voice.

Fanny swallowed hard. "Yes."

"Do you think this will work?"

Of course, she spoke of their plan. *Focus on what really matters*, Fanny admonished herself.

"I don't know," Fanny answered truthfully. "But I suppose nothing will happen if we don't try."

There was a quiet rustle of bedclothes as Mary turned, and then Fanny sensed she was much closer. "I'm nervous," she admitted. "What if we go to all the effort, and—"

"You don't have to do this, you know," Fanny hurried to reassure her. "You and your brother only arrived after my uncle died. This is not your mess."

"But I feel like I'm a part of it," she whispered, and Fanny had never felt more warmed by that. "Henry always gets what he wants, and he takes advantage of opportunities wherever he can. I should have told him to not insist on offering you representation."

"That wasn't your fault," Fanny protested.

"I know, but . . . I've kept quiet about his misdeeds for so long. I told myself it was because it never made any difference if

I spoke against him or not. I think I even convinced myself . . ."

Fanny strained her ears against the darkness, hoping to pick out what Mary would say next. But there was nothing. "You convinced yourself of what?" she prodded gently.

"That . . . if Henry represented you, then it meant I didn't have to say farewell for good when we finally left Mansfield and returned to London."

It felt like a confession and an invitation all at once. Fanny's heart thudded with wild joy, but she was afraid of saying the wrong thing again. "I'm sorry," she whispered. "For how I acted that last night."

"Are you . . . apologizing for what you did, or what you said?" Mary asked.

Fanny desperately wished she could make out Mary's expression in the darkness. "For what I said. It was cruel, and I only said it because I was scared. As for what I did . . ." That kiss was seared into her memory, and it would be until the day she died. "I hope that I didn't overstep."

"No." The word was quiet, but lonely.

All her life, Fanny had been timid and anxious, prone to overthink every word and action. But now, she wanted—no, *needed*—to explain herself. The prospect was terrifying, but somehow, she found a deep well of courage within her to say, "What I feel for you . . . I have only felt for one other person before, and he . . ."

She was unable to finish. Not because she didn't want to,

or she'd lost her nerve, but because she didn't know what to say.

"And he . . . was a he," Mary said.

"Yes," she whispered. She was holding herself so still her muscles were beginning to cramp, but she was so afraid of what Mary might say next that she couldn't relax.

"And what I feel for you . . . I've only ever felt that way for other ladies. Do you suppose that means there's something wrong with me?"

"No." The word sprang to her lips without conscious thought. How could Mary be wrong? If she was, then this part of her, the part of Fanny that longed to close the distance between them and kiss her again, was wrong, too.

"I'm glad to hear you say it," she whispered. She felt Mary move again, and then Mary's hand was brushing her arm, reaching out for her. Fanny extended her own hand, and their fingers curled around each other. The reassurance of Mary's touch made Fanny's muscles relax slowly, and eventually Mary's breath steadied into the deep rhythm of sleep.

But sleep eluded Fanny for what felt like hours. She couldn't help but stare into the darkness, holding Mary's hand, and wonder how she could bottle up this feeling of small, quiet bravery to hold on to until tomorrow.

As Mr. Darcy's carriage drew closer to London, the landscape gave way from fields and farms to homes and buildings, all packed closer and closer together. It was on a much larger scale than Portsmouth, and Fanny felt the return of her nerves. Soon, she would be confronting her family once more. Soon, she'd see Edmund again. She'd didn't want to think about what it meant that his letter hadn't mentioned that her paintings had been brought to London. Perhaps he hadn't known? Surely he *must* know. Or had he simply assumed that a sale would be to her benefit and therefore she would thank him later?

Fanny didn't want to think that Edmund, her oldest ally, would consciously hurt her.

As they drew into the city proper, it seemed as though everything from storehouses to stables, residences to restaurants, had been pressed up against each other like some giant hand had nudged them closer and closer until the streets and paths were nothing but narrow ribbons, jammed with people. Their progress slowed thanks to the thick traffic, and Fanny's eyes felt permanently widened. London seemed to unfold unendingly before them, and she marveled that the driver had any clue where he was going.

"It's all so much," she whispered.

"You get used to it," Lizzie assured her. Then she added after a pause, "Or I suppose you don't, and you leave."

Fanny could scarcely imagine choosing to live in such a place. "There are no trees!"

"Not here," Lizzie agreed. "But some gardens have them, and there are plenty in Hyde Park."

"Where's that?" Fanny asked.

"Far from here," was the response.

What struck Fanny the most was how many people there were on foot, winding in between carts and carriages in such a way that suggested they did not value their own lives. One such figure, a dark-skinned boy of no more than twelve or thirteen, jogged alongside their carriage and then leapt onto the footboard, pressing his face against the glass. Fanny jerked back in surprise. "Um, Miss Bennet?"

But the young solicitor showed no sign of shock or dismay at the sight of their stowaway. "Please, call me Lizzie. That's just Fred." To the young boy, she said, "Fred, you gave us a fright! What are you doing here?"

"Been watching the main road for you," he shouted through the glass. "Bloody conspicuous, this carriage."

As if this were a completely reasonable response, Lizzie leaned across Mary and Fanny and slid open the glass. "You're supposed to be watching the postbox!"

"Aye," he agreed, sparing Mary and Fanny a brief glance before saying, "About that."

The carriage kept rolling through the streets, but the air went still inside. "What happened?" Lizzie demanded.

"Someone set fire to a clothes peddler's stall outside the postal station this morning," the boy said.

"Tell me they didn't," Lizzie said. She didn't sound mad per se, but Fanny shivered at the commanding tone.

"Sorry, miss. I figured it for a distraction, but the entire street is wood and wares and it was pandemonium. Lucky the fire didn't spread, but whoever it was emptied the box and was gone."

Lizzie let out a very unladylike curse and leaned back against the seat. "It's not your fault, Fred. Someone was desperate indeed if they were willing to risk a fire like that. Keep your ears open, and see if you can rally a crew to the Pantheon tonight, will you?"

The boy nodded and then leapt from the moving carriage into the busy street. Fanny let out a small cry of surprise, but when she leaned forward to look out the window, he was nowhere to be seen.

"Don't worry about Fred, he's like a cat," Lizzie said. "Always lands on his feet. Now as for our case . . ."

"If someone took the money," Mary said, "that means—"

"Could it have been Mr. Rushworth?" Fanny asked, even though she wasn't fully convinced.

"Possibly. But whoever it is, they're taking more risks and acting desperate. That usually only means one thing."

"What?" Fanny asked.

Lizzie wouldn't meet her eyes. "They're getting ready to cut and run."

TWENTY-TWO

In Which Fanny Finds a Missing Link

"WE'RE GETTING CLOSE TO your family's house," Mary observed, peering out the window. "Are you ready?"

"No," Fanny answered. "But I suppose I never shall be, so we might as well get it over with."

Sometime between arriving in London proper and now, the sun had slunk toward the horizon and evening settled onto the streets. They found themselves in a more genteel neighborhood—the streets were cleaner, people weren't lingering on stoops, laundry was not aired outside where anyone could see, and children didn't play in the gutters. The houses were grander and spread farther apart. The carriage slowed to a halt before a respectable-looking stone town house with tall, narrow windows and a black door that made Fanny feel uneasy somehow. This was a very buttoned-up residence compared to the sprawling and casual grandeur of Mansfield.

They had agreed it would be best for Fanny to go inside alone, so as not to raise suspicions. It would be up to her to get herself to the masquerade that evening. Despite her fatigue at spending nearly two full days on the road, anticipation rushed through her. Lizzie watched her closely. "All right?"

Fanny nodded and gave Mary a reassuring smile. "Yes. I'll see you both in a few hours."

"See you then," Mary echoed, reaching out to squeeze Fanny's hand. That simple gesture sent the blood rushing through Fanny's veins and gave her the strength she needed to step down from the carriage.

The driver handed over her valise, and with one last wave, she turned to face the house. She hadn't even reached the stoop when the austere black door was opened by the familiar face of Mansfield's butler. If he was surprised to see her standing in the street, far away from where she ought to be in Portsmouth, he didn't show it.

"Hello," Fanny began, suddenly uncertain. Would he deny her entry? But she needn't have worried.

"They're in the drawing room, miss," he said, stepping aside to allow Fanny entry. Out of the corner of her eye, she saw the curtains twitch.

Fanny had never been permitted to travel with the Bertrams whenever they left Mansfield Park, and so she had never set eyes on their London residence before. She had been expecting some small, outdated little town house just a bit too neglected to be considered fashionable. But although the furnishings and the wallpaper weren't new by any stretch, it had an air of sophistication to it. She was led to two double doors, which were opened to reveal a sitting room full of her family members.

"Fanny!" Julia cried from her position near the window. "I thought that was you, but I wasn't sure until I heard your voice. What on earth are you doing here?"

"It's highly improper," Aunt Norris announced, already standing from her seat on the settee. "How did you get here? Who accompanied you?"

"No one sent for you!" Maria proclaimed from her position by the fire. "What are you doing here?"

Tom sat on a divan, his leg propped up and encased in plaster. "Let her speak, why don't you?"

"I can ask a reasonable question, Tom!"

"Right, like anything you say is—"

"Would you two stop squabbling like children?" Aunt Norris cut in.

Fanny merely waited out the chaos as she scanned the room. No sign of Edmund, and Mr. Yates was sitting in a chair near Tom, too engrossed in his newspaper to do more than glance up.

Finally, they seemed to realize that Fanny had yet to explain herself and turned to her expectantly. Aunt Bertram stroked Pug's head and said, "Oh, Fanny, why come to London at all? It's a terrible place."

"Because I believe I have some unfinished business," Fanny stated.

That sent them all into another round of rapid-fire questions and exclamations.

"Business!"

"What does she mean?"

"Well, isn't this just rich. . . ."

"Fanny doesn't have—"

"Ahem!" Fanny cleared her throat rather dramatically. "If I may, please?"

Her family looked upon her in astonishment. Fanny wondered if this was what Maria felt like all the time, demanding attention. It was rather a lot of pressure, but she felt powerful, too. "I received word that my paintings were to be shown at Mr. Crawford's masquerade this evening, despite my *explicit* wishes that my work not be showcased," she said, not having to work too hard at sounding disapproving.

Her family exchanged confused looks, and Aunt Norris appeared as though she'd been sucking on lemons.

It was Tom who spoke up first. "Edmund said it was all right. He said that before you left for Portsmouth, you'd given permission."

Now it was Fanny's turn for shock. "But, he wouldn't . . . no.

It must be a misunderstanding."

"It's too late now," Maria told her. "We've already had them framed, and everything is all set up for tonight. You can't pull them." The look on her face dared Fanny to argue.

"Well, then I know you'll agree that I have a right to be there." She stared Maria down, trying not to show how satisfied she was to turn her own dirty tactic against her.

"You don't have the right to *insert* yourself," Aunt Norris began, but shockingly, it was Maria who interrupted.

"If she wants to come to the masquerade, why should we stop her?" Maria looked at Fanny's muddy hem and said, "I am certain you won't be the only . . . bohemian artist to ever show up uninvited to a society party."

At one time, Fanny might have wilted under such an insult, but now she kept focused on her goal. "How kind of you, Maria," she said, which startled her cousin enough that all she did was shoot Fanny a look of disgust before flouncing out of the room.

Aunt Bertram tutted. "Julia, surely you can find something for your cousin to wear tonight?"

"Does that mean I can get a new dress from the modiste before we leave?"

Fanny rolled her eyes, but Lady Bertram merely waved her hand in acknowledgment.

Julia grinned. "In that case, you can have my violet gown. But you better not spill anything on it."

Her aunts rose and swept out of the room, likely to see

to the arrangements and discuss Fanny's audacity, and Fanny decided that she'd had enough of standing in the doorway. She took the chair across from Tom and Mr. Yates and helped herself to a cup of lukewarm tea from the service on the table. She didn't even care that it had clearly been sitting for a while—the day's travel and her nerves at facing down her family had been surprisingly draining. But not so much that she felt like crawling into a corner and hiding. She felt . . . determined.

"Portsmouth has changed you, Fanny," Tom remarked with an amused smile. "Has the sea breeze blown the meekness out of you?"

She went still, the teacup half raised to her lips. "And so what if it has?"

"No complaints from me. Although I suppose you've always had a stubborn streak. Aunt Norris hasn't been able to stop going on about your refusal of Crawford."

Fanny made a tiny face as she sipped her tea, and Tom laughed as he sat up, shifting carefully so as not to jostle his leg. "It's quite rude to anger her and then go off, leaving us to endure her moods."

Fanny set the teacup down with a neat clink. "I didn't leave willingly, if you'll remember."

"Don't be cross, Fanny. Maria was furious at you for exposing Rushworth. Probably best you left and let everyone calm down."

"I would think you'd all be grateful," Fanny said. "Or would you rather happily consort with criminals as long as no one's reputation is ruined?"

"It's not so simple as that, and you know it," Tom began, but Fanny didn't want to hear his excuses.

"I've decided that I can no longer wait for my inheritance, Tom," she announced, careful to look him in the eye and not waver. "I trust that after the success of the auction and this evening's opening, that shouldn't be too inconvenient for you?"

"I . . . what? I mean, Fanny. Why the hurry?" Tom swallowed hard, then forced a laugh. "I mean, surely there's no need for such a trifling sum right away? A new dress can wait. . . ."

"I don't intend to buy any dresses, and no, it cannot wait." Fanny kept her voice firm but light. "After all, I have no idea when I might be turned out during the next temper tantrum."

"That was a onetime affair, Fanny. And no one *truly* meant to leave you at Portsmouth forever."

Fanny was certain that was exactly what the Bertrams intended, and she decided that it was time to stop playing into their hands. "Even so, I think it's best that I take the money for safekeeping now. You understand, surely? You wouldn't deny your poor, penniless cousin her trifling sum, would you?"

Tom gaped at her and then seemed to realize the trap he'd walked into. "Of course not. I'll . . . see what I can do."

"Thank you," she said with a smile as sweet as the sugar

339

she'd stirred into her tea. "And I trust that will be in addition to the proceeds of the sale of *my* paintings?"

"Less the dealer's fee," Tom said without missing a beat.

"I could still pull the paintings," she reminded him. "It would be a terrible nuisance just hours before the event, but I have been told I can be quite bothersome at times."

"Fine," he gritted out, and even Mr. Yates had put down his paper to stare at her in surprise. "But you'll have to deal with Crawford if you expect him to give up his fee."

"Oh, I look forward to speaking with him later," Fanny promised, even though the exact opposite was true. She'd just downed the last of her lukewarm tea—who knew standing up for oneself could be so draining?—when she heard footsteps stomping through the hall and Edmund burst in.

"Tom, has something happened? Aunt Norris is in a state, and— Fanny!"

She rose and turned to face Edmund, heart racing. "Hello, Edmund."

He wore an evening jacket, which felt incongruous with the early hour. His hair was neatly combed back and seemed to shine unnaturally in the light. Was he wearing hair pomade? Fanny felt the old familiar pangs of excitement and longing when she saw him, but they were curiously diminished in the moment, so much so that she wondered if she truly felt them or was just recalling the sensation of them.

He blinked in surprise. "What . . . how did you get here?"

"Coach dropped her off a quarter of an hour ago," Tom said dryly. "Apparently a little bird told her that Crawford is showing her paintings."

Tom was winding Edmund up for a reaction and Fanny decided to cut him off before he could stir up any more drama. "Thank you for explaining the situation, Tom. Edmund, could I have a moment?"

"I can't stay," Edmund said with a quick shake of his head. "I agreed to get to the Pantheon early, for a rehearsal. I'm performing."

"I understand," Fanny said, but she was persistent. "But it would just be a moment."

"Please don't be cross with me," he begged. "I only let him have your paintings because I thought that if they sold, you could have the proceeds and then you wouldn't have to stay in Portsmouth."

As far as an explanation went, it was reasonable enough. She wanted to believe him, to forgive him. But a small part of her wondered in what world Edmund would take such actions without once consulting her. "That was very . . . thoughtful. But it wasn't your decision to make."

"Listen, Fanny, I know it's hardly ideal. But nothing about our circumstances has been ideal . . . lately." He seemed nervous speaking in front of Tom and Mr. Yates, who were clearly watching the pair of them as though they were actors in a play put on for their own private entertainment. "I want to make it up to you. Did you get my letter? I was going to come to Ports-mouth after the masquerade."

"I got the letter," she said, and then the clock struck half-past five, and Edmund swore under his breath.

"I'm late, Fanny. Shall we talk about this tonight? No, in the morning would be best. I'll go down on my knees and apol-ogize a thousand times if you want, but a coach should be out front for me, and I mustn't be late." He turned and looked about the room, his mind clearly elsewhere. "I'm missing a sheet of music, and surely it must be . . . Aha!"

He plucked a sheet of paper from under a stack on the table and held it aloft. He flashed a grin at Fanny, but she couldn't match it. His betrayal was too fresh, even though he'd done it for her. "Now, wish me luck!"

"Luck," Fanny said without much feeling.

"I'll see you there tonight?" he asked Fanny as he strode across the room. "I'm so glad you're here, truly, and we'll—*Ahh!*"

Edmund was upright, walking across the drawing room one moment, and the next he was sprawled out on the carpet, flat on his face. "Edmund!" Fanny cried out, and rushed to his side while Tom and Mr. Yates erupted into laughter. Fanny helped Edmund to his feet and then spotted the cause of his tumble at the same moment Edmund did—the tip of one of Tom's crutches. It had been placed strategically in Edmund's path.

"Grow up," Edmund growled at Tom as he straightened his

jacket and brushed off his knees. "We aren't schoolboys any-more."

"Too bad," Tom said through laughter. "You knew how to take a joke back then."

Edmund gave him a venomous look and strode out of the room. They all heard the slam of the front door, and Tom and Mr. Yates burst into another round of guffaws.

"That was cruel," Fanny declared, turning to fix Tom with a glare. "I don't care if you're upset at being laid up with a bro-ken leg, you could have hurt him."

But neither Tom nor Mr. Yates paid her any mind. "I've been waiting years for someone to bring Edmund down like that," Mr. Yates crowed. "I won't give you full marks for style, but for managing a face-plant, I salute you, sir!"

Tom took a mock bow in his seat, and Fanny shook her head in disgust. "The two of you are horrid."

"Turnabout is fair play, Fanny," Tom said. "Your precious Edmund and his mate Rollins were hellions at Eton. Quite the reputation, those two."

Curiosity got the better of her. "What do you mean?"

"All they lived for was pranks. The only reason Edmund never got kicked out was because Father sold the headmaster a Weyn portrait at a criminally low rate. Poor Rollins lost his spot eventually."

This was a side of Edmund she'd never heard of before. "What kind of pranks?"

343

"The usual," Mr. Yates mused. "Frogs in bedsheets, swapping out pie fillings for table scraps."

Fanny wrinkled her nose. Is that what boys got up to at school? It sounded positively juvenile. "That hardly seems remarkable," she said.

"Well, it was Rollins who pulled off the most infamous prank of all," Tom pointed out.

"He once tripped the headmaster," Mr. Yates said, a note of reverence in his voice. "At the beginning of the term, during chapel. He laid a trip wire across the floor and wound it around a pew. No one noticed a bit of wire on the floor, so the whole procession commenced without issue, and then, just as the headmaster was getting ready to walk right back out, the sneaky bugger pulls the wire taut and down he went!"

Tom and Mr. Yates burst into another peel of laughter, but Fanny's veins ran cold.

"It was a moment that went down in school history," Tom continued. "In the ruckus, he tossed the wire aside, so it looked like it could have been one of fifteen lads. No one thought that *Rollins*, of all people, had it in him. Boys were blaming each other left and right. It wasn't until he showed a bunch of us how he'd done it that anyone believed him."

"It's always the quiet ones," Mr. Yates added. "His father was what, some kind of inventor? Handy with pulleys and all that."

"Was," Tom emphasized. "Didn't I mention? Old Mr.

Rollins was in debt up to his eyeballs. The only way he got the bailiffs out of his house was by selling it out from under them."

The two of them were too busy reliving their schoolboy antics to notice that Fanny had gone still with horror, but when Tom finally realized that she wasn't laughing along with them, he took one look at her face and faltered. A peeved expression crossed his face. "Oh, Fanny. Don't be such a wet blanket. It was just a prank."

A strange sense of calm descended upon her. *Maintain your composure*, she told herself sternly. And so she gave herself a little shake and said with as much condescension as she could manage, "Prank or no prank, someone could have gotten seriously hurt."

"Edmund was fine just now. Ruffled, but fine."

"And his friend . . . Rollins?" Fanny asked. "What is his first name?"

"Why, do you want an introduction? I have to warn you, he's looking for a future wife with a little more than twenty pounds to her name."

"Answer the question, Tom."

"Percy. Why?"

It had to be a horrible, awful coincidence.

Did Tom and Mr. Yates realize what they had just revealed? Clearly not—they were still chortling to themselves. She closed her eyes and tried to recall precisely what Edmund had said that awful night when he accused Mr. Rushworth—she was fairly certain all Edmund had revealed was that someone had set up a trip wire.

Fanny relived the moments in the warehouse, trying to place everyone at the moment of the fall. Tom and Mr. Yates had stood a few paces from the bottom of the stairs, and Maria had been right next to them. Sir Thomas had been a stride away from the top of the stairs when he'd tripped. And Edmund . . .

Edmund had been nowhere near the bottom of the stairs.

But he had been almost directly underneath Sir Thomas.

He would have had the opportunity to set his trap, she knew. Just as any of them would have had an opportunity. And if he laid the wire on the floor, no one might have noticed it in the dusty, busy storehouse. Stray bits of wire, errant nails, and sawdust collected everywhere. It explained how they all had been trooping up and down the stairs without tripping. All Edmund had to do was ensure he was in a position to pull the wire taut at the right time.

And then later, when they'd gone back to the storehouse, he'd not wanted Fanny to follow him upstairs after Pug. Had it been because he'd needed to remove the evidence?

How could she have gotten things so miserably wrong?

Suddenly, Tom stopped laughing. He looked at Fanny, eyes wide. "Wait, you don't think . . ."

"Unfortunately," Fanny said, "I do."

TWENTY-THREE

*In Which Fanny Realizes More
Than One Plot Is Afoot*

ON ANY OTHER OCCASION, Fanny would have been delighted when the Bertrams' carriage stopped before the Pantheon on Oxford Street. The square front was elegantly adorned with pillars and the long rectangular windows cast a warm glow on the street below, where partygoers awaited entry. Inside proved even more lavish. They passed through a fine vestibule, where Fanny, Maria, Julia, and Aunt Norris left their cloaks with the attendant, and through a cardroom before coming upon the Pantheon's crowning glory: a rotunda that served as an assembly hall, with a sloping grand staircase leading to a second-story gallery, crowned by a dome.

But Fanny couldn't appreciate the architecture or the fine decor, nor did she take note of the artwork up for auction, carefully staged along the gallery. She barely registered the finely dressed attendees with their flamboyant masks. She needed to find Lizzie Bennet.

"Stay close," Aunt Norris grumbled when Fanny tried to slip away. "I don't want to have to be chasing after you all evening."

"Then don't," Fanny told her, and she couldn't even enjoy the look of shock on her aunt's face as she stepped away, desperately searching the crowd.

Fanny was supposed to tail Maria all evening while Mary stayed close to her brother. Lizzie promised to be in attendance, and she had made vague references to "resources," should they need them. But Maria could steal the crown jewels from under the nose of the mad king himself, and Fanny wouldn't care.

She needed to find Edmund.

She didn't *want* to believe him responsible. Just because her cousin and his friend had told her a story of schoolboy shenanigans that just so happened to match the exact method by which her uncle died didn't *prove* anything. And Lizzie Bennet was the one who'd urged her to chase after proof, not just circumstantial evidence.

And yet.

Fanny couldn't help but recall all of the instances during which Edmund seemed just out of reach. The way he'd been reluctant to believe her. How he'd just so happened to show up at the storehouse during the ball—to make sure she was all right. But what if it was to ensure she didn't discover anything? And he'd been the one to arrive at the conclusion that Mr. Rushworth must be responsible, despite the lack of evidence and, frankly, common sense.

However, planting the false lead in Fanny's mind had been successful in making her impatient. She'd broken into Mary's room looking for evidence of their collusion and had been caught. Mr. Crawford had offered Fanny representation as a way to control her. And when Fanny had refused . . . Edmund had recklessly accused Mr. Rushworth despite knowing that Maria would have been so angry, she would have done exactly what Edmund had long predicted: find a way to send Fanny packing.

But *why*?

Why would he want to harm their uncle? Certainly Sir Thomas was not without his faults, but he'd been kind to his two young wards when everyone else dismissed them.

Fanny had no clear answers, and so she wanted to believe that she'd gotten the wrong end of the stick, somehow. But when someone grasped her elbow, she was so on edge that she whirled around and caught the hand that had startled her. It belonged to a beautiful figure resplendent in very light pink silk with gray beading and pearls. Mary lowered her pink mask, revealing a furrowed brow. "Are you all right?"

"Oh, thank God," Fanny said. "Have you seen Lizzie?"

"Not yet, but I'm sure she's not far off. You look as though someone stepped on your grave. What's the matter?"

But there were far too many people pressing closely around them for Fanny to unburden herself. She shook her head and said, "Not here."

Mary nodded her understanding. "Come with me. I have something to show you."

The tone of her voice suggested that it was serious, and the strength of her grip conveyed urgency. Mary wound her way through the party, leading Fanny to a large painting. A painting that Fanny recognized straightaway. They stopped to the side, several paces away from the other guests, while Fanny gaped.

"But . . . what? How?"

It was the Millbrook painting, boasting a new gilded frame and placed in a position of honor in the rotunda. Fanny's eyes welled up to see the familiar picture that she'd so loved, that she never thought she'd see again. And she had to admit . . . it was nice to see it in such a fine hall, where it could shine.

"While I was in Portsmouth, my brother persuaded Lord Allerton to allow him to display it for one evening only, as a show of his success. Lord Allerton agreed, but . . ."

Fanny tore her gaze away from the painting to look at Mary. "But?"

"Fanny . . . I don't think that's the Millbrook."

Her words were whispered, and Fanny almost didn't hear

her. The implication of what Mary was saying was slow to reach her, and Fanny looked back at the painting with horror. "You're saying . . ."

"I think that one is *yours*."

"No," she whispered. Not because she didn't think that Maria and Crawford would stoop that low, but because she couldn't believe that her version of that painting would be good enough to fool a crowd of people. "They can't have switched them."

Fanny had never seen Mary look so serious. "I'm pretty certain that they did. Millbrook's signature is on the painting, but . . ."

"I never signed my replica," Fanny insisted. "I wouldn't have gone that far."

"Come look."

Doing her best to appear casual, Mary linked arms with Fanny and pulled her closer to the painting. It had drawn a throng of art appreciators, so they had to wait to get close enough. All the while, Fanny was studying it, recalling every dissatisfied brushstroke or tiny spot where she hadn't quite been able to get the color right. There were a hundred different ways to tell if this canvas was hers or the real thing, but as they drew close, Fanny looked to the second sister's eyes.

They were blue. Blue like Mary's. Not the brown of the original painting.

"It's mine," she whispered to Mary, pulse racing. "You're right."

Mary had to pull her away and steer her to a seat. She couldn't hide her excitement. "We've done it! We've discovered them." Then, she seemed to realize the full extent of what they'd discovered—a plot to *steal* a very valuable work of art. "Do you think the original is close by?"

"I don't know," Fanny whispered. "Do you suppose this was their plan all along? Sell the Millbrook, pocket the profits, then steal it back?"

"All along?" Mary asked. "No. My brother didn't know anything about your replica until Edmund brought it up."

Edmund really must learn to keep his mouth shut, Fanny thought.

"But I won't pretend that my brother is not an opportunist," Mary allowed. "He would have seen your replica and thought that there must be some advantage to be had, somehow."

"Unless . . . ," Fanny said, and she stopped to think very carefully. "Unless it wasn't entirely his idea."

"What?"

She looked up at Mary. "All those paintings sitting in Aunt Norris's cottage. Maria supposedly sold them, remember? And we know that someone came and picked them up, because Anna told me about the man with the Scottish accent. But then she bought them back at the same price. What if . . ."

"You think she's running some kind of forgery scam?" Mary's voice dropped to such a whisper Fanny could barely hear her last two words.

"I think that's exactly what she's been doing."

They stared at each other, and Fanny felt her heart race as her mind swirled with questions. Had Mr. Stewart approached Mr. Rushworth and Maria with a proposition? Or had Mr. Rushworth not even known? Who was the artist? How many paintings had they forged? How many hapless collectors had been scammed?

And were the paintings in Aunt Norris's cottage originals or fakes?

"How are we going to put a stop to this?" Mary asked. "Without you revealing . . ."

Fanny hadn't thought of that. If she told the truth, it would look as though *she* were in on it. "I don't know. But you need to find Lizzie and tell her what you've discovered."

She stood, but Mary didn't move. "Fanny? What's the matter?"

Somehow, being presented with the betrayal of her artistic work paled in comparison to her suspicions about Edmund. Fanny didn't know how to tell her. Fanny didn't want to believe it herself. If she could just find him, demand an explanation, give him a chance, then . . .

"I have to find Edmund," she managed to say. "If this is true, then surely he's involved in some way. He told me that he thought I wouldn't mind having my work sold, because I could use the money, and then he ran off. I have to find him."

Mary's gaze was absent of jealousy or suspicion—there was

simply concern. At some point, Fanny would have to tell Mary about . . . well, about her complicated feelings for Edmund. And the kiss Mary had witnessed the morning she left Mansfield. She'd have to be honest about what she wanted, but right now, she didn't have time.

Mary leaned in close and brushed her lips against Fanny's cheek. "Go. But be careful."

Fanny knew Edmund well enough to know that he would not be found socializing among the partygoers ahead of his performance, no matter how much he might want to make connections. Since he was not on the stage, where a string quartet was currently playing something sedate and pleasant, he was likely behind the scenes, pacing off his nervous energy.

Fanny circled the perimeter of the rotunda, searching any door or hall that might lead off to a private staging area. She found one behind a drape of red velvet curtain, and with a furtive glance to ensure that no one was watching, she slipped behind the curtain.

It concealed a shadowy hall that had a few closed doors on both sides. Fanny crept along, trying each door as she went. They were all locked, but the third one was ajar with a small bit of light peeking through. She hovered outside, listening carefully. There was no sound from inside, and she was caught between wondering if she ought to knock or nudge open the door.

In her indecision, she didn't notice anyone behind her until she caught a tiny flash of movement in the corner of her eye. She startled in surprise, an excuse already flying to her lips, but the person behind her was no partygoer or master of ceremonies demanding to know why she was snooping about: it was a man, dressed for a party with a full, unadorned white mask covering his face. The effect was uncanny, and it stunned Fanny into momentary speechlessness. This gave the masked figure enough time to advance on Fanny, and she realized in a sickening instant the man meant to grab her.

She stumbled backward with rough gasp, back hitting the door that had been previously ajar. The man's gloved fingers caught on her necklace, and with a frustrated grunt he yanked at the strand, as if she were a dog on a leash. A sharp burn against the back of her neck made Fanny cry out, followed by a heartbreaking snap as pearls scattered everywhere. Fanny felt the door behind her give and she tried to keep her balance as she stepped into the room, scrambling away from the figure. Her pulse was thudding, and fear had taken over her body. The masked figure had her cornered, and the only thing to do now would be to call out, scream, hope that someone would hear her over the sound of a hundred mingling voices and the string quartet. . . .

But just as she drew in a breath to scream, the man brought up his gloved hand over her face. Fanny caught a glimpse of something white in his hand, like a rag, and then it was over her face. The chemical burn filled her nose, and against her will she inhaled the noxious scent. Her head swam around in the horrid smell, and her knees went weak.

The last thing she saw before she passed out was that curious white mask, blank except for two dark slits for eyes that watched as she succumbed into unconsciousness.

TWENTY-FOUR

In Which All of Fanny's Worst Fears Are Confirmed

IT WAS THE PAIN, more than anything, that brought Fanny around.

Her shoulders ached, and her fingers tingled. Her tailbone felt numb, and her legs and bottom were cold. Her head hung forward in a way that made her neck scream, and there was a fuzziness to her thoughts that made her feel as though she was experiencing everything in slow, exaggerated motions. As the confusion cleared, she could smell traces of that nasty chemical that had so neatly taken her out, and her stomach churned.

But worst of all was the panic that set in as she took in her surroundings. Where was she? What had happened? How long had she been asleep?

Gritting her teeth, she forced herself to breathe evenly, and eventually her stomach decided *not* to empty its contents in her lap. As she slowly brought her head up, she took inventory of her circumstances: she was seated on a dirty, scuffed marble floor, legs straight out but her skirts and dress neatly arranged around her, as if she'd decided on her own to sit on the floor. Her back was against something hard and unyielding, and her wrists were tied behind this thing—she craned her neck around and determined it was a pillar.

As she attempted to roll out her shoulders, she gave a soft hiss of pain. Beyond her, something rustled in the shadows. She went still, eyes searching in the semi-lit room for any sign of life.

The room was narrow and long, with tall ceilings and only a few candles sputtering on stands, and a single lantern near a faraway double door. Crates lay strewn about, along with tools and makeshift tables. It looked like a receiving area for shipments of artwork. *Not good*, Fanny thought, *but better than some unknown cellar.* She must still be at the Pantheon, perhaps in a back or side room. That meant that whoever had knocked her out hadn't taken her very far.

Of course, no one knew *where* she was, either.

She heard footsteps and her first instinct was to call out for help, but she resisted. She didn't know exactly *who* might hear her, and what if the wrong sort of person, the man in that dreadful mask, came running and gave her more of those horrible fumes?

Fanny just had the thought that maybe she ought to pretend

to still be unconscious when a figure in an evening suit stepped out from behind a tall stack of crates. Fanny caught sight of his face and nearly whimpered in relief. "Edmund!"

Edmund didn't hasten his pace. He was strolling, she realized, as if he were making the rounds at a party. The sickness she'd managed to calm returned in a torrent and she had to swallow the bile rising in the back of her throat. But curiously, she wasn't scared. Horrified, confused, heartbroken. But she'd never *truly* been afraid of Edmund.

Maybe she should have been.

He stopped inches from her feet and crouched down to look her in the eye. He was wearing a bemused smile. "Oh Fanny," he said. "You seem to have a knack for getting caught."

It took her a long moment before she found her voice. And then, the only word that warbled out was, "Why?"

He sighed as he stood, and Fanny thought for a moment he might be leaving her there without an answer. But he just reached for a plain wooden chair and dragged it over so that he was several feet away when he sat down. He regarded her with a wry smile and said, "I told you no good would come of your investigation."

Unexpected laughter bubbled out of her, surprising them both. "That's rather rich, coming from a murderer."

Edmund's genial expression slipped, and she caught a glimpse of the same cold fury she'd seen earlier, when Tom tripped him. "I don't know why you're so caught up in that man's death. He wasn't that good of an uncle, you know."

"Why would you even say that? He was a fine uncle to us both."

"Little Fanny, always so blind to the real world around her," Edmund continued in a mocking tone she didn't recognize at all. "I suppose I can't blame you entirely. I didn't see it, either, until I went to school. You were trapped in your fantasy of Mansfield, but I got to see the wider world and understand the situation for what it truly was."

"And what's that?" Fanny managed to ask through her shock and pain.

"Our uncle was using us." The words were blunt, but not cruel. "Of course he took me in because I was his nephew and his poor younger brother's only son, but I also had a trust. Money that he was supposed to guard. Only he didn't safeguard it very well."

Fanny thought to the moment the will had been read and it was revealed that Edmund's trust had been substantially drained. She tried to remember his exact expression when the news hit—shock, anxiety, betrayal? She couldn't picture it exactly. "You knew? Before the will?"

"Of course I knew. I overheard him talking with his solicitor—the old one, not Miss Bennet—ages ago. Things were tight with the business, and the solicitor told him to dip into my trust. As long as he could pay out when I came of age, no one would be any wiser, he said. But that was not how it's supposed to work. It's my money, and it shouldn't have been touched."

It took Fanny a moment to reconcile this new information with her own theories, but this was a missing link, she realized. Everything began to slot into place. "So you began blackmailing him?"

Edmund smiled as though she'd answered a math problem correctly. "Very good."

"But how did you know what Maria was up to? And Tom and Mr. Yates?"

He laughed, as if he were truly delighted by the question. "I figured you knew about them and were holding out on me! Come, Fanny. We all went to the same school. It wasn't that hard to figure they were more than friends. As for Maria, do you remember two years ago, when my coach was delayed coming home for the holidays, and I ended up walking home from the village?"

"Yes," Fanny whispered. She'd fretted about him not arriving on time, but everyone had told her to go to bed and worry about it in the morning.

"Well, I was walking past Aunt Norris's cottage when I saw a wagon pull up. My first thought was that the old lady had a secret beau, but I hid behind a tree and quickly discerned that it was some kind of business dealing. All it took from there was to keep my eyes and ears open. It was enough to formulate blackmail letters, but I admit that I took a few liberties with my accusations—I had no idea Maria was in that deep. But the point wasn't to get her to stop. I just wanted as much of my trust in my hands before our uncle could spend it. I needed that money, Fanny. For our future."

Our future. He had done all of that . . . for them? "But you killed him," she whispered.

"Yes, well, that was an accident. He wasn't meant to die." Edmund waved off his words as if they were pesky technicalities and not the truth.

"How can you say that? You tripped him at the top of the stairs."

"He stopped paying," Edmund countered. "And by my calculation, I was still owed four hundred pounds. There must be consequences, otherwise what's the point of threats? I honestly thought he'd merely break an arm or something. I didn't expect him to smack his head on the way down—nor for you to notice that he tripped."

"But you must have known that it would have been a possibility." Fanny could feel her voice edge into hysteria. How could Edmund be so cavalier about *murder*? "You murdered him!"

"Come now," he said. "The most anyone could charge me with is manslaughter, and besides—life is not without a bit of risk. You should know that, Fanny."

"It's not an accident if you orchestrated it."

He crouched down before her with a heavy sigh. "You're getting hung up on the details, dear. You're not seeing the bigger picture. Our uncle's death offered me a new opportunity."

"What do you mean?" she asked, chilled at the thought that Edmund's scheming was not over. "You have your money and your freedom now. What more do you need?"

"Need?" he asked. "I need very little. Want, however . . . You see, it strikes me as unfair that Tom, who has no idea how to run a business, gets to inherit. If there was any justice in the world, then those with the skills and knowledge to continue the family legacy ought to inherit."

"Tom's riding accident—breaking his leg," Fanny gasped, suddenly remembering Edmund's letter. *Better his leg than his neck.* "Did you . . ."

"Pity that wasn't nearly as effective as Sir Thomas's accident, but I suppose it's for the best. I got impatient. I'll keep my distance for a couple of years before trying again. Tom isn't inclined to marry and produce an heir, so I stand to inherit Mansfield next."

Fanny was too horrified to produce words. It all made sense now—getting rid of Mr. Rushworth so Maria wouldn't marry him. Edmund couldn't risk her shares of the business passing to Mr. Rushworth if she declined to leave them in trust to Tom. Fanny had a sick feeling that if Maria announced her engagement to Henry Crawford, he too would find some awful end. How long before Maria's coach crashed or some strange illness befell her?

"You're a monster," she whispered.

"No, Fanny, I simply chose to look after myself. And I

would look after you, too. Much better than Sir Thomas. But you had to go poking into things, consulting a solicitor, asking questions. And I can't let that stand."

His last sentence chilled Fanny. She looked into his eyes and she no longer saw the childhood friend, the trusted confidant, her ally at Mansfield. She saw a stranger with blind ambition and a cold heart.

"And what now?" she asked, because it seemed to be the most logical question left.

"What now indeed," he said with a sigh. "I hope you understand what a difficult position you've put me in, Fanny. I never wanted to drag you into this. I always thought of you as an innocent soul. But there's no undoing the past. I suppose I shall leave the choice to you. Shall we get married?"

"What?"

Over the years, Fanny had dreamed that Edmund would one day propose. To her, it seemed like the perfect solution to everyone's happiness, a way to ensure that they ended up together forever. And not too long ago, she would have even said that she fancied herself in love with him. But now, the mere thought of being bound to him forever shocked and repulsed her.

"You're not keen on the idea," Edmund remarked dryly.

"I . . . I mean, you want us . . . but . . . why?"

"You surprise me, Fanny," Edmund said. "I could have sworn you were in love with me. You have always been like a burr sticking to my coat the moment I set foot on Mansfield. Are you telling me that I misread things?"

Even now, faced with everything he'd confessed to, Fanny couldn't lie. "No."

"Then there you have it. Our solution is simple. I had wanted to wait a few years until perhaps Tom was out of the way, but no matter. We shall marry straightaway. I can get a special license tomorrow morning, and once we are married you will not be able to testify against me in a court of law. In fact, you will go back to being the quiet, timid, shy little Fanny we all know and love. You can keep up with your painting, and as long as you don't stand in the way of my plans, we shall have a very successful marriage."

"And if I say no?" she asked.

"Do you plan on saying no?"

Her mouth was dry, it was hard to get the words out. "I would just like to understand all my options."

He laughed at that, and the sound sent a cold spike of fear down her spine. "If you say no, then I'm afraid I won't be able to trust that you'll keep my secrets."

"You'll kill me?" she asked, her voice barely a whisper.

Edmund sighed. "I'm not completely heartless, and I do care for you, Fanny. However, I *will* be forced to tell Aunt Norris and Aunt Bertram that I fear so much change and excitement has had you telling the most spectacular tales. Tales that couldn't possibly be true, leaving me to draw the conclusion that you'd suffered a nervous breakdown. Add on to that a most indecent fascination with Miss Crawford . . . and, well, I think we can all agree that an asylum will be the best solution. It would be the safest for you, and everyone around you. Because anyone else you might tell will likely meet their own series of unfortunate accidents. I've gotten quite good at orchestrating them."

Death was a chilling enough threat, but somehow this was worse. The thought of Edmund turning on Mary . . . the fear rushed over her, filling her lungs and spreading throughout her limbs, turning everything numb. So this was what it had come to, then. The tired old insanity excuse, an age-old solution for any meddlesome woman.

"What will it be?" he asked.

Even though the idea repulsed her, she gulped and said, "I accept your proposal."

"Good," he said, rising to his feet and dusting off his hands. "But I hope you'll understand that I can't let you go back out there and tell anyone the truth. I'll leave you here. Percy is coming any minute now to pick up the true Millbrook—thank you for your very cunning replica, by the way, Maria and Crawford were enamored of it—and he'll take you with him. I'll tell Aunt Norris you went home with a headache, and I'll see you tomorrow. I expect you won't cause any trouble. Percy can be a bit rough, but he'll leave you alone if you behave yourself."

"But—" Fanny forced herself to bite down on what she

had been about to say. *Mary and Lizzie will notice I'm missing.* Edmund couldn't know that.

"Are you going to make things difficult?" he asked, and she shook her head.

"Good. Now, I'm going to gag you. Be a good girl, and we'll come out of this unscathed."

Before Fanny could protest, he tied a white rag tightly around her mouth, nearly making her gag. Mercifully, it wasn't laced with the same chemical concoction that had knocked her out.

He'd no sooner finished this task when the distant sound of hundreds of hands clapping reached them, and he tossed her a charming grin.

"That's my cue."

TWENTY-FIVE

In Which Fanny Makes a Confession of Her Own

DESPITE WHAT FANNY HAD promised Edmund, she had no intention of allowing herself to be kidnapped and forced into marriage with a confessed *murderer.*

She tried screaming, but that only seemed to result in a sore throat and no rescuers. She attempted to wiggle free of her bindings, but she'd lost all feeling in her fingers and the ropes seemed to grow tighter the more she moved. She managed to work her way into a standing position by bracing her back against the pillar and lifting herself up with her legs; however, now she was just standing with an aching back and throbbing wrists. Still, it somehow seemed better to face a kidnapper while on one's feet than sitting down.

All the while, Fanny fumed. She seemed to have bypassed

her initial shock and denial, and now she was just angry. Angry at Edmund for concocting this plan, for getting greedy, for taking such reckless action with their lives. And . . . well, angry at herself, too. Why hadn't she seen this sooner?

Because she hadn't wanted to, that's why.

And Edmund had played her like his viola, right into his master plan. Now she was getting what she wanted for half her life—marriage to Edmund, security, the ability to paint. Only now she didn't want to marry him, the security was ill-gotten, and he'd probably make her paint forgeries for the rest of her life. Out of the frying pan into the fire.

Faintly, she heard the scuffing of footsteps. She closed her eyes against the burn of tears. Well, this was it. She'd be defiant, not compliant. And while she wouldn't do anything stupid—she wanted to get out of this alive, after all—the last thing she wanted was to make it easy on Percy Rollins.

Another soft scuffing, hesitant, reached her and her eyes flew open. The sound was coming not from the back door, but from the hallway that Edmund had disappeared down. And it was not his heavy footfalls.

She began screaming in earnest, as loud as she could with a mouth full of linen.

"Fanny?" a voice called out, soft and scared.

It was Mary. She screamed again, feeling the force of her sound trying to make its way past the gag. She strained against her bonds, even though doing so sent spikes of white-hot pain up her arms and down her back. She kicked her feet, anything to make a sound.

And then Mary was in the doorway. She dropped her masquerade mask and cried out in horror as she ran toward her. "Good God, Fanny! Who did this?"

When the gag fell away, Fanny gasped, trying to wet her mouth. "Edmund," she managed to get out. "Can you get my bindings?"

"But why—"

"We don't have time, Mary! Please, please, untie me as fast as you can!"

Neither of them had a knife or sharp implement, so Mary began working at the knots anchoring Fanny to the pillar. "Your fingers are purple! You were gone so long, and then Edmund came out and I still couldn't find you. I slipped down the hall he came out of when no one was looking and I found the pearls of your necklace on the floor."

"Thank goodness I didn't pawn it in Portsmouth," Fanny murmured.

"Very funny. But wait—Edmund did this?"

"Yes, and I'll explain everything, but first we have to get out of here. He's sent someone to come collect me."

"Collect you? What does that mean?"

Fanny was casting about desperately, looking for anything that might aid them. Her eyes caught on a toolbox in the corner, and she saw what was the handle of either a paintbrush or palette knife sticking out of it. "Mary, over there. Look in that box and see if you can find something sharp."

Mary ran to do as she was bid, and Fanny did her best to catch her up. "We got it all wrong. Edmund was responsible for everything—the blackmail, my uncle's accident, framing Rushworth. I suspected this afternoon after something Tom said, but I wasn't certain until I came back here and he caught me."

"And now he means to kidnap you?" Mary asked. The palette knife wasn't very sharp, but it seemed to be making progress.

"Yes, and force me into marriage. He threatened you and Lizzie otherwise, and said he'd place me in an asylum if I didn't— Wait! Shh!"

She listened carefully. There was a scraping sound coming from the back door. Fanny twisted around and met Mary's terrified gaze. "Hurry!"

Mary had clearly been taking care not to harm Fanny as she attempted to release her from her bindings, but now she sawed at the rope with a force that made Fanny clench her teeth. Finally, blessedly, the ropes fell loose and her arms were free, although they burned with pain.

The back door opened.

Mary yanked her forward, and Fanny stumbled but caught a glimpse of a dark-haired young man wearing a laborer's uniform. Surprise was on their side, for he clearly hadn't expected to find two terrified young ladies fleeing the scene. "Hey!" he shouted, but Mary and Fanny were already running as fast as their skirts would allow. Their only hope was to reach the assembly room and raise the cry for help.

Mary half led and half dragged Fanny down a darkened hall, around a corner, and through an unfamiliar door. Then there was the hallway that Fanny last recalled, and the only thing that separated them from the assembly room was a thick drape. The man was fast on their heels, but Fanny gambled that he wouldn't chase them into a crowded room full of society members.

They didn't so much burst out into the assembly room as tumble—just as the final strains of Edmund's viola warbled throughout the hall. The music faded and applause soared as Mary yanked her behind a colonnade. They garnered only a few curious looks, thankfully, and Fanny didn't want to think about how disheveled she looked.

"Where's Lizzie?" Fanny whispered.

"I'm trying to spot her," Mary hissed back, craning her neck. She kept one arm around Fanny's waist, for which Fanny was grateful. She needed the support—her knees were still shaking. "There! On the other side of the hall!"

Fanny peeked around the colonnade and saw Lizzie Bennet standing almost exactly on the opposite side of the rotunda, a crowd of people between them. She wore green silk and no masquerade mask, and her arms were crossed as she looked about the crowd with an impatient expression.

Meanwhile, everyone's attention was focused on the platform to one end of the rotunda, where Edmund took a bow. Behind him was the Millbrook painting, and as the applause died down, Henry Crawford stepped forward, commanding attention.

"Lords, gentlemen, and ladies, thank you so much for coming this evening. My name is Mr. Henry Crawford, and I am an art dealer and your host this evening. But more than anything, I am a fine appreciator of the masterpieces on display tonight. And I imagine that you are as well, if you are here!"

This earned him a gentle round of polite laughter. "Can you signal her?" Fanny asked. "She said that she'd have *resources*."

"I'm trying," Mary said, waving her arms about. But enough people stood between them that Lizzie wasn't able to see Mary's gestures, and they were drawing more dirty looks from other partygoers than anything.

Fanny kept an eye on the hall, looking out to see if her potential kidnapper had followed them. Then she glanced up at the platform, where Mr. Crawford was still going on and on about his business and successes, and her heart stopped.

Edmund was looking straight at her.

"He's spotted us," Fanny hissed.

Mary dropped her arms and they both watched as Edmund stepped back from the platform. He began to slowly, but determinedly, make his way around the rotunda to them. "If he reaches us, he'll claim that I'm hysterical," she hissed. "He'll start his whole charade of how I need to be put away. We need to get Lizzie's attention, *now*."

"Should we cause a scene?" Mary asked.

Fanny shook her head quickly. "That would play directly into his hands."

Just then, Mr. Crawford announced, "And I am pleased to present an early, untitled painting by none other than the elusive Mr. James Millbrook, which is generously on loan from Lord Allerton, who purchased it at my last auction. I'm sorry, it's not for sale—but please consider it as an example of the wonderful treasures that I am able to source, and an example of the quality of art you can expect when you turn to me for your art needs."

Everything came to Fanny in flashes.

Edmund stalking toward her.

Lizzie looking about and not seeing her.

Mr. Crawford smiling before a rapt crowd.

Mary's face, twisted in fear and desperation.

And the Millbrook—no, her replica of the Millbrook—on display.

She stepped out of the protective circle of Mary's arm and called out in as loud a voice as she could muster, "It's a fake!"

The hall went deathly quiet, and then the hum and buzz of gasps and whispers rose to a quiet roar. Henry stood on the platform, a confused smile on his face as he searched the crowd.

"Fanny, no!" Mary whispered, but Fanny was already

striding toward the platform where he stood. The eyes of everyone in the room were focused upon her. It was, without a doubt, her worst nightmare. Actually, no—her worst nightmare had been replaced with Edmund's threats and the cold gleam in his eye as he told her about how easily he could arrange for an accident to befall Mary. This, this was merely an embarrassing dream.

She marched toward Mr. Crawford with her head held high, trying to emulate confidence and poise. She had to keep an absolutely level head if this wasn't to backfire on her. When she was just steps away from the platform, she saw the flash of fear on Mr. Crawford's face. But before she could climb the steps, someone grabbed her arm.

Fanny spun around, heart in her throat. But it was only Maria, who glared at her with fire in her eyes. "What are you doing?" she hissed.

But Fanny shook her off and closed the distance between herself and Henry. She looked out over the crowd. "This Millbrook painting is a forgery! The real one was stolen!"

"I don't know where this is coming from," Mr. Crawford said, still trying to laugh off her accusations. "What an absurd claim."

"It's not absurd," Fanny said, her heart racing. She looked about until she saw Lizzie, who stared at her in open-mouthed shock. Behind her stood Mr. Darcy, grim-faced, whispering in her ear. "Mr. Crawford and my cousin Miss Maria Bertram colluded to steal the original painting, which they sold to Lord Allerton at the auction at Mansfield Emporium. They switched it out with a replica, which is on display before you."

Lord Allerton was near the platform and he was marching toward her with fury twisting his face. Maria stood right below her, hissing at her to *shut up* while Mr. Crawford proclaimed, "How absurd! I have never cheated in my life."

Fanny couldn't see Edmund in the crowd, so she added, "And Mr. Edmund Bertram, whom you just heard perform, has conspired to steal the original out from under all of their noses. And he's guilty of much more." Fanny hoped that Lizzie would understand her meaning. "So if there is anyone in this hall who can secure the premises, I suggest they do so immediately."

Mr. Darcy was already striding off toward the front door, and to Fanny's surprise, so were many more men in the room. They blended into the crowd quite well, but now as they began to move toward the perimeter Fanny could see that they must be working with Lizzie. In short order, it seemed as though these men had encircled the crowd, and judging by their tall statures and efficient movements, they knew exactly what they were doing.

But where was Edmund?

The crowd of partygoers pressed even tighter into the center of the room, and in all of the mayhem, Fanny spotted Mary's dark hair. She seemed to be fighting her way to the platform, but Fanny's relief turned into horror when Mary was jerked back suddenly.

"Mary!" Fanny shrieked.

The room seemed to stop for the space of a breath, and then ladies began screaming as Edmund stepped forward, dragging Mary with him. His arm was around her neck, and he held something to her throat that glinted in the candlelight. Fanny felt faint, but she kept her eyes locked on Mary's.

"Get back!" Edmund growled. "All of you!"

A space quickly cleared around them and the room fell quiet except for the odd sob. Edmund was yanking poor Mary around left and right as he spun about, searching for a way out. "I'll hurt her unless you clear a path!" he shouted.

But no one moved. The perimeter of the room was guarded by Lizzie's men, and the partygoers didn't make an effort to get out of his way.

"My sister!" Mr. Crawford cried out.

"I need a clear exit," Edmund said. "And she comes with me. You all stay inside, and if you try to follow me before I'm clear of the building, I'll slash her throat."

Fanny had never known such fear. She had felt afraid so often throughout her lifetime—fear for herself, fear for William or Edmund, fear of an unknown or uncertain future, but never had she felt the frantic surge of terror for someone else that made her step forward and say, "No! Take me."

Edmund wheeled around to glare at her. "A little too late for that, Fanny."

"Let's be reasonable," Mr. Darcy said, stepping forward. He cut an imposing figure through the crowd with his serious, dark expression and tall stature. "No one needs to get hurt."

"I agree, so let me pass!"

Fanny found Mary's terrified gaze. As they locked eyes, Fanny tried to convey how sorry she was for dragging Mary into this. She tried to pour an entire painting's worth of feeling into that one look, so that if this was one of Mary's final moments, at least she'd know how much Fanny cared for her and how sorry she was.

Mary, for some reason, kept flicking her gaze downward.

Mr. Darcy was still trying to reason with Edmund, but Mary locked eyes with Fanny once more, then looked around the room. Then, her eyes rolled up briefly, and she stared straight back at Fanny.

What on earth?

"I'm done negotiating," Edmund declared, taking another step toward the door. "Are you going to let me pass, or am I going to have to kill her?"

Suddenly, Fanny understood.

"Edmund!" she cried out.

He wasn't expecting her to call out for him, so he half turned to look at her. In that moment, he loosened his grip on Mary just enough that she fell into a spectacular swoon. The combination of the distraction and Mary's dead weight on his right arm sent him off-kilter, and Mr. Darcy seized his moment. He leapt toward Edmund, very effectively disarming him from behind. Then he was down on the floor and Mary was scrambling away from him, straight into Fanny's open arms.

"Are you all right? I'm so sorry! I never imagined he'd try something like that. Did he hurt you?"

Mary wrapped her arms around her and clung to Fanny, her lilac scent mixed with sweat filling Fanny's nose. "I'm all right. Didn't I tell you a well-timed swoon could get you out of all manner of things?"

"I shall never doubt you for as long as I live," Fanny promised.

"That long?" Mary asked. Her voice was a little shaky, but when Fanny drew back to look her in the eye, there was a sparkle of amusement there. "Does that mean you hope to continue our acquaintance, even knowing that my brother tried to cheat you?"

"Well, Edmund tried to abduct you, and I think I might have just ruined your brother's reputation. And probably yours. And mine will likely never recover. So really, the choice is yours."

"What you're saying, then, is that we can be two scandalous ladies together?"

But before Fanny could respond, reinforcements arrived and bound Edmund and hauled him to his feet. He cast one last hateful glance in Fanny's direction and, seeing the way that Fanny and Mary embraced, spat at her feet. Fanny flinched, but Mary stepped forward with a menacing look, and then he was hauled away, out of sight.

The crowd was now abuzz, and Fanny would wager that they'd provided enough entertainment that night to fill three society papers, at least. The poor printers of London would be very busy tonight. Lizzie was marching her way toward them when a male voice called out, "What about my painting?"

They turned to find Lord Allerton standing next to the Millbrook painting, rage turning his cheeks pink. "Crawford, if that man was guilty of all she claimed, then I need your absolute assurance this painting is genuine!"

The whispers rose again as Mr. Crawford fought his way toward the painting once more. "I have no idea what that spectacle was all about, but any claims of fraud are the ravings of a madwoman."

"I'm not mad." Fanny turned to confront him head-on. But this time, she wasn't alone. Mary stood beside her, and she took Fanny's hand in her own. That gave Fanny the strength for what came next. "And my proof is this: I know the painting is a forgery because I painted it."

That got more of a rise out of the crowd than anything, but Mr. Crawford merely laughed. "You! Ladies and gentlemen, this young lady, this poor, sick young lady only fancies herself an artist. These are the mad ramblings of—"

"I spent weeks replicating the painting for my own practice and edification. Any expert would be able to tell the difference between it and the original."

"That is the original, and unless you can produce another painting like it, no one believes you." But Mr. Crawford was starting to sound desperate, and he kept looking about as if hoping to find someone who would agree with him.

But now there were murmurings in the crowd, and one man shouted, "Can someone come retrieve that hysterical female?" Others grumbled their agreement, and Fanny closed her eyes briefly against their censure. In trying to save herself and catch Edmund, had she played right into his hands yet again?

"I can authenticate it."

The voice that rang out was young, female, and clear. Fanny's eyes flew open and she saw a lady push her way to the crowd. Her posture was impeccable and her expression was bland, but there was something familiar about her. She stepped up next to Lord Allerton on the platform and repeated to Mr. Crawford, "I can authenticate the painting this instant, and put to rest any speculation."

"You?" Mr. Crawford asked, not able to disguise a laugh. "Who even are you to—"

"You'll take my word for it, because I am James Millbrook," the lady said, and her expression remained curiously bland. That shocked Mr. Crawford into silence and set up cries of surprise among the crowd. "And before you engage in the tedious argument that James Millbrook is male while I am clearly female, please know there are several respected members of society in attendance tonight who can verify my claim."

She then stepped around Mr. Crawford and studied the painting. Fanny was so shocked at the revelation that one of her favorite artists, the person who had captured a scene so perfectly, was a lady, she very nearly forgot that she'd admitted to copying the artist's work in front of her. And now her own shallow attempts were now being evaluated by the person she'd admired for *months*.

It felt like hours, but in reality it was probably only a minute before the strange lady—Millbrook—stepped away from the painting. She turned to address the crowd, and Fanny could feel that everyone was on edge for her judgment.

"It is a very good fraud," the artist declared.

Pandemonium broke out.

In the front of the hall, Maria and Aunt Norris were wild-eyed and strangely silent as a furor rose among the crowd. It turned out that wild accusations, an attempted abduction, a daring maneuver to escape said abduction, and an arrest were enough to push the crowd to the brink, and now they were chanting for Henry Crawford's arrest. Men with more sense than passion were whisking wives, daughters, and sisters out of the Pantheon as quickly as they could manage, while others stood on for the entertainment. Somewhere in the madness, the Runners had shown up as well, and they were now approaching Henry Crawford.

Lizzie finally fought her way to the front. "Are you all right?" she demanded, throwing her arms around both Mary and Fanny. "That was mad, and utterly brilliant!"

Fanny returned the hug, then said, "Don't let Maria escape! And Aunt Norris, too!"

Lizzie nodded and turned on her heel. She drew her fingers to her lips and let out a piercing whistle that got the quick attention of several Runners, and she pointed to Maria and Aunt Norris, who were trying to make a run for it. She wasn't proud of it, but Fanny knew she'd treasure the sight of Maria and Aunt Norris being arrested for all her days.

Mary tugged her away when it became clear that Lizzie and Mr. Darcy had things under control. As they moved away from the platform, Fanny looked up to see the face of the artist she'd copied, staring straight at her with unabashed curiosity.

"Miss Millbrook?" Fanny ventured, mouth suddenly dry. "I'm very sorry. I never meant for that to happen. I only copied your painting because I loved it so, and I wish I could paint as well as you. It was never meant to be seen by anyone else, and I certainly never signed your name to it."

"I see," Miss Millbrook said, and she didn't sound angry, exactly . . . but there was a steeliness to her voice that made Fanny want to look away. "I've always hoped to have a famous work one day, but not like this."

"I'm sorry," she said again. "If there is ever any way I could make it up to you, anything at all. I don't have any money, but I would make restitution. I could sell some work—my own work, naturally, and pay you back slowly. . . ." She ran out of ideas. All she knew was that standing before the actual artist herself, she was more desperate than ever to be taken seriously.

"I don't want your money," Miss Millbrook said bluntly, but not unkindly. "You aspire to be an artist?"

Fanny glanced at Mary, uncertain of why Miss Millbrook asked. Mary squeezed her hand encouragingly. "Yes, miss. Or rather, I am an artist. I mean, I've not sold anything, but . . ."

She resisted the urge to explain away and belittle her work. If she wanted others to take her seriously, perhaps it was time to take herself seriously. "Yes. I'm an artist."

"Hm," Miss Millbrook said, but there was the faint hint of a smile around her eyes. She reached into her reticule, withdrew a calling card, and extended it to Fanny. "I'm in London another three days. Call on me before I leave, and we shall discuss this matter further."

Then, with a quick, appraising glance at Mary, she swept away.

Fanny stared down at the card in her hand. It read "Anne Millbrook" and listed a London address. "What just happened?" she asked.

"What happened," Mary said, "was that you did it. You solved your uncle's murder and you met your favorite artist all in one night."

"And he's a she!" Fanny exclaimed.

"Indeed," Mary agreed.

And then they were both giggling, then laughing together. As Fanny tried to catch her breath, she said, "Why is it that I'm always caught laughing at inappropriate moments with you?"

"I don't know," Mary said. "But I like it."

Fanny felt herself falling into Mary's blue eyes. "What do we do now?"

Mary took a step closer. "Now? I think we wait for Lizzie. It looks like she might have some questions for us, and reports to write."

"And then?"

"Then . . . we'll figure it out. But you don't have to return to Bertram House or Mansfield Park, not unless you want to."

"Heavens, no." Fanny suppressed a shudder. "I don't want to see anyone from that house. If I go back there, all I'll do is think about Edmund and how he deceived us all."

"I'm sorry," Mary said. "I know you two were close. I never understood exactly how close. . . ."

It was a question, but she didn't press Fanny to answer. Yet Fanny wanted to anyway. "I always thought we were close, but now I don't know. I thought I loved him. I thought we'd have a future together. And now . . ."

"You were deceived," Mary said gently.

"I was," Fanny admitted, "but it wasn't just that. When you arrived at Mansfield, I began to question *everything*. At first, I thought I was jealous because Edmund seemed fonder of you than he was of me . . . and then, I realized too late that I was jealous because *I* was fonder of you than I was of Edmund."

Mary stared at her with such an expression of hope and happiness that Fanny could barely breathe. She was opening her heart and laying it before Mary, something that had long terrified her, but now, having just escaped a very terrifying fate, she didn't want to waste another second of her life hiding how she felt.

"You made me reconsider everything. I think you're clever and charming and you make me laugh, even if I don't always show it. And I think you're beautiful. I couldn't stand it if you believed I thought otherwise."

"Fanny," Mary breathed, and for half a moment Fanny lived in fear that she'd completely misread the situation. But then Mary leaned in and said, "I think you're marvelous. And brave. And you look very fetching in violet."

Fanny thrilled at the compliment and the confirmation that Mary's feelings were returned. But because she was herself, she protested, "I haven't felt brave. I've been fumbling my way through all this time, asking myself what Lizzie would do."

"I think," Mary said, stepping even closer and dropping her voice so low that Fanny had to lean in to hear her, "that it's all right to borrow bravery from others while looking for your own. But Lizzie didn't expose Edmund and your family and my brother. You did. Even though it upended your life. That's true bravery. And right now, I'm going to borrow some from you."

And she kissed Fanny.

It wasn't like their first kiss, when Fanny had been full of miserable confusion and inexplicable yearning. This kiss was confident, but gentle. It was also brief, for concealed as they might be off to the side, they were still in public after all, and society was reeling from enough scandalous revelations that evening.

But when Mary drew away, Fanny knew that it would not be their last kiss, not by a long shot.

EPILOGUE

In Which Fanny Finds a Happiness Beyond Hope

IT WAS ON A balmy August evening that Fanny found herself headed to Vauxhall Gardens for the first time. It was toward the end of the season when the trip could finally be arranged, and her excitement at visiting the famed pleasure gardens was rivaled only by her eagerness to meet the person who'd invited her there.

It was late afternoon when they set out, timing their arrival to the edge of dusk. Vauxhall Gardens were close enough to London proper to attract quite the crowd, and Fanny thrummed with excitement and nerves. "We'll never be able to see anyone in this crowd," she remarked in an anxious tone.

"You'll find her," came Anne's quiet reassurance, and Fanny flashed her a grateful smile.

After that fateful night at the Pantheon—"Pandemonium

at the Pantheon," as the papers had dubbed it—Fanny spent three days in London seeing to the aftermath of her family's criminal activities. She hadn't forgotten about Miss Millbrook's card, slipped to her that night, but she'd been reluctant to face the artist in the light of day. It had been Mary and Lizzie who had convinced her to go on the final day that she was to be in town, and for that Fanny would be forever grateful.

She'd been ushered into the drawing room of a modest town house that was filled to the brim with artwork. Fanny had come alone, feeling strongly that if she were to face judgment, it would be best she did so on her own, and later she wished she'd brought along Mary so that she could confirm that all of the paintings that covered nearly every inch of the walls were in fact real. She took it all in with wide-eyed awe as Miss Millbrook served tea and then was taken aback when Miss Millbrook asked, "What do you think?"

"Oh, which one?" Fanny asked.

"That one." Miss Millbrook pointed, seemingly at random, to a painting of what appeared to be an Italian maiden brandishing a sword.

Fanny stared at it, and at first she was inclined to grade it according to her uncle's scale. Was this a very good painting, or was it only passable? But then she shook her head. Miss Millbrook asked for her opinion, not her uncle's. "I like it."

"Why?" Miss Millbrook asked.

As Fanny fumbled through her reasoning, Miss Millbrook

watched her with an appraising eye. And then she pointed to the next painting on the wall. "And this one?"

The exercise was repeated until they'd covered every painting in the room, and Fanny was half-afraid that Miss Millbrook was questioning whether or not Fanny planned to replicate them all when she set her teacup down and said, "Miss Price, I would like to offer you a position."

"A position?" Fanny echoed, uncertain of what she meant.

"Yes. Your responsibilities would be assisting me in my work—ensuring I have the adequate supplies, some light cleaning, and perhaps a bit of housekeeping. I keep a very small staff, and live simply when I'm not in London. In exchange, I am willing to provide room and board at my country home, a small stipend, and share in my expertise."

Fanny nearly dropped her teacup. She'd half expected that when she arrived, Miss Millbrook's solicitor would bring legal charges against her. "You mean . . . painting lessons?"

Miss Millbrook finally cracked a very small smile. "Yes."

"But . . . why? After what I did?" Fanny still couldn't shake the fear that this was all an elaborate joke to punish her for her part in the scandal.

Miss Millbrook appeared surprised by Fanny's question. "I bear you no ill will or resentment. You were following an instinct that is, in fact, correct. All good artists imitate before they find their own vision. In fact . . ."

She looked into her tea, as if deep in thought. Fanny waited, afraid that she was about to rescind her offer. But when Miss Millbrook spoke again, it was with a surprising revelation.

"Some months ago, I was in a small gallery where a friend was displaying my work. I met a man who I assumed was a collector, and he was taken with the painting that you copied. We struck up a conversation—he did not know that I was the artist. It was, for a time, a closely guarded secret."

"I am sorry about that," Fanny said.

Miss Millbrook waved her hand. "This man complimented me on my knowledge of the art displayed, and asked if I was an artist. I told him I was, though I didn't tell him we were discussing my piece. He asked me if I had any advice for a young lady who also aspired to paint. He said his niece had a measure of talent, and he hoped to see she was successful one day."

Fanny could hardly draw a breath.

"I told him to advise the girl to keep working. To get her lessons, if possible. And to paint her own versions of paintings she loved, so that she may learn to develop the skills she'd need in her own work. The man thanked me, and then he bought the piece. So I can only deduce that he was . . ."

"Sir Thomas," Fanny finished. Tears pricked at her eyes and she withdrew a handkerchief to wipe her eyes. "So he really did believe I was talented after all. I often wondered if he was just humoring me."

"I didn't know him, but I believed him genuine," Miss Millbrook said. "And I do care about fostering new talent, especially young female talent. But if you are to be my apprentice, you must promise me you'll work hard, and find your own vision. No more copying."

It was a promise Fanny was happy to make.

A week later, Fanny arrived at a modest country cottage in Sussex—grander than Aunt Norris's cottage, but nowhere near as fine as Mansfield Park. And though she was loath to leave Mary behind in London and she regretted not being able to return to William in Portsmouth, she found true happiness in Miss Millbrook's unconventional household. Her mornings were spent sweeping and mending and doing various household chores, and her afternoons in the company of Miss Millbrook, who taught her what she knew about art.

Miss Millbrook lived with a young widow named Mrs. Green, who was as effusive as Miss Millbrook was reserved, and Mrs. Green made Fanny feel very welcome, banishing all notions that Miss Millbrook harbored any secret resentments toward her. They grew close quickly, and Fanny was grateful every day that she had gone to call on Anne Millbrook in London. And the best part was that Sussex was much closer to Portsmouth than Mansfield Park, and she got to visit William and her family at least once a month.

The only thing missing was Mary.

When they arrived at Vauxhall Gardens, Anne paid their admission fee and they wandered onto the grounds. A large wooden structure brightly painted and adorned with unlit lamps greeted them, where an orchestra sat. The musicians were tuning their instruments and warming them up, and the effect was a dissonant yet musical cacophony that made Fanny wince—more out of bad memories than anything else.

The last she'd heard, Edmund was being held in Newgate for manslaughter, but Lizzie Bennet would not rest until she managed to get the charge upgraded to murder. He'd written her only once, and when William told her his letter had arrived in Portsmouth, she'd asked him to burn it.

She looked beyond the orchestra to where a rotunda stood. Mary's last letter had said that she'd wait for them there, and Fanny longed to break away from Anne and Mrs. Green and run to it. It was difficult to listen to her mentor explain how the gardens would be lit with twenty thousand lamps and the whole place would glow with candlelight. She didn't care about the grottoes, the statues, the paintings—some of which Anne had painted herself. She had eyes for only one person.

Fanny didn't spot her until she was nearly at the rotunda. Mary stepped out from behind a colonnade, her dark hair gleaming in the setting sun. Her dress was dark and service-able, not as fine as she once wore, but her blue eyes were full of amusement and they lit up when they alighted on Fanny.

Fanny couldn't walk—it was impossible. She broke into a trot and Mary met her halfway, and they embraced and spun about from the force of their affections. Fanny didn't dare kiss her in public—it was best to be cautious. Men who loved each other found the law against them, and while ladies didn't often face the same persecution, there were an abundance of ways that society could punish an unconventional woman.

"You're here!" Mary declared. "I can't believe you're really here."

"In the flesh," Fanny promised. She turned to properly introduce Mary to Miss Millbrook, who had seen her only in passing the night of the Pantheon pandemonium, and Mrs. Green.

"We'll let you two catch up," Mrs. Green said with a quick wink to Fanny. Where Miss Millbrook was a still, deep well of contemplation, Mrs. Green was more of a bubbling stream, quick to smile and tease. "Shall we meet back by the orchestra in time for the fireworks display?"

They agreed on that and bade farewell to Miss Millbrook and Mrs. Green, who walked arm in arm down a gravel path bordered by tall hedges. "They seem very nice," Mary remarked as she pulled Fanny down a quieter path, framed by larger, leafy trees.

"They're incredibly kind," Fanny agreed, feeling suddenly shy now that it was just the two of them. "They live a quiet life, but they've opened my eyes to a completely different way of living than I ever knew at Mansfield, or back in Portsmouth. I'm grateful to them. But, tell me about you—how are you liking your work?"

After Henry Crawford had been arrested for fraud, his

entire operation had gone bankrupt as former clients and buyers came around, demanding compensation for falsified works of art or simply demanding proof that their works were originals. Mary, with the help of Lizzie, quietly ducked away and used her meager savings to set herself up at a ladies' boardinghouse in London, owned by none other than Charlotte Lucas. Miss Lucas was still working at Longbourn & Sons but had recently spent her savings on a home of her own and took in Mary as a boarder. Mary made her living teaching drawing and painting to the daughters of middle-class families and offering harp lessons to the few families who owned the instrument. Mary regaled her with stories of her students—their talents, the artists they studied, their work, and the funny things they said.

"I love my students, and they work hard," Mary said. "I like to think I might be mentoring the musical version of the next great Anne Millbrook or Fanny Price. Maybe one day I'll be sending one of those girls on to you."

"Hopefully none of them will have as rough a time as we have," Fanny remarked.

"Oh, but we made it out all right in the end, didn't we?" Mary asked, her grip tightening on Fanny's arm.

"I could have done without being drugged and tied up," Fanny joked. "But otherwise . . ."

Mary laughed, but then her grip on Fanny's arm tightened and she drew her off the path and under the drooping branches of a willow tree. "But are you happy, Fanny? I am, for the most part, even though my life looks very different these days. But I worry about you. I didn't grow up in a grand estate, so I didn't ever have to suffer losing it. In fact, I feel like despite my fall in status, I have gained so much—a home, a purpose, friends . . . and you."

Fanny took her time, choosing her words with care. "I think back to how timid and afraid I was before I met you, and how I hoped and wished for things that would save me from my fate as the penniless, spinster companion . . . and I am glad I didn't get my wish. I don't relish bringing about the ruination of Mansfield Emporium—"

"But your family mismanaged the business, not you," Mary cut in.

"You're right," she said. "However, if you're asking me if I regret how things played out because I've lost my home at Mansfield, the answer is no. Because Mansfield, for all its fine amenities and treasures, was never truly my home."

"And . . . where is your home?" Mary asked, her voice shy.

That was a good question. Because home wasn't exactly Portsmouth, either, at least it hadn't been since Fanny was small. But was it Miss Millbrook's house in Sussex? Certainly, she felt very welcome there, and she had the feeling that Miss Millbrook and Mrs. Green would share it with her for as long as she'd like to stay. But it wasn't truly hers, either.

"I think that home isn't exactly a place so much as what you make of a place," she said. "How you inhabit a house, and whom you choose to inhabit it with, that's what makes a home. Perhaps I don't have my own home . . . yet."

Mary bit her bottom lip as she smiled and said, "And perhaps, one day, home could be somewhere . . . with me?"

Fanny felt as though her cheeks would ache from smiling. "I would like that very much."

"Good," Mary said, casting a furtive look about before stepping in closer. "Me too."

Evening had fully set in by now, and they were quite concealed beneath the drooping willow branches. Fanny closed the distance between them, hungry for the feel of Mary's lips on hers, for the warmth of Mary's hands at her waist, for the chance to wrap her arms around her and feel the curve of her back. They kissed for what felt like hours and mere seconds at once, breaking apart only when they heard the approach of the lamplighters come to light the glass lanterns that seemed to be tucked into every corner of the gardens.

When they stepped out of the embrace of the willow tree, they discovered that the gardens were aglow, burning softly with the light of countless wicks. They walked arm in arm back to the orchestra, where the first fireworks exploded above, and into a future brighter than the night shining around them.

FINIS.

AUTHOR'S NOTE

I have a confession to make: If I had to rank all of Jane Austen's books, *Mansfield Park* would probably come in as my least favorite.

When I first read the novel, I recall being rather disappointed by Fanny Price. She lacks the verve and wit of other Austen heroines, and while she has my sympathies for all she endures and my admiration for how closely she adheres to her morals, I always felt as though she was a bit too timid, and that she was cheated on the romance front. It wasn't until I revisited *Mansfield Park* many years later that I began to have a deeper appreciation for what Austen was trying to convey in the book. It's a novel about what it means to be principled in situations where morals are lacking, the contrast of vice and virtue, and of course, the friction between social classes and the friction between families. And it turns out, those are some interesting themes to reshape into a murder mystery.

As with *Pride and Premeditation* and *Sense and Second-Degree Murder*, the circumstances of the characters have been changed somewhat dramatically, and they aren't perfectly historically accurate. It is unlikely that a man of Sir Thomas

Bertram's status would run an art emporium, but it allowed me to explore the art world and a topic that has always fascinated me: art forgery. Art forgeries have occurred for almost as long as we've had art, whether due to popular demand for said art (it hasn't always been accessible) or because there was money to be made, or both. Considering that the Bertrams are largely motivated by money in both Austen's original text and in my retelling, I thought it would be interesting to explore how the various characters might use art for profit, whereas someone like Fanny Price would have nobler ideas about what art can and should be.

The paintings by Millbrook were somewhat inspired by the work of Edmund Blair Leighton, whose Regency art of everyday scenes were famous in the latter half of the nineteenth century. Many descriptions of the artwork in Mansfield Emporium have been inspired by my research into the types of paintings and objets d'art one might find in a Regency-era household, although most artist names are of my own creation.

As with my first two books, the protagonists are deeply affected by property and inheritance laws that often overlooked women. This was a large factor in keeping women socially constrained and preventing them from obtaining (much) independence. Fanny is completely reliant on her Bertram relatives' willingness to host her, but other characters are equally constricted by the need to either make, inherit, or marry into wealth, and it's not just the women who found themselves in tight spots.

In Austen's original text, Maria Bertram is looked down upon for marrying a man she does not love in order to secure her financial future, and is socially ruined when she turns her back on Mr. Rushworth in favor of Mr. Crawford, who does not wish to assume the social shame of consorting with her. Now, I am no Maria Bertram apologist, but I do think the options for women were exceptionally bad during this time period, so it was my intent to explore a few different ways that unmarried or widowed women attempted to find security—either through latching onto family despite their misdeeds, resorting to criminal schemes, or masking their identity in order to sell their own artwork. In my version, Fanny Price observes this all, but must figure out her own path.

And speaking of Fanny forging her own path—I confess I have never been much enamored of Edmund Bertram, but Mary Crawford has always fascinated me. Her attachment to Fanny in Austen's original text, despite her flighty and sometimes inconsistent actions, is something that stirred my imagination. When given the opportunity to retell *Mansfield Park*, I couldn't resist making Mary a love interest.

While little is known about the lives of queer women in early nineteenth-century England, we do know that many queer and transgender individuals did exist, as they have throughout time. Anne Lister is a notable figure during this time period, and she kept detailed diaries written in code that were finally published during the twentieth century, becoming the basis of the TV show *Gentleman Jack*. Because women were so dependent on men for financial security, it was more difficult for them to live together and many lesbians of the time were forced to marry and carry out their relationships with women in secret.

Society and history also tend to diminish romantic relationships between women throughout history as passionate friendships, so it's impossible to know just how many lesbians and queer women lived in secret. Homosexuality was very much a crime punishable by death during this time period, and while women were less often targets of the law, many women have been institutionalized over the years for what was considered deviant sexual behavior—Edmund's threat to send Fanny to an asylum at the end of the book certainly has its basis in history. And men like Tom and Mr. Yates could all too easily be arrested and even hanged on sodomy charges. However, just as history is full of many instances of queer suffering, it's also full of queer joy and resilience. For this book, I chose to focus on that joy and resilience and imagine that Mary and Fanny could create a happily ever after they both deserve.

ACKNOWLEDGMENTS

Many thanks to my friends and family who offered support, enthusiasm, and encouragement throughout writing this novel, particularly my fellow writer friends Monica Roe, Anna Drury, Nora Carpenter, Melissa Baumgart, Emma Kress, Emily Martin, and Annika Barranti Klein. Thank you to Jaclyn Swiderski, Paul Grosskopf, Joey Crundwell, and Taylor Carlson for listening to me talk about writing and obscure Regency-era facts whenever we're together. And thank you to my family for being so encouraging, particularly my partner Tab, who often herded our many pets out of the office so I could write without a cat on my keyboard.

Thank you to my agent, Taylor Martindale Kean, for being such a wonderful supporter of my work and sounding board. Thanks also to the incredible team at Full Circle Literary.

Thank you to my editor Claudia Gabel for her patience and guidance throughout this book, and for running with the idea of Fanny being queer. Thanks to Sophie Schmidt for all the encouragement and enthusiasm for this book. I also have to thank all of the amazing people at HarperCollins who work hard to bring books to shelves and who had a hand in

Manslaughter Park and my previous books: Anna Bernard, Sabrina Aballe, Nancy Taylor, Sona Vogel, Jessica Berg, Josh Weiss, Corinna Lupp, and all others who I don't have direct contact with, but whose efforts I greatly appreciate. Thank you also to Jess Phoenix and Filip Hodas for yet another stunner of a book cover.

Thank you to all of the bloggers, content creators, librarians, booksellers, teachers, and book champions who've shared my work with readers. You have my respect and gratitude, and you're the reason why my TBR pile will likely bury me alive one day.

Finally, thank you to Jane Austen for writing *Mansfield Park*. I'm sorry I didn't fully appreciate it the first time I read it, but I do now.